D0122863

THE
POLICEMAN'S
DAUGHTER

ALSO BY TRUDY NAN BOYCE

Old Bones
Out of the Blues

THE
POLICEMAN'S
DAUGHTER

TRUDY NAN BOYCE

G. P. PUTNAM'S SONS
NEW YORK

PUTNAM

G. P. PUTNAM'S SONS
Publishers Since 1838
An imprint of Penguin Random House LLC
375 Hudson Street
New York, New York 10014

Copyright © 2018 by Trudy Nan Boyce
Penguin supports copyright. Copyright fuels creativity, encourages diverse voices,
promotes free speech, and creates a vibrant culture. Thank you for buying an authorized
edition of this book and for complying with copyright laws by not reproducing, scanning,
or distributing any part of it in any form without permission. You are supporting
writers and allowing Penguin to continue to publish books for every reader.

Library of Congress Cataloging-in-Publication Data

Names: Boyce, Trudy Nan, author.
Title: The policeman's daughter / Trudy Nan Boyce.
Description: New York : G. P. Putnam's Sons, 2018. |
Series: A Detective Sarah Alt novel ; 3
Identifiers: LCCN 2017027533 (print) | LCCN 2017031285 (ebook) | ISBN
9780698140721 (epub) | ISBN 9780399167287 (hardcover)
Subjects: LCSH: Women detectives—Fiction. | Policewomen—Fiction. |
GSAFD: Mystery fiction.
Classification: LCC PS3602.O927 (ebook) | LCC PS3602.O927
P65 2018 (print) | DDC 813/.6—dc23
LC record available at https://lccn.loc.gov/2017027533
p.   cm.

Printed in the United States of America
1 3 5 7 9 10 8 6 4 2

BOOK DESIGN BY MEIGHAN CAVANAUGH

This is a work of fiction. Names, characters, places, and incidents either are the product
of the author's imagination or are used fictitiously, and any resemblance to actual persons,
living or dead, businesses, companies, events, or locales is entirely coincidental.

For Rick Saylor

*I am saying that a journey is called that because you
cannot know what you will discover on the journey,
what you will do with what you find,
or what you find will do to you.*

—JAMES BALDWIN

THE
POLICEMAN'S
DAUGHTER

WITHDRAWN

WITHDRAWN

1.

IMPROPER CROSSING
OF THE GORE

They were always close to hard times. So she and Pepper invented a game to play before the calls piled up. Beginning of shift, late afternoon, before the zone began to bust up, before the adrenaline hours, they ran from roll call, scrambling to get to their Crown Vics, eager to get a traffic case on some obscure charge. The winner would be the first one to have written at least one ticket for each of the violations in the traffic code.

Running her finger down the worn list, Salt had made all the easy ones a hundred times over: "Stop Sign," "Failure to Yield," "Improper Equipment," and she had made the harder ones, *A* through *H*. Her favorite so far was the "Lewd Bumper Sticker" case she had made last week. "Fuck Up," it had read. "Improper Crossing of the Gore" was on her agenda for the afternoon. If she could make this one she'd keep her slight lead on Pepper.

After shift, on the nights he had ticketed for some obscure

infraction, Pepper would make his entrance to the precinct giving her the business and calling himself "Hot Pepper," inviting the rest of the cops to rain insults, Pepper playing straight to the champions of put-down. "I am black and proud and red-hot tonight," he said, pimp-walking into the precinct, underscoring his street name.

Now idling on the expressway, Salt sat parked beside an entrance ramp wall, watching for a gore violation. The vibrations of the concrete ramp beside her reverberated to her hand on the gear arm. Hearing Pepper on her shoulder mic calling out a tractor-trailer-rig stop, she could imagine some weird "tonnage" charge he'd be carrying on about at shift change. Highway dirt blew up from a ragged hole in the passenger-side floorboard. A fine dust coated her arms and everything in the car, one of the Atlanta Police Department's finest vehicles. The city was playing its budget games again this year, this season with the police vehicle acquisition contract.

Still smiling at the thought of "Hot Pepper," she saw a Maxima come shooting from the entrance ramp, sending roadside trash whirling, its draft rocking the patrol car. The driver ignored the thatched lines of the gore island and had to break sharply before he was able to pull into Atlanta's fragile, rule-dependent, rush hour commuter derby. "As improper a crossing as it gets," she declared out loud as she hit the blue lights and fell in behind the violator, calling the stop. "Radio, hold me out southbound on the Downtown Connector at Fulton Street on a late-model black Maxima, New York tag, one, X-ray, Mary, two, two, five, occupied one time, white male driver." The car pulled slowly into the emergency lane, the driver seeming uncertain, brake lights on, off, on, off, his silhouette leaning right. Her foot copied his, on the brakes, on the gas, off, on. She followed him a hundred yards or so until he pulled to a stop in the right emergency lane.

Beginning of rush hour was always the most dangerous, traffic just fast enough so that accidents, occurring at the higher speeds, were more injurious. She stepped out of the cruiser, hypervigilant of the roaring freeway on her left. An eighteen-wheeler's big tires, head high, whooshed close. Speeding cars and a hot wind swirled dust and debris across fourteen lanes. She put her hand up to shield her eyes as she approached the Maxima. Muscle memory took over: coming up close on the rear of the driver's side, touching the trunk with her entire palm flat on the warm metal, watching the barely visible print evaporate. The oils from her body could be evidence if a driver made a run for it. The safety films at the academy had perps hiding there ready to spring out: "Make sure the trunk is latched." She pressed the lid but in the noise of the traffic, which wasn't in the training film, couldn't be certain what she heard—something, a click?

She moved to stand just behind the driver's window and, leaning down, began a polite, "Sir, the reason I stopped you is because you merged illegally, crossing the gore."

The driver, about forty years old, didn't look at her but stared straight ahead, his large hands hovering over the steering wheel. "I crossed what?" His lips were badly chapped, pieces of skin peeling off with some tiny, fresh bloody spots.

"The gore, the diagonal lines between the ramp lane and the traffic lane. Could I see your license and proof of insurance?"

His jaw muscles clenched beneath gray-stubbled cheeks. "You stopped me for crossing some lines?"

She focused on his hands. On the back of his left hand was a fuzzed-line tattoo of a joker with the hat points on the knuckles. A jail-type tattoo of blue-gray ink. "Sir?" Checking the interior of the car. "Sir, do you have your license?"

"You stopped me for that?" The points of the hat spread as his fingers tightened around the steering wheel.

"Sir, it's a violation."

"I apologize, Officer. I didn't know it was against the law."

"May I see your driver's license." There was a can of carburetor cleaner and a black case on the passenger seat.

"I said I was sorry. Give me a break." His eyes were on hers as it registered, all wrong—carburetor cleaner for a new car? No. Carburetor cleaner, the lazy man's gun cleaner, the black case.

"Sir, do you have your license?"

"Look, Officer"—he was beginning to spit his words—"I pulled over, I apologized for breaking a tiny rule that I didn't know existed. Now why don't you give me a fucking break."

She'd already heard it in his voice anyway: his wires crossed, now pulled too tight, a jailhouse joker, a convict. Now they both knew he couldn't con her. His right hand went to his jacket. Backing away, she reached for her weapon, unsnapping the safety strap, fast-drawing. "Radio, start me another." Before she could finish the transmission he was moving, opening the car door. She backed toward her cruiser, seeking cover, careful of the rubble of the freeway under her boots. As quickly, before she could get to the car, he was out of the Maxima, both arms in a shooting stance, short barrel, a glint of fire.

The world slowed, the expressway faded, and the sounds of traffic were gone. She saw gray-white smoke from her gun, saw the rounds entering the blue cloth of his shirt, and watched as he fell backward in the blowing dirt. Then there was only her own breathing and the weight of her weapon.

Like a phone ringing in someone else's house, radio was calling: "3306, 3306, 3306."

"3306." Her mouth formed words but she couldn't hear them.

Still in tactical mode, her focus was on the driver, though he had to be dead; she had clearly seen the rounds entering exactly where his heart should be. She moved closer to him, slowly, still pointing the nine, keeping the sights trained, her eyes gritty from the flying dirt and not blinking. She kicked his weapon away, breathing heavy, her mouth open, smelling and tasting gunpowder.

The stream of time eddied and broke as she pointed her gun at the motionless man. Eventually, she dropped her arms to a waist-high position. Then Pepper was there, calling out as he ran up, "Salt, Salt." He touched her shoulder. Only then did she holster. But the wind had blown something into her eyes, making it hard for her to see.

Pepper took her elbow and made a cradle with his arm, guiding her down to the dirt-coated asphalt. "Radio, 3306 has been shot. Ambulance. Code 3!"

She wanted to tell him it was okay but she got distracted trying to clear her sight. She touched her eyes slowly, carefully. They felt sticky. One eye cleared enough for her to see that her hand was covered in blood, and she was confused because she hadn't touched the dead man. His blood wasn't on her. Now her lips were wet and tasted of gun smoke, a sharp flavor mingling with her own trickling blood.

Pepper was telling her, "You're okay. You're going to be okay." She felt his hands moving her hair, tracing through her scalp. The words to a childhood prayer had been trying to surface. "Lead me," was the only part she seemed to remember. And then she lay back and rested on the hot pavement, not far from the gritty white lines of the gore.

2.

DREAMS

She was a chair maker, alone in sepia-tinted woods, wearing overalls and gloves. In the distance, seen through a mist, were trees, their almost black trunks visible in a light fog. The trunks of the closer trees, their limbs bare, appeared darker. The ground was covered in brown leaves. A clearing, her workspace, room for materials and the work.

She had just finished the first chair of rough, gray, uneven boards that stuck up at odd heights on the back, a chair of the folk, not a standard size but larger, with an unusual elegance.

Then someone faceless, nameless, but important, came into the clearing and admired the chair and then vanished.

She began to decide what to use for her next chair, whether to use some rough tree limbs, some shiny painted-primary-color boards, or the same rough weathered boards that the first chair had been made from. She chose the rough boards and began again.

The dream shifted. The mist swirled back revealing the upstairs of her house. Trees gave way to walls. Leaves blew back from bloodied flowers on the rug. Terror crept into her gut at the realization of what was coming. Her paint-stained hands were sticky but now with viscous blood.

Her father's skull rolled at her feet while she stood frozen, unable to move, call out, or cry for help.

3.

RECOVERY

Salt woke to twilight and tentatively made her way from the hospital bed to the wide window tinted with an aqua color that washed the panorama, high above the city of Atlanta, with a softer, cleaner light, a vastly different perspective than from the streets of The Homes. She touched the crease in her scalp, which in her reflected face seemed to continue down over her forehead, eye, and cheek, effects of the anesthesia still lingering.

Grady Hospital, called "The Gradys" by some old Atlantans, plural from a time when the hospital was divided by segregation, was all too familiar. She frequented the trauma center to interview victims and witnesses and sometimes for wounded colleagues. It never seemed to change: the muffled sounds, soft-soled shoes on linoleum, the muted opening and closing of the doors, and the sick smells underneath disinfectant.

But her first time here she had come to see her father. He was restrained with bandages that tied him to the bed and she'd over-heard someone say it was so he wouldn't throw furniture. "He's a jumper," she remembered someone saying and she'd thought they were wrong because she'd never seen her father jump or even run anywhere. He was a walker.

She had worn her Sunday dress. Her mother told her, "Smile and tell him you made an A on the math test."

"But I—" Salt had said.

"Put on your best face. Do you want him to worry?" Her mother pushed her into the room.

The room had been too warm, too close, as this room was now. Arms spread, she pressed her body and the stitched wound against the cool glass.

"You look like an angel."

She jumped, startled, then realized there had been a knock but she'd thought it was part of the memory.

"I didn't mean to scare you. Shouldn't you be in bed?" At first Salt didn't recognize the chief, the big guy himself, his uniform blending into the darkening room. Only his shiny brass badge and insignia caught the light. He was a huge man with terra-cotta skin and gray eyes. Her father's face began to recede though she held on.

"Where were you?" her mother had asked. Her father moaned in the bedroom. His voice heard from anywhere in the house.

"Stay here with him," shouted her mother.

Salt had given a little push to the door of her parents' bedroom and stood looking through the barely cracked door. Her father was lying on the floor and when he lifted his head to look up at her there was sticky blood on his face.

She shook her unbandaged head to get out of the memory, then quickly realized that her backside might be exposed through the loosely tied hospital gown and tried to sidestep her way back to the bed. "I think I'm still a little confused, the drugs maybe. No one told me you were coming."

"I always make my way here ASAP when my officers are injured. How's your head feel?"

"They said it's superficial, a mile—mild—concussion."

The chief walked to her side at the bed and put his hand out. "Good, that it's not so bad. Bad enough," he said, shaking her hand, the movement jarring her eyesight. "If there's anything you need, tell Major Townsend. At the window, what were you looking at?"

"Just looking. The city is really different from up here. You know 'A kinder, gentler, city,'" she said.

When he smiled it was like the grin of the Cheshire cat, all teeth gleaming through the dimness. Closer now, his eyes looked tired. Salt felt groggy from the anesthesia, trying to work out if the chief was part of the memory or the here and now.

"It's the whole picture, not just one perspective, that makes it really beautiful. You did what you had to do on the expressway. I hear about your everyday work, Officer Alt," said the chief. "I hope you know the regard your fellow officers have for you." He turned, walked over to the window, and stood looking out.

After what seemed a long silence Salt said, "Chief?"

It was his turn to snap back to the moment. "Some days it's hard to tell the forest for the trees," he said.

She thought of the trees in her dream. "Yes, sir," she said, and fumbled for the light switch pinned to the hospital pillow.

As the fluorescent light flickered on, the chief turned to leave. He stood with his back to the door and snapped to attention. He saluted her: "Salt," then made an about-face. Before she could return the salute he was gone and she realized that he had used her street name.

The door hadn't even clicked shut before the department chaplain stuck his head in. "I'm ready for the prayer. I had to wait for the chief to leave," he said, walking in and sitting down in the chair next to the bed. He opened a black notebook with the city seal on the front. The preacher was wearing a clerical collar with his dress uniform suit coat. Little white tufts of hair sprang randomly from his pink head.

"Chief was here," she said, sorting the dreams from the present.

"'The Nondenominational Prayer Specified for Police Officers Shot in the Line of Duty.'" He cleared his throat. "'Yea, though I walk through the valley of'—no, wait. That's the one for 'Killed in Action.' Oh, here it is," he said, turning the page. "'Officers Surviving Injury in the Line of Duty.'" "'Yea, though I walk through the valley—' It's the same one," he said, dismayed.

"Chaplain." She tried to gently interrupt him. "Could you get me some water?"

"Oh, sure," he said, and stood up quickly, searching the room. The notebook fell on the floor and the prayers scattered. He bent down to scoop them up and banged his head on the food tray as he tried to stuff most of the prayers back into the notebook. "I'll put those in order later," he said, and continued looking for water. "Where do they keep the ice?" he asked, picking up the hospital cup with its flexible straw.

"I think the ice machine is next to the nurses' station."

"Oh, right," he said.

"Is Homicide here?" she asked before he opened the door. He was having trouble with the cup and the notebook with the loose prayers.

"They've been waiting until I finish."

"Could you tell them to come on in?"

"I'll get the water." He seemed relieved to be going rather than praying. He pried open the door with the edge of the notebook, then wedged it open with his foot, calling out to the detectives in the hall, "She said for you to come in. I'm bringing her water."

In all police-involved shootings Homicide processed the scene, took statements, completed the initial investigation, and presented the results to Internal Affairs, which then conducted its own investigation.

The two detectives from Homicide filled the doorway. Salt tried to even out her breath, like she had been taught on the firing range, right before squeezing the trigger, a breath in, part of a breath out.

The detectives, Hamm and her partner, Best, were two of Homicide's most respected and they were both fat, really, really fat. But neither seemed to mind all the jokes: "Their basic food groups? Glazed, powdered, jelly, and chocolate." "Is that your belly or did you swallow the suspect?" "Two pigs in a poke." In fact they both wore little pig pins: hers on her jacket lapel, his as a tie tack. Their reputation as detectives was exceptional but they had additional high visibility because of their size. Both were almost as wide as they were tall. Hamm, now at Salt's bedside, quickly tried to put her at ease. "We just want to get the basics and we'll be out of here. From what we could tell from the scene, you did all the right things."

"Why did he do it?" Salt asked. A flashbulb of memory went off, bringing into focus the hairs of his knuckles spreading from the joker hat as he'd tightened on the steering wheel.

"He was a 'three strikes you're out' candidate," answered Best, "twice convicted of violent crimes committed with guns. Name, Johnny Mitchell, out of New York. They have him linked to a major drug cartel, but only as a contract worker, very low rung. His handlers won't give a shit that he's gone. He was known for pinching off something for himself anyway. He had a trunkload of guns, mostly handguns and a couple of rifles, all with altered serial numbers."

"I'm starting the tape," said Hamm, placing a mini-recorder on the tray table and rotating it in front of her. Best gave the date, time, and place of the interview, as well as the names of those present.

"Officer Alt, tell us what happened on the afternoon of April 18th," Hamm said for the record.

Salt began with the gore violation, leaving out the rules of the game she and Pepper had been playing, trying to give them every other detail. When it came to the part where the perpetrator jumped from his car with the gun pointed at her, she remembered to say, "He put me in fear of my life," the phrase that justified the use of deadly force by a police officer.

"He put me in fear of my life," she repeated, took in a few short breaths, then let a long breath come slowly, controlling her breathing, still seeing the rounds going into his chest. She looked down at her fingers pulling the trigger on a frayed edge of the bedsheet. Hamm lightly covered Salt's fist with her own soft, fleshy fingers. The tape recording would not reflect that touch.

"Do you know how many rounds you fired?" asked Best.

She was tempted to say "enough" but conceded, "I don't know."

"You fired four rounds center mass," said Hamm.

The words were posted on the walls of every classroom in the training academy: *Ability. Opportunity. Jeopardy.* In every deadly-force situation an officer had to instantly evaluate: *Ability. Opportunity. Jeopardy.*

"Salt?" Detective Hamm reminded her that the tape was running.

"I didn't know I had been shot but I saw my rounds go into his shirt." She felt the stitches stretch on her scalp as her jaw moved.

"That concludes the preliminary interview with Officer Sarah Alt. The time is seven-forty-five p.m.," said Best, shutting off the recorder.

Salt didn't want to ask but did anyway. "How long before I know how it's ruled?"

"You did fine," said Hamm, collecting the recorder and their interview notes. "We took the guns to the crime lab. They'll do what they can to raise the serial numbers. But since the perp's not at large they won't be in any hurry, backed up like usual. When and if we get some numbers ATF will do traces."

Then they were gone and it was all fuzzy, like they were moving too fast and she was in slow motion.

The notebook with the prayers wasn't with the chaplain when he came back with her water. Placing the full cup on the food tray where the recorder had been, he asked, "Is your family here? Do you need me to talk to them about anything?"

"No, my mother lives in North Carolina." Salt hadn't listed any family on the emergency call section of the personnel form. Pepper would know who and how to call if something worse happened. It was good of the chaplain not to mention her father. Or maybe he didn't know. She often wondered how much talk there was of him. It was a long time ago and not many people were left that had worked with him.

She looked to the window, where the sky had changed from satiny pink and orange to deeper violet and gray. The chaplain asked if he could get her something other than water. She told him no and thanked him for coming. Closing the door softly, he left the room.

Her stitches were without a bandage so that air would help them heal more quickly. Alone now, she reached up and touched again the line of shaved scalp. It was on the opposite side from her father's wound. She thought about having to cut the rest of her hair to match the shaved part.

From her bed Salt watched through the wide window as a searchlight scanned the oncoming night, moving back and forth across the low clouds above the skyline. What was it they wanted you to see that you hadn't already? Another searchlight from some opposite location crisscrossed the first light and the two lights came together, then spread back out over the city sky.

4.

COODA POTPIE

Their fear for her had been great and this was her first day back at work. Individually and as a group they were formidable, huddling, large arms encircling her, hugging in turn, badges snagging on silver buttons, batons tangling, their vests buffering breasts and chests.

"Nice hair," said Big Fuzzy, punching her on the arm. But at the hospital he had stumbled over his words: "When you came on the radio, I could hear it in your voice and since you never—I mean I knew. Oh, hell . . ." his voice trailed off and he looked away before continuing. "When you said, 'Radio, start me another,' I knew it was bad."

"Fuzz," she had said, and laid a hand on his arm.

They were guarded in their tenderness. Blessing and Pepper had started a play fight at her bed, jostling for position at her side, going for their batons, threatening moves to their holsters.

"Unhand her, you vile piece of excrement!"

"You, sir, are a scalawag!"

They had a baton sword fight with swashbuckling moves, jumping on chairs and the bed across the hospital room. The nurses threw them out, laughing and charmed by their antics.

These fools were all assigned to the "War Zone." Every police officer in the city would tell you that if you could work the Third, you could police anywhere. They were one-man cars, answering more calls per officer than in any other area, with a higher percentage of the calls violent. They had more projects than any precinct. Salt had never worked or wanted to work anywhere else—her shift, the four p.m. to midnight, busiest of all. Proactive policing and patrolling were luxuries. Most nights it was a struggle just to keep up. Radio would advise, "We have pages pending," which meant ten calls per screen, or pages, calls waiting to be dispatched to the approximately ten officers who were already working other calls. "Can any unit clear?" radio would implore. On the rare occasion that they were caught up, the officers would try to get something to eat, take a restroom break, or check on problem areas. Socializing happened on calls, cars pulled together, driver's window to driver's window, briefly passing gossip, complaining about command, or quickly catching up on off-duty lives.

Almost every night was an adventure. She often felt like Alice falling down the rabbit hole. In the culture of poverty things sometimes appeared upside down. Citizens elsewhere never left their houses without identification in purses or wallets, while an ID for denizens of the zone might mean incarceration for outstanding warrants or going to jail under the correct name. Rookies became veterans when they learned to ferret out real names and dates of birth. For new officers, even the language presented a barrier. Accents of the ghetto, street slang, and the rapid-fire conversations of disputants left many rookies mystified.

Sarge, their watch and sector supervisor, yelled, "Watch, fall in!"

Salt turned to the roll-call room mirror, checking her newly shorn hair and the part left by Mitchell's bullet.

She and her shift mates formed the line for roll call.

Theirs was the southeast quadrant of Atlanta. For policing it was divided into two sectors and ten beats, many of which had become ghettos of housing projects and poverty, testaments to the legacies of slavery, Jim Crow, and economic discrimination. Salt had policed beat 306 for ten years. Third shift, four to midnight.

"Okay, 3301, your regular, 3302, 3305," said Sarge, going down the assignment sheet. "You, 3306"—he looked at Salt—"you'll be on the desk."

"Sergeant," she responded, roll call formal. "I've been cleared for full duty."

"Don't you—"

"Sarge, request permission for my regular."

"First day back and you're already a pain in my ass. See me after roll call. 3307." He continued down the roster.

After they broke she walked to the podium where the sergeant was signing forms and gathering his work. "Sarge, SOP says I can resume full duty."

"Fuck the SOP and don't quote it to me. Hell, I wrote the damn SOP. I just want you to take it easy for a while."

"Sarge, I want to get back on the horse."

He shook his head and crossed out a line on the work roster. "3306, your regular."

And so she was back, carrying gear, clipboard, report forms holder, ticket books, and water bottle, and heading to get 306's car. She loaded her utility belt with a large flashlight and her baton and checked the pepper spray and weapon clips in the leather pouches. The heaviest items were the radio with the attached shoulder mic on her left side, and the Smith & Wesson 9mm on her right. The belt fit snug against the bottom edge of the bullet-resistant vest under her uniform shirt.

The big white patrol cars were all Crown Vics and her car, which she shared with two other shifts, like many of the War Zone cars, had scraped doors, a smashed front bumper, and a siren that sounded more like a hiccup than a scream. But when she got all her gear settled and got behind the steering wheel, and as she strapped the belt over her chest, she felt the familiar giddy high of anticipation. All those dings and damage to the car were evidence of some adventure, some often-repeated tale of comedy, terror, heroics, or brotherhood. This dent or that bullet hole on a car could be read like a "How To" or "How Not To" manual of police work, or could be fine material for the next precinct comic. They couldn't wait to get the rookies, fresh out of the academy, so the veterans could compete for who got to embellish the stories first and how much.

Radio gave her a couple of minor highway accidents back-to-back and she milked the last accident by not telling radio she had finished the call, so that she and Pepper could meet up for a six o'clock "afternoon" lunch. An easy afternoon, and a whole thirty-minute lunch at the Big Buddha. Then, as always, toward evening and on, the calls started and they responded and ran and tried to keep ahead of the violence.

On Thayer, in the very deserted darkness, Salt slowly steered the cruiser, tightening her bladder, and hoping for a quiet last ten minutes till the end of the watch. She touched the still raw scar on her forehead and at the same time saw her father's hand as it had moved toward his bloody head. She'd seen him before in the cruiser with her, riding shotgun, while she'd remember him talking about the streets. *"Oh, you shoulda been there, girl,"* he'd say with a laugh. Then she'd imagine telling him, thinking he could see it through her eyes. Her eyes, her vision gained starry speckles. She shifted in the broken, low driver's seat, distracting herself by trying to remember the childhood prayer. Just as some of the lines were coming up, something about *lambs* and *through the darkness,* a skeleton-like woman appeared under the dim rays of the lone working streetlight. Salt stomped on the brake pedal of the battered patrol car and felt the vibrations through the sole of her boot. She heard the scraping of the worn brake shoes and the grinding of bare metal. The pieces of the prayer vanished. As the woman came more fully into the light, Salt recognized Shannell—prancing, knees high, like a majorette—now in the narrow street, right in front of the still-moving patrol car, her giddy motions uninterrupted by the approaching steel bumper. Salt pumped the mushy brakes and brought the heavy police car to a stop. Shannell kept coming, and leaned toward the open window of the cruiser. When she stopped, her arms continued swinging, like a little girl being cute. Her head shook and swung in an impossible arc and reminded Salt of those bobbing toys that attach to the dash of a car. She was all bone, sweat shine, and skinny legs. Her scalp alternated between wild sprouts of hair and bald patches. A slipping tube top flattened what little curve of breasts she had and black leggings hugged the bones of her thighs.

"Big D cut," Shannell said.

"How bad?" Salt tugged at the open neck of her navy/black uniform shirt, pulling it to get some air beneath her vest, undershirt, and athletic bra. Whoever had decided that dark wool-blend uniforms were the way to go for officers in a Deep South city had obviously never worked the streets. The humid heat had come early to the usually fine Southern spring and now the car's barely working AC was already on overload. Salt kept the windows down anyway so she could see, hear, and smell the streets better. Except for Shannell, Thayer Avenue seemed deserted, although voices, children's hysteria, harsh laughter, and fighting words echoed down from the corner. Salt recognized Etta James's "Tell Mama," but the music was thinned, coming from cheap or old speakers and a player that skipped and repeated.

"You got to help my man. My Big D he bad cut." Shannell had stopped but her body continued its involuntary disjointed gyrations. Her teeth clicked the downbeat over her words.

In this Southside neighborhood, on the doomed periphery of The Homes, it was really risky to be alone on the street at night. The doors and windows of the small sad houses that still stood were shut against predators that roamed the dark, like roaches seeking an opening to slide through. Every other lot was vacant, houses torn down as nuisance properties. No one sat on stoops, no children ran around catching fireflies.

Shannell grimaced, her lips pulled wide over her clenched teeth. "He's bleedin' like a faucet and walkin' roun', and bleedin' lots and walkin' and I'm tryin' to fine him. You got to hep me fine him, he bleedin' and walkin' roun'." She smiled, coy, some part of her brain reminding her that life would be harder if her D were found dead.

She held on to the car, swaying, lost her balance, then leaned closer. Clown-like, her eyes squinted, her mouth opened in an oval. "Oh, you Salt," she said, sounding pleased with herself.

"Shannell, you couldn't tell it was me? You get something bad in your bump tonight?" Salt's hands felt sticky as she lifted them from the steering wheel.

"You poleese car all muddy." Shannell ran her hand over the windshield. "I couldn't see." She held up her hand, dirty, then wiped it through her fierce hair.

Salt shifted again in the seat as she moved the gear arm up to the park position. Even though at five feet eight she was as tall as some of the male officers, she could barely see over the steering wheel of this old cruiser because the seat was broken down to the floorboard. The big day-watch guy had been driving this car for a couple of years.

Cutting through Shannell's crack chatter, Salt tried to get to the necessities. The best way to catch sight of Big D on these night streets would be by his clothes. "What shirt does D have on?"

"That Raiders one he love and always wear."

"Black with the silver lettering? Where's he cut?"

"Just his arm. Yeah, he love them Raiders. They go to jail almost much as he do."

"Where on his arm?" Salt pictured Big D in his old Raiders shirt, old OG.

"His top arm, near his pit."

"How long since he was cut?"

"Just a minute."

"Who cut him?"

"I diiiid." Shannell dragged out her last word, just like a kid, sampling the consequences of a partial confession.

"Why this time?"

"We just always fight."

"Get in the car and help me find him. Where's the knife?" There was no place on her skinny body to conceal much of anything.

"D took it." She grabbed the door handle before Salt could press the automatic lock release. Then she had one leg in the open window of the back door before Salt saw what she was doing. "Aw, Shannell, don't come through the window, let me get the door unlocked."

"Oh, I can." She had one leg in and one out, all jittery, she couldn't be still even when stuck. Finally, she got all the way back out. "I can't never decide which way to go."

"Just get in the backseat on the other side so I can see and talk to you while we look for Big D. I don't know why you stay with him."

"I'm not scared of him. He the one cut."

"He's always the one cut. Why doesn't he move out?"

Shannell passed in front of the headlights to get to the other side of the car. "'Cause I'm Shannell and he luuuvv my cooda potpie!" she sang, grabbing her crotch, hoochie dancing and laughing. When the skin-and-bones woman opened the back-right door and plopped onto the seat, Salt was overwhelmed by Shannell's odor: metallic crack, recent sexual encounters, and the reek of days without proximity to any body of water larger than a shot glass. She tried not to smile or breathe in the "cooda potpie." Salt exhaled as she tripped the auto lock system, the simultaneous clicks of the four locks ensuring Shannell's containment in the caged backseat. She turned her head to the open window, scanning the street while she took in air.

Everyone in and around The Homes knew Shannell cut Big D on a regular basis. Big D never showed for court because he almost always had warrants out on him for some crime or other, usually receiving stolen autos. But now he had to be found quick. With a cut to the upper arm he might be bleeding heavy. Shannell might go down for his murder tonight rather than next week or next year, though the opportunity would probably come to her again.

Salt's hands on the steering wheel were still just for a moment before she shifted the gear arm to go into the urgent search for Big D. As she checked the rearview mirror something in her own reflection, in her eyes, reminded her of the skinny kid she'd been when she'd needed that prayer. Along with an adrenaline surge, she saw herself watching from the twilight woods, her hands on rough tree bark, the lights of her own home. *Lead me through the darkness.*

The call log, open on the console beside her, was going on three pages long now. It was almost time for the shift to be over. The gun belt cut into her hips. Her water bottle in the console had been empty since around eight, when the zone busted into violence. Calls rolled, one not over before they were called for the next, every one somebody's emergency. Her bladder shot her a sharp reminder. Unlike the men, she couldn't just unzip behind an abandoned building. And now she and Shannell would be tracking Big D and there would be reports, tickets, and the logs to finish after either finding D dead or something close to dead.

Shannell's funk stewed in the patrol car. It was hard to keep watch for D and roll fast enough to get fresh air through the window. They crawled through The Homes trying to pick up a blood trail or a sighting of D in his Raiders shirt. Back to the alley where the fight had ended, asking each corner gang, passing the dope traps, asking after D, bloody minutes dripping away. These five- or ten-block streets were filled with the scrapings of the young who had nothing to lose and the old who'd already lost everything. Here blood was cheap. People had stopped taking much note of it when it was splattered on the ground. While a halo of bright city lights illuminated the sky above, the lights of these sorry streets were either shot out or so few and far between that there were more shadows than light. At the corner of Moury and Thirkeld, Shannell shrieked, "I see him, there he is, look by the barrel." Salt turned the exterior spotlight over the vacant lot and there beside a rusted fire barrel was a huge mound, Raiders silver dimmed by dirt. D, on the ground, not moving. She pressed the accelerator, tires grabbing the curb, undercarriage scraping metal against concrete, driving the car into the lot as glass popped and cracked in the short weeds beneath the tires as they crossed over to D. Shannell screamed to be released to get to the man she'd stabbed. "Deeee." Salt caught glimpses of her in the rearview mirror, twisting in and out of the reflection. Swiftly she refocused the spotlight on D, then manually lifted the single lock on the driver's door and left all other doors locked. Shannell screamed again when she saw that she was being left in the prisoner compartment.

In a couple of strides Salt was out, leaning over D, her fingers feeling for a pulse in the sweaty rolls of his neck. She was both relieved and furious when D groaned and tried to push up with one hand. Blood left his brain again and full consciousness eluded him. He rolled and slumped back toward the ground. Keying the radio mic on her shoulder, Shannell's muffled screams in the background, she called out the location for the ambulance: "Emergency Code 3."

"3306, raise 3394. Sarge, I'm out on a person stabbed. Ambulance en route." D went still again, his eyes rolling back under half-closed lids. Salt sprinted to the cruiser for the first-aid kit and scene tape. She snatched the keys off her belt and popped the trunk. The lid jumped up, blocking Shannell's smeary face, plastered to the rear window. The car rocked with Shannell's attempts to change her status, to argue her case to get out.

"3306, you okay?" Sarge checking on her.

"Af-firm."

Inside the trunk she found a ridiculous plethora of highway flares, a garbage bag of stuffed animals, a bicycle wheel, no kit, and no yellow ribbon. "Shit fire," she muttered. The car had been to too many crime scenes and no one had mustered the energy to replace supplies. She fantasized briefly about lighting the flares around Big D. If he went south, Homicide would give her hell about not stringing the tape and preserving physical evidence. Again, she hoped D would live.

Over the radio she heard the Code 8s announced for other cars going out of service. Her shift was en route to the precinct, their night over, done. The next shift would be in no hurry to enter the melee. She was now officially on overtime, slogging through a haze. If she had to run it would be slower; perps could catch a corner sooner. Her brain on overload, she registered the checklist of crime scene duties. There wasn't much benefit to police overtime. She needed to pee worse than ever.

Salt slammed the trunk. Shannell's face strained toward the dark crumple of Big D. She would cross the *t*'s and dot the *i*'s to make sure Shannell would spend at least the next month in jail, before the judge would get tired of D not showing up for the hearings. During that month or so Shannell would cool down and be off the pipe, and Big D would stay alive and his wound would heal. Then they would have a fresh start at the same games all over again. Unless D died. Then Homicide would take it and Shannell would never have another chance.

Salt walked around Big D, reminded of his large circumference, needing to turn him to check his breathing. He just might survive, and if he was not in shock but just passed-out drunk, he could still have the knife Shannell stabbed him with. Although the ursine-looking man was normally gregarious and easygoing, he could be a mean drunk, and at three-hundred-plus pounds he could do damage. She'd once seen him tear a door off its hinges with a single swipe.

"Where are you hurt, Big D? Can you hear me?" She hoped he was conscious enough to recognize her voice. No response, just his labored breathing. Blood was pooling under his body. "D, it's Salt." Carefully she knelt closer. "D?" She touched his arm, thick as a ham. "D, it's Salt." Keying the mic again she asked for the ETA of the ambulance. She pulled at his meaty shoulder to turn him but he didn't help her, his dense body was close to deadweight, his left cheek stayed pressed to a patch of dusty weeds. She succeeded only in moving his torso half an inch forward and back. His old Raiders jersey was torn and losing pieces of the luminescent lettering. Then he groaned, opened his eyes, and said, "Bitch, I'll—" and then lost his words as the blood ebbed in his brain. But his hand had inched to the ground under him.

Finger on the radio transmit button, it occurred to her to ask for a backup. But she couldn't see a knife, just bright blood soaking into the dirt. Shit, she didn't need this. She rubbed at her gritty eyes and reminded herself to keep her hands off the itchy scar. Tired, hungry, and on her last nerve, she was too near to having the night done, ready for relief, and here was D reaching underneath his chest.

"He done dropped the knife." The voice, bitter and strained, came from behind her. Darrell, aka Lil D, son of the D on the ground. She'd seen him earlier at the dope hole near Sam's Chicken Shack. Lil D, named after his father, Shannell and Big D's twenty-four-year-old, on a sure path to dying in the streets and unlikely to reach twenty-five. He showed what he had—a smeared butcher knife. "He done dropped it and I picked it up after him." Small, thin, and shirtless, he held the knife, blade out. His body, like that of his mother, was small but muscles tensed and twisted beneath his deep brown skin. With one hand he held a towel, ever present around his neck, covering a port-wine mark; with the other he kept swinging the knife forward and back in the same rhythm as his mother's arms when she'd flagged Salt down earlier. Lil D was a holder for the dope boys, lowest rung on the crack ladder, paying off his mother's debts when she couldn't.

"Put the knife on the ground," Salt ordered. This family couldn't stay still. Lil D kept moving and saying that D had dropped it. "Lil D, put it on the ground!"

Shannell yelled something sharp; Salt could just make out "D" and "My baby." The big car rocked with her exertions.

Lil D stopped where he was and, still holding the knife, looked toward Shannell's muffled screaming. "What you pick her up for?"

"Lil D, knife on the ground."

Last thing Salt wanted was to tell Lil D his mother was under arrest. Big D began moaning again.

"My daddy just laying there like a dog. Where's the ambulance?"

"I called. It's on the way. Put the knife on the ground." Salt was trying to keep her eyes on the blade as well as on Big D's attempts at regaining consciousness, hoping that Big D didn't have anything else under his huge belly that could be used as a weapon.

Now she keyed the mic, asking for backup. "3306 to radio, start me a unit," and then, talking to Lil D, "Lil D, he's okay. I need you to put the knife on the ground."

"My mama ain't goin' to jail."

Salt kept close hold of the mic, her safety net, the antenna biting into her cheek, everyone at the precinct changing shifts, worst time for trouble and she was calling, "Radio, give me a backup." She really didn't want to start a move to her holster.

"She ain't goin' to jail," repeated Lil D. Several more members of the gang and gang wannabes came up from the street.

"You know she won't stay more than a month. She'll get rehab." Salt tried to reassure him.

A crowd was forming. People came to watch. Word was out. Shannell was still screaming in the car but wasn't visible because the windows had fogged over; Salt added possible heatstroke to the growing crisis. Big D moaned louder. Lil D still held the knife. Rocks, bits of glass, and the rough stubble of weeds bit into Salt's knees as she knelt at Big D's back. She kept her eyes on the crowd, on their eyes, all wide and glittery, reflecting light from the cruiser's headlights. The crowd grew: gangbangers, dopers, users, children, all watching, turning eagerly to one another with predictions, excited to see how it would play. One of the gang members, Stone, his face permanently frozen in anger, jaw muscles bulging, eyes squinting, brow furrowed, called out like a hellfire preacher, yelling to Lil D and for the crowd's benefit, "You gone let your daddy just lie there? You gone let Miss Poleese take your mama to jail?" He walked closer, four yards and closing, crowd following, mouths moving, necks straining. Someone, a man's voice in the middle of the group, testified back, responding to Stone's excitations, "That's right." Several women loudly joined the call and response: "They don't care," in support of Lil D, identifying with the too-long wait for an ambulance and D on the ground in the broken-bottle grass. The crowd now closer, within stride distance, arms gleaming with sweat, hands making whirling gestures.

"Y'all, please, give him room to breathe, let some air get through." She swept space with her arm.

A far-off siren wailed; it was hard to approximate distances because of echoes off the city hills.

Careful not to interact with Stone; one wrong word, one stupid
move, by anyone, could ignite the scene. One misjudgment could
tip her hand toward her holster; she already had the "in jeopardy"
reason to draw her gun. But it wouldn't go over well with the crowd.
She was on empty and desperate, grabbing for anything. She thought
of the prayer and Shannell, dancing in the headlights. "Cooda potpie," Salt said out loud.

"What?" said Lil D.

"Cooda potpie. Big D loves her cooda potpie."

"That bullshit." Lil D looked toward the car and his mother.

"Listen, Lil D. She said he loves her cooda potpie. Big D is
going to make it, again. He's going to be okay. He's more drunk
than cut."

From the crowd, someone laughed, and seized the chance to
have a speaking part. "Tha's right, she always says he loves her 'pie.'"

The prayer, the way her father would calm her when she was
little, when she was scared something would happen to him, when
she was on the edge. *"Lead me,"* Salt said to herself again. She said
to Lil D, "He's okay. Your daddy's okay. He's okay."

A close siren yelped as blue lights spangled the block—Pepper.
His cruiser spun up, slinging dirt, grass, and gravel as he slid the
car into the lot. The car rocked from the sudden stop and Pepper
jumped out, leaving the car door swinging—cool. The crowd
loved his entrance and began yelling, "Pepper, Pepper, it's Pepper,"
calling out his street name. The ambulance, on the tail of his
cruiser, turned and crossed the curb. The kids in the crowd got
louder, sing-songing the street names of the two cops, "Salt and
Pepper, Salt and Pepper," laughing at each other.

"Now! Lil D! Put down that knife. The paramedics need to get to Big D. You can talk to your mother, let her know Big D is going to be okay," Salt kept telling him, watching for his shoulders to lower, watching for the slack in his arm.

Lil D let it go, slung the knife to the ground, close enough to where Salt could grab it. And the paramedics were on Big D in an instant.

Pepper joined the inner circle, pointing to Salt's holster. "Sometimes you too cool. You didn't even unsnap? Must have been hot what with the crowd and all. Girl, you can't cut shit so close, so soon." He tapped her head with his knuckles.

"You're the cool one. Great entrance. Thanks," she said, and went to catch up with Lil D, walking toward his mom in the car.

Lil D's head tilted forward as they walked, pulling the towel to wipe his face. Though his skin was a shade of dark mahogany, the port-wine birthmark, darker, stood out clearly from below his left ear to his collarbone. Salt and he both reached for the door handle at the same time. Shannell jumped out and up against her son.

As they lifted Big D onto a gurney, Pepper stood by with the paramedics, one of whom gave a thumbs-up that Big D would make it. Lil D dashed from his mother to the ambulance. The gang members, including Stone, walking backward, still watching, began to leave the scene.

The crowd filled the hot air with a chorus of, "Cooda potpie, Salt and Pepper, cooda potpie, Salt and Pepper."

Pepper, grinning, walked up to Salt at the patrol car. "What's that they're yelling?" he asked, motioning toward the crowd. "'Pie'?"

5.

FADED LIGHT

It had been two a.m. by the time Shannell was booked and the paperwork completed. Except for the 9mm on the seat beside her, Salt's gear, uniform shirt, belt, and all its accessories were stowed in the trunk of her Honda. With her T-shirt drying from the wind coming in the car's open windows and the city lights fading in the rearview mirror, Salt concentrated as the rest of the prayer came to her:

> *Jesus, tender shepherd, lead me*
> *Through the darkness be Thou near me*
> *Guide thy little lamb tonight*
> *Wake me with the morning bright.*

Halfway into the late-hour commute, flashbacks inserted themselves between the words of the prayer: Big D's ragged shirt, Shannell coming *through the darkness*, her "cooda potpie," and the birthmark on Lil D's thin neck—a regular Homes family. She'd arrested every one of them, except a daughter who was young, living with a grandmother. She'd tried to get social services for them, particularly for Lil D, when he was young and she'd been, what, naive?

"Ten years now," she said out loud. "My first night back. What difference will I have made, Pops?"

As one of the tires bumped over something, Salt jolted back from her altered state, slowed, looked in the rearview mirror but couldn't see anything except a change in the hue of the pavement. The dark trees in the distance, backlit by some dim source, seemed foreign, one of those moments when, even though the road is right, the mind doesn't recognize a familiar way. Then the sign appeared that announced the little town, Cloud, whose rural address was hers and she felt a quick flutter of relief. Construction of a new mini-mart presented itself, a skeleton on the country landscape. The city was spreading toward her small town and its fields and farms.

The trees grew closer to the road as Salt came to her home. Light from a full moon that had just begun to wane struck the glitter of gravel and turned her drive into a sparkle of gray white. The moon seemed to perch on one of the chimneys of the three-story Victorian house that had been in her family for almost a century. To the right of the house there were only woods and fields. Her one neighbor was across a field to the left. The car window still down, appreciating the silent view, she turned off the headlights and air conditioner. She parked behind the house and sat listening as the engine cooled and as the quiet night unfolded with a chorus of tree frogs and night birds.

Still half on alert, she eyed a plump grocery bag by the doorsteps that hadn't been there in the afternoon. As she got out of her car and approached, she recognized the recycled bag that Mr. Gooden, her old neighbor, often left for her. This one held three large sweet onions. She picked up the bag and unlocked the door. A midsize all-black dog bounded out and repeatedly, purposely, bumped into her. He kept up the bumping until she had put the onions on the kitchen table. She dropped her gear bag at the bedroom door and went down the long hall to sit on the living room couch, where the dog buried his head in her lap, blowing his breath onto her until she had run her hands all over him, scratched his ears, rubbed his eyes, and vigorously patted his flanks. Some of his soft fur floated onto the hooked rug. Salt lowered her face to his muzzle and Wonder, with a light flick of his tongue, washed dried sweat from her cheeks.

He followed her back down the hall to the bedroom and jumped on the old iron bed, eagerly watching her moves. He knew the sequence of the nightly rituals. With each divestiture—thirty-pound utility belt unloaded and hung on the closet hook, uniform stripped of brass (department insignia, nameplate, expert pistol pin, and badge) and dropped into a pile for the wash—some of the night's exhaustion abated. Wonder knew his time had come as she slipped on torn jeans and laced up old work boots.

Salt carried the clothes, smelling faintly of urine, to the kitchen, where she dumped them into the washer. Then she and Wonder stood at the screen door and looked out to the pecan grove that spread from the backyard for three and a half fenced acres. As soon as they stepped out she gave the dog a "lie down" in a quiet, almost inaudible voice, then walked to the edge of the yard and clucked softly. The dog, low to the ground, snuck to her feet. Using old Gaelic commands she gave an "away to me" and the dog ran quickly and quietly off to the right, and, even with the moonlight, seemed to disappear. Then they came, like apparitions from the far end of the orchard, five fat mostly white sheep, stepping firmly through the trees with the dog back and forth at their heels. *Lamb . . . Through the darkness.* She thought of Shannell coming out of the dark into that streetlight. When the tiny flock was about ten yards away she gave the dog a "down" and he dropped to his belly.

Salt went over to a small paddock and opened the gate. The sheep jostled each other at the edge of the yard. A soft "walk up" to the dog and he raised slowly, staying exactly where he had lain but forcing the sheep to turn toward her. The lead sheep stepped forward and the rest followed through the paddock gate, which she closed. Wonder settled in to watch his "Sheep TV."

The little flock grazed under the trees during the day. She fed and watered them at night. Closing the gate, Salt walked to the porch, calling, "That'll do, Wonder," and the dog pulled himself from watching through the slats and came with her into the house.

The oak doors of the library were darker where over the decades her family had placed their hands to push them apart, the spots smoother, slicker than the rest of the blond wood panels. As the doors glided easily back into their pockets, Salt was enveloped by the fragrance of cedar. Family lore had it that it was her great-grandmother who insisted that the library shelves, which were built six high on each of the four walls, be made of the aromatic red lumber. For more than two centuries the family had had their roots in this property. Salt was the last to live in the old house, built after the Civil War to replace the original homestead cabin.

The library was bereft of all furniture, bare except for a worn Asian carpet and books from each generation. A few of her great-grandmother's had survived, some in Latin; pocket editions of Tennyson, Browning, and Shakespeare, pages brittle and crumbling, leather bindings cracked and flaking, were on the same shelf next to the plastic cases that held her father's blues and gospel cassette collection. There were also books of her grandfather's. But most of the shelves were taken by her father's books. He had had a unique and personal method of organizing and shelving his books: on a waist-high shelf near the door he kept a ledger that listed which books he'd read each year, and the books were shelved accordingly, by year, on the east-front wall; the books he'd read as a child were on the low shelf of the north wall. On the middle shelves of the east wall were Eudora Welty, Richard Wright, Flannery O'Connor, lots of William Faulkner. "Find out where people come from," he'd say. Walking around their property he'd remind her, "We've got a lot more than some folks ever had." Other than on the streets, this was the place where Salt felt closest to him.

She took a worn copy of *Tarzan and the Lost Empire*, sat down cross-legged with the book open on her lap, and leaned back against the shelves, remembering the smell of her father's flannel shirt as they sat together in a big leather chair, light from a pole lamp holding them in its warm halo. She was still tired and sad from the post-shooting dreams, her vision not really up to focusing on the words of the book. On the heels of the incident on the expressway, images of her father's death had been asserting themselves. Her hand flattened on the open page and she lifted her eyes to the rest of the room, the closed brocade drapes, the deep burgundy rug blurring.

There had never been doubt in the family about how the children paired with their parents. After her brother, John, was born her mother became absorbed with the baby and left Salt to her father to raise. But it seemed now to Salt that she'd been her father's child anyway, even from her birth. He'd talk to her about Howlin' Wolf, about the blues. "Honey," he'd say, "if you know how people feel you can understand why they do what they do." He would tell her stories of what happened at work. "Honey, you can predict what someone will do if you understand how they feel. She just needed someone to talk to. It wasn't me she wanted to cut." He'd explain about the pecan trees out back. "Hundred years old or more. Their flowers are called catkins." He'd talk and she'd ask for more.

She looked over at the last books he'd been reading, some of the titles on their spines in large enough print that she could see them from where she sat: *Depression, Abnormal Psychology, Living with Someone with a Mental Illness.* Her mother believed Satan had taken hold, kept after him to let the preacher lay his hands on him. "You care more about those people than you do your own family," her mother said once. "It's making you sick."

"How did I not know, Pops?"

Wonder lay in the hall at the entrance to the library. It was the only room he never wanted to enter. Salt thought it was the cedar, that maybe he didn't like the smell. It had always made her think of old things: old people, winter clothes, jewelry chests, cedar chests, and coffins.

Wonder, his head on his paws, kept his eyes open, glancing at her, then back down the hall toward the door.

Salt's memory turned to one sharply held incident. It must have been an off-duty day because she was with him. They were going back into the city, going to a movie. She couldn't remember why her mother and brother hadn't come but it felt special. She couldn't remember what the movie was about or much else about the day, except that on the way he told her they needed to stop somewhere, and he said something like "where he worked," not the precinct house but where he patrolled. She remembered that the façade of the building where they stopped was like that of buildings in The Homes, brick with a small porch. She vowed that one day she would go to the police records office and find out if she could retrieve old assignment sheets, find out what beat he'd worked.

He'd held her hand as they walked up to a door. "This is my daughter," he'd said to a woman on the other side of the screen. In a deep, soft voice, "I see that," had been the woman's exact reply. Salt was sure of that. It was what she remembered most clearly from that day. There had been a little more talk between her father and the woman, something had happened the day before, something about money and milk for the baby. There was a very dark baby on her hip and more children at her skirt, their hands against the wire mesh at Salt's level, their skin so dark almost all she could see of them through the screen were their shiny cheeks and eyes. The woman stood behind the screen until he pulled a green envelope, like the ones that had gone with their Christmas cards the year before, out of his shirt pocket and handed it through the slightly opened door.

It was all she remembered about that day, except that back in the car he took a blue bandanna from his pants pocket and wiped his eyes.

Salt closed *Tarzan* and leaned back against a set of Harvard Classics. She tightly clutched the book to her chest. "The streets, depression, this house, all of it you let go. And along with all the rest, Pops, you let go of me."

6.

KNIGHT

The following day, at the outset of their shift, she and Pepper were standing at the intersection of Moury and Thirkeld, in the dense project, buildings close and distant, as far as the eye could see. Water gushed from a couple of open hydrants into the gutters, evaporating in the heat before it reached the bottom of the block.

The project, constructed in the early 1950s, was crammed onto one hundred hilly acres. Sturdy old live oaks reached their limbs high above the buildings they shaded, lining the ten avenues and two through streets along which The Homes were built. From the packed red dirt of the small yards the big trees thrust up the knobby knees of their roots. The buildings were all brown brick, each unit with a small five-by-seven concrete porch hemmed with iron-pipe railings. There were seven hundred families, give or take an eviction or two, in one-, two-, and three-bedroom apartments.

Only a few miles south of Atlanta's downtown business district, the two hundred buildings housed more citizens than any other development in the city. At the highest point, on Shaw Street, the city skyline and tall buildings appeared like a distant smoky mountain ridge.

Salt was the first female cop to be assigned to The Homes and the first white officer since two white officers had shot and killed an unarmed black man there five years before. She had asked for the beat, knowing no one would ever be able to say she had had a cushy rookiehood if she worked The Homes. Since she was the only one to request it, they had to give it to her or explain the discrimination. The defined community and even the name, "The Homes," appealed to her, and it was a bonus when Pepper had been assigned the adjoining beat of warehouses and failing businesses.

In the years just prior to Salt's assignment there had been several instances of children killed by stray gunfire in The Homes. Now she and Pepper watched while the kids played in the spray from the illegally opened hydrants, enjoying the luxury of being there together and with the kids, before the calls took them alone and apart. Soundtrack of the shift, their shoulder mics, crackling every now and then with calls for other cars on other beats. Later it would get constant. They were supposed to report open hydrants; instead Pepper's eyes were on the street above, watching. There was a ten-mile-per-hour speed limit, but the crests of the hills were only half a block away.

You could hear the beater before it came into view. Thump, blum, thump, blum. Bumper, grille, hood, tires. The driver slowed as the blue strobes of the patrol cars reflected off the windshield. Daylight was no guarantee of sufficient visibility. Things could be missed in the sun's glare just as in the night's darkness.

Sun-shot streams of water ran down the bodies of the twenty or so children darting from sidewalk to sidewalk and filling the street with jumping, dancing, squeals, screams, and happy shouts. They were oblivious to any danger and to the detritus—medical waste, Big D's scissored shirt, and all that was left from the drama that had occurred in the lot across the corner the night before. Shannell never explained what the fight had been about, only that Big D "had a problem with it," but she never said what "it" was.

Some older boys came roll-walking down toward them. This year's Homes identifier, limited to the east side of Pryor, was wearing a tennis visor turned upside down, with the bill sticking up, graffiti-marked in multicolor. Along with baggy pants this was the uniform of local gang life, worn with arrogance, defiance, and anger, and more often than not predicting its wearer's future.

"I know what you're thinking," Pepper said, taking a glance at the approaching boys. A trickle of sweat ran through the slick valley of a scar along the left side of his dark, dark brown face. "Some things change and stay the same."

When Salt had started at the police academy, Pepper's face had been seamless, all of them fresh-faced rookies. They discovered their birthdays were only a day apart and that they were the same age, both having just graduated from college. He had drawn her in, though they were an unlikely pair. He was gregarious, lighthearted, and handsome, she reserved and determined. Classmates' curious eyes would hold a second longer, noting a shared laugh between them or their pairing off at meals when Pepper's wife, Ann, had packed extras for Salt in his lunch.

There was only one other woman in their class of thirty rookies and Tonya had been the flirty type. Salt was not. Some of the guys hit on her, a few were hostile, some indifferent. But Pepper teased, setting her up so she could have the good lines, getting her in on the rowdy back-and-forth. He was tall and athletic and the other rookies liked him, wanted him to like them.

One day at the firing range, second month into their training, Salt had asked him why he included her. "I like the way you think is all," he had said, and laughed it off. "Everybody needs good backup. Me too." It was Pepper, whose real name was Greer, who had given her the name that stuck, the only name any cop remembered to call her: "Salt," from the shiny nameplate she wore opposite the badge on her brand-new uniforms. The night of their graduation ceremony they'd inspected each other. "'S. Alt' it says. Salt," pronounced Pepper.

Today Pepper's smile was directed at the squealing children, the same hundred-watt grin that made people want to tell jokes just to keep that light on. She thought of that one rainy night in their first year, after they'd both received their assignment together in what was known as the War Zone. The call was to a possible burglary. They had run from the rain to an overhang outside the building. Pepper leaned over and sniffed. "You don't smell like a wet dog." Salt asked what the hell he was talking about. "You, you don't smell like a wet dog. Black folks say white people smell like wet dogs." With Pepper's smile reflecting the bare bulb of the overhang light, she felt like she had been given a perfect gift.

She smiled at the memory and caught the eye of a little girl with wheat-colored hair and honey-brown skin, who smiled back from the middle of the wet, jumping kids.

She and Pepper rescued each other regularly. Not much they learned in the academy had prepared them for these streets. Even Pepper, at first, wondered what they had gotten themselves into. He, at least, understood the language, the accents, the culture of poverty. Though he himself had come from a middle-class home, his parents had come up hard. In the beginning, except for memories of her father's stories and admonitions, Salt felt not much of her own background prepared her for the job and these streets. They both stumbled through their rookie days, comparing experiences, commiserating and consoling. She thought he had taught her more, but he claimed she helped him to sort things out.

Two of the littlest boys from the hydrants ran over to Pepper and slung the water from their arms on him, daring each other to stay while the big cop made mock monster lunges at them. He grabbed them up, one in each arm, their slippery giggling giving way to looks of amazement at being so far off the ground and so near his face. The boy on the opposite side from the scar leaned around Pepper's face to watch as the smaller boy traced his fingers down the long-healed wound.

Six years ago his face had been slashed. Pepper had made his official statement at the hospital where the skin and muscle of his face had been reattached with three hundred uneven stitches. He told the rest to Salt.

A late-in-the-shift call, radio had given it out as a domestic disturbance. No weapon had been described to the 911 call taker and so no weapon was indicated to the dispatcher, who therefore sent only one car. In this city one car meant one cop, had almost always, except when a trainee was along. Though they paid lip service to supporting the men and women in blue, the politicians chose: one-person cars meant more cars available for calls. Even though Hot Pepper was aggressive, he was careful. And it was no different that night. He told Salt that he had scanned the area as usual when he got out of the patrol car in front of the project apartment building. He saw nothing except the dark breezeway, the busted bulbs under the stairs, a tunnel of danger on each of the three floors. But while climbing, entering those breezeways with his flashlight in his left hand, right on his holster strap as he ascended to the second level, a warning voice slightly prickled his brain. That was all it was most of the time, just a tiny pinch, not thought, not complete or conscious. He told Salt that this other voice had said, "Blood." It was hard to know whether it was a smell, or some motion barely seen or heard. He brought up the flashlight and caught the gleam of a blade coming at him from under the stairwell. Pepper cleared his holster and the man with the knife was blown backward just after the blade left Pepper's chin.

Salt and Pepper spent hours dissecting the "other voice." They knew of other cops who hadn't recognized the voice quick enough. Some were alive and would tell you they had heard it. Some wouldn't tell. Some were dead. Pepper's yet beautiful face was testimony to his having listened. They had theories: angels, God, ESP. But the one they put the most faith in was "You know more than you think you do."

So after a tough or confusing call, or when they wanted to connect with someone who understood, one or the other would say, just between them, "You know more than you think you do."

Now standing at Moury and Thirkeld, Hot Pepper saw her eyes roll up at the sight of the baggy-pants boys with the ludicrous visors. He released the squirming boys, who joined hands and ran together into the hard spray of the hydrants.

Not long out of their rookie probation period she and Pepper had been in line in a fast food burger place when one of the gangbangers walked in wearing a coonskin hat, about eighteen years old, he had exposed nostrils, a lower lip that hung excessively under a smaller upper lip. She had wondered aloud, "Does he think that hat makes him look better?"

Pepper had looked at her for just a second and in a neutral, quiet voice said, "He's without hope. He's never known better and is angry without knowing why." Salt, stung by her ignorance of the simple truth of what he said, turned, looking for judgment, only to see that he cared enough to have told her.

The wheat-and-honey girl came out of the group and stood in front of Salt. "You got black curly hair and you white. I got yellow hair and I'm black." The girl giggled behind her hand and ran back to her friends. Salt turned, still smiling, to Pepper.

Pepper, smiling back at her, said, "Yeah, where did you get that black curly hair? From my daddy?"

"From your mama." She threw and pulled a punch at his scar while he laughed and ducked. He was quick to laugh but also took to her serious side, backing her always, and to others.

There had been other times when they talked about chaos and dirty apartments, about the energy it takes to get clothes clean when the washing machine is four blocks away and you have five children to take with you. They traversed the land-mine topics of race and gender and why it took Salt longer to tell Half-Dead from his brother, Cat-Eye. Both admitting the inaccuracies of eyewitness information across races, speculating that folks of different races didn't fine-tune their observations, didn't get or didn't choose to get close enough, didn't look at others in their faces. They were both learning.

Standing there watching the kids play in a prism of sunstruck water, she said to him, "I do know more now," and looking up, "Thanks to you."

Pepper looked at his shoes. Then tried to hide a smile as he stepped away a few feet and pulled out his expandable baton. He swung it fiercely in an upward arc so that the metal sections extended, caught, and reflected some of the bright sunlight. He made it, as he often did, like magic, like the light came from his own secret source.

He was playing with her. "Now kneel down, Blue Knight."

And she, playing along, despite the children and now adults forming an impromptu street party, knelt on one knee. He tapped her once on each shoulder with the baton. Since her head was properly bowed, as any good knight's would be, she couldn't see what he was doing, although she thought she heard the sound of Velcro separating and then she felt him place something around her head.

"Rise now, thou Knight of The Homes," he proclaimed.

Salt stood up and felt for what he had crowned her with. The children and the Homes residents laughed, and so did she when she removed the visor of Pepper's police hat, which he had separated from the cloth crown and placed on her head upside down— a moment to carry them through the night, secretly superstitious that the magic would hold. She checked the crowd and saw the visor boys had disappeared.

7.

MARCY STREET

They were just finishing their soup when radio started asking, "Can any unit clear and start for 541 Marcy Street, apartment B-4 on a person down, possibly 48?" Salt held the last gulp of soup in her mouth. Signal 48 was the radio code for a dead person, and apartment B-4 was Shannell's place. She swallowed, grabbed her shoulder mic, and responded, "3306 to radio, I'm clear and en route." Pepper yelled to Mai, "Hold the satay," throwing money for the check and tip on the table.

On the way Salt imagined talking to Shannell: *You can't have. You didn't. You better not have killed Big D.* Just last month Shannell was in her patrol car, eyes crack bright, knowing that even though she'd stabbed Big D, he loved her. She could still hear Shannell's pronouncement: *He luuuvv my cooda potpie.*

But it didn't save you, now did it? Salt thought. She lifted her foot from the gas, the familiar sadness causing a moment of breathless sluggishness.

A crowd was gathering as she turned onto the short street. The Marcy Street apartment was where Shannell stayed with Big D most of the time, and it was as bad a shit hole as it gets. It didn't matter that this call was inevitable. Salt felt flattened by it. She watched for the players and snitches and to see who walked away as the patrol car pulled into view. Witnesses would be quick to disappear when the questions started. Salt parked along the curb perpendicular to the dingy redbrick apartment building.

Pepper made his entrance, tires squealing to a halt behind her car.

The Hope Apartments were a short row of three four-unit buildings in a development that would have fulfilled only the smallest of hopes. One of the peripheral blights around The Homes, they had been built about ten years before but, in her ten years in the zone, these apartments had never looked anything but worn out.

Before she could get out of the car, Sister Connelly, who was the tallest woman Salt had ever known, appeared at her car door. She owned the little old house across the street and could tell you who was kin to who as far back as Jesus. "Lawd, that child done found Shannell dead," said Sister, patting the crown of braids on the top of her head with thin, knobby hands, polished with age to a shiny brown. She was a revered elder at the nearby church and had earned the title "Sister."

Salt faced forward and focused on a tiny crack in her car's front window. "Damn," she said, shaking her head. Without looking up she asked Sister Connelly, "Who found her? How do you know she's dead?" She forced her voice to be professional. The weight of another grief made Salt feel her body was too heavy to get out of the car.

"Her girl come over to my house. I called 911 and then went up to that apartment and I saw her. She been dead 'cause they flies on her."

"Where's the girl?" Salt asked, getting out of the car, trying to focus on anything other than the body she'd have to see.

Sister Connelly pointed up at the apartment. "She the one standin' at the door. She followed me when I went up and I couldn't get her to come away."

A girl of about eleven or twelve, wearing all pink, was barring the doorway of the apartment. Also there were at least a dozen people on the stairs, compromising the crime scene. Pepper was already out, wading in, calling for the people to come down from the stairs. The crowd was murmuring, "Salt and Pepper, that Salt and Pepper," as she and Pepper fell into a familiar rhythm.

On her way Salt noticed that all of the apartment's window-panes had been painted red on the inside, the paint chipped where there were cracks. She imagined Shannell with a dripping brush of red, jittery and covered in paint. The screen door was broken, just like the last time she had been there, the wire mesh of the screen missing, boards left hanging from one hinge.

Sounds came from inside, like someone breaking Sheetrock. Lil D stomped out, kicking and slamming his fists into the walls as he came. He knocked into Salt as he rammed the door, causing her to hit her newly healing head on one of the dangling boards, yelling, "I'll kill him my own goddamn self!" Salt put out her arm to stop him. He jerked away. "Don't touch me! Fuck the poleese!"

"Hold on, Lil D."

"She in there dead, man." His face contorted with anger and grief. He was trying to put on a fierce look, but the tight muscles around his eyes couldn't hold back the tears.

"Show me where she is. Did you find her?" Salt sounded harder than she felt.

"You poleese don't give a damn. And you ain't gone fine Big D 'cause he don't want to be found. But I'll find him and then you can arrest me." He punched the air as he stomped down the stairs past Salt. "You just lock her up and she gets out and they back in the same old shit."

"How do you know Big D killed her? Were you here when it happened?" Salt called out to him, then dropped her shoulders in exasperation.

"I jus' know. Who else? They always fightin' all the time." He was halfway down the steps, knocking into people as he went.

"Lil D, help me here. Maybe your daddy didn't do it. Did anybody see him kill her? Who was here?" She shouted to Pepper, "I've got to go see where she is. Hold on to Lil D." Lil D continued punching the air, trying to make his five-feet-five thin frame tough. Pepper grabbed him and opened the back door of his cruiser.

Salt tried to ignore the ache that was starting in her scalp.

"Shush."

She turned to the girl in pink, whose finger was in front of her lips, the sound coming from her puckered mouth, the rest of her face stiff. Salt couldn't tell to whom the admonition was directed. The girl's eyes were focused past Salt on nothing Salt could see.

"That my sister," Lil D yelled from below, looking up as Pepper closed the car door.

Salt turned back just as the girl was blinking, as if her vision were returning, surprised to find herself here.

She reached out for the girl's arm, asking, "Are you—?"

The girl interrupted; answering the questions Salt had asked Lil D: "Wasn't nobody here. I found her."

The girl seemed familiar. Salt then realized that the girl looked like Shannell.

"Where is she?"

"She in the closet, in the bedroom."

"Do you have a key?" Salt asked as the girl turned away. Pink barrettes held two thick, neat braids tight against her head. Her blouse, pants, and sneakers were all the same color pink, cheap clothes but clean, starched, with ironing marks visible on the cloth.

"No key. They don't ever lock the door. Ain't nothing worth stealing anyway. I went in and called her. When she didn't answer I thought she might still be asleep, 'cause she sometimes doesn't get up till late."

"Wait for me at the bottom of the stairs." Salt touched the girl's shoulder.

The apartment was grim. The entrance was through a roach-infested kitchen, the stench oppressive, something meat-like rotting in the filthy sink. Salt hurried through the living room, to the right, and down the short, narrow hall. The bedroom door on the left was open. She stood looking into the room, her eyes adjusting from the daylight to the dark inside. The room was a dim blur. Crumpled dirty blankets in the middle of the floor took shape, a soiled bare mattress under the thin rectangular windows on the wall opposite.

"Then I went in there"—the girl appeared at the door, pointing without looking to the inside of the bedroom—"and saw her in the closet." Her eyes were scanning memory, not the present.

"There's no need for you to go farther." Salt stepped alone into the bedroom, leaving the girl in the hall. Wet molding clothes were in piles in every corner of the bedroom and the blanket mound was empty. The closet door was open, Shannell's familiar patchy scalp visible on her bowed head. Slumped on the floor and there was no doubt she was dead: thick, dark, crusted blood covered her chest and pooled, congealed, in her lap. Flies had begun the work of taking Shannell back to nature. At least eight hours, Salt thought. Where was I? She swallowed, her throat tight as if she needed an alibi.

Something flew in front of her face. She lifted her hand to ward it off. But when she turned the flutter was still there in her vision. The girl stood in the hallway, steadily pulling on each of her fingers, not cracking knuckles, but with a stripping motion. "It's Mother's Day. Shannell is my mama. I live with my grandmother over in Lakewood. So I took the bus to see her. I came in." Her voice got so soft.

"I went out and called Lil D from the corner. Then I went over to Sister Connelly's. Lil D's gonna kill Big D if he can."

"Let's go back outside," said Salt, stepping out of the room.

The girl just kept pulling at her hands, like she had to finish both of them, one finger at a time. Salt reached out. "We can go now." Shannell's daughter nodded, still looking but not seeing down the hall. The girl couldn't be more than twelve, slender, with skin that shone in the dim apartment. She possessed the frightening calm of some children who have seen too much. Salt touched her back to escort her down the hall. As they moved through the apartment the girl seemed to be talking to someone, not Salt. "She wasn't careful."

"What?" Salt said to the girl's back.

"Shush," sounded the girl again.

She had gotten the girl back outside and down to Pepper. The paramedics had arrived, and Salt and one of them, her friend Sherry, went back into the crime scene so Shannell could be officially pronounced. Back in the bedroom, Sherry approached the closet and snapped on a latex glove. She batted a fly away from her face. "God, God, God," she said, almost like a prayer as she knelt and put two fingers to Shannell's throat. For half a second she looked at her watch. "Time of official pronouncement, 7:22 p.m." Salt wrote it down in her notebook. Sherry turned and took off the glove.

"How long?" Salt asked.

"Rigor has set in. Ten hours or more," Sherry answered. "Looks like a bullet wound to me."

Back out on the landing, Salt stood blocking anyone from going back in. Below, Pepper was guarding Lil D, locked in the patrol car with his face turned away from the outside. Pepper bent his head toward Shannell's daughter, talking to her.

"Radio, raise a Homicide unit," Salt said into her shoulder mic. Seconds later a unit came on: "4125. Was someone trying to contact Homicide?"

"3306 to 4125, we're at 541 Marcy Street on a 48, probable GSW," she responded.

"En route." Detectives were on the way.

Sister Connelly had gone back across the street to her yard and was looking up at Salt. The tall woman just kept staring, so intently that Salt turned to check the apartment door behind her to see if there was some sign or problem that Sister Connelly could see from her viewpoint that she was missing. There was nothing different, the screen door boards still held to the frame by that single hinge. She carefully pushed them well clear of the entrance.

In the crowd of thirty or more people to the left, exactly straight across the small street, the gang lieutenant and enforcer Stone stood, leaning against another apartment porch support. Wherever there was trouble he seemed to catch wind of it. He was eating from a bag of chips and looking at the action, his red-brown face impassive, like he was watching a movie. He and Sister Connelly were about the same height and build, with about a sixty-year age difference. Stone glanced up, looked over to check out the crowd, then again at Salt, making eye contact. He sprinkled the rest of the chips around the porch, threw the bag in the yard, and loped toward the street, looking over his shoulder like a stray dog that's marked its territory.

In the patrol car Lil D knocked on the window. Pepper opened the door, listening while Lil D, face wet and taut, gestured broadly. Pepper motioned for him to move back and closed the door again. Salt thought again of Shannell, her last time in custody, in the patrol car backseat.

An unmarked detective car pulled up. Wills and Gardner got out, checked with Pepper, then looked up. They had been on other homicides Salt had worked. Both were white guys. Gardner was older and never had much to say, and even though he had classic male-pattern baldness, he was the only Homicide detective she knew who didn't wear the signature fedora. He and Wills, both always slightly rumpled, were enough alike in their bad sartorial choices to have been shopping from the same thrift store. But where Gardner was thin and lanky, Wills was built like a high school football coach, hard-boned and muscular without the definition, and always seemed to be looking in your eyes. Gardner began taking notes while talking with Pepper. Wills started up the stairs toward Salt.

"We've got to quit meeting like this," he said when he reached the landing, smiling at her.

Salt, caught without a comeback, glanced at her notes. "Her

name is Shannell McCloud, pronouncement time, 7:22 p.m. Call came in at 6:45, we arrived at 6:55."

"How's your head?" he asked.

She touched her scalp and felt a piece of scab that was hooked in her hair. "Okay, till I knocked it against that board there." She gestured toward the screen door. "I'll show you in."

He followed her. Salt left him at the bedroom and went back out to protect the entrance, back to where she'd first seen the girl standing. Gardner came up and went in to join Wills. The crime scene van got there and the scene technicians brought their equipment up, banging their black cases against the wobbly stairs. The funeral home employees, contracted by the city to transport bodies to the morgue, waited down the block in a black hearse. The crowd waited for the high point when the body, locked in a medical examiner's bag, was carried out, covered with a fake velvet cloth. The girl was below, stiffly leaning against Pepper's car. Sister Connelly came over to Pepper, then turned and pulled Shannell's daughter with her toward her house.

The girl, her words, the tight braids. Salt ran her fingers through her hair. The scab wouldn't come unstuck, though she kept worrying it. Then with a sudden rush of guilt she remembered: Mother's Day. She thought about calling her mother, who still didn't know she had been shot. She thought about the last phone call. *"Are you enjoying the Crock-Pot we sent for your birthday? I use mine all the time. Jake loves a roast cooked slow. I'm getting our kitchen painted over. John and Susan took the boys over to the beach. Do you see your friends from college? Are you keeping your doors locked? Mr. Gooden told us he would look out for you."*

"Mom, I'm a cop. I look out for Mr. Gooden. He's eighty years old,"

she had said, speaking of her next-door neighbor. He and his deceased wife, Peggy, had known her family for generations.

"You don't need to remind me that you're a cop."

"No, Ma, I'm sorry. I know you worry. It's just. Well, I love you guys, too. Tell John, Susan, and the boys hello."

"Those boys are so cute. You should see them in the pool."

"Mom, I love you."

"Why don't you come visit?"

"I will. I will," she said, knowing she wouldn't. "Best to Jake."

The gurney was being lowered down the steep, shaky iron stairs. Because of the rigor, Shannell's body made the cloth cover stick out in the wrong places. Just like Shannell, Salt thought.

The detectives talked to Lil D. Gardner went over to Sister's house and after getting from the girl that Lil D hadn't been in the apartment when she found Shannell, they cut him loose. Wills told her Shannell's daughter's name was Mary Marie McCloud.

Walking back to their cars, Salt asked Pepper, "Did you get your mom and Ann something for Mother's Day?"

"Roses for Mom and tulips for my sweetie."

"I need to go to the precinct for a minute. Can you cover my calls?"

"You feeling okay? Your head bothering you?"

"I'm okay. I'll catch you in a few."

Milking the Shannell-is-down call, Salt drove behind the old stone church, parked, and turned on her phone. She reached her mother's recorded voice and left a message. "Hi, Mom, it's Salt, Sarah." Her voice tightened. "Mom, I'm at work but I didn't want you to think I forgot you today." Her voice felt strained, thinning out. "Mom, happy Mother's Day," she said, trying to mask the relief she felt to be talking to the machine that asked no questions and made no comments.

She laid her head on the steering wheel and let the memory come—of her own discovery of a dead parent, her tenth birthday, left with her father while her mother and brother went to get the trappings for the celebration.

She sat for a minute, then turned on the car and the wipers. The night had come on, accompanied by a pre-rain foggy mist. Waiting for the window to clear, Salt pushed back the image of trying to clear the blood from her father's eyes and mouth. She struggled to remember something about boards, another memory snagged by the broken door on Shannell's apartment. The patrol car windows were clear enough now, she just wished she had a way to clear the cloudy flecks from her eyes. She put the car in gear, hoping to catch a break between calls so she could go look for Big D. And she needed to find Lil D and ask him to pump the street for anything that would lead to who had killed Shannell. Homicide would do their job, but murders on Marcy Street just wouldn't get the same attention from the detectives as a murder on the north side.

She prayed softly to Shannell. "Your daughter didn't forget. She came to find you."

8.

THE WAR ZONE AND LIL D

Salt pulled into the precinct parking lot ready for the Friday night fights and found the whole shift leaning against their cars, trying to act casual, all early. They cut their eyes to her and looked quickly away. Then she saw her beat car. The big white cruiser was covered in gauze, thin cotton strips wrapped the tires, trailed like streamers from the windshield wipers, flew like banners from the antennas. On the driver's-side door, taped across the city emblem, was a sign that read DUCK DOES NOT MEAN LOOK UP! Salt got out of her Honda, walked over to the decorated car, and in full uniform, boots, hat, gun belt, radio, and baton, put one foot on the push bumper, hoisted herself to the hood, and assumed a calendar-girl pose. The pain in her head rattled slightly, then settled. "I wondered when you guys would start in on me." She laughed. You knew you were loved when they made jokes about your misfortune. Pepper grabbed his phone and took the picture, all the guys behind her, making faces, telling her to say "duck" instead of "cheese." The photo showed her sitting atop the bandaged car, the crease of a scar running through the dark beginnings of her newly grown curls.

Officers got worn out, baffled, and scared but never, ever bored. But it was frustrating to pass by the drug dealers night after night, the PD without enough resources to clean up the problem areas, the war on drugs a joke. Some nights officers would ask other officers to cover for them, stealing time while they tried to identify the players and how they ran the dope traps, their efforts quixotic attempts to gather enough information to either pass on to Narcotics detectives or obtain enough probable cause to get their own warrants.

Before roll call was over, radio was already asking for units to pull in for calls. Salt didn't bother to unbandage her car. She just rolled out of the precinct, trailing gauze. Another sign on the trunk read JUST RECOVERED.

She handled several calls. On one domestic some kids had unbandaged her car while she made peace. Then Salt drove to an alley parallel with the front row of some project buildings. Occupied units alternated with the unoccupied and vandalized. Windows were dressed in broken shards. She got a pair of binoculars from her gear bag, hung them around her neck, got out, and started down a dark path. Watching for gang members and dopers who could run to tell the dealers she was in the area on foot, she tried to stay in the shadows. The old-fashioned word *ambush* came to mind as she put her hands over the silver buttons and badge on her shirt to cut down reflections. "Radio, hold me out on foot in the area of 222 Moury," she whispered into the radio mic. The shift would be listening, nervous until she came on radio and advised she was back in her car. Pepper had agreed to try to catch her calls while she was out.

As she watched for the gang, a sizzling awareness of shapes, shadows, and movement sang in her veins like she thought meth might feel. She switched off the radio.

On the rutted and gullied downhill to the abandoned, burned-out apartment, aware of the rubble, she was careful with her footing. Glinting liquor bottle glass crunched under the tread of her heavy work shoes. Rotting boards that had been used to seal the doors and windows of the stripped and vandalized building were lying in the grass, as they had been for the last year. Vacant units were supposed to be sealed to protect them from thieves and to keep children out. But as soon as the boards went up they came down.

Salt had often used this place to watch the drug transactions across the street at the corner walk-up food shop. Careful to avoid the condoms and human feces that littered the concrete floor, she stepped from the doorway to the broken window facing the street. Lifting the binoculars, she focused, bringing the players, surrounded by a yellow haze from the streetlights on the corner, into view. Man-Man and Johnny C, light-skinned brothers, handsome in red jerseys; heavyset Bootie Green; skinny and quick Lil D and Half-Dead; and Q-Ball with his shiny head. All the usual gang members except Stone were running the trap tonight. She scanned the shadows, hoping to locate Stone leaning against some corner or sitting in a car. He'd get her vote for most dangerous. Sometimes he'd walk up close to her on calls, staring and crossing the line into a scene. He gave her hard looks, constantly challenging with an unspoken threat, and had recently pointed his finger at her and mimed pulling the trigger. Searching and not finding him in the lens of the binoculars, she became aware of a breeze on the back of her neck. Propped on the sill of the window, viewing the action, left her back exposed to the doorless entry. She counted on the bits of glass on the floor to serve as warning. Her ears were on hyper-alert.

Lil D moved into focus. He was wearing fresh new clothes, maybe he'd moved up in the gang. Mainly he'd just held and done hand-to-hands, usually in the same baggy jeans, shorts, orange jersey, and worn sneakers. He was wearing shiny black-and-red shorts, a matching jersey, number 38—police code for drugs—and new sneakers, two-hundred-dollar red flashers, presenting him as an equal, mid-level in the drug gang chain. Salt sat back, waited, watching.

Nine years ago Lil D had been living with his grandmother, his father's mother, Mrs. Mobley, in The Homes, the largest part of Salt's then new beat. She had gotten a domestic disturbance to Mrs. Mobley's apartment and when she got there Lil D was bad-mouthing his grandmother, whose apartment was a known shot house, where illegal booze by the glass and loose cigarettes were sold. Card games and gambling were other sidelines and the two-bedroom apartment was almost always a chaotic place filled with people trying to numb some kind of misery.

That call wasn't the first Salt had gotten involving Lil D fighting with Mrs. Mobley. For several weeks radio had kept sending her to respond to either the grandmother or Lil D or someone calling 911 about their back-and-forths. But that day was different. Lil D, there on the stoop, with the towel around his neck, tired and scared, wasn't a hard case yet. He seemed to Salt to hold a recognizable hope for some adult to give him a childhood, that day struggling to swallow, trying to be angry so he wouldn't cry, afraid to trust one more person. She took his despair hard. She had needed to believe a kid from The Homes could make it, could have a real childhood. So she jumped at the first idea that came to her. To buy the time she thought she'd need to get him help or to find a program, Lil D would have to go to Juvenile lockup. She explained that he would have to be arrested, that a placement could be found for him from Juvenile. As they talked he began to look more at her and less toward the apartment, away from his grandmother's and the pressure to work the Avenue and toward the possibility of escape by arrest.

"I got to get locked up so I can get what?"

"I'm going to make some calls, get you in a program, a group home, maybe good foster care. Get some recommendations to the judge."

He looked back at his grandmother's, then shrugged. "Anything would be better than tryin' to stay here. Looks like I got no choice."

"Come on. I'll charge you with a hummy, a bullshit charge," Salt had told him. "Call me a bitch."

"What?"

"Call me a bitch."

"You want me to call you a bitch?"

"You have to so I can take you to juvenile. You have to commit a crime. Call me a bitch."

"Bitch," he said flatly, then sniffed and wiped his nose.

The next day Reverend Bradford's voice dripped with world-weary heaviness, delivering a "No Room at the Inn" speech that sounded rote. It was the same with all the other contacts and agencies Salt called. Any program had a wait of at least thirty days. Refusing to give up, Salt went back to Juvenile on her lunch minutes, between calls, hoping they would hold Lil D until a spot opened up, only to find that an anonymous caseworker had disregarded her request to contact her before releasing him. Big D had been allowed to get his son and take him back to The Homes, his grandmother's liquor house, and the street.

It wasn't like she'd given up; she kept asking, kept knocking on the doors of the system. Lil D and his family were bound, brick and bone, mortar and marrow, with and by The Homes. Every encounter with Lil D since, he'd look away, move away, or spit on the street and put on a street face. Lil D and Salt, nine years.

Through the jumpy, jittery binocular view she focused on him, all these hard years later, now selling on the Avenue full time. It was difficult to hold a steady image with the powerful binoculars. Any slight movement on her part caused ghosts to run through the focus and people to jiggle around unnaturally. His features in a blur, Lil D could have been his mother. He'd never grown much taller than the five five he had been as a fourteen-year-old, still rail thin, but the scared kid was locked beneath the hard lines of his face. He cocked his chin defiantly, his eyes hooded, his mouth puckered in a permanent scowl, a study in street-tough anger. The birthmark was barely visible in the shifting focus.

He leaned against the dingy white bricks of Sam's Chicken Shack with one foot propped behind him. A dark blue sedan pulled into the parking lot and stopped near Bootie Green, tonight's deal man, who gave a nod to Lil D. Lil D pumped himself off the wall, going to get the product from behind the food joint.

Nearby, a decked-out yellow low-rider truck shimmied with bass beats as Lil D sauntered around the building. He was at the back side of the building for about twenty seconds and returned with a cool walk, arms dangling, fingers loose, except the thumb of his right hand was tucked into his palm. He went over to Green. Arms touching, they leaned together into the open window of the dark sedan.

Green and Lil D backed away and returned to their positions, the thunk, thunk of the low-rider vibrating the prismed light of the corner, the blue sedan rolling out of the lot.

The Ghetto Girls Gang, with their neon-red and blond hairdos, shook into the scene, pretending to ignore the come-on calls of the corner boys. Salt heard glass crunch. She slid from the window to avoid backlighting from the street. Weighing the risk, she'd turned off her two-way so that the radio traffic wouldn't give her away. She waited in a squat. Two figures stumbled into the door. The couple didn't see her as they went past into the next room, probably searching for a mattress and a safe place to share a pipe. Salt breathed and quickly stepped out of the apartment, back onto the path, and back up the hill toward her car thirty or so yards away.

Illuminated by the streetlight, Stone sat on the hood of her black-and-white, his bony shoulders curved in toward the cigar he was lighting. His profile was instantly recognizable. In addition to the winglike shoulders, his head was very round and too small for his build. Sitting on her car was an arrogant street insult. Salt switched the radio back on: "3306 to radio. Can any unit meet me at Moury and Thirkeld?" Stone knew the rules and was challenging her again, both of them knowing how long it would likely take for another cop to get there.

Stone's white T-shirt was loose, plenty of room to conceal.

Salt continued up the hill, knowing that to stop or back off would concede Stone ownership of territory. It felt like a clichéd confrontation from a movie, but she could not afford concessions.

Careful of the language of the street, the moves, she didn't draw any weapon but surreptitiously unsnapped gas and gun.

There were no private moments in these streets. Someone always passed the word. Someone could always testify.

"Get off the car," she said, moving in, giving him fair notice.

Stone pretended to be listening to the loud rap from the corner, kicking his leg to the beat, keeping time, and mouthing the words *Fuck the police. Fuck the police.* His cheekbones shone in the light, making it hard to tell whether his eyes were open or closed.

"Off the car," she repeated at the curb. She came around the trunk.

He lifted his chin, ignoring her, looking away down the street.

He's caught in his own game, she thought.

He propped himself, stiff armed, leaning on his hands.

Her hands were free. There were gunshots in the distance.

He pushed off, slid his bone-and-muscle body from the hood.

She touched leather.

He brought his left hand up. His right touched the hem of his T-shirt. He pointed his left barrel finger, keeping it trained on her while he slipped past the streetlight circle into the shadows of the building.

Stone must have passed the word because the boys on the corner were ignoring both the walk-up customers and the cars pulling into the lot looking to score. She stopped her cruiser in the chicken place parking lot, close to where Lil D was standing. He watched her arrival, then turned his face and, as he often did in front of his boys, spit on the pavement. Salt got out and stood there until she was sure everybody on the corner had noticed, and was paying some kind of attention. So many people out on this warm summer night, a kind of insurance. There was plenty of light from the food shop and the streetlights. Mr. George, sitting on the curb nearby, nodded slightly. She had delivered his grandchild when his daughter went into premature labor last year. Sitting on the curb beside him was Crazy Sue, who counted on Salt to get her to the city hospital when her medication ran out or just didn't work anymore. There were enough people here, maybe not to stop a bullet, but to at least drop a dime, to bear witness that she was doing her job, occasionally interrupting the dope traffic for a minute, messing with the gang. She walked, still cautious, to the back of the building where from her vantage point across the street she had seen Lil D go to get the single rocks for the buyers.

She stood behind the dirty cinder-block building for a few seconds, kicked at food bags and take-out boxes, knowing that there were too many places to conceal dope for her to find the stash. After a few more seconds, enough for a show, at random she picked up a paper sack and walked to the front of the store. The rest of the gang was drifting off, but the stash was Lil D's responsibility tonight and he couldn't leave it or the geek heads would steal it before he got back. Lil D, of course, would know what kind of container the crack was concealed in, so he wasn't particularly worried when Salt came back around holding the brown bag. But the fact that she had some kind of bag caused him to grow watchful and less casual. He dropped his foot from the wall and fell away from his leaning spot, less cool, now not trying to ignore her.

Salt, running the routine, radioed Pepper. "3306 to 3307, come on in." The pressure was working on Lil D but it was too late for him to leave cool, his timing was off and he had to protect the dope. Pepper pulled up and was quickly out of his car, moving toward Lil D. They hemmed him in between the building, their cars, and themselves.

Lil D said, "You got nothing in that bag, 'less you took it back there with you."

Salt responded, "But you don't know, do you, Lil D."

Pepper: "Get your hands on the car."

Lil D appealed to Salt. "You always been straight, now you plantin' dope on folks? What's up with you?"

She stepped toward him. "Put your hands on the car."

Outmaneuvered, Lil D assumed the position, hands on top of the cruiser, legs spread. She patted him down, ignoring what felt like a small bag of weed in his right pants pocket. She leaned close and told him quietly, "A little bit there, huh, Lil D?"

"You ain't got no charge to take me. You can't do this, man." Lil D knew the rules of probable cause as well as any defense attorney. He had been arrested and through the system many times for minor stuff. But he had never done more than a few months.

"Get in the car," Salt said, opening the back door of the cruiser.

Pepper stepped closer, his six-foot-plus frame diminishing the slight dope boy.

"Man," said Lil D, getting in the car.

Salt shut the door and Lil D leaned his forehead against the backseat cage. As they moved out of his hearing, Pepper asked, "You want me to hang around?"

"No, I'm just going to talk to him. Ask some questions about how he got all those fresh clothes, what he knows about who Shannell was hanging with before she was killed. Then I'll turn him loose."

"Homicide's working Shannell. They don't need you messing around in that."

"It's my beat. I don't like folks getting murdered on my beat."

"You keep messing with these dope boys, they're gonna make things even more rough for you out here."

"It's my beat. I'll raise you after I let him go," Salt said, turning to get in her car.

With Lil D protesting, Salt left the parking lot, drove a couple of blocks, and turned into the drive of the elementary school that served The Homes. Spacious frontage and playgrounds put acres between the school and the apartments. Around back was dark except for one dim bulb above a steel-bolted door. Lil D asked, "What we doin' here?"

Salt stopped the car, put it in park, turned around, and faced Lil D through the metal screen. "I could have stood around at Sam's trying to ask you about your mom's murder. Would you have talked to me in front of your boys? I could have asked you about your new clothes. Would you have talked to me? This way they don't see you talking to me."

"I ain't got shit to say to you anyway. I ain't got to answer. Ain't no crime to have new clothes." Lil D's face in the low light was shadowed through the latticework steel. He avoided looking at her and instead kept his head turned toward the dark side of the car.

"You're right, but it is a crime what you do to get those clothes, and even if you don't believe me I do want to find out who killed Shannell. Your mother probably died because of dope, yet you're out here slinging."

"I ain't talkin' to you about my business and you can go ax Big D 'bout who killed my mom," he said, gritting his teeth, breathing heavy, and for once looking at her.

"And how do I find Big D?"

"I don't give a shit. You the poleese."

The minutes clicked by and the car air conditioner began to fail, putting out a powdery odor. Sometimes she thought of her police car like a church, or a confessional.

Lil D said, "Let me out or take me to jail."

Radio was dispatching and asking for units to clear for backed-up calls. She couldn't keep sitting there, hoping that Lil D wasn't too far gone.

How long? she wondered.

She could just add Mother's Day to a mental calendar on which the holidays were blighted: malnourished children at Thanksgiving, mothers robbed of their children's toys at Christmas, a grandmother raped coming home from Easter services—a calendar of grief, starting with January, the worst.

How long?

Five years ago in The Homes, working New Year's Day, first call out of the precinct, baby, dead, two months old, another broken child. Salt wouldn't remember his name, would not. Left in the apartment with some guy who paid for a room, the witness who testified that he told the mother he wasn't going to "watch after no baby while she was out getting high." Mother had come home geeked up and drunk, had passed out on top of her baby, found him suffocated underneath when the hangover woke her New Year's Day. In Salt's custody the mother cried, not over the baby but for her broken bottle of gin.

How long?

For months after she would sit in her car or in some fast food place between calls, trying to hide the silent tears running down her cheeks. One day Pepper said, "You have got to be able to close the door on these calls once they're over. You have got to shut the door or you'll never be able to stay doing this job. We bleed enough for our own. I refuse to bleed for all the rest of these people out here."

"How long?" she said out loud.

"How long the fuck what?" Lil D kicked at the steel partition.

Now she tried to close doors. Sometimes it worked. Here with Lil D, she didn't know what was possible, couldn't decide if the hope was more for him or herself and if hope should depend on one person.

She had invoked a prayer and Shannell, his mother, had walked out *through the darkness*. And she'd taken her to jail for stabbing Big D. And now she was dead.

"Let me out or take me to jail. What you just sittin' here for? It's my mama was killed. Now you jammin' me up."

She got out, slammed the door, and threw open the back door. "You're jammin' yourself up, Lil D. You want to stay out here until you get put in jail or killed, have at it."

"You tryin' to help me now?" Lil D stood and started to walk away. When he was about five yards out she heard him say, like he was reminding her of nine years ago, "Bitch." He kept walking, not knowing she'd never needed a reminder.

"Say it again, Lil D," she called out.

"Bitch." His voice barely heard, soft even, as he started in the opposite direction from Sam's.

9.

THE GANG

Billy's knobby head bobbed above the semicircle of cops that surrounded him. As Salt got out of the cruiser she could hear how angry his words sounded. "King Silver of mine," he shouted. It was hard for people, his family, cops, to understand the fear that drove Billy's rage. "You ain't my own." Billy's bare long arms swept the air above him as he roared.

She walked up behind almost half the officers on the shift. "I'm here, Sarge. I heard the call come up but I was on a kiddie call and had to make the run to detention. You ready for me to talk to him?"

The afternoon sun, at its hottest, burned through their dark uniforms. Sarge tugged at his sweat-soaked shirt and eyed the teenagers joining other Homes residents gathered to watch "The Billy Show." "It worries me that you and this crazy fucker understand each other, but he's under arrest and we need you to get him in the wagon. We might as well write an SOP to raise you when a Billy call comes up." He turned sideways to let her pass through the line.

Billy Wallace picked up one of his huge feet and stomped. "You take my fish and eat them, too." He turned toward the apartment he was standing in front of, turned back, lifted his leg, and stomped another threat toward the cops. Tributaries of sweat ran from Billy's face, merging in long streams on his completely naked body.

As soon as Billy noticed her he shook his fist. "You," he shouted. "You heard me calling you. Didn't they tell you, King Silver?"

At six feet seven and weighing over two fifty, Billy towered over Salt by nearly a foot and outweighed her by at least a hundred pounds. He was more or less psychotic, depending on whether he had taken his meds or smoked crack or both. He had an ongoing paranoia about his family and was known to fight cops. Six months ago Billy had broken two of Sarge's ribs.

"I came as soon as I could." She never lied to Billy, he'd be sure to remember the next time. And there was always a next time.

Billy turned his back to her then, wide-eyed, jerked his head over his shoulder. He began to run in place as if warming up. Salt heard the clinks of metal batons behind her.

"What happened today, Billy?"

He made a rope-pulling motion with his arms. "I called you, King Silver. They ain't my own."

"I'm here now." She took a step toward him.

He lowered his arms but kept his fists clenched.

"I did the best I could," she said.

Billy sat down on the steps of the apartment's entrance. "King Silver." His voice went down, some of the rage dissipating.

The children sang, "We see you thang, Billy. We see you thang."

Billy's genitals swung between his bent knees. His chest rose and fell with rapid breathing. As she walked closer he took in a long slow breath, even while his eyes jerked over the other cops, the children, and a few others in the crowd.

Salt said, "What's going on?" She took a step closer.

"I want all them, King Silver"—motioning at the other cops—"to leave."

"They can't leave, Billy." Salt moved forward another step. "How 'bout a cigarette?" she asked, keeping her eyes on his arm and leg muscles, watching for any increased tension, watching his eyes, his breathing.

Billy let his arms loosen and said, "I want a fishy, Orange Fanta."

"We'll get it for you." Salt nodded to Sarge, who motioned a rookie to go get the drink.

Salt shook out two cigarettes from the pack she kept in her pocket. She lit them and offered one to Billy. As he took the cigarette she nodded. "Before you get in the wagon, your drink will be here by then."

"I don't want to go in the fishy wagon."

He didn't say he wasn't going. "You know when all this fuss happens you have to go. But you can have another cigarette and your drink." She carried cigarettes for the street, mostly. The urge to cough rose when the smoke reached the bottom of her throat. Billy inhaled, then lowered his head. Still careful, Salt sat down on the step about three feet from the big man. They sat there smoking, the other cops and Sarge watching and beginning to relax, edging out of the circle toward any available shade. The rookie got back with the drink and Salt went over, got the can, and came back to Billy. "I'll walk you to the wagon." He stood up, jerking one side of his face forward, giving the other cops the evil eye, his movements and matching eye threats parodying a bad guy. Just because he was crazy didn't mean he'd lost his sense of humor. She walked with him to the paddy wagon, opened the rear doors, and when he was seated inside waited until he gulped his orange drink. "I'll see you in a few days, Billy. I'll come by." She gently shut the cage door.

The rest of the cops and the small crowd, drawn to the drama, mostly folks from the 1400 building where Billy had been cornered, began to drift away. Salt sat in the air-conditioned car catching up on paperwork. She looked up from the report forms and saw Man-Man standing not five feet away. He began to applaud as she lowered the window. "You good, you good, Salt," he said, smiling and walking toward her car. He wore his usual always new long white T-shirt, spotless baggy jean shorts: gang garb, but simple, never any flash. Hairline precise, his hair was cut so close it was hard to tell the color. He was average height and build, five feet nine and muscular without showiness. But he also had something that the girls loved and in the projects he was considered the epitome of sexy. He had just slightly bowed legs, which gave him a natural swagger as he walked.

"Hey, Man," Salt said.

He stepped back, making room for her to open the car door.

Smiling, she got out of her cruiser, eager to grab this opportunity to find out what Man knew about Shannell. Anyway, she was always happy to see him when they met like this, on neutral ground. He was charming with his beautiful wide smile and tight light skin. He and his brother, Johnny C, were the top dogs of The Homes. They controlled the crack market. And lately there were rumors about guns. She'd just heard the word *gun* here and there, just pieces. Man and his brother were successful because of two things. They were loved and they were feared.

Salt liked them both on a personal level. Man especially was always friendly during their noncombat interactions. The two of them had an ongoing discussion about life in the projects. He had been born twenty-five years ago in The Homes. He had a sharp sense of cause and effect and knew bullshit when he heard it. Man had only finished seventh grade, being truant most of the eighth and ninth until he completely stopped going to school by tenth grade. By then he was organizing the crack sales. Salt understood that if it came down to it, Man would kill to keep what he had built in The Homes. He was the leader of the gang. But these realities didn't keep either of them from enjoying their occasional conversations.

"Why do you care 'bout Billy Wallace? Don't nobody in the rest of this city care 'bout him," Man said, lazy like, his way of leading into a discussion.

"Do you care about Billy?" Salt said agreeably.

"Billy choose to use."

"If it wasn't here he'd have a hard time using."

Man came back with, "He'd just use somethin' else to smooth out his head."

"You may be right about that, or maybe he'd be so desperate he would get real help."

"Yeah," Man said. "And where that help comin' from?"

Salt didn't have an answer and instead turned the conversation toward Shannell. "You talked to the Homicide detective yet?"

Just then, about a half block up, Stone, his distinctive shoulders hunched, walked across the street in front of them. He turned his head in their direction. Man lifted his chin, acknowledging his lieutenant. Stone kept his face toward them even as he continued to wherever he was going. He didn't return Man's gesture.

"What's up with him?" she asked.

Man answered, "You know Stone be Stone." He shrugged, watching until Stone was out of sight. Man looked back to her, at her scalp, eyes narrowing. "I see you got a new hairdo." He tapped his own close-cut scalp in the same place as her scar.

"You changed the subject, dude. How's Lil D doing?" she asked.

"Lil D all right. He calm down."

"You normally keep things cool around here. But you got a lot going on. Lil D's not happy. Stone a wild card." She was fishing. "Shannell's murder. You know murders tend to bring heat."

Man's pleasant face changed. His eyes narrowed and he gave her a hard look as he said, "You ain't no detective. What do you care 'bout no ho?"

She flashed on Shannell's dead bowed head. "She was more than a whore. She was one of your boys' mother. Lil D isn't going to forget." Salt stopped, realizing her voice was sounding strained.

Man's face got harder. "Shannell wasn't much of a mama," he said.

"Yeah, but she was his mama. And this is my beat, Man. The way I see it, doesn't much happen around here that you don't have some way to find out about. I just thought you might be willing to help me on this," she said, trying to lighten her tone while wondering suddenly if she hadn't just given Man too much. Now he might figure out that Shannell meant something to her.

"You got your job and I got mine," he said.

Salt came back to the issue they almost always ended their encounters discussing. "Man, you could do anything you want to, yet you choose to run the gang. You're smart, you look good, and you know how to get along. Why not try something else? Go back to school."

"Why you a cop? It's what you know. I know the street. Rich people do what they know. They get their share. I'm just getting my share."

"Yeah, your share comes off people like Billy and Shannell." She ground the heel of her boot in the hot dust.

Man pushed off her car, turned, and started walking off. She called after him, "I guess that means you either don't know, don't want to know, or won't help me about Shannell." He threw back an *end of discussion* wave as he turned the corner of the 1400 building.

Like any effective CEO, Man knew about all significant events in and around The Homes. Marcy Street was only a few blocks out of the actual projects. Every addict in the area was hooked in to Man and his gang. And although his gang was small, his network, considering the number of people who used his product, was huge. The actual gang members included his brother, their cousin Bootie Green, Q-Ball, and Half-Dead, all of whom had grown up with them in The Homes, and of course Lil D and Stone. The structure of the gang was simple. Man and Johnny C made the deals for the product in bulk or "weight." They arranged for it to be cut, packaged, and sold. Bootie, Q, Half-Dead, and Lil D were the street-level dealers. Though most people in the projects were cautious around any of the gang members, they knew you could talk to Man and his brother. Stone was the one they avoided, he was unpredictable, volatile, and seemed to get off on hurting people. So Man and Johnny C used the threat of him to keep other dope heavies out of The Homes, and used him to make sure debts were paid. He was feared by everyone but Man. Salt wondered as she sat in her car what that told her about Man and how good a hold he had on Stone.

Her head was starting to throb. Light grew around the edges of her vision. In her mind's eye, Shannell's face, shiny with sweat, the shadows of the patrol car screen crisscrossing her dark skin, came into sharp focus. Man would have to be pushed. Salt had friends, Narcotics, Vice, and the Gang Unit.

Man, so big on claiming his share—she saw his point. But what share or justice was there for Billy, for Shannell?

Pepper pulled up. "Why you just sittin' here? Calls are backing up."

"I just got through talking to Man," she answered.

"I worry about you," Pepper said. "You're closer to people here than outside the job."

"Come on, Pep."

"I keep telling you, you got to let Ann fix you up. You clean up pretty good." He reared back with that smile. "I'm not gonna get into all that girlfriend talk but as I remember, your last date was what, five years ago?" He bugged his eyes out at her.

Salt shook her head and said, "McKinzie was a jerk. I tried."

"That was one guy."

"I might clean up on the outside but I'm more at home here than in some club on the north side. I'm no good at small talk. I end up frozen, trying to keep from saying something that sounds freaky, cop talk or Homes talk."

"People like to hear police stories. Sex and violence, you know."

"I don't like trotting out some misery from 'Tales of The Homes' for entertainment." Salt shook her head. "It feels sleazy."

Pepper turned his face to hers. "Unless there's a point to the story, something to be learned." He was serious.

"That's what I'm talking about. I don't do small talk. And I'm not getting on the precinct dating circuit."

"Okay, Hot Pepper's 'Psychiatrist, Five Cents' sign is down. But you get me worried, spending more time talking to gangers than to regular folks."

Radio was calling for units to clear to answer a robbery in progress the next beat over. They simultaneously slammed their cars in gear. Salt switched on her blue lights and watched as the strobe found and washed over Stone. He hadn't gone far but stood leaning against the wall in the growing shadows of the 1400 building. He was watching Man, who was laughing with someone on a stoop two rows down.

She reached to switch off the cruiser's AC both to give the car more power and as a reaction to the sudden sensation of a chill from cold sweat underneath her vest.

10.

THE IMPRESSION

A disturbance call brought Salt to the Thirkeld Avenue buildings. Night clouds were boiling high, backlit by lightning, like some old black-and-white horror movie, rain holding off until the climax. Young teenage boys were swinging fists, sticks, rocks, whatever they could pick up or put their hands on to bash one another. It would only be months before some of them would have guns instead of having to make do.

"3306 to radio, I've got a fight in progress. Start me another unit." She waded in to stop the beatings. Her hands, strong from holding sheep shears, hoof clippers, and feed bags, firmly grasped young muscles, slippery with sweat and dirt, inserting her body as a barrier between the determined combatants, their grunts and growls like those of deep-throated infants.

Stone was on the steps of a nearby apartment, his red-brown face gleeful, the rest of his tall, thin body invisible, out of the light of the porch bulb above him. "Tom-Tom, get him!" he yelled over and over.

The blue lights of Pepper's cruiser added to the flashes from the sky as he pulled up to the brawl. "Which ones?" he shouted.

She had two on the ground, one of her boots between each set of legs. "All." Her breath short with the fight.

He was already cuffing two together with his hand on a third. The boys, shirtless, their pants pulled or torn, still strained to get at one another. The ratcheting of the steel cuffs around slender wrists was accompanied by wincing as the metal restraints pinched skin against bone. Separation led to silence once the boys were herded into the car cages.

Stone had disappeared.

"I thought I saw the vulture," Pepper said, referring to Stone.

"He was here." They were writing out the detention forms on the trunk of Pepper's car. A distant roll of thunder brought more surety of a storm.

"That guy bothers me. He always seems to be around on your calls. Where does he stay?" Pepper asked, pulling out another form from his clipboard.

"I don't know. With anyone he can. Man takes care of him. I lost track of whatever family he had about eight or nine years ago. I'm not sure he ever had much of a family."

Salt looked toward Shaw Street, a street on a steep hill in the project. A flash behind the clouds of the Shaw buildings lent them starkness. Her first memory of Stone, her first Christmas in The Homes. Little kids on their new bicycles and tricycles. As much to cheer herself as anything, she had started singing into the car's outside mic, "*Here comes Santa Claus. Here comes Santa Claus.*" The children would laugh or hide shy smiles behind their hands. She had just turned the corner onto the top of Shaw. Two children were sailing down the hill on new Big Wheel bikes. She began to sing, then saw the boy sitting halfway down the hill on the gray stone wall that fronted the apartments. He was naked from the waist down, his skin the same color as the bricks of The Homes. His hands were in his lap, in one hand a thing that glinted. Her voice caught midnote. The kids sat quiet, watching from the bottom of the hill as she drove and stopped the car beside the boy. His pants were around his ankles, his erect penis in one hand, a mirror held close to his erection in the other hand. By the time he looked up she was out on him. His lowered pants would have kept him from running but there was no evidence of panic in his demeanor. He ejaculated immediately, as if her arrival was just the stimulus he needed. He held the cum-covered mirror up to her. She jerked his arms behind his back to cuff him and the mirror fell and shattered on the pavement. He wasn't wearing a jacket in the bright, cold day, just a dirty tan sweatshirt that looked like it wouldn't hold up to another wash. Wrists locked together, his already broad bony shoulders jutted up and further gained the appearance of curved vulture's wings. She hoisted his pants and led him to the cruiser. As he climbed into the car cage he checked the interior, as if for future intelligence, in his small eyes the shine of a feral thing. Her mind worked to accommodate the experience of him. She'd been a rookie, not naive but a believer: salvation was around the corner. But that day something hard formed in her chest.

"Curtis Stone," he gave his name when she asked. That was the first and last time she could recall hearing his first name.

"Where do you stay?"

"At 1248," he answered, "around the corner, two buildings up, at my auntie's."

She took him there, looking for a guardian to accept custody so he wouldn't have to go to detention, not on Christmas Day.

Most of the Homes residents made some attempt at Christmas decorating: a string of lights around a window, a plastic Santa in the yard, foil paper covering a door. At Stone's auntie's place there was nothing. Salt hit the auto lock and got out. In the back cage Stone put his lips against the window and mouthed, *My auntieeeee, oooh. I'm scared*, as he peered from the smeared window of the locked car.

Salt knocked and called out but couldn't get anyone to the door. A television blared at maximum volume from inside the apartment. Her baton dented the metal door and finally got results. Two little kids in underpants and dirty shirts opened the door. Behind them the apartment was dark, the only light coming from a flickering TV, colors bouncing off the dingy walls. She shepherded the children into the apartment. Immediately inside the doorway, to the right, was a small kitchen. There was no odor of roasting turkey, only an iron skillet emitting a rancid smell from a quarter inch of congealed grease. Heat turned too high amplified the smell. The refrigerator door hung half-open, its interior light harsh among empty shelves. A roach or two dropped while families of roaches skittered from the walls.

Her eyes adjusted to the dim interior. "Hello," she yelled. "Anybody home? Police." Farther inside the hallway the metallic odor of crack, old sweat, dirty feet, and wet diapers overrode the old-grease smell from the kitchen. The short hall emptied into the living room, where a large-screen TV with bad color glowed with ghosts and lines. A commercial heralded the superior qualities of beer in a pink can by featuring a blue basketball player driving a sleek purple car to a maroon ocean.

In the rainbow light from the TV two men, washed by blues, greens, then red and purple, slept sitting up on a ripped leather sofa. Across from them, a teenage girl in panties and a large T-shirt was sitting in a recliner not more than two feet away from the TV, just to the right of the blaring set, mesmerized by the screen, barely glancing at Salt before turning back to the next commercial, a lavender-haired woman earnestly preaching the importance of wise investing in a mutual fund.

Salt walked over and turned the volume down. "Where's your mother?"

The girl stared at the TV. "She dead."

The two little kids followed Salt's every move, standing beside her and staring up as if she were Santa Claus. "Whose kids are these?" said Salt, pointing at the silent toddlers.

"The girl, she mine. The boy, he my auntie's."

"Where is your auntie?"

"She upstairs."

The men hadn't stirred. With the sound down on the TV the voices of other children could be heard coming from the second floor. Salt climbed the stairs to the first landing. The two toddlers from below were trying to follow her, so she had to take them by their damp, sticky little hands back down to their mother/cousin. "Watch them," Salt told the TV girl, who reached for a pink plastic baby bottle lying on its side on the floor beside her chair. She gave it to one of the kids and the other child immediately tried to grab it.

"Is there another bottle?" asked Salt.

"I put enough in it for the two of them," she said, turning the volume back up.

The housing authority–mandated smoke detector upstairs sounded. Neither the TV girl nor the men on the sofa stirred. Salt sprinted up the stairs and found a small stream of smoke in the hallway coming from under one of the closed bedroom doors. Kids were yipping and laughing from behind the smoking door. The door flew open, spilling five children sprinting for the stairs. "Biggie did it, Biggie did it," they screamed. Inside the dim room there were blotches of color all over the floor. Salt's first thought was that a Christmas toy had been left unassembled. Then she saw that broken crayons had been fed into a portable heater, which was dripping green and orange onto the worn rug. The crayon papers had produced smoke but hardly any fire, which was now out. Other than the heater, there was little else in the room except for some bare mattresses. She yanked the heater plug from the wall, then crossed over to the window to check on Stone below. She pulled back the dingy sheet that served as a curtain and found the window boarded up on the outside.

Still hoping to find a real parent, Salt followed music: "O Holy Night" coming from behind the door to another bedroom. Again there was no answer to her knock. She pushed on the door. It stuck at the top corner. She pushed harder and the door gave way suddenly and slammed into the wall. A skinny man and an even skinnier woman, both naked, jumped up from a bare mattress. The woman grabbed at a tattered curtain to cover herself, then quickly turned around to determine how much of herself she was exposing to a window. The man, seemingly relieved to see only a police officer, slumped back down on the bed. The radio on the floor beside the bed now rattled out a tinny "Here Comes Santa Claus."

"Are you Curtis Stone's aunt?"

"What's that little bastard done now? No, I ain't acceptin' no custody. Take him to Juvenile."

"Merry Christmas." Salt turned, slamming the door behind her, and walked back past the now smoke-cleared crayon room and down the stairs. The scene there was just as it had been. The men slept through the smoke. The kids were screaming. The teenage girl glared at the purple-screened TV. Christmas wasn't going to come to that apartment. The fire-starting kids who'd fled the upstairs were outside, dancing around the police car, making faces at the impervious Stone. He watched them and her without expression. "What, my auntie busy," he'd said as she got behind the wheel. It wasn't really a question. He flashed her a wide-eyed parody of a smile in the rearview mirror. Salt struggled to keep her face neutral while a trickle of fear prompted the beginnings of despair. She felt he'd somehow tricked her, taken something from her, let something loose or was holding a secret she should know.

On that Christmas Day she delivered Curtis Stone to Juvenile lockup. His bony twelve-year-old shoulders hunched against the cold as she walked him across the fenced, razor-wired enclosure of juvenile detention.

Salt wrote the report, notified Child Services, and was reminded that it was not against the law for kids to have no gifts at Christmas but she still thought it was a crime. That was the first holiday she had gone to buy toys in a convenience store. It was the first time she had gone to the city jail with take-out dinners. And the first time she became aware that her faith in the redemptive power of Christmas might be insufficient.

Ten years.

Now as the first hard drops of rain fell Pepper was saying, "We need to get these guys transported."

Salt shook her head. "Right." Then she and Pepper, cars loaded, drove through the storm, out of the projects, headed once again for juvenile detention with angry, battered boys.

11.

DOGS

They had only been one beat away, finishing another call, when radio gave out "person down/shots fired." Now, about three minutes later, Salt watched with a sense of the absurd as Pepper in front of her almost ran over one of the bodies in the parking lot. He locked his brakes and slid on turned wheels, inches from the body of a young man. It was his beat. She would be second officer on this one. She stopped her car, blocking the entrance to the apartment parking lot on Cohen Street. The bodies of two other men lay farther into the lot. The dead men must not have been residents of the complex; no mothers or girlfriends wailing or trying, in their grief, to grab their bodies. Nothing, no one moved in the still gun-smoke-filled air.

One beater, its motor running roughly, was stopped parallel with the building, stopped not in one of the faded parking spaces but across a couple of them, three of the car doors open. The trash-strewn parking spaces, adjacent to the two-story brick apartments were empty except for a few rusted-out cars. A tattered baby bassinet with broken front legs lay crumpled against the nearest corner. Three poles, one in the middle of the lot and one at each end, provided the only lighting. Beyond the broken asphalt surface, the dingy buildings were lost in darkness.

She and Pepper got out in the otherwise quiet night, their flashlights flickering briefly over empty shadows. "God, I thought you were really gonna mess up the scene. Running over one of the bodies—not good form, Hot Pepper."

"My lightning-quick reflexes," he said with a short grin, wiping the sweat out of his eyes.

They cleared the idling car for possible perps and began checking the victims for vital signs, four fingers pressed under a jaw, drawing zeros on all three, no pulse, no breathing. Each young male had been shot multiple times and each had sustained at least one shot to the head. The bodies lay approximately twenty feet from one another in an almost perfect triangle around a sunken place in the pavement. The blood from each victim was seeping in slow streams toward the low spot.

Paramedics arrived, confirmed and pronounced the official deaths; flicking their cigarettes with relief, they drove away with empty buses. By the time the scene tape had been strung Homicide arrived, Gardner and Wills again, the same guys who had been on Shannell's murder. The Homicide Unit was street-named "The Hat Squad." Some years ago a dapper detective had started the fashion statement and it had stuck, though Gardner was sans hat as usual. They both wore short sleeves and Wills had on a red tie dotted with what looked like little femur bones. Salt and Pepper began working with them, marking the crime scene, collecting evidence, and trying to find, in the half-abandoned building, someone brave enough to be a witness.

Pepper was canvassing the apartments. Salt was helping Wills make the measurements, using one of the light poles in the lot for a reference point. Like shadows themselves, they all moved in and out of the light. She was holding the carpenter's tape while he wrote the numbers. Without looking up from his notes, he asked her, "You got any dogs?"

She paused a second, uncertain she had heard him right. "Dogs?"

"Yeah, you seem like a dog person." He smiled and looked up at her. She remembered his solid body and steady eyes from Shannell's.

"How can you tell? I do have a dog."

"That's why they call us detectives. What kind? I've got two myself." He moved to place the tape at the right toe of one of the victims.

"He's a stray I found in The Homes, but I've been training him for three years and he's working really well." She called out the distance from the toe to the pole, "Eight feet, three-quarters of an inch."

"Either you're lucky or a good trainer. Strays can be iffy. How old was he when you found him?"

"I think he was still pretty young. I know what you mean about strays, especially from The Homes. Some have been too abused to rehabilitate."

He moved the tape to the nose of the body. "How long you gonna stay uniform? Why don't you put in for detective division?"

"I don't know. I've still got unfinished business on my beat." She tightened her hold on the measuring tape. "You got anything on the Shannell McCloud case?"

"Who?"

"The woman in the closet on Marcy Street. Eleven and a half feet," she read from the tape.

"Nope, that's a complete who-done-it and we've caught four more, not including these three, since then. Gardner did find out from somebody that the victim's boyfriend—what's his name?" He jotted the numbers down on his pad.

"Darrell Mobley, Senior."

"Yeah, some neighbor said he was living in one of the shelters downtown. They didn't know which one and we haven't found him." He followed the retracting tape, walking toward Salt.

She looked up quickly. "How long ago was that?"

"Huh? About a week ago. Why?" Wills reached for the tape measure.

"Do you think he killed her?" She shrugged to cover her eagerness.

"We just don't know. Right now all we want is to talk to him. What kind of dog?" He stopped in front of her.

"What?" She was thinking about which shelter she could check to find Big D.

"What breed is your dog?"

"Since he's a rescue I'm not sure." She smiled as the image of her dog changed her focus. "He's all black with longish fur. He's got the body of a Border collie, although the Borders are seldom all black. I called him Wonder 'cause you wonder." Her eyes were almost level with Wills's.

He'd paused from taking notes. He was medium height, about five ten, but with a heavy, hard-boned look, maybe forty-something but he could be younger. Homicide detectives were notorious for not aging well. He wore the requisite fedora of the Homicide squad but otherwise didn't appear to care about his clothes. Each time she'd seen him he'd been wearing khaki pants and a short-sleeve shirt of indeterminate blend. He glanced back at the bodies, then back to Salt. She thought she saw something familiar there in his look.

She broke eye contact and asked, "You think maybe you can let me know if you get anywhere with Shannell's—the McCloud—murder?"

Dropping his head, he shrugged. "We won't get anywhere with that homicide. No witnesses coming forward, forensic evidence in a crack apartment—forget it."

"What about the autopsy?"

"Two gunshot wounds, 38-caliber, one in her shoulder, one to the heart. From the angle of entry it appeared she was crouched in the closet when she was shot."

"So she wasn't put there to hide her body and she didn't run there after she was shot?"

The contract hearses arrived to cart the bodies away.

"Looks like she was trying to protect herself, covering her heart with her arm." He held his arm over his chest.

She looked away from his gesture. "Did anybody hear the gunshots?"

"If they did they're not saying. We did the door-to-door but on Marcy Street . . ." He shook his head.

"Yeah, I know."

"Why are you so interested in the case? Did you know her or you just got a thing about your beat?"

"Both. A .38 is not the gangster's choice these days," she said.

"You're right. We usually see more 9s and .380s used by the gangs and dealers."

"You got any likely suspects?" he asked.

She didn't answer right away. "Not really."

Wills nodded to the body snatchers who began to load the bodies onto gurneys. He helped Salt tear down the yellow tape and bundle it into a dented Dumpster. "My dogs are Pansy and Violet," he offered.

"You're kidding me, right?" She laughed.

"No, what's so funny? Who wants to hug on something named Spike or Killer?"

"Well, Homicide detectives are not normally known as huggers."

"I can hug." He feigned hurt feelings.

"Okay, okay." She laughed again but couldn't quite let go of this chance for information on Shannell. "Don't forget, if you get anything more on Marcy Street let me know."

They stood side by side at the rotten-meat-smelling Dumpster, looking out at the crime scene. After a few awkward minutes, Wills broke off and headed toward his car. "Be careful," he called to Salt.

"Okay." She lifted her hand and watched as Gardner came out of the building, looked at Wills, who was still watching her, and grabbed Wills's arm, laughing and pulling him toward the detective car. Gardner shoved Wills in the unmarked and drove off, Wills waving back toward her cruiser.

Pepper came up, smiling. "What's with Wills?"

"Just talkin' about dogs."

"I'm glad you're finally having conversations with somebody about something other than Shannell," he said, dropping into his cruiser.

"Yeah, looks like he and I have something in common," Salt said, lifting a strand of crime scene tape into the trash.

12.

SISTER CONNELLY AND BOOTIE GREEN

On Saturday afternoon it was raining hard when Salt stopped the cruiser in front of Sister Connelly's. One small, blimp-size cloud seemed to be dumping its heavy load here on Marcy Street only, on the old woman's all-garden yard, like God personally watering Sister's forsythia, azalea, jasmine, wisteria, honeysuckle, and Cherokee rose. New-growth plants were scattered around in make-do planters—coffee cans and old buckets—inching green sprouts above their rims. The cloudburst had not had the breadth, duration, or strength to wash the grime off the projects. Salt lowered the car window to catch the fragrance of rain on green.

Sister's yard shamed the worn dirt in front of the apartments on the other side of the street. A plyboard cover had been nailed across the entrance to Shannell's building. Someone had finally, in a way, fixed the door. Slanted graffiti blurred into the fake wood of the barrier, words scrawled in various colors, hard to decipher, capital letters and lowercase letters, random, some backward, like an ancient language, the handwriting of some ghetto god: *mENe, MenE, tekel, PARSIN?* Shannell's building, like Babylon, ready to fall into ruin, walls cracked, windows broken, forsaken by anyone who cared.

In contrast, Sister Connelly's small, hundred-year-old folk-Victorian cottage seemed bursting with energy, with its one-gable front, on what was probably once a shotgun house, and a twenty-foot wing added to the right of the original structure. Rivulets poured from the narrow porch. Hanging baskets crowded one another, vying for the rain and sunlight and shading a two-seater swing. Precisely cut, neat patches of tin and old advertising signs had been added here and there to cover spots where the wood siding had fallen off. One rusted piece read SKOAL with a faded picture of a snuff can.

Salt sat for a while in the car, waiting for the rain to let up; the storm beating and beating with hard fast drops for a few short minutes. Then it was gone; the hot sun appeared and began turning the puddles into steam.

Sister Connelly was on the porch by the time Salt had started up the steps, the wood worn so that water puddled in the middle of each plank. "I know you ready for some ice tea," the tall woman pronounced. Like the house, she seemed steady and durable.

"Yes, ma'am, if you've got some made."

"Always keep tea in the Fridgidaire. Come on in."

Salt had to adjust her eyes once she passed into the house. All the shades and drapes were pulled shut, keeping the little house cool. The front parlor was crowded, upholstered furniture, pillows, doilies, afghans, throw rugs over the woven carpet, a maze of objects and shadows. Framed photographs of individuals and groups, decades represented in aging hues, hung on walls and propped on tables and shelves. Sister was a woman who knew most everybody, their families and their history.

"Sit, sit," said Sister.

The old woman went down a dark hall, disappearing into the dim, like Alice's rabbit. Salt's sense of her own over-average height and proportion began to grow in the close room. "Radio, hold me out on an information-only call," she spoke quietly into the mic on her shoulder.

Sister returned with two jars. "You here 'bout Shannell," she said, offering the tea, then bending her body into a worn armchair.

"Just asking around. Have you thought of anything more? Remembered anything else? Did you hear the gunshots or see anybody over there around the time Shannell was killed?" She took a sip of the iced tea. It was sweet, sweet, sweet, almost like cold syrup.

"You know now, I've known Shannell's family for a long time. Fact is, her mother, Mrs. McCloud, is a cousin of mine, second or third, on my mother's side. They was always a righteous family." While Sister Connelly always seemed open and forthright in their previous encounters and conversations, Salt often had the feeling that Sister's native language wasn't modern English but something else, though she had no particular accent. It was as if she was translating in her head before she spoke. She was doing it now, looking upward and to the left before talking, a pause, a look up, her clear, bright brown eyes lifting above wire-frame glasses, Daniel interpreting for Belshazzar.

"Are you there, 3306?" radio called.

"It wadden till Shannell fell in with Darrell Mobley, Lil D's dad, that she started on the downslide."

"Yes, 3306 here," answered Salt.

Sister Connelly smoothed her loose flowered shift over her knees, then took a snuff tin off the side table. She offered the opened tin. Salt smiled, shaking her head no. The old woman put a pinch between her teeth and lower lip. "Them Mobley kids always been bad but I had hoped Big D would turn around. I had hoped he would not be loose like his mother."

"Ah, 3306, meet Narcotics," radio said.

Sister's voice was lower when she continued. "He had no daddy to speak of. Shannell was good for him but life kinda pulled them both down. You might say history caught up with them." She leaned and spit into a pink ceramic vase on the table beside her, then took a sip from the tea jar. From somewhere in the shadows a clock ticked in the muffled silence. Sister turned toward the sound of the ticking clock. "Shannell got away from Big D and for a while was doing all right till she got pregnant with that little girl. She and Big D already had Lil D, so she gave the girl to her mama to raise and Lil D went to Mrs. Mobley, too, when Shannell took to the street."

"3306 copy. Meet Narcotics," Salt responded, eager for the call she'd been listening for, ready to go and taking a long drink of the tea to finish it in a hurry.

"They callin' you?"

"Yes, sorry," she said, standing. "Thank you for the tea."

"You stop by again. Us old folks don't get many visitors and most people 'round here I don't want on my porch, much less in my house. They act like dogs."

"No, ma'am. My dog is polite. The people act like nobody trained them right or cared about what they did."

"You right, you right. But Shannell loved her girl. She wanted Mary to have something. Didn't want her ever in the street like Lil D. Hoped her mama would be a better mama." Sister stopped mid-sentence, looked away as if at a sudden memory.

Salt hurried to the porch, radio asking for her ETA to the corner. She bounded the steps to her car, waving to the old woman as she drove off. Halfway down the block with the odor of green leaves, new flowers, and damp yard still following her, she realized Sister had never answered her questions about whether she saw or heard anything. She backed up, inhaling the exhaust from her own vehicle. Sister Connelly was still standing on the porch. From the car window Salt asked again, "Do you know anything that would help us find out who killed Shannell?" Her mouth felt dry and sticky. The sweet tea had made her thirstier than before.

"You come back to see me again, Miss Salt."

Pepper was answering radio, starting for the corner, the sergeant calling her radio number, asking for her location. She pulled off again from Sister Connelly's and, with a screech of the siren, busted past the stop sign at the corner.

The only people in the parking lot at Sam's were a couple of uni-form cops, some plainclothes detectives in takedown masks, and Bootie Green, handcuffed, shackled, and lying facedown on the pavement. A wiggle of elation and apprehension bounced around in Salt's chest. Bootie would be the first gang member to fall in her campaign. She'd missed the takedown but wanted to be there to deliver a message for Man-Man.

She got out of the car and went over to Sol Chambers, her Narcotics friend. "Thanks for the help, Sol." Hugging him, in part, for the benefit of the shadows across the street.

"No problem. We have to put in eight anyway. It was easy, just like you said. He"—Sol pointed at Green—"sold to Junior and we watched him get the hit from a stash in back. But better, he was carrying a stolen .380 pistol. He'll be in the federal system because of the gun and won't be getting out on bond."

Salt had known Chambers since her academy days and they had kept up with occasional phone calls, usually work related, and running into each other in the street and in court. When she had called asking for his help with the gang's corner, he was eager to make a dent there and to be able to report results from that location. He had been even happier that the surveillance, which took so much time, had already been done.

She walked over to Green and the Narcotics detective standing over him. "I'll take him to the wagon," she offered. He nodded and walked away to join some of the other cops. She knelt down. Green turned his face toward her, sweat pouring down his forehead, causing bits of dirt and small pieces of pavement to stick to the side of his cheek. He was overweight by about fifty pounds and breathing hard.

"You can blame Man-Man for this, Bootie. So when you call him from jail tell him that."

Green glared at her. "You dead."

She stared back. "Bootie, the only way you can help yourself on a federal charge is to give me what you know about who killed Shannell."

"Man, I don't know anything about that."

"Yeah, maybe, maybe not, but if anybody comes forward for

you with the information you can get your sentence reduced. That's the way the feds work."

"Fuck that."

"Think about it. Here's my card and phone number." She rolled him on his side, tucked the card in his shirt pocket, and hoisted him to his feet.

"Get your hands off me, bitch." He jerked his tethered arm from her grasp.

"Who's the bitch, Bootie? You're going to jail 'cause Man tells you to jump and you say, 'How high?' Call me if you want some years of freedom back."

Salt left him to the wagon driver, then walked to the edge of the parking lot, knowing that they were watching from across the street. She lifted a hand, a challenge, to the watchers in the dark.

Pepper came up. "What are you doing? You gone crazy?"

"I was just helping Sol." A sharp pain in her head made her eyes start to water.

"Your hormones actin' up? First you're late on an in-progress call and now I catch you waving at UFOs."

Laughing with relief that he hadn't figured out what she was up to, she turned to him. "No, just practicing my salute for when you make chief," she said, resisting the urge to wipe her eyes.

"When pigs fly. So, are we on for this weekend? Ann's already cookin'."

"As long as you promise no unexpected guy will show up."

"Oh, good grief. Danny wasn't that bad."

"He wanted me to handcuff him, for God's sake."

"So, what's wrong with that?"

She flipped him the finger and went to thank Chambers and the other detectives again.

As the wagon pulled off with Bootie, the scene began to clear and she went to get in her own car. Pepper came over again. "You gonna tell me now what you're doing?" He was standing close in the wedge of her open car door. Seemed like he wasn't in the dark after all.

"Community Policing, the new trend in the war on crime." She smiled, quoting a recent department directive, trying to make light of her action.

"I'm serious. What message are you trying to send? What did you say to Bootie?"

She looked up, and feeling crowded by his tall body, said, "You're in my door."

He lifted his hands and backed away. "Don't get jammed up with them," he said, sounding like he'd let it go for the moment.

"Pepper."

"I mean it. You work too close sometimes."

"That's what works here. You know it. You have to get close, close enough to—"

"Get hurt," Pepper stopped her. "Don't try to do this by yourself." He turned to go to his car, then turned back. "Why do you take stuff on all by yourself? You don't have to prove anything." He got in his car and slammed the door, windows closed.

She rolled the car windows down to better hear the night, drove out of the parking lot, following Pepper while radio was giving out a call to another unit. There was a loud blast and Pepper, a couple of car lengths in front of her, swerved and came to a stop. She hit her blue lights, braked beside his car, got out, and ran up to him, then realized that his car was leaning to the right. "Damn, I thought it was a gunshot. I didn't think tires still blew out that way," he said, looking up at her from the window. He puffed his cheeks, blew out a long breath, and got out. They both went to the passenger side of the car. The front tire was ripped open. "Radio, start me a wrecker for a flat," Pepper advised dispatch.

Salt walked back to her car trying to calm her breathing. On the hill above, something in motion reflected light from the street.

She yelled back to Pepper, "I need to go finish a report. Do you need me here?"

"I've got blue lights. Go."

The car hung in first gear on the short drive around to the Homes' entrance. She drove until she got to near where she thought the flash had come from. A sharp right turn led to the buildings that faced the chicken place dope hole and overlooked the street where Pepper waited for the wrecker. She drove slowly, straining to see in the shadows. Parallel with where Pepper was stopped, she parked and got out. There was no one in sight. Her flashlight covered sequential sections of the area as she walked toward the hill lined with water oaks and low, leafless shrubs. The beam caught movement at the far edge of the tree line, an arm, light brown shirt, slipping back around toward the apartments. Picking up the pace, she followed her flashlight's beam skipping over the ground. Around the corner of the end building whoever had been on the hill had disappeared.

Back to where the brown shirt had been when she first caught sight of him, she found herself standing directly above Pepper, the wrecker now parked in back of his cruiser, the driver and Pepper changing the tire.

The ground around her was rutted and ugly. In the dirt, littered with cigarette butts and food wrappers, were shell casings, most dull with age. But glinting brightly, there was one that caught the glare of her light. She grabbed it up quickly and held it in her closed palm. It still held the faint heat of being recently struck, fired, and ejected.

From the other side of the building, behind her, little girls' voices echoed: "Red rover, red rover. Let Cee-Cee come over."

"Pepper," she said, exhaling quietly.

13.

HUNTING BIG D AGAIN

She took a personal leave day on Sunday. Other than the red digits of the clock on the dresser that glowed 5:00 a.m. the bedroom was dark, only a little gray-blue light coming from the moonlit hall. Wonder groaned at the foot of the bed. The dreams of boards had recurred, boards swinging, dangling from that one hinge on Shannell's apartment door, merging with the dream of her own hands on rough boards trying to fit them to a chair in a foggy forest clearing. An electric, needle-like pain sizzled along the scar in her hair. Since the expressway, when she tried to get to sleep at night, psychedelic beads would cross under her closed lids, like involuntary sheep counting, and during the day fuzzy white movements blurred her peripheral vision. Salt kept thinking it would clear up. Sarge would stick her behind a desk for sure if there was any question about her fitness for duty. She'd be of no help to Shannell in the office.

Standing at the kitchen sink she drank a strong cup of Cuban coffee while looking out to the still dark backyard, the silent sheep, and black-trunked trees. She fluffed the dog's fur and admonished him to stay before closing the door.

The sky to the east began to grow a peachy haze as she drove toward the city. It felt strange to see, odd to make the trip this time of day, on her own time, wearing her own clothes rather than the uniform. Coffee buzz zinging in her veins, she hoped it would keep her clear-eyed for a while.

At six a.m., she made a turn off Peachtree onto Pine Street. People who mistakenly turned off Atlanta's much-celebrated main street onto Pine quickly realized their error. Dozens of men were hanging out in front of a building that spread over a city block. In the parking lot across the street dejected men sat along all the rest of the sidewalk, their legs in the gutter, possessing the curbside. She parked next to a hydrant, the only close space, looked at the faces of the two guys closest to her Honda, then closed and locked her car doors.

For men only, Haven House was the largest facility for the homeless in the city. It was downtown and out of her precinct. Her beat had several other shelters and Salt had been able to check all of them during duty hours. But she hadn't found Big D. Like most of the shelters, Haven House emptied out in the early dawn hours. She'd gotten there forty-five minutes past her cup of coffee.

Weatherworn, ragged men sat against the wall, sandwiched by garbage bags of belongings. Wild-eyed men guarded grocery carts filled with cans and pieces of metal. Flattened men in the parking lot across the street slept on cardboard beds next to the scraggly bushes.

She crossed the narrow street. Just before the curb in front of the entrance, a man in a dark shirt and dark suit stepped in front of her. "I'm Reverend Black. Do you know where you're going?" Salt tried to step around him. He moved back in front of her.

She said, "You're in my way."

"You searchin' high and low, here and there." Reverend Black waved his arms.

She moved to go around him again and again he jumped in front of her. "Sister, we all searchin' but you won't find what you need here."

Salt pulled out her badge and as the light struck the silver, Reverend Black stiff-armed a Bible in front of his face. "And lo, the angel of the Lord came upon them, and the glory of the Lord shone round about them: and they were sore afraid." She passed by him, badge to Bible.

Just inside the entrance, a guy sitting at a dented metal desk traced his finger down the rows of a ledger book. He had on a dingy T-shirt and there was a cigarette hanging from a corner of his mouth. Ashes had spilled on the front of the shirt, on the shelf of his stomach. He didn't look at her or the badge that she had kept open in her palm. Someone yelled from the back of the hall, "Rev. Gray, he's stinking the place up." The deskman yelled back, "Either get him the fuck out or I'm calling the cops." He looked up and saw Salt. Before he noticed the badge in her hand he said, "Lady, the entrance for the soup kitchen volunteers is around the corner. You got the wrong door." Then he noticed the badge. "Wow, a cop when you need one. I'm Reverend Gray." Stretching across the desk, he shook her hand and stood up. "Come on, let's get this guy out of here." He got up and rushed her down the dim corridor.

Salt stopped midway down the hall. "No, you don't understand. I'm not on duty. I'm here because I'm looking for a guy."

Reverend Gray said, "Lady, I need a cop now. This guy is tearing the place up and shitting on the floor. I need you to get him out of here one way or another."

"Is there more than one exit?" Salt thought of Big D's propensity for wandering away.

They came to the entrance of a cavernous room that looked to have once been used as a warehouse. In spite of the roaring wall fans, it smelled of dirty feet, urine, and rotted flesh. Sleeping pads lined the space, four rows on each side of the room, as far as she could see into the deep corners, a corridor half a block long down the middle. With the early morning turnout, most of the spaces were empty at this hour.

"The only other exits are alarmed, ring like a freaking banshee," said Gray.

Squatting ten mats away was a troll-looking, blond-bearded guy. He had his pants down and was letting diarrhea onto one of the sleeping mats. "Goddamnit. That's the fifth pad this week," Gray said.

"Call 911 for an ambulance. He's got DTs."

"We already called. They take their time coming here."

Paramedics hated these shelter calls. The patients were often drunk and belligerent, and left terrible odors in the ambulances for the rest of the shift. She pulled out her phone and identified herself to the 911 call taker. "ETA five minutes." She pocketed the phone.

The sick man groaned and swatted at his demons.

Sunday-morning light was filling the space. An old hymn bored its way into Salt's consciousness:

> *Will there be any stars, any stars in my crown,*
> *When at evening the sun goeth down?*

Outside Reverend Black shouted, "We all searchin' . . ."

Salt turned to Reverend Gray and pulled out a mug shot of Big D. "I don't want to arrest him," she said, handing him the photo. "I'm looking for information on the murder of his son's mother."

The smoke from Gray's cigarette rose back toward his face and he squinted with one eye, studying the photo. He looked out into the long room. "He's there, at the back, by the window."

Salt's worrisome eyesight was strained by the growing light from the back of the huge room. She could just barely make out a figure illuminated in a shaft of sunshine. Whether it was the coffee wearing off or her impaired vision, she began to feel sluggish.

Reverend Gray coughed. "Blah." He hung his head and leaned on the door frame. "Damn." He struck his chest, clearing the phlegm. "There are a few residents that are allowed to stay during the day. He's one of them."

"Why?"

"Special circumstances." Gray left her, coughing his way down the hall.

She walked toward the back, her head pulsing with each step. Fuzzy images merged and converged the closer she got; Shannell trapped in the backseat while they searched for Big D after he'd been stabbed, trying to find a pulse on his heavy bleeding body. By the time she reached the back of the room the peripheral had become tangled with what was in front of her.

It was him, barely. It had been almost two months but she had found him. She had. And Big D wasn't big anymore. He would have been hard for anyone to recognize. His clothes hung on his bones. He was gray and ashy-looking, his eyes bloodshot and watery. He sat on a metal folding chair staring out the meshed-glass window and didn't seem surprised to see her.

"You ever have a dream where somebody appears where they usually don't belong?" He turned his head back to the window. "How did you find me?" One arm was pressed against his chest, flat resignation in his voice.

"They pay us to find people, you know," she said, trying on a small smile.

Salt looked out the window so that she and Big D were sharing the same view, a large Gothic stone church loomed near, the city hospital in the distance. When she turned her head to look back at D her vision blurred again. She forgot for a moment what it was she was there to ask and stammered the first thing that came to mind, "What about Lil D?"

"I done the best I could. I didn't know no other way."

"D, did you kill her?"

"You askin' if I shot her, the answer is no. Life kilt her and it's gonna kill me, too. Ain't none of us gettin' outta this shit alive."

"Lil D thinks you killed her."

"He's a kid. Kids see so much they don't know how to reason out."

Salt shut her eyes for a second. "Do you know who might have wanted her dead?"

"Shannell whorin' for crack, whorin' to pay Man. Last time she cut me you arrested her and I stopped being with her. I'd see her though, on the corner hangin' with that skinny red ho." He pressed his long arm against his chest, then reached across to hold his left side. "You wouldn't think I'd grieve for her."

"I would," she said. "But I have to ask. Do you or did you own a gun?"

"I don't own nothin', no gun. I don't care 'bout no gun. Never have."

"Is the woman Shannell was hanging with called Dirty Red?"

"Yeah."

The fuzzy light flashed. "You staying here because of Lil D?"

"Yeah, Lil D. If I go back to The Homes we both get hurt, or dead. So until you lock somebody up for killing his mama, it's best I stay here." His arm looked tired, hanging down beside him.

"That still bothering you?" She nodded to the side where Shannell had cut him.

"No, it's my heart. They can't do nothin' for me," he said. "Doctor called it a arrested heart, something like that. That's another reason I'm here. Lookin' to die." He turned back to the window. "I'd like it, to die next to that church out there and not in jail."

For a second Big D came into clearer focus, inept car thief, dying man, father, Shannell's love. He stared out to the filigreed church spire. Pigeons were taking off from stone petals and catching drafts between buildings. She put a card with her phone number on the sill and quietly walked back between the rows to the front of the shelter. The troll man hovered in a corner.

The two reverends were standing one on each side of the exit, Reverend Black with his Bible, Reverend Gray lighting another cigarette. Both turned as she got to the door.

"Was it him?" "You still searchin'?" they asked simultaneously.

Salt said, "Still searching." Not directing it at either one, she walked out to the sound of a siren soaking the Sunday-morning air. The church bells competed, sounding more like a clang this close to the skyscrapers. In her car she squinched down to look up one more time at the steeple. Big D had a better view from the window above.

14.

A GIRL, A DOG, AND ESCAPE

The flowers—catkins—of the pecan trees dangled like tiny ornaments from the deepening-green branches of the orchard. Salt stood underneath watching the sunlight and breeze turn the trees into a jade-and-yellow-white kaleidoscope canopy. She'd just gotten home from locating Big D and paused for a minute after getting out of the car, sorting through the possibilities and thinking about how to find Dirty Red when Mr. Gooden came from around the side of the house with Wonder, a loose lead rope around the dog's neck. The old man and his now-deceased wife had been her parents' longtime neighbors. At eighty years old he was still tall and always seemed sunburned. A small belly pressed out over the top of his wide, tight belt.

"This rotten beast was staring at my cows again," he said with a grin, nodding toward his pasture to the west and the brown impressions of the loosely scattered herd on the green far field.

"I'm sorry. Did he hurt anything?"

"No. Like usual, he just watches." He ruffled Wonder's fur and slipped the rope off.

She bent down and took her dog's snout between her palms. "I'm not sure why he gets the notion, but sometimes I catch him looking longingly toward your herd. He's too smart for his own good." Straightening, she remembered. "Thank you again for the onions and the flowers."

"Let me have a look at you." He took hold of her shoulders and held her at arm's length while he studied the crease in her hair. His survey parodied one he might make of prized stock. "From the outside that wound looks to be healing." He turned his head, eyeing her first with one eye, then the other. Salt stood under his scrutiny, feeling childlike, awkward but good in his large red hands. "I'm just sorry there wasn't more I could do." He dropped his hold on her. "How's your mother?" he asked. "I'm surprised she didn't come down when you were injured. It must add to her worry something terrible."

"I talked to Mom a couple of days ago, I guess." She bent to pick burrs from Wonder's coat, trying to untangle them rather than pull his fur. "She's as good as can be. I didn't see any need to tell her I got shot." She didn't look up at the old man, who was silent while she picked at the burrs. She mumbled to Wonder, "You get all these watching cows?" As she stood she gave the dog a firm spank on his haunch that sent him into a tail-wagging frenzy. Wonder shook himself and trotted to the fence and the sheep.

Mr. Gooden had his lips between his teeth like he was holding back words, silently watching the dog. "Lord, nobody but you and the dog. Alone. Again." He cleared his throat. "I read in the paper that you were by yourself when you pulled the car over. Don't you have partners?" He didn't stop for her to answer. "I'm going to say this now even though you might see it as minding your business and I might say it wrong but you just almost got killed, part because you were alone. I'm not trying to play amateur shrink but I wonder if you've gotten too used to, well, taking on too much by yourself. I remembered how much your mother loved flowers and that made me remember Peggy picking some just like those from the field back there." He pointed to some splashes of red and yellow at the back of his property. "She asked me to bring some to your mother. You would have been about ten."

Hearing "ten," she immediately put up her hand, palm out. "That was a bad year for my parents. Dad was sick a lot and then there was the accident. They didn't want people to know, especially my mother. Wanted to keep their privacy."

Mr. Gooden pointed his finger at her chest. "Privacy is one thing, Sarah, but at the expense of a child. That's not right."

She interrupted him. "I grew fast that year. They counted on me and I didn't want to let them down. Hindsight is twenty-twenty."

Mr. Gooden kept on. "I knew your folks well enough by then, I thought, to just drop in. But that day when I got here and knocked on the back door and didn't get an answer I came on into the porch. I stood at the screen door to the kitchen. Your dad was sitting beside the table and you had a pan and were on the floor washing his feet. Before I even said hello your mother came to the door and stood like she was blocking out you and your dad, like you weren't there. I've thought about that day over and over. It wasn't that you were taking care of your dad. It was the way your mother held herself. Even though she's a small bit of a woman she seemed that day like a rock wall with her hands on her hips, elbows out, and her feet wide apart." He shook his head. "I handed her the flowers. I can't remember anything we said, just the way she stood." He shifted, looking again way back to the end of his property—to where the blur of flowers grew. "You had too much of a burden for a child. Peggy and I talked about it. We both worried about how alone you seemed after your dad died. Before he died I used to see the two of you everywhere together."

Salt scattered the pile of burrs with the toe of her boot. "I'm not sure I understand," she told him. "My dad was worn out from work that year. He loved soaking his feet and getting a foot rub. That's all."

"Your mother didn't want anybody to know how bad things were with your father."

"Mr. Gooden. I don't see how dragging all this up—"

He held up his hand, palm toward her, to let him finish. "Sometimes, whenever your father got really bad, she'd call Peggy to come over to stay with you and your brother. The night of your father's accident she ran to our house. She left you with him again, even with you finding him and all." He shook his head. "And in the years since she moved away and Peggy died, I've wanted to say something."

"Day," she corrected him, turned, and started walking for the house.

He walked beside her. "What?"

"It was daytime when my father shot himself."

Salt was at the back door and turned to face the old man. "She did the best she could."

"No, Sarah." He looked at her straight on. "She should have asked for help. Not left a child, you, with him. That was no time to let pride get in the way. She left you with something a child couldn't handle. What's that saying? 'Those who cannot remember the past are condemned to repeat it.' And now here you are. I don't know. I don't know."

Salt reached up and touched her scalp. "It was my birthday. She went to get a cake and balloons for me. I haven't really forgotten anything."

They both looked down, then out toward where the dog was looking. The cows were far away. Finally he laughed. "Nobody but you would have rescued this crazy dog or put up with him, even buying him sheep to herd." He coiled the short rope and slapped it against his leg. "I'd best be getting to the cows. I hope I didn't overstep." He kept whipping the rope against his jeans as he headed for the field between the two houses.

"Mr. Gooden," she said as goodbye.

"Keep safe, Sarah." He climbed the fence, crossed to the other side with the agility of an eight-year-old only with locked knees.

She had thought about telling him that her mother said he would look out for her.

There was a brief ruffle of a breeze. Wonder lifted his snoot. Salt took a breath, inhaling a trace of old roses.

The Sunday-noon sun made the wind blow hot and dry, but Wonder didn't notice. He was standing perfectly still, ten yards away from her, his dark eyes focused on the sheep, his black fur blowing almost horizontal with his body.

She loved the place: the old trees, the connection with her father's family, the orchard. This was her father's. She sent the dog around to the far right of the sheep and as he ran she felt her own muscles as if she were running with him, a black-haired girl again, pretending to catch a bad guy and protecting the innocent.

"There," she called. He stopped, facing the sheep. Salt asked him to do only what he wanted, what he could do, gather the sheep. The little flock moved toward her as the pressure of the dog at their backs increased. She turned to lead them toward the paddock near the house.

The big white house loomed sweet and aging. She loved the way it looked from here, all worn but well put together, white on white, trim and dormers, porches over porches. The downstairs drew in breezes and the central long hall kept a stream of cool air circulating.

Her gaze was drawn upward to the second floor. It felt good for Mr. Gooden to have told her, "Keep safe." She remembered her father's voice: *"Your eyes are dark blue, like a newborn baby's. Where did you get those eyes?"*

"From you, Papa." Then he would sleep in the afternoon. Her mother would tell her, *"Watch your father."* She had done what her mother had asked most of the time. It made her feel powerful but unhappy.

Now she turned back toward the sheep. Her breath evened out. Her skin collected the sun while the wind tousled her hair over the healing scar. The black-haired girl had run, climbed, and jumped and in exhaustion found peace. Now, when she was on duty, after a street fight got settled, a successful arrest made, she felt release. A car or foot chase sometimes let loose a memory of some story her father had told.

Mr. Gooden may be right, she thought. I haven't handled it.

15.

OF THE FEMALE PERSUASION

As soon as she came down the drive to the precinct, arriving for her evening shift, Salt saw Sister Connelly with Major Townsend, their area commander. They were standing on the south side of the precinct, the major looking up at Sister, who not only had the advantage of being taller but was also above him on the incline. They were accompanied by several of the supervisory staff, two lieutenants and three sergeants, all sweating, mopping their brows, and looking at the base of the bushes beside the precinct wall. Salt headed up the banked yard as soon as she got out of her car, just in time to see Sister push the major into a stoop while she pointed at the base of one of the hydrangeas. Salt had never seen anyone touch the major. He wasn't that kind of person. She hurried up the hill to the group just as Major Townsend asked, "Where do I get the manure?" He sounded uncharacteristically frustrated and maybe a little shrill.

"I can bring some sheep manure from home," Salt said, arriving just as Sister handed the major a handful of dirt.

The brass all turned at once to look at Salt.

"Sheep manure, it's just as good, maybe better than any other, than cow or horse," Salt explained.

"Sheep manure," repeated the major.

"Yes, sir."

Sister acknowledged Salt. "There you go. Right under your nose, one of your officers has what you need to start getting this yard to where it should be, setting an example. After all, this is city property. You could also grow vegetables with all this yard, give some to the homeless shelters. At least take care of these shrubs and bushes, make them shine." She showed no sign of letting the major off the hook.

"Shine," repeated the major. He seemed incapable of getting ahead in the conversation.

"And plant some perennials and annuals both, raised beds. All these young folks, strong men, and you got a sick yard like this. Is this the way you take care of your zone? Your employees? No wonder those uniforms look so shabby. Crime off the chart." Sister was wearing a simple blue cotton dress without a wrinkle, and she was carrying a pocketbook on one arm, like the queen. White gloves were folded over the handle. The major was in trouble.

"Sister," Salt interrupted, "are you here to see me?"

The major stumbled down the hill toward Salt. "Yes, Sister Connelly, Officer Salt can help you with whatever you need." He held up his hand as Sister started to speak. "With what—what we need for the precinct yard." He was on his way up the back steps before he finished the sentence. He turned to his administrative lieutenant. "Make sure we get this situation resolved, Lieutenant."

While the sergeants and lieutenants dispersed, Salt walked with Sister around the back and to the other side of the residential-style precinct house. "Sister, you didn't come by just to give us a gardening lesson." Salt grinned. "Not that we couldn't use it." She picked some yellowed leaves off another plant.

"This yard is a mess. But I came by because I remembered how I recognize you."

"I'm sure you've seen me on the beat. I've been your evening watch officer for about ten years now. And of those ten years I've probably spent, total time, months or so just answering calls on Marcy Street. You and I have talked several times."

"Of course, but it wasn't till you came asking 'bout Shannell that I really got close enough to you to know that it was your daddy I was remembering."

"My daddy." Salt heard herself say the words before they sank in. Sister Connelly talking about her dad?

"I remember him for a couple of reasons. You all right? I'm sorry if I upset you, but I thought that since your daddy died so long ago—what, twenty years?—that you'd be okay if I brought it up. Is your head healing proper? I heard about the expressway."

"I'm fine. It's just that not many people remember my dad and even if they do they don't talk about him to me. I just was caught off guard. I'd like to know more about him, especially about his work."

"You're like him, you know. Even though I met him after he became a police officer, I also knew of him before because some of my family come from around Cloud, where his family had that big farm."

Salt smiled. "It's not so big now, just the house and a few acres. I'm the only one left living there. That's where I have the sheep."

"I see." Sister took a couple of steps away and then turned sideways to Salt, looking off in the direction of Cloud. "Too many folks in this town forget that we, lots of us who grew up in Atlanta, come from or have family that came from the country. And in this town the country is not far, half an hour, or a year or so or half a century or a century past the railroad tracks. And in some directions the country is right up against this big city, little places like Cloud. Not that I'd want to go back. No sir." Sister slapped her hand and arm against her thigh, the sound like wet cloth hitting a river rock, and stood there looking away.

Salt said, "I've got about thirty pecan trees in the orchard. I feed the sheep but they also graze."

"Oh, I know 'bout those big ol' pecan trees around Cloud. My sister had one of the big ones where she lived, right next to her and our auntie's house." Sister Connelly went back to looking off. A screechy cicada signaled an early evening, beginning his ratchety crescendos and diminuendos. Sister turned her head back to Salt as they walked to her preacher's big sedan parked at the curb. He didn't look up as they approached, just kept reading the Bible propped on the steering wheel, its soft leather binding bending to fit between the spokes.

"You said you knew my dad through his work, right?"

"That's how we figured out about our Cloud connection. But yes, yes, I met him because of his policing. You're like him about that. He'd talk to people, get to know them. Atlanta is not so big a city. Some want to call it a city, it's just a railroad town."

"I'd like to know what he talked about. Was he asking you about cases he was working? How often did you see him?"

"Our roads didn't cross all that often. It was usually over some crime problem he was working on nearby. Marcy Street used to be real nice, especially before they built those apartments. He'd drop in whether or not he thought I'd know anything or about anybody involved. That's why I realized who you were—didn't recognize your name since everybody calls you Officer Salt. I know you better now that I know who your daddy was." She made a sound, "hummft," something between a laugh, a cough, and a grumble, and settling into the seat, she said, "You come by. We'll talk." She pulled the door closed and nodded to Reverend Stevenson, who put down the Good Book and put the car in gear.

. . .

Jesus loves the little children,
All the children of the world.
Red and yellow, black and white

Red. She needed to find Red. All night the old Sunday school song had kept running through her mind. It was a hot night and Salt was now surrounded by whores. Calvin's Motel was one of her regular stops. It was called "Calvin's" even though Calvin hadn't been in evidence since Pepper found him seven years ago and served him on a warrant for pimping a nine-year-old. It was a one-story building of twenty single-door rooms, L-shaped, and set up on a hill overlooking the Avenue, a south-side street notorious for its sex trade. A driveway made a U from the street up the hill around the front. Johns would drive through and take their pick from the girls, hoping the dress of the whore indicated their willingness to cater to a particular fetish: leather and spike heels for the

S&M crowd, frills for the shy, bright lips for blow jobs, plaid skirts for the spankers.

They laughed and played like kids do when they're desperate to get in just a little more fun before they're called for bedtime. Like little girls in dress up—high-heel shoes, bright blouses and skirts— they twisted and pranced for potential customers. They wore wigs that were unnaturally straight or blond or red.

Salt's mother had always dressed her up for church in dresses that felt like Halloween costumes. Sometimes she liked them.

They are precious in His sight
Jesus loves the little children of the world.

These ladies were probably not the "children of the world" the Sunday school teachers had in mind. Glenda wore a Day-Glo-green tube dress that conveniently rode up her broad backside, which rumbaed when she walked. Rocksand was in pink pleather. Black Sally with her thigh-high boots. JoJo in feathers. There was a new girl. Salt rubbed her eyes and got out of the patrol car.

Salt had worked Vice details, dressed up, done the stroll in front of this place, escorted johns into the shabby rooms where they were arrested by her partners. She could feel how her feet hurt in whore-heel shoes, feel the anxiety of how it would go down once the man or men were trapped in the room, the takedown team, flipping out shields. Johns almost always fought, unsure if it was an arrest or a robbery.

On a detail last year a man had presented her with a cat-o-nine-tails, beautifully wrapped in florist's paper. "Beat me?" He also wanted pins stuck in his dick.

"You costing us dates, Salt," the girls protested weakly, pointing at the black-and-white parked in the drive. But none of them turned down the bottled water she brought. The hot air was dry and gritty.

"Where's Pepper tonight?" Rocksand, the only white whore at Calvin's, asked.

That started them all on a roll.

"That man so fine I'd do him for free," said Glenda, the street-smartest, oldest on the Avenue.

"Ooowee, he shine like new money."

"His mama and daddy was makin' love when he got made 'cause don't nobody that good lookin' come from just fuckin'."

Salt was laughing, drinking her water, sitting on the trunk of the cruiser, her boots propped on the bumper while the cars passed by. It was like having friends as a kid might have felt, someone to play dress up with. All these prostitutes she knew except for the new young one who had on such heavy makeup it was hard to tell her age, her arms and legs smooth and unbruised. She was wearing a tight black miniskirt and a see-through black lace top. A blond wig fell to her shoulders and she kept swatting the hair back from her eyes, like she'd never worn hair that wasn't her own.

Salt caught her attention and asked, "What name do you go by?"

The others answered, laughing. "We call her Peaches 'cause she just got fuzz down there."

"How old are you?"

Peaches didn't seem to know whether to stay or go back to her room. The mood with the girls was still light but she kept looking from Salt to the girls, all laughing together.

Peaches answered, "It's my birthday. I'm seventeen today."

The laughing stopped. They looked to Glenda, who opened the snap of a tiny purse she had taken from where it was hidden in her tight top. "Come here," she said to the girl, and gave her a five-dollar bill. "You take this and go buy a cake. You ain't workin' tonight."

All the girls retrieved money from their various caches and each gave something to Peaches. Salt slid off the trunk and took a five from her uniform pocket. "Happy Birthday, Peaches. You got your ID?"

Peaches went into a room and came back with an out-of-state ID card that listed her age as seventeen today. She probably had other IDs, and any number of birth dates. Salt moved her own birthday around when anyone came close to making her celebrate. But here in Wonderland, Alice or Peaches or most anyone could be as big or small or old or young as she wanted to be. Many of them had followed the white rabbit of cocaine down the hole.

Several more cars came through the motel drive and then sped up at the sight of the patrol car.

Rocksand was the first to say it, serious: "You messin' with business now."

"I'm outta here, ladies." Salt ambivalently turned toward her car, the festive mood broken. They were getting antsy for her to move on. Pimps had to be paid. Drugs had to be scored. Babies needed milk.

Glenda moved the girl with the five-dollar bills in her hand off to the side while the others went back to their doors. Salt had cut Glenda breaks over the years. Famous for blow jobs, missing two top front teeth, she smiled often but with her lips closed until she was ready to work.

"Question, Glenda," Salt said, and waited for her to come close. "You seen Dirty Red lately?"

A blue sedan with two older men drove through. Glenda stopped smiling. "We ain't seen her in a while."

"Where would she hang when she wasn't here?"

Glenda shifted from one hip to the other. "She sometimes turn tricks over on Jonesboro."

"She have a house or apartment to use?"

"Her sister stays around there somewhere." She bit at a cuticle while she watched the entrance.

"Did you ever know her real name?"

"Matter of fact I do. I know 'cause she had to tell it when we got arrested together one time. Her real name is something Stone. I don't remember the first name since everybody calls her Dirty."

Salt stood very still. "How do you know she gave her real name?"

"The Vice guys know her already so she can't give no false name."

"You know if she has other family nearby?"

"Yeah, 'cause she told me one time her brother put her in the hospital, he beat her so bad. It was her little brother but I guess he musta not been too little."

They stood together, both stiff, arms folded across their chests, and watched while a cab pulled in. The birthday girl, now with money, got in to go get her cake.

"You want my card or anything? Can you call me at the precinct and leave a message if you hear from Dirty Red?" She moved to the cruiser.

Glenda held out her hand, waggling her fingers. "You done helped me before. Give me your card."

A part of her wished she could just sit the rest of the night joking with the girls. But they and Salt knew it was time for Salt to go; she was keeping the johns away. And they had dues to pay on debts they'd never owed.

Glenda took the card and walked down the drive toward the entrance. Radio was calling on a dispatch for possible child molestation in The Homes.

16.

SAM'S AND THE CAPPUCCINO CAFÉ

The next day, first thing out of the precinct, she went down Pryor, under the abandoned rusting train trestle, the railroad easement thick in kudzu, past a city equipment yard, rusting iron and steel beams, bars, rebar, and rails visible above the latticed fence. She left after roll call with the purpose of letting Lil D know that she'd found his father, that Big D was sick, and to relay Big D's claim of not having killed Shannell. The drug trade slowed around this time every day, only one runner needed in the hole. She was fairly sure it would be Lil D, like it was most days.

At the intersection next to Sam's Chicken Shack, street signs had been down for so long some said it was now the corner of Nothing and Nothing. Sam's faced East Nothing. The street on the north side of Sam's was actually named Joyland, and the irony of the street name was not lost on those who frequented the area.

There was a hollowness in Salt's stomach, a hungry-sick feeling. She couldn't guess if Lil D would listen to anything she had to say.

On one side of Sam's there was a concrete foundation of some former building. Beside it was a pole with a small raggedy billboard that depicted a young woman with a prominent rear holding a sweating can of malt liquor. Among the debris in the lot was an upholstered rose-floral pillow.

On the other side of Joyland was a strip mall of vacant shops, a small market for meat, produce, and beer, a closed beeper business, and God's World Ministries church. Here most legitimate businesses failed. What survived was the drug trade. God's World had the earth and its continents amateurishly painted on the front window. Clouds obscured parts of North America. Florida was shaped like a penis.

Both sides of Sam's were covered in graffiti that overlaid peeling posters for rap shows and horror movies. One piece of graffiti in black contained the word NECK, the rest of the lettering indecipherable. A crumbling low concrete wall circumscribed the perimeter of the business. There was no drive-through or sit-down, only the walk-up window under an overhang that dangled sections of aluminum roofing.

Sam's was not inside The Homes proper but yet was its center. Everyone went to Sam's. The drug boys ate and took their own orders at Sam's. Courtships, friendships, and neighborliness happened at Sam's.

Another afternoon storm was passing as she pulled into the parking lot. Patches of light came and went between the parting clouds. The rain had cleared most people from the dope corner but Lil D was standing alone under the ragged overhang eating from a Styrofoam box. Sam's chicken sure wasn't making him fat.

She parked in front of the take-out window and got out. No other customers. Sam's face and shoulders filled the small window under the ORDER HERE sign.

Lil D gnawed the last bite from a drumstick and flipped the container into a trash can.

"Let me have a minute to decide," she told Sam. He flung a greasy hand towel over his beefy shoulder and lumbered toward the back.

Lil D was close under the overhang. Keeping her face toward the empty order window, Salt said, "I found Big D and talked to him." She put her hand on the buckle of her belt at the hollow of her belly.

"I know you ain't tryin' to speak to me." He looked away, his expression making it hard to tell if he cared. There was a little smear of grease on his chin. Salt resisted the urge to take up a napkin to wipe it. He was again dressed in fresh clothes, his small frame engulfed in shiny, baggy blue mid-calf shorts and matching shirt. Being in the hole was paying something.

"Meet me over behind the school in twenty minutes," she said.

Lil D pushed off the wall and sprinted out into the receding rain. He went in the opposite direction from the school.

She waited a minute, then called Sam. "I'm not hungry. Could I just get a can of soda?" Sam handed it to her unopened, knowing cops were particular that way, didn't take it personal.

She got in her car and sat watching Lil D's figure recede in the distance.

Pepper pulled into the lot, his tires making splashes through the craterlike potholes, then parked so they were driver's side to driver's side. The rain-streaked windows made Pepper look like he was melting. Quickly as it came, the rain stopped completely and steam began rising from the pavement. As they lowered their windows the washed air offered welcome refreshment. "Be sure to tell Ann that I enjoyed the afternoon."

Saturday she had taken Wonder to Pepper's suburban two-story house for a backyard picnic. Pepper's boys, Theo and Miles, loved her dog and their energy was a match for his. They had thrown the Frisbee till their arms were worn out. Pepper had the grill going. The backyard grass had been recently cut and the sprinkler was on for the boys and dog to run through. Another water hose was attached to a Slip 'N Slide and Wonder chased along as the boys skidded on their bellies. The day had felt light and she was a part of it. Her head and eyes were clear the whole afternoon.

Rhythm from the boom box was under it all. After a few beers, unable to resist Aretha Franklin's "Respect," she'd grabbed Wonder's Frisbees and began a routine with Wonder jumping for multiple discs, flying over her arms to make catches. Pepper and Ann were yelling, "What on earth!" and "Oh, no!" laughing, falling out of their chairs. The boys clapped and danced, skinny legged. It had been a good day with the smell of sunlight, damp boys, and her dog.

"You and that dog are quite a pair. I think you need an agent." Pepper smiled from his window now. "The boys loved it but it makes me think you spend too much time alone with that dog."

"Oh, here we go again. 'Salt, you need a man. When you gonna go on a date? I've got somebody you need to meet.'"

"Well, excuse me if Ann and I want you to be happy," Pepper said, actually looking hurt.

"I know you want me to be hooked up." She was sneaking a glance in the rearview mirror, briefly considering how she looked to a regular guy, when her attention was drawn to a car passing the corner. "There goes Johnny C in a car with a broken vent window."

She was already moving her foot to the gas. Pepper slammed his car in gear and took off, following her out of the parking lot. She'd bet a paycheck that was Half-Dead in the passenger seat. Johnny C, Man's brother, and gang member Half-Dead would definitely be a score for Salt in her war with Man. She was logging onto the computer, screen set to run tags for stolen, while she drove.

"Run, run," she said, vibing the boys in the car, anticipating the chase, her body confident. Then she thought about Lil D waiting behind the school. What if he had turned the corner and changed direction. There was no time to choose. She bore down on the boys whose arrest might lead to information about who killed Lil D's mother.

After going north, then making a few turns, they changed direction and went south on Hill at just under the speed limit. She was following a pace back, holding off, until the computer reported the status of the Buick. Johnny C's silhouette kept turning toward his rearview mirror.

"Radio, I'm following an older-model tan Buick, busted vent, occupied two times, tag, Adam, Adam, Michael, 236. Confirm status. South on Hill from Park." She kept her movements casual, the speed low, timing radio transmissions so that Johnny C and Half-Dead wouldn't notice she was on her radio. Pepper had turned off and was following on a parallel street. The screen on the computer lit up.

The familiar high rush of excitement was in her breath. "Radio, I have confirmation."

Pepper responded, "Radio, I'm close by for an assist."

Several more officers jumped at the chance to be part of a pursuit. Salt heard them reporting locations, whether they were or were not precisely there, making sure to report nearby so they could reasonably be part of the chase. Sirens wailed behind their transmissions. She held off on the blue lights until other units were in place, not wanting to spook the boys any more than they already were. "Radio, we're still southbound, approaching Englewood."

The Buick slowed. Johnny C signaled for a turn into the Englewood projects when he noticed Pepper's cruiser at the intersection. Englewood was an area notorious for harboring car thieves—experts, juveniles as young as twelve and thirteen heisting vehicles. On the hills above, the streets had been cut to dead ends when the projects had been built, perfect drop-off points for stolen cars. Perpetrators chased by police could jump out and have a downhill run through the kudzu and into the apartments below.

"3305, I got the dead ends covered," reported Big Fuzzy.

"3304, I'm at the bottom," Blessing called out.

She turned on her blues. Pepper responded with his.

"Come on, give us a real run," she prayed, not wanting to lose her high. Salt was a short skid mark from the stolen car. Pepper blocked their access to home base and Johnny C shot past, south on Hill, Salt and Pepper on his tail. She grinned and felt lifted on buzzed air. "We are running."

Hill came to a T at University, where another unit was screaming up at them in the opposite lanes. The Buick made a fishtail right onto University, barely avoiding eastbound cars. They busted the light at Pryor and beat the cops to the only available route, the entrance ramp to the expressway. It was the ramp nearest her beat, one she'd traveled many times and one time too many. Without warning, a blur caught the edge of Salt's vision. She held her breath, lips tight, but the smell and taste of gunpowder filled her mouth and nose. Instead of slowing, she gunned the Crown Vic past the scene of her shooting. Gritting her teeth, forcing air to her lungs, pumping more adrenaline, tightening her hands on the wheel, and clearing her eyes, she found herself inches from the bumper of the stolen car. Tires squealing, the boys gunned it into the downtown connector filled with commuters.

In an attempt to lose the cops, Johnny barreled across six lanes, leaving in his wake swerving cars, braking, screeching tires, and a few broken bumpers. Salt and Pepper, sirens yowling, were joined by two cars from the adjacent zone.

Traffic parted for the blue lights. These boys, trained to steal close to home, were now headed toward the rest of the city. She backed off in caution but continued to call the chase. "Radio, we're northbound on 75/85. They've caused a minor accident at Pine Street. Notify Zone Five. Injuries unlikely. Suspect is doing about eighty miles per hour in the HOV, passing Tenth." Now there was no exit available for the pursued. They were blocked in an HOV lane that would carry them to another expressway and out of any territory familiar to them. She gunned it, settling on the perps' tail. Pepper pulled up on their right side, showing them there was no way out. They swerved, feigning a swipe at Pepper, who was grinning. The speed racers were likely lost. The expressway divided and 75 went off to the left with the HOV lane. Pepper had to drop back at the split and the perps saw their chance. They shot into the right lane and headed for the exit.

She advised radio, "Notify Zone Two, the perps have gotten off at Northside." The Buick rode up the left-hand side of the exit ramp, eating shrubs, squealing past cars stopped at the light, then turned left. "Radio, they're southbound on Northside, fifty miles per hour, their undercarriage is damaged, dragging metal, showing sparks." Salt was right on Johnny C, hugging every turn. A voice-over, the academy instructor's commands: *Threshold braking, shuffle steering, hands at two and ten,* as natural now as lifting her feet to run. Then in an instant, an echo voice, *I wanted to teach you to drive,* her father's plaintive whisper. She inhaled smoking rubber, blinking to silence his ghost.

The lost boys took a left on Tenth, heading toward the tony midtown restaurant area. Two more patrol cars joined the pursuit, all following her lead.

Barreling east, the caravan picked up speed, busted red lights, whipped around, and scattered traffic. Pedestrians jumped back. Some drivers came to a dead stop, paralyzed by the lights and sirens. Salt was not missing a beat, avoiding the obstacles, cool on the radio, hot on the road, riding the high, and feeling the release.

They were headed straight toward Peachtree Street and its skyscrapers that emptied out to trendy shopping and chic restaurants. Northside is fixin' to meet Southside, Salt thought. The boys veered around a stopped car at Spring Street, scraping a light pole with the rear-left wheel. Tire going flat, riding on a rim, they took the turn onto Peachtree. They lost steering and headed across four lanes. Tires squealing, brakes screaming, sparks flying, they were on a collision course with the high brick wall of the Cappuccino Café.

It was a moment suspended. Northsiders sat under bright flowered umbrellas that shaded their tables, sipping lattes and frappamochas, looking fine and sleek in dresses and shirts that cost more than a month's rent for the families of the boys in the stolen car. In short seconds it registered on the coffee drinkers' faces that the metal noises they heard were emanating from a vehicle that was not going to stop in the street. Their mouths and eyes formed little *o*'s.

"You're wrong boys. But you're my wrong boys. It's not often we bring the battle here." Johnny C hit the wall at just the right place to do no real damage, bricks busting and flying; she was laughing. She'd seen these boys scramble unscathed from many stolen cars. They knew how to wreck and roll. Dust filled the shining sunlit afternoon. Patrons scrambled against overturned tables, dodging spilling drinks. Both doors of the stolen car were pinned shut, the car wedged between the wall and a parked car. Salt went left, Pepper right, both cruisers coming to a stop on the sidewalk beside the rear fenders of the car. Simultaneously, they swung from their cars, guns drawn, and scrambled up to the driver's- and passenger-side windows. Pepper ordered Johnny and Half-Dead to keep their hands where they could be seen.

It took the rest of the shift for Salt and Pepper to write the reports, impound the car, and get the boys in the wagon bound for the Gray-Bar Hotel.

Other than the Buick and the brick wall, there were no injuries except coffee stains on the stylish couple who'd jumped quickest mid-sip. A good-looking crowd gathered to watch Johnny and Half-Dead do the perp walk to the wagon. Smiling Pepper announced, "Your tax dollars at work."

Later that night, the precinct humorists were swearing that Salt and Pepper had asked Johnny C and Half-Dead at gunpoint, "Will that be caf or decaf, boys?" Or that while they cuffed Johnny and Half they told the waiter they would take their lattes to go.

But as she was transferring her gear to the Honda, she wondered if Lil D might have waited for her behind the school, that he just might have cared enough to want to hear about his dad. It gnawed at her that once again she might have let that family down. There seemed no way to do right without collateral damage.

17.

DIRTY RED

I t was toward the hottest part of the day, late afternoon sun still baking the streets, when Salt drove down Meldon looking for Dirty Red's sister's house. She rolled the lobe of her right ear, still tender from a pavement scuffle the night before, between her thumb and finger, and felt herself overly annoyed by the loss of the little silver stud earring whose mate she still had in her left ear. Hot wind came in through the four open windows of the cruiser.

The houses on Meldon were cousins to her own old house out in the country, built in the same era and style. But here, near The Homes, the houses were vulnerable and falling fast. Some of the roofs were caving in on a third story or attic. Windows were boarded up, decorative trim rotted. They were unevenly spaced on the street because so many had been torn down.

Using Glenda's backstory on Red, she'd asked around and had been directed to a house on Meldon where people said the sister

lived. Next door to the house, weeds overran the lot and grew between piles of bricks. Vines wrapped an old fire-scorched chimney.
The instant she got out of the car she was startled by a loud snap,
a crack in the air above. Salt grabbed for her holster. With quick
relief she saw that a blue plastic tarp covering at least half of the
house's gabled roof had come loose on one side and was flapping
loudly in the wind. The gaudy blue stood out in bright plastic contrast to the gray, weathered siding. A broken concrete walk led to
the front steps and up to an ill-fitting hollow-core door that someone had put their foot through, leaving a splintered hole in the
bottom panel. The original door would have been solid oak. She
stepped to the side and knocked on the cheap wood.

A large, light-skinned, freckle-faced woman partially opened
the door. "Is Red here?" asked Salt, not being sure if she or her
sister would like her being called "Dirty."

"Which Red, me or Dirty? I'm Big Red."

"Well, I was wanting to talk to Dirty Red." Salt hid her grin
with a cough.

"What the poleese want with her?" She didn't open the door any
farther.

"I'm Officer Salt, and first I wanted to make sure she's all right."

From behind the large sister, another woman's voice: "Let
her in."

Opening the door only a little more, Big Red turned to speak to
whoever the second voice belonged to. "As if you ain't brought
enough trouble to this house."

Salt stepped in just barely clearing the door before Big slammed
it shut behind her. The house was dark and cool. A small tunnel of
light coming from the kicked-in hole in the door shone down the
hallway, where a skinny woman was leaning with her shoulder

against the wall. The woman's features were hidden in the dim. But she had the disjointed, jittery posture and stance of a crack user.

"Shannell," Salt said, even though she knew better. Before she could adjust her eyes to the dark rooms and the bright backlighting, the figure moved and turned into the woman she assumed to be Dirty Red, completely naked. She went through a doorway, sauntering past Salt, and into a large living room, lifted a dusty drapery, peeked out the front window, then turned back and told Salt, still standing in the hall, "You in now. You might as well come all the way in."

"Good God, girl," said Big Red. "Put some clothes on. I ain't gonna hear this. Best I know nothin'." She plodded out and down the hall, leaving them alone.

Flopping down on an old brocade sofa, Dirty Red said, "Ain't nothing the poleese ain't seen before. 'Sides it's too hot."

Salt felt her sweat-soaked undershirt plastering itself under the bulletproof vest and felt a familiar admiration. In her, like Shannell, there would be no pretension, which was always a relief. She pulled at her vest to let some air get to her skin.

"Why you say 'Shannell' when you come in?" asked Dirty Red, flinging her limbs around an arm of the sofa, swinging her legs open and closed. Salt was used to this lack of modesty, having searched so many whores after they were arrested; the male cops were always calling female cops for the close body searches of female arrestees. The whores, most of the time without even being asked, pulled their pants down and their shirts up, displaying breasts and "showing pink" without the least bit of inhibition. *I never even saw my own mother naked*, Salt realized.

"You and Shannell hung together," answered Salt, feeling the weight of all the gear on her belt.

The streets forged strange intimacies. She, who'd never argued with her parents, now had this job, which sometimes involved close combat. Salt had lain on top of Man when she and other officers struggled to get him handcuffed. Just after the cuffs were on, Man asked in a friendly manner for a quarter for his jail phone call, like nothing unusual had happened, no hard feelings, both of them doing what they do. This conversation with a naked Dirty Red, who wasn't literally dirty or red, seemed not out of the ordinary.

"Yeah, sometimes. But I hang with lots of folks. Shannell did, too."

"I need your help." Salt shifted her utility belt, adjusting gun, nightstick, gas holder, and radio, then sat down in a chair close by.

"I can't even help my own damn self. I'm down and dirty." She grinned and grimaced, her nerve endings so shot that she could no longer hold even a simple smile.

"Shannell was pretty far down herself."

Red looked away. "Nobody know that better than Shannell. Nobody know better than us how low we gone. We the first to tell you."

Salt pictured funky Shannell and her "cooda potpie" booty shake.

Without the drug tics Red actually looked very like her sister, freckled and light-skinned, but much, much thinner. Crack gave her grin an unnatural width. "You don't remember me, do you?" Red asked.

There was something, another dim memory. "I'm sure I've seen you on the street a couple of times." Salt stood and moved over to the mantel, on which was a photo with curling edges of a school class, one girl circled with a pencil. It was hard to tell which sister it might have been. There was also a ceramic cat meant for a plant but holding a crack pipe.

"No, I mean a long time ago, when I was a kid."

Salt turned back, a vague memory forming. "Your sister looks familiar, like a girl I interviewed once."

"That was me. We looked alike before I got hooked."

With the memory sharper now, she looked at Red, past the dry broken hair, past the contortions, the tics, the ashy skin, to the child in the penciled circle.

"I was raped," said Red, still smiling.

"You're Stone's sister. You and he lived with your auntie on Shaw."

"I was ten."

"Your uncle and his."

"His daddy. You gave me a teddy bear."

"I remember," Salt said, as if words would shatter something already broken.

"I still have that bear. But I've forgotten where."

Salt had more bears in the trunk of her car. "I guess by now he's seen better days."

"Hell, I ain't," said Red. She swung her feet to the floor and leaned toward Salt. "I ain't. Shannell dead. She ain't hurtin' no more but I'm still here."

"Whoever killed Shannell needs to get caught. I heard your brother beat you up a little while back."

"You know what? He dead before he dead," said Red. She flung her herky-jerky body to the far side of the room. For a moment Salt thought she might be searching for the bear, but Red grabbed a pack of Kool cigarettes off the mantel.

"Are you staying here because your sister can protect you?"

"Yeah, Stone won't mess with my sister 'cause she really his mama."

"You mean your sister is your brother's mother?"

"You a smart poleese."

Salt's head was beginning to hurt. It had started again last night and now the wavy lines in her vision were back. She wanted to do right for Shannell, but at the same time wanted to be away from the images of little girls who had to make do with nothing for a childhood and who ended up easy to get killed. "Who might have wanted Shannell dead?"

"Shannell like me. One wrong turn and we liable to get a bad surprise. We at the bottom, like nothin'. But I still got Big till she don't have no mo money. Then I got the street again. I ain't quite at the real bottom. Shannell ruin what she have with Big D. She was on the last step. Anybody coulda kilt her."

"Was she doing something different, something that would have put her next to a killer?"

"Now, Officer, you been 'round these streets. Every next person might be ready to kill. Say a person don't get their piece of the chicken, don't get a decent night sleep, get disrespected by the boys on the corner. Don't take much more and they just kill. Question for me is, 'When they ready?'"

"Did Stone or Man or any of the gang have regular contact with Shannell?"

"I ain't answerin' on the grounds that it might intimidate me. I know my rights." She swung her legs again, open, closed, like a child, a twenty-four-year-old crack child, on short time.

The white shimmers in Salt's sight danced faster. She gave it another shot. "I'm not trying to intimidate you. You're not under investigation." She tugged again at the ear missing its silver.

Red lit the Kool and blew smoke up toward the ceiling. "I know when to shut up. I learnt that a long time ago. I never had no protection. I had that bear for a while. I always did what I was told, till that bear. I told that bear what I wanted. Then he got lost."

Salt had found the right house and now she wanted out. She stood suddenly and turned toward the dim hall. Red said, "You find you own way out."

At the threshold of the living room she half-turned. "It's my job. To find who killed Shannell. Just like if you were killed. I'd keep on until I caught them. Little girls don't get too much say around here and they damn sure don't say much once they're grown and dead." Salt's muscles tightened. Her boots hit hard on the old floor, heading into the shaft of light from the damaged door. Behind her she thought she heard Red say, "Bears ain't no protection."

Outside, as Salt hurried to the privacy of the cop car, the hot wind continued to pull and lift the blue tarp covering the Red sisters' house.

18.

ON THE WAY HOME

Wednesday night was brutal. Nothing major, but radio had been relentless. Call after call, dispatch constantly asking units to clear, advising that there were numerous high priority calls pending. There had been no time to needle the gang. It worried her that she had not caught sight of Lil D. Salt had gulped a power drink on the run and had to milk a call to take a bathroom break and to refill her water bottle. By the time the shift ended her vest was soaked. Her gear bag felt like it carried a ton of Homes bricks when she hauled it from the patrol car to her Honda.

None of the guys were joking, hardly even talking. They were all exhausted, too exhausted to complain about manpower shortages in the PD or the dearth of patrol cars, or the politics that at times played hell with the police budget, as they had in the most recent years. Mostly it was just the muffled sounds of trunks closing. Uniform shirts came off, then the vests. White undershirts appeared disembodied in the dark parking lot. Salt stowed her gear, vest, and bag. Her T-shirt began to dry. Her skin breathed again.

Pepper stumbled to his minivan parked next to Salt and sat with the door open, his head on the steering wheel. "I'm so tired I don't think I can get the key in the ignition."

"I don't know how I'm going to make the drive home. Thank God it's Friday," she mumbled.

"It's Wednesday," Pepper said.

"Well, it's our Friday and I'm going home," she said, eager for the pecan trees, the sheep, and her black dog.

"Good night, partner."

Salt steered out of the drive and cut through a few short streets to get to the expressway. Stopped at the last light on Love Street, before the expressway entrance ramp, her hand moved to cover the butt of her 9mm and she realized that, distracted by fatigue, she had left the gun on her belt in the trunk. But she was so close to open air, close to being away from the city. She headed onto the expressway, her mind gone to thoughts of the coming days off, her dog, and home.

Half an hour later, waiting for the light at the top of the off-ramp exit to her country town, she was jolted out of her reverie by the heavy thump, thump of a loud car speaker, its vibration shaking the frame of her Honda. With the windows rolled up, air conditioner on full blast, no words came through, just the jolting bass beats. In the rearview mirror, behind the car directly behind her, she could see the top of a yellow truck, shaking with the blaring sound. When the light changed she made the right turn onto the rural two-lane that led directly home. The decked-out Chevy truck turned behind her, sped up, and filled her rearview mirror. It was familiar, from the corner, from the chicken place. A gang car.

The windows of the truck were dark tinted so it was impossible to tell how many people were in the cab. She maintained her normal speed but her heart began to race. There were five miles of unlit blacktop before her winding dirt driveway, but no way would she lead them to her home. The truck began to accelerate around her. In a split second Salt considered her options. There were only old farmhouses between the expressway and home. If the truck pulled alongside her she would be an easy target. If she slowed to turn back, same possibility. She would not put some old farm family in danger by turning into their drive. That left one option. She floored it.

The Honda seemed to gulp a second before responding to the infusion of fuel. The six-year-old sedan was not built for speed, but Salt felt she had one advantage. She had been driving this road since she was sixteen and it was a sticky blacktop. She knew every turn, how they were banked. She'd slipped off its shoulders enough times to know where the ditches were deep and where they were shallow. If she could make it, ten miles out there was a small-town speed trap where the local sheriff filled the town coffers with fines levied on unsuspecting out-of-towners. The truck rammed her from the rear. Salt's chest hit the steering wheel as the car jolted toward the right ditch. How to make the ten miles? The first of the curves appeared and she knew exactly how far into the curve she could keep up speed. She anticipated the apex and maximized acceleration coming out of the bend. Salt watched in the mirror as the truck decelerated too soon and for a brief moment she lost sight of it as she hit the gas coming back on the straightaway.

But it was a mile to the next real bend in the road and the headlights were shining closer again in the mirror, hurting her eyes and messing with her night vision. She downshifted to get more grip for the car, risking the transmission, turned the AC off to get more power, and left the windows up to minimize air resistance. Sweat poured from her face and neck. She couldn't think of any way to get more advantage for her small car. The truck rammed her again and knocked the rear-right wheel off the edge of the road. She fought to hold the car straight before angling back onto the road surface.

No longer tired, her body flooded with adrenalized instinct, the earlier longing for the soothing silk of dog fur and home now replaced by primitive determination. For an irrational second, she considered the sheep and that their hooves needed to be treated for rot.

This time when the truck slammed into the car she felt the jerk and then a tug from the bumper biting into her left-rear tire. The next curve appeared and she remembered one more accessory to eliminate. She flipped off her lights coming out of the curve, hoping that she was far enough ahead that the truck occupants would, at least briefly, lose sight of her, that there was enough moonlight to see by, that her eyes would adjust quickly enough, that the tire wouldn't go flat, and that the Honda would hold up for a few minutes more.

She knew that another curve would come almost as soon as this one ended, and she quickly accelerated, decelerated, downshifted, and tore out of the apex, following moonbeams on the white lines of pavement.

Sighting down the bridge over the recently dry Billy's Creek, crossing the bridge, she slammed on the brakes, cut the Honda sharply to the right just as the bridge railing ended, and fishtailed down the bank to the rocky creek bed. She dared not lose momentum on the sharp dry rocks, keeping the car grinding and bumping for traction back up the incline, timing it for just after the truck passed over the bridge. Now she was following them, her lights still off, as the truck poured on speed, searching for her ahead. The sharpest curve on the stretch loomed unannounced because the SHARP CURVE AHEAD sign had not been replaced after the last accident victim took it down coming out of the curve from the other direction.

Even with her windows up the impact was loud, and seconds later the explosion vibrated to her car. The glow became visible as she drove slowly, car limping with the flattening rear tire. Then around the bend, the night lit up by the truck burning against the base of a large pine tree. Salt stopped on the shoulder at a safe distance. The truck had struck the tree sideways on the passenger side, just behind the cab. The doors had crumpled inward but the windows had somehow stayed unshattered. Fully engulfed, fire filled the cab. It was impossible to see if it was one person moving behind the tinted windows or two people being consumed by the flames. She got out and went to the trunk for her phone in a side pocket of her gear bag. She held the phone in her palm, popping sounds from the burning car murder on her ears, fire shooting up the trunk of the tall pine. Needles caught like white sparklers, spraying the ground. She pocketed the phone, closed the bag, pushed aside the gear belt with the 9mm, and grabbed for the spare tire. Using the light from the fire, she worked as fast as she could with the rusty jack. She pounded the lugs loose with the wrench, changed the tire, and then sped down the road to home.

In the hall the first lavender light of day was showing, coming from between the top of the living room curtains and the sills. She sat at the kitchen table in the faint light, a half glass of red wine, a black gun-cleaning kit, and the chrome 9mm laid out in still-life. Salt took a sip of wine and released the clip from the gun. She separated the slide from the frame and drained the glass. Her nostrils filled with the smells of gun oil and fermented fruit as the first rays of sun crept down the hallway. The light played attractively on the chrome. With the weapon still in pieces she put her head on the table and fell into a sleep without dreams.

There was a large turnout, seventy-five or more, for the funeral of Q-Ball. Salt kept out of sight, on a street crest overlooking the attendees, above the stone church where a good number of dope boys had been eulogized in the past. Two columns of young men in colors filed into the church. A floral spray in the same blue was carried behind them, the number 13 outlined in white carnations.

Blessing had mentioned that he'd heard Q-Ball was killed in a wreck. "Highway 14, isn't that out where you live?" Pepper noticed the pulled-out dent in the bumper of her Honda. "How'd you get that?" Nobody that she knew of put it all together, though. The county sheriff didn't come asking. There was no record. She had not made the call. Nothing to tie her to Q-Ball and the chase on the road to her house. Salt would not risk being seen as not able to handle her beat. She would not risk being taken out of The Homes. There were still supervisors who felt protective of the women cops and would see this kind of incident as too much of a threat. She would deal with it.

No one in the city cared where Q-Ball had crashed and died, just another dead ganger. No one, except maybe Man, and Salt.

19.

SISTER CONNELLY

In the dark heat Salt slowly trailed along Marcy Street, windows down in the black-and-white. A hot misty rain had fallen during the day and now a heavy fog hung over the night. The streetlights had halos, and the white noise of the city was muffled. The tires crunched on bits of gravel and glass. An ethereal cloud cloaked the street. There hadn't been much radio traffic, the mic on her shoulder mostly silent. From where Salt parked down the street, low visibility made her view of Sister Connelly, in a red choir robe, all the more startling as Sister approached from the apartment side of the street, moving toward her house. The colors of the houses, the street, a close-by mimosa were hazy and muted to shades of dark and gray, all except the bloodred of Sister's robe and the cracked red of Shannell's windows across the street.

Salt used the outside car mic to announce herself: "Hello." Her greeting floated, disconnected. Sister stopped in front of her gate and waited as Salt drew up, her robe redder the closer Salt got, the pleats folding and unfolding as she moved. "You're out late tonight. Coming from church?" Even her unamplified voice seemed to expand.

"Prayer meeting and choir practice. You don't think I wear this just to wander around in, do you?" Her words were also magnified in the muted night. "You making fun of something with that microphone?"

Salt turned off the ignition and got out, her hands on her gear belt to keep things from jangling. She shut the car door quietly, only the click of the latch audible, and moved closer to Sister, who seemed in this light both younger and more ancient. "You didn't really answer my questions about Shannell when I came by last week."

Sister stepped closer. "You ever go to church?"

"I was raised in the church," Salt said.

"'Salt,' now that makes me think of Lot's wife who got herself turned into a pillar of salt when she looked back at evil."

"It's my job to look."

Sister turned with a swish of red and started up the steps. "Come with me."

The porch light flickered with moths; one hit Salt in the mouth as she followed up the steps and into the dark house. The old woman switched on a dim lamp beside her worn armchair, sat down, smoothed the robe over her knees, and motioned for Salt to sit on the flowered divan across from her.

"You say it's your job to look at evil. What do you really know." It didn't come out like a question. "You been around The Homes for ten years. That's a blink of an eye for me. My eyes saw evil before your daddy was born."

"I don't see how this relates to Shannell," said Salt, realizing the conversation was getting away from her again. The place where she sat on the divan was sprung. She was sunk in a low spot, her knees higher than her lap.

"Tell me what you see that's evil," demanded Sister.

"Stone hurts people because it makes him feel good."

"Oh, I know that, and how did that get in him?" The old woman was asking questions in the rhythm of a catechism. Then, sitting forward, her face above the lamplight, her red robe shining, she said, "I'll tell you answers you don't have questions for. I knew his great-granddad from down in Hahira, before they all come up here to find work. He whipped his grandchildren like he whipped his mule. And he whipped his mule hard leaving Hahira." She picked up an old scrapbook and began to turn the black pages of yellowed newspaper clippings stuck in between the seams. She stopped at one clipping, handed the album to Salt, and pointed: NEGROES BURN SHARECROPPER STORE. It was from an old county weekly dated 1959.

Salt studied a photo of burning shanties. "Why are you showing me this? What does it have to do with now?"

"You say you think you've seen evil, but Stone carries a curse. Curse different from evil."

"I can't undo what's past and it doesn't explain what happened to Shannell or what will happen to the next person who gets in Stone's way." Salt handed the scrapbook back.

Sister Connelly leaned over the book, into the light, and said, "You got a curse, too, maybe just like your daddy, I'm sorry to say. You think you cursed same as your daddy? You have to get close to people, maybe too close?"

Salt shifted to the front edge of the couch, readying herself to stand—talking about her father in a conversation about Shannell's murder was making her uneasy.

"Hold on now." Sister motioned her down. "We all got some kind of curse. Don't take it personal. Curse can be a blessing depending. Why you think Stone killed Shannell?"

"Because he likes to hurt people. Because he hurt his own sister. Because Man and the gang aren't talking, even though I've arranged for some of them to be in jail. I've always suspected that Man doesn't understand how damaged Stone is, how he's a double-edged sword."

Sister held up her hand to stop Salt. "Why? Why would he kill her? Why would anybody kill her?" Posing the questions like teaching, not asking.

Salt sat there silently staring at the hem of the choir robe, then said, "I don't know. It doesn't seem like a killing for pleasure. She wasn't tortured, didn't have anything to steal. Maybe she was shot because she did something to somebody, or as a warning."

"Maybe as a lesson, like a Sunday school lesson," Sister Connelly said.

Salt was getting tired of the cryptic nature of the conversation. "What do you know? Also, the way you talk makes it seem like you knew my dad pretty well."

Moving her face back into the shadow Sister said, "All's I know is what I know. Your father and I talked about our old families, how they were and all—hard. Wasn't his daddy, your granddaddy, a preacher?"

"I didn't know him but heard stories how he was hard on my dad, some kind of hellfire-and-damnation type. Was Shannell dealing?" Salt tried to mask her irritation, laying her words out smooth, not biting them off like she felt.

"I didn't say nothin' 'bout no dealing. I'll tell you what she cared about—that daughter. So much so she gave her up."

"Did Mary Marie come often?"

"Every other week or so. I always knew when the girl was coming 'cause, crazy Shannell"—Sister chuckled to herself, shaking her head—"she'd walk over and put on like she was admiring my flowers. I'd see her out my window. But she was no good at sneaking around, all exaggerated, sweeping her arms through the weeds, like on some TV commercial, making faces into the blooms. I'd notice later some kind of pitiful something would be missing, not the biggest flowers, but things that grow on their own, dandelions or honeysuckle. Then later I would see Mary Marie leave with the little weeds. It wasn't much she could give her. I don't know why she didn't just ask me. I'd've let her pick the good flowers."

"Did you—do you know if anybody saw or heard anything the day Shannell was killed?" Salt rubbed her head in frustration. Johnny C and Half-Dead were in lockup. Q-Ball's funeral was Sunday a week ago. Bootie Green would stay in federal custody. Still nobody was coming forward with information. And now here she was sunk into an old divan begging this mysterious woman for some straight answers.

"Oh, don't you go thinkin' anybody gone testify to any of what somebody might have seen, or might have heard."

"I'm not asking you to testify. I just need something to go on."

Sister Connelly looked past Salt's shoulder at the window facing the street and the apartment where Shannell had lived. "A car with New York tags would sometimes be over there. A white man and sometimes a black man would go in Shannell's and come out. They carried suitcases, sacks, or boxes."

"Guns, drugs, dirty money?"

"Don't know 'bout any of that either." And without pause she asked, "Why you called Salt?"

Her encounter with Johnny Mitchell on the expressway had been at the entrance closest to Marcy Street. Mitchell, guns, and a New York tag. Salt answered distractedly, "Sarah Alt. Our nameplates here"— Salt touched the metal above the pocket opposite her badge—"it's just my initial *S*, and 'Alt'. We got the nameplates in the academy. Officer Pepper saw it first. He made a joke about it then and it stuck."

Sister picked up an old church fan from the side table and began to fan herself. The fan had a picture of Jesus standing in the middle of a flock of sheep with his hands raised upward, his eyes focused on something otherworldly. Sister fanned faster, then stood up and unzipped the top part of her robe. "Whew, rain didn't cool things off much. 'Scuse me, I don't wear a dress under this robe when it's too hot." Salt caught a glimpse of Sister's chest. Right above the lace edge of a white slip, her skin was crisscrossed with long scars, like yellow rubber. Sister walked to the window and peered out. "It's still foggy. Old folks used to say another thing about salt. 'Salt of the earth' meant a good person."

Salt pushed up from the divan, old springs popping, and walked to the door. The fog outside seemed to have doubled. But every week her eyesight had been worsening, she'd been seeing what wasn't there, obscuring what was with floaters and mist. She put a finger to the corner of one eye to try to clear a speck that probably lived in her brain. "New York tags," she repeated.

Sister Connelly asked, "What makes Shannell important to you? What makes Lil D different than Stone?"

Salt looked over across the street, at the red windows. *In death Shannell appeared to have been praying.* "Shannell's place. No flowers, not even weeds. Dirt's hard-packed, walked on, walked over. Even the dirt's dirty. The only door to that apartment has been broken since before I can remember. But she painted those windows red, to fix it. Lil D tries to hide that mark on his neck with a towel. Those close-up little things make them different to me. Stone was raised in chaos. Maybe he had a curse on him like you say, but he also got lost and twisted. I never knew anybody in The Homes that cared for him, except maybe Man, and he just uses him and his twistedness. I'm afraid that Stone is beyond saving. I know the Bible says different, but he's beyond my power to help. Lil D, Big D, and Shannell have kept being put in my path, in my streets."

Sister opened the door and they walked down the steps together. Sister looked out and began to recite: "'Even so it is not the will of your Father which is in heaven, that one of these little ones should perish.' Matthew 18:14."

The radio mic on Salt's shoulder barked, "3306, radio check."

"Matthew 8:12." Sister began another Bible quote. "'But the children of the kingdom shall be cast out into outer darkness.'"

Salt answered, "3306 loud and clear."

The night had been so slow, radio was checking on the units. "3307," called radio. Pepper's number.

No answer.

"3307, radio check."

No answer.

Then, "3307," he answered.

Salt was lowering herself into the driver's seat and for a moment experienced doubt about the reality of the conversation she'd just had with the woman on the porch, moths swirling around her head. *Did she make up that quote about children being cast out into darkness?*

"3307," Pepper mumbled again. He sounded groggy, like he'd been asleep. Not good. He'd been working off-duty jobs to send the boys to summer camp. She needed to get coffee for the two of them. After he'd had a hot sip or two she thought about asking him to listen out for word in the street of guns and The Homes.

20.

VICTIMS

From the road the house, under a clouded moon, looked reassuringly the same: yellow lamplight on in the front window, brighter back porch light outlining the corner of the house. She parked, cut the engine, and sat there listening to the small clicks and pops of the motor cooling. The oak and pecan trees were old, the lowest branches high, their limbs swept up toward the night, trunks solid. The sheep, their distant baas echoing, were far out beyond the light from the house, in the quiet, dark orchard. She tucked the 9mm into her waistband, then popped the trunk of the Honda and got all her gear: belt, vest, and uniform shirt.

At first there seemed to be moonlight spilled into the kitchen, but then she saw one glass panel from the back door shattered on the floor, reflecting the porch light. The door was ajar.

"Wonder?"

She dropped the load in her arms, grabbed the flashlight, and pulled the 9mm. *Just because it's your own house, don't panic*, she told herself. *Always call for backup to search a house.*

"Wonder?"

Salt tamped down a tide of fury, stepping carefully over the broken glass, bent down and touched a finger to one of the drops of viscous blood that smattered the shards and pieces. Wonder's, or the perp's? Had Wonder managed to get a bit of flesh? She blinked. Her dog would have presented himself here, lips raised, showing his teeth, barking. Horribly she imagined his body jerking, saliva flying. She imagined him but heard only silence and the ticking of the mantel clock in the living room.

The kitchen almost looked unfamiliar. She swept the flashlight with her left hand. She held the nine in her right hand down close to her leg. *I live here.* In the flare of the flashlight, details in the ceiling medallion stood out in black and white. Not many places of conceal-ment in the kitchen. She left the room dark behind her as she moved through to the rest of the house. A board groaned under her foot as she stepped into the hall, straining to listen. Something, someone inside, or were voices coming from a distance, an idling engine?

"Wonder?" There was no blood, no drag marks, beyond what she had seen in the kitchen. He'd never allow himself to be picked up if he was conscious. "Wonder?"

Her back against the plaster wall outside the bedroom, flash-light held high, she squatted low to quick-peek around the door opening. Simultaneous with a scramble into the room she brought the nine to waist level and scanned the room with the light. The closed closet door was as she had left it. The drawers of the dresser appeared undisturbed. Then the mirror burst in reflection of the light beam as she stood. She grabbed the closet doorknob with a jerk. Empty.

Out to the hall, dining room, library, living room, upstairs. Tactically clearing each space. "Wonder." Everything was as she had left it. "Wonder?" She breathed his name. The weeks, the day, the night, the hours, the minutes, now seconds, began to register with shaking exhaustion.

There was no blood anywhere else in the house except for the kitchen. She retraced her steps and found drops that she'd missed coming up, on the steps to the porch. She looked out to the orchard. And listened. The sheep sounded like their usual selves—their usual selves as they made their way from the back property—herded. By Wonder. His animal eyes caught a bit of light, glowing red and gold out of the darkness. She flew the beam of the light all around and over the back lot as she ran toward her dog. "Wonder." He lifted his head, panting, and pulled his lips back over his teeth at her approach. She swallowed a cry that was building in her chest. "That'll do, Wonder." He was torn from his ear to his lip, across the right side of his face. Blood, caked and oozed, black, red, and pink flesh. The lid of his right eye was split, his black muzzle spackled with dripping and drying blood. Still he stood facing the sheep that were now huddled against the outside of their pen. She flashed the light toward the side of the house, but impatient to touch her dog she lowered the light and knelt. "Hey, baby, hey baby." He collapsed to the ground. "Good boy, good boy." She touched him lightly, carefully inspecting the damage. Her fingers touched grit and stickiness. She picked up the flashlight and again slung the beam toward the road and across the orchard. She'd yet to check around the sides of the house. Staying low to the ground, she dashed to the back of the house and around to check the south, east, north faces of the house, and all the shrubs and bushes. The sound of a car starting came from the distance but she couldn't see headlights or taillights.

She opened the pen and the sheep, somehow sensing a different threat, scurried to their shelter. She went back to her dog. "Good boy." There was blood oozing through scraped places all over his body. He whimpered and began panting, hard. An ache to wail rose up in her throat, already raw from breathing hard. Wonder's eyes showed white at the edges. She knelt and turned the flashlight over the dog. He began to thrash, trying to gain purchase in the dirt, each sound from him like salt to her own wounds.

A rush of fury filled her head. She was losing the order of things that kept bad situations under control, pushing herself to where she could make mistakes. She soothed her dog with her left hand and with her right drew her gun, pointed it out into the night, focusing through the tiny luminous sights at nothing. Stunned, frustrated, and helpless to ease the dog's pain, she blinked and pleaded, "That'll do, Wonder, that'll do," repeating the command. He obeyed her and lay still. "That'll do."

"I've gone too far," Salt choked. "It's my fault. I should have known when they followed me in the truck." Angry for Wonder and for what might be waiting. Nothing moved, no one in sight, everything silent. "You've stepped into my space."

She slid her hands over Wonder's head, snout, legs; she shone the flashlight in his eyes. They rolled back and his tongue drooped from the corner of his mouth. His head hung limp over her arm as she picked him up and carried him to the back porch, where she laid him on an old quilt.

Inside, trying not to think about how he'd received the injuries, she grabbed cotton balls and hydrogen peroxide from the medicine cabinet. When she returned to the porch Wonder lifted his nose and tried to stand but his wobbly legs failed. He stumbled and yelped. The dog looked up at her with fuzzy confusion, sniffing the air, smelling the sheep. Wanting to go back to his little flock, he tried to get up again. "No," she said softly, and he stayed, like a good dog, his damaged side up. The wounds were no longer bleeding but were raw and dirty. She sat between his front and back legs and began to sing while carefully lifting his matted fur.

Little Bo Peep has lost her sheep
And can't tell where to find them

Night insects smashed into the porch screen. She sang to calm him. He moaned in the silence between verses. She sang until her vision blurred. Home wasn't safe. Wonder's normally sweet earthy dog odor was diluted with something like the stink of sour clothes.

Leave them alone,
And they'll come home . . .

Stone? Over clenched teeth she hissed the *S* out loud. *Cursed*, Sister Connelly had said.

Maybe it was time for her to leave The Homes? Lil D? Shannell? Every crack path, mapped in her mind, the victims, the perps, the gang? It just got worse, more violent, more drugs. Was The Homes her curse? She tightened her fist. *No*, not until she got at least one, one little salvation.

And dreamt she heard them bleating

Even her teeth hurt. Her voice was going hoarse. She sang softer, then went to a low hum.

But when she awoke . . .
For they were still all fleeting

She squeezed peroxide into his side. Wonder raised his head at the sting. "Stay," she said. Her eyes began to lose focus.

Determined for to find them

The thought of Stone hurting her dog made her throat tighten.

She found them indeed,
But it made her heart bleed . . .

Wonder lifted his head again and briefly pulled his lips back, showing his teeth, telling her she was hurting him. The peroxide bubbled. She imagined Stone hitting him, cutting him. Wonder looked at her with narrowed eyes. She finished his leg and lifted her hand to his head. He jerked his snout back and snapped. Salt stopped with a sharp intake of breath and slowly pulled back her hand. But in a faint voice, she continued with the last verse.

And tried what she could,
As a shepherdess should . . .

By morning Wonder seemed mostly back to his usual dogginess, staring at her until his breakfast bowl was filled, barking to work the sheep, and quarreling with her when she pointed him to the car for the trip to the vet. Dr. Withers assured her that Wonder had sustained no life-threatening injuries, and after the doctor gave him some stitches and preventive inoculations she gathered her dog and drove directly to Mr. Gooden's.

The old man was in his neat garden when she arrived. He waved as soon as he saw her car in his drive and propped the hoe he was carrying on a small, rusting tractor. "Let that dog out," he said as she parked. "He can't hurt anything. The cows are way in the back."

Salt got out while Wonder stood in the backseat with his nose pressed to the window, eyes darting.

"Sorry to come by without calling first," Salt said.

"Nonsense. We're neighbors."

She took a quick deep breath, getting ready to ask for his help, but he was squinting at her, looking with his keen old eyes.

"How have you been? How's your head? Your hair looks good short. You can't hardly see any scar, just looks like a part."

Salt knew that with his old-fashioned manners her hair could look like, well, like Wonder's fur, and he'd still find something nice to say.

"I'm fine, thank you. But I could use your help with Wonder."

"What's he been up to? Getting on top of the house again?" He laughed.

Wonder liked high places and one day she had come home and found that he had slipped out of the upstairs window onto the back porch roof and had made his way to a perch beside a chimney on the very highest point atop the house. Mr. Gooden had been in on the rescue, proud that at his age he could climb a ladder to the gable. He'd find other things to help her with. And then would go on for days about how the "next time" she needed her dog off the roof, or the sheep doctored, or the weeds mowed, she should call sooner.

"No, I'm keeping those upstairs windows closed now but—" Salt hesitated and looked toward her house.

Mr. Gooden stood patient, still smiling.

"I don't know how to ask you without just coming right out with it. I need to ask you to keep Wonder at your house for a couple of weeks, I'm not sure, while I'm at work."

"Of course, Sarah."

She opened the car door. Wonder jumped out and she told the dog, "Stand."

"My Lord," Mr. Gooden said. Wonder's fur was all matted around the wounds.

The old man slowly came over to the black dog, bent over, and scratched his good ear while he examined his damaged head. When he looked up at Salt there was a purple tinge beneath his sun-weathered face.

"How did this happen?"

"I'm afraid I've brought my job home. Someone came to the house last night while I was at gone."

"Son of a—"

"I was hoping that he could stay here, only while I'm at work, until I take care of the problem."

"You put your mind at ease. Who wouldn't love this dog and I enjoy his visits, even if he does rile the cows sometime. He's company. We'll take an evening walk. It will give me good reason to check your house before I go to bed and I'll leave him on my screen porch so you can walk over to get him when you get home."

"That's very generous but no need to check the house. I don't want to chance putting you in harm's way. When I come by to pick him up we'll be quiet."

"Goodness, Sarah." He hardened the lines in his face to a fierce frown. "I get to feel like Dirty Harry. I got my .357. I'll have a good time. I can look forward to maybe getting to shoot a bad guy." Mr. Gooden gave her a Clint Eastwood ready-to-tangle grin.

"I don't think they'll be back. But if you insist. Do you have a mobile phone so you can call the sheriff at the first sign of anything wrong?" She would not insult him because of his age and besides he was fit and no fool.

"Sarah?" he asked, stepping closer to her. "Have you reported this, told anyone? And yes I have my pocket phone."

"They would reassign me and I wouldn't be able to do what I need to do. I know this situation better than maybe I should but I think I've been given this for a reason." She put her hand on his shoulder, his muscles somehow both hard and soft. She dropped to one knee beside Wonder, lifted each of his ears, planted a little kiss on the soft inside pink tips, and swiped a drop of one tear that escaped from her right eye.

Mr. Gooden held on to Wonder's collar while she got in the car. "Sarah . . ."

"Thank you, neighbor." She gave Wonder the hand signal to stay and drove back to her house, alternately fantasizing about laying her head on Mr. Gooden's shoulder and Mr. Gooden and his .357 facing down Stone.

21.

WILLS

The terrain of the city seemed to slump under the weight of the huge building that housed its police headquarters. There was no view that provided an accurate perspective on the size of the massive structure. Once the warehouse for a catalog and retail company, it had later been a hub for rail transport all over the Southeast. The building belonged to the 1930s and '40s. Twenty-first-century technology didn't function properly between the nicotine-stained walls. Computers glitched, high-tech communication wizardry failed. The behemoth wanted swing music and a cigarette. The ghosts of girl clerks in ankle-strap heels and managers with pencil-thin mustaches walked the floors while night workers sorted police reports, stored evidence, answered the 911 calls, and dispatched cops to crime scenes.

Salt parked near the patrol car graveyard, where mutilated vehicles sat on wheel-less rims, engines and doors missing from some, wrecks waiting to be cannibalized by motor pool mechanics, slumping on tires rotting in oily puddles of water. She hummed the first notes to "As Time Goes By" as she entered the code on the electronically controlled "Restricted" door. She accessed a short hall, stacked with discarded monitors and keyboards, that led to a large, elaborate freight elevator, another relic from the '30s. The more modern elevators at the building's main entrance were unpredictable and when they failed employees had to walk up seven or more flights of stairs. Salt ran her hand over the tarnished brass filigree of the cage as the outer doors rolled shut and the floors scrolled past the smoky window of the slow-moving lift.

Conjuring Humphrey Bogart in trench coat and fedora, she got out on an empty floor with columns that took the eye up to a ceiling twenty feet high. The elevator door clanged and the echo spread in the cavernous space. Yellow lines on the floor specified the layout for the ghosts of old shipping pallets. She wound her way through to the stairwell, where the floors were designated, inexplicably, with conflicting numbers. She walked up one flight to the fourth floor, marked as both the fourth, in red, and the fifth, in black. At the double doors to the Homicide Unit a receptionist with long fuchsia nails buzzed her in the outer door and gave her the code for the inner door.

The whole look of the office betrayed the work that went on there. There was something incongruous about Wills, spokesman for the dead, sacred work, Bogey's heir, working from an open, 1980s-era, shoulder-high cubicle, his space delineated by cheap, flimsy materials. She found Wills at his cubicle, surrounded by brown paper evidence bags, guns with red tags, and murder books. She'd never seen him without the fedora, never seen his hair, which was light brown, thinning, and looked accidentally cut. Across the aisle, Gardner was asleep with a violet file covering his face. Both their cubicles were stacked with files of various colors, the colors denoting the years of the murders. They worked scenes as partners, but each investigation had only one lead detective, one to hold responsible.

When he saw her Wills smiled and put his finger to his lips, motioning for silence, pointed at the sleeping Gardner, and led her to the coffee room. His tie was loosened and there were smudges of what was probably print powder on his left shirtsleeve. "Gardner's been working twenty-four hours straight on that triple in the West End. What brings the legendary Salt to our humble office?" His smile widened, as he looked her in the eye. "Are you just getting off shift?" He pulled out an orange plastic chair for her.

In the microwave window on the counter, Salt caught a glimpse of her after-the-shift, still-growing-back-in hair. She looked down at her scuffed boots. "Yeah, it wasn't too hectic tonight so I thought I'd try and catch you before you got off."

He had a happy, expectant look, his eyes wide, bright, smiling.

"Are you making any progress?" she asked.

He laughed, still smiling. "I don't know. Am I?"

"I was wondering if I could see the crime scene photos from Marcy Street? And I wondered if you could get the ATF trace on Mitchell's guns, the perp I shot?" she said.

His smile wilted. He shrugged and turned to get coffee from a stained pot on the counter. He turned back to her with a wrinkled brow and handed her the cup. "No wonder you're the Legendary Salt. Do you bleed blue?"

"Did I catch you at a bad time?" Salt sensed his mood change.

"Oh, no." He shrugged again and looked down into his coffee.

"'Cause you can just call me at the precinct if this is a bad time for you."

He interrupted her. "Salt, do you ever think or talk about anything but what goes on in The Homes?"

"This is a bad time. I can see you are busy." She stood to leave.

Wills put his hand out. "I'm sorry. I just get tired of talking and thinking murder all the time. When you walked in, my mind left death for a minute and I was reminded of some trees."

"Trees?" She suddenly recalled her dream of making chairs in the woods.

He shook his head. "There are some sweet gum trees in a place I go to in the mountains. You know those trees that drop those prickly balls? Why are they called sweet gum anyway? You just brought those trees to my mind."

Doing her best Scarlett O'Hara imitation, Salt said, "Why, Rhett, you do say the sweetest things, 'trees.'" She tilted her head, smiled coyly, and batted her lashes.

Wills laughed. "Well, the Old Salt has a funny bone."

"My bones can be as funny as the next guy's," she said, still smiling. "In fact, my dog finds me quite humorous." She was struck with a sense that this might be going in a direction other than what she'd intended. She worried that she was being disingenuous.

"And how is the Wonder dog?"

"You remember his name."

"How about letting me meet that fine canine?" He raised an eyebrow.

Her breath wouldn't sync with the words she was saying. She bit her lower lip, concentrating.

"What does the pause mean? Does he bite?"

"Not unless I tell him to," she said.

Wills leaned closer but not too close. "I don't."

Slowly, Salt said, "Okay," and noticed that his eyes were dog brown.

"Okay what? Can I meet your dog or okay that I don't bite?"

"Okay, you are welcome to meet my dog and okay, I don't think you bite."

"Well, that's settled. When?"

"When what?"

Wills threw up his hands in playful exasperation. "God! When can I come meet your dog?" He laughed.

They both turned as Gardner poked his murder-file-marked face in the break-room door. He covered his eyes and abruptly turned back out, playing like he had caught them in an intimate moment.

"My suave partner," Wills muttered, and she saw her chance to get back to her mission. "Can I see the photos?" she asked, searching for safer ground.

"What are you doing Saturday?" Wills asked.

"Saturday is okay but can't I see them now?"

"Perfect. Saturday it is, but I meant to meet your dog. Yes, you can see the photos now. I'll also try to light a fire under the crime lab so ATF can do the trace." He put his hand on the underside of her arm and steered her back to his cubicle.

Salt wasn't sure what she had agreed to, but was relieved when he retrieved Shannell's murder file from the bottom of a violet pile. He handed her the large photo envelope and watched as she slid the photos out. They were color eight-and-a-half-by-elevens, taken in sequence from the outside moving in: Shannell's run-down building, her apartment door with the hanging boards, the kitchen entrance, ratty living room, dark hall, sad bedroom, closet, and last, Shannell's bloody body. The photo began to blur in 3-D, her fingers seemed to go beneath the blood on Shannell's forehead, a smear between her brows, like the ashes of penance. Salt's hand lifted to her own head, finding the tender spot in her scalp.

"I hadn't noticed the scar," she heard Wills say.

Her hand responded to gravity and dropped to where the breast-plate in the center of her bulletproof vest usually was. She shuffled the photos back to the living room and hall shots. "I thought I remembered flowers on the floor," she said both to herself and Wills, and pointed to the floor in the kitchen shot.

"Flowers? Yep, those look like flowers," he confirmed.

"Do you know what kind?"

"What kind?"

"I think they're wisteria," she said mostly to herself. She thought she could make out the little lavender blossoms, some still clinging to small cuts of vine, scattered on the floor. Rolled against the hall wall was a jar that might have held them, although it was hard to discern recent clutter from what appeared to be the normal chaos. Flowers—she pressed her hand to her chest again, unconsciously, feeling the rise of her breath.

"Salt?"

She took one last look at Shannell and put the photos in the envelope. As she handed the pictures back, Wills was telling her, "The gun traces, I'll have them by Saturday when I come to your place."

"I'll be working on the sheep. I guess I could use some help, so you'd be best to wear something you won't mind ruining," she said, making up her mind.

"Sheep?"

"Take I-85 south to the Tree Haven exit, turn right, and go about five miles. My place is an old house with 'Alt' on the mailbox on the right. I'll be in back by eight a.m."

"Can I bring my dogs?"

"Maybe I'll meet them some other time. Saturday is sheep business and Wonder won't have time to socialize."

"Will you?"

"Let's see how it goes." She was walking backward toward the Homicide entrance.

"You're a bit of a mystery yourself, Salt." Wills followed her, talking.

"I thought you were getting tired of mysteries."

"Only the ones I can't solve"—he laughed—"and when the stack on my desk falls over. I'll see you Saturday."

He walked her out to the stairwell, marked four and five, held the door for her, and as she started down, leaned over the stair rail above. "Saturday, eight a.m.," his voice echoed down.

Salt looked up. "Saturday," she said, and headed down to the third/fourth floor and Humphrey Bogart waiting in the shadows.

22.

MARY MARIE McCLOUD

There was a small chain across the narrow opening of the door, a chain that looked old and corroded, the plating coming off. Through the two-inch opening Mary Marie McCloud, Shannell's daughter, blinked one eye. The light behind her showed briefly as she changed to the other eye.

"I'm Officer Salt. I was at your mother's apartment the day you found her."

"Mother's Day," said the girl through the opening.

"I'd like to talk to you. Can I come in?" Salt said gently.

The chain tightened, then drooped. "My grandmother says not to let anybody, not anybody, in this house. She don't want dirt tracked in. That's what she says." Mary changed eyes again.

"I'm sure she didn't mean not to let the police in. What if there was an emergency?"

"Is this a emergency?" Her eye looked bright.

"It's kind of an emergency," Salt told the girl behind the door. "You can at least take the chain off. I'd like to see how you're doing. All I can see like this is one eye at a time."

Mary closed the door with a bump. The chain slid out of the keeper, a rusty scraping sound, then a small clack when it fell against the jamb. Then nothing. Silence.

"Mary?"

The door slowly opened. Mary stood facing her in a plaid school uniform jumper, white blouse, and white socks. She wasn't wearing shoes. The hall floor behind her was one long gleam and there was an odor of pine cleaner.

"You can't wear your shoes in this house," the girl said, turning to walk toward the back of the house, pretending to skate on the shiny floor.

"I'm a cop. These are high-top lace-up work shoes. It will take time to get them off and longer to get them back on right. I might get an emergency call."

Mary moved her feet to slip back down the hall, slipping for a slide, awkward though, like she had to practice being a kid. "You said this was kind of a emergency. Anyway my grandmother doesn't care who you are. Nobody wears shoes in this house. And I don't care if you are the poleese 'cause I'm not getting a whippin' and having to polish these floors again because you lied about this is a emergency." She was disappearing into the back of the house.

Salt sat down on the floor just inside the door and began unlacing her boots. The floors were just as spotless at this level, not a speck of dust. She shaded her eyes from the light reflected from the shining boards and experienced a fragment of memory, her father lying on the floor, his blood seeping into the flowers on the wool rug, roses turning pink to red.

Salt placed her lace-loosened boots beside the door, then pressed her hand to the immaculate floor, leaving the print of her palm fading as she pushed to stand. Remembering the last time she'd purposely left a palm print. She followed Mary, passing rooms with furniture covered in sheets so white they bordered on blue. The house seemed to echo silence.

Salt paused at the doorway to the kitchen. Mary had sat down at the table, head bent over, spooning cereal and milk from a plastic container into her mouth. A shaft of sunlight from a window fell across the back of the girl's neck and head, highlighting the short soft hairs that had escaped her braids.

"You took me away from my cereal. It's soggy now," Mary said.

A lid was lying neatly beside the container. There were no dishes or other kitchen paraphernalia visible. Schoolbooks were stacked, squared with the edges of the table.

There didn't seem to be any air circulating in the house. Salt was beginning to feel queasy. She could feel sweat beads break out on her lip and temples. "What time does your grandmother get home?"

"She works two jobs, cleaning a white lady's house in the day and at a store till nine."

"Summer school over yet? Regular school starts soon, doesn't it? Not much of a break?" Salt asked, looking at the neat books. She pressed the back of her hand to her forehead to stop the sweat from slipping down her face.

"What's the emergency? I'm not talking anymore till you tell me." Mary's voice was louder than Salt's or was stronger than Salt felt at this moment.

"I'm trying to find out who killed your mother," Salt said, and watched as Mary put the spoon carefully, slowly, back in the plastic container. The weight of the handle tipped its balance spilling some of the milk. A small puddle began to form on the white table-cloth. The girl pushed away and began to pull her fingers like she had done in Shannell's apartment the day she found her mother dead. "I'm in trouble, I'm in trouble," she said, watching the damp spread on the cloth.

"Milk will wash out," Salt said, alarmed at the girl's reaction to the soiled cloth. Mary's confident façade vanished.

"She'll know," Mary said. "Look, there it is." Staring at the tablecloth.

"Here," said Salt, picking up the books and putting them on the counter. She grabbed the end of the tablecloth, thinking of magicians who pulled cloths from under whole table settings. "Where's the washing machine? It'll be done in no time."

The radio mic on her shoulder spit static, then began calling for units to respond to a burglary in progress. "3306, are you in service?"

Salt eased the volume knob lower and turned her head toward the mic, "Radio, do you have any other units available?" Mary watched with worried eyes.

"Negative," replied radio.

"Damn," Salt said to herself.

Mary shivered, like she was trying to fit back in her skin.

"I have to get my shoes on. They're calling me. I'll come back." Salt headed toward the door and her shoes. "Do you have any idea who might have killed your mother? Did you see anything that might help me find out who killed her?"

"I'm not allowed to use the washing machine," said the girl, following Salt, who kept looking back over her shoulder to check on her. Mary pulled at her fingers, one at a time, as she kept up with Salt, going down the hallway. "I heard that word you said."

"What? 'Killed'?"

"'Damn.' You said 'damn.' If you talk like that you'll be damned in hell, my grandmother says. Then you lied and said there was an emergency in here." The girl's face grew stern.

"You're not allowed to use the washing machine?" Salt sat down on the floor in order to get into her shoes.

"My grandmother wants to see what gets dirty." Mary looked down at the floor, then cut her eyes to Salt.

"Handwash the tablecloth now. It might dry before nine. I don't know how long this other emergency will take but I'll be back if I can." Already she could feel the shoes were tied too loose. She tried to jerk the laces tight without untying and starting over. "Radio, I'm en route to the call. ETA five minutes." She ran down the steps. Just before she ducked into the patrol car, she saw the girl close the door and open it again with the chain between the door and the jamb. Salt sped off with blue lights, no siren, to catch a burglar who she hoped might have loose shoes.

It was late in the shift when she had gotten her calls caught up and could get back to the McClouds'. She'd caught the burglar after all but had not saved the baby in a burning car. The grandmother came to the door, quickly looked at Salt through the opening, and slid the chain off.

"Good evening, Officer. What can I do for you?" Mrs. McCloud, with a slight smile, stood perfectly in the middle of the door frame. "I didn't call the police. It's late." She filled the entrance, square and solid in a big black dress with a purple sheen. Salt looked for some similarities between Mrs. McCloud and Sister Connelly, who'd said they were cousins. But where Sister was tall and thin with movements either too quick to catch or so slow you didn't notice them, Mrs. McCloud seemed a barrier, broad and thick. Sister had a deep plum shimmery color. Mary's grandmother was light brown, blond hair pulled back in a twist, and green eyes.

"May I come in?" Salt asked.

"Oh, my heavens. I just got off work and this place is a mess," said the grandmother, smoothing the tight sides of her hair.

"No, it's—" Salt halted. "I just wanted to check to see how Mary is taking her mother's death. I was concerned."

"You don't have to worry yourself," said Mrs. McCloud. "Shannell wasn't much of a mother anyhow. I mostly raised the girl, though it's hard with all the trouble these streets bring. I keep Mary off the street though. I keep her busy. She takes extra classes during the summer."

"Does she make good grades?"

"Oh, yes. I see that she does. Why, she's gonna go to Bible college someday." The woman hadn't moved from the doorway.

Salt shifted on her feet to unobtrusively try to see around the large woman. "Mrs. McCloud, I'm also trying to find out who killed your daughter. Do you know anything that would help me? Anything that would help me understand why, or who might have wanted her dead?"

Mrs. McCloud thrust her face out directly at Salt, chin first. "The devil and drugs killed her. She killed herself." She kept her hands open and together, like she was holding a hymnal or Bible. "I did what I could to keep her straight and on God's path but she was just like Mary Marie, didn't want to do right. Now the devil got her full-time. Mary Marie knows that. She seen the way her mother died."

Salt interrupted the woman's tirade. "Did Shannell help you? Give you money for Mary?"

"Now where would a crack whore get money?" She swiveled her head toward the inside of the house. Every hair was held by her tight bun. "Who said she gave me money?"

"When is the last time you saw Lil D?" Salt asked quickly to the back of Mrs. McCloud's head, some instinct to draw her attention from the inside of the house.

"I don't know Lil D." She snapped her head back toward Salt. "You seem to know so much about my business, my family, then you should know Darrell Junior was claimed by his daddy, not me. Darrell Mobley never claimed Mary 'cause my Shannell was whorin' by then. Mary doesn't even know who her father might be."

Salt took one step back with her right foot, but leaned forward on her left, close enough to Mrs. McCloud to notice a dry sweat smell. She went quiet and checked the fierce resentment she'd begun to feel toward the old woman, then dropped the questioning that felt dangerous to Mary.

A car with loud music thumped by. Rapping the words: *kill*, thump, thump, *kill*, thump, thump, bouncing out into the night air. She faced the grandmother again but Mrs. McCloud was watching the car at the traffic light.

With only half her attention Mrs. McCloud said, "You, Salt, don't come back to my house 'less you got some business here. 'Less you got some business, and you won't. Don't come back." The big woman backed inside across the entrance and closed the door.

Salt stood there listening. But there was no sound of the chain sliding back in place. Mrs. McCloud was also waiting, close, on the other side of the door.

Salt did a reluctant slow turn to go down the steps, feeling worry for the lonely, sad girl on the other side of that silent door.

23.

FLOWERS THAT GROW
IN DITCHES

The hardest part of treating the sheep for foot rot was getting the dusty, smelly animals to stand in the tub. But Wills was gamely holding the biggest of the five sheep steady in the trough of water and zinc sulfate while Salt clipped the hooves of the dam in the iron cradle. The sheep he was holding kept trying to step out of the trough, splashing the solution on the detective's jeans.

That morning Wills had pulled up to her house at eight o'clock on the minute. The day was already bright, morning sun promising heat. She'd heard the truck as soon as he turned off the highway onto the gravel drive. By the time she met him at the side of the house he was already out and reaching back into the cab. The truck shone, looking freshly washed and waxed. His jeans looked new and had a sharp crease down the exact middle of each leg. He turned, pulling a bouquet of orange tiger lilies, trailing green ribbons, from the passenger seat.

Salt was already muddy from mixing the footbath and the dust of the backyard. Wills's jeans and the flowers made her anxious. Her fingers curled around the grip of the hoof trimmers in her hand.

"My God, what are those for?" Wills asked, looking at the sharp, narrow-bladed clippers.

"Sheep feet," she answered, looking at the lilies.

Wills held out the orange flowers. "These used to grow on the side of the road when I was a kid. Now they sell them in florist shops."

Salt put the clippers in her back pocket and received the lilies in her arms. "Some still grow in a ditch in back of my property. I never thought to bring them inside. They're really pretty." She was drawn by the soft throats of the striped blooms. "Pistil, stamens," she said softly as her fingers examined them.

"Sounds like the evidence list in a murder book." He laughed. "Your house. Look at that second story, dormers and gables." His gaze swept upward.

"Come in. Let me put these in water." Careful of the flowers, she could only dust one side of herself as they walked toward the porch.

Wills followed, then stopped when he saw Wonder in his obsessed, stretched-snout stare, holding the sheep in a tight group in their night pen. The dog's ears quivered but he never looked away from the sheep.

"How long until I can introduce myself?" Wills asked. "He doesn't even seem to know I'm here."

"He knows more than you think but he lives to work the sheep. Today he'll get to help us single them out."

"Us?" Wills raised his eyebrows.

"We're clipping the sheep's hooves and giving them footbaths today."

"We?"

"In return for the ATF information I can trade you how to take care of sheep hooves." She smiled and started up the steps.

Wills followed. "Dogs, sheep, who knew."

In the doorway of the old kitchen he stood looking around, scanning the ceiling, the tile floor, the old table. He met her eyes as she stood at the sink. She was adjusting to the idea of him being in her house; she'd not imagined him here. She looked up at the blue enamel pitcher that sat on a high shelf.

"Want me to get it down? This is an amazing place. Did you do all the restoration?" he asked.

She pulled over a footstool for him to stand on in order to reach the pitcher. "No restoration. Over ten or so years I've upgraded the plumbing and electric. I finally tore down the old outhouse when I built the sheep pen. The place has belonged to my family since it was built after the Civil War and before that there was an original homestead." She filled the pitcher from the deep sink and put the flowers in it. The powder of the pollen felt like new skin when she touched the soft surfaces of the lilies, and it left her fingertips stained yellow.

Wills walked to the hallway. Wiping the pollen on her jeans, Salt came up behind him, carrying the pitcher and flowers. "Would you like to see the rest of the downstairs?"

He turned to let her pass. "Very much." For a moment they faced each other over the orange flowers. She lowered her eyes and turned down the hall.

"This your living room?" he asked at the arched doorway. Again, not having planned on Wills being in the house, she had left her nightshirt and the old afghan on the sofa, a clear indication to a smart detective where she had slept. She put the lilies on the table beside the sofa, picked up her nightshirt, then didn't know what to do with it and threw it back on the sofa. "Yes, living room," she said, ready to be back outside with the dog and sheep.

Wills turned to the stairs that led to the second floor. Just as he put his hand on the banister she herded him in the opposite direction. "I keep the upper floors closed off, too expensive to cool and heat." She quickly crossed over the hall to the library doors and spread them with a slam. "And this is the library." Wills started to go in but Salt was already heading back down the hall. "The dining room, which I don't use, is here." She pointed to the middle room on her left. Wills lagged. "That's the real bedroom." She pointed to the room on the right, not stopping until she was back in the kitchen. She was already at the door to the porch, looking out at the sheep, when Wills caught up with her.

"That was fast," he said. "Remember, I don't bite."

He seemed so confident and steady. She felt edgy. "I need to get to work." She pushed the screen open.

Wills followed. "I'm at your service, sweetheart," he said, with a Bogey accent.

She brushed hair from her eyes and jogged down the steps.

Salt opened the gate and the sheep almost jumped over one another to get away from the stare of the dog, who hadn't moved.

Wills hooked one boot over a bottom rail. "This is beautiful and amazing. What a puzzling policewoman. You keep sheep because?"

"To train the dog and fertilize the orchard. Equipment is minimal, the clamping cradle to hold the sheep for clipping their hooves, the tubs for the footbaths." She shrugged and called Wonder into the pen, putting him in a "stay," and then pulled the cradle to the gate. She signaled Wonder to maneuver one of the sheep against the cradle, made of two small iron grates. She clamped the cradle shut, then rotated the lever so that the dam was on her side.

"Poor sheep," said Wills. "I don't even like that ride at the fair."

She pulled the clippers from her back pocket and started on a hoof. Wills watched closely while she clipped the rough edges. "That takes a lot of hand strength," he said.

"Same muscles you use to pull a trigger." The sheep tried to jerk her leg from Salt's grip. Her hand slipped and the clippers dug into the soft part of the sheep's hoof. It let out a bleat.

"It's bleeding," Wills said.

The dam struggled in the cradle, its hooves clanking against the metal clamp. "Clipping almost always draws a little blood. I hate hurting them but it comes with the job. Speaking of the job."

"Why do their hooves have to be trimmed? I've never heard of it. 'Course what I know about sheep comes from movies."

"The ragged, overgrown parts make places for bacteria and infections. When the hooves are cut back the medication can get in there and the exposure to air helps keep bacteria from growing." The dam had gone quiet and was panting. Salt lowered the cradle and opened the clamp to let it walk into the adjoining footbath pen. "Just steady her for a few minutes." She showed him how to hold the sheep.

He grabbed the sheep's wool through the iron bars. It let out a sharp bleat like a burp and immediately kicked a foot out and bucked. Zinc sulfate water splashed Wills's jeans. He grappled with the sheep but didn't let go.

"Were those your good pair?" Salt asked.

"Well, yeah. I was hoping to make a good impression." He smiled. "Do all your dates get to bathe sheep?"

"I'm ready to clip the next one," she said, going back for another sheep, ignoring the sheep's chorus of complaints, pink mouths opening and closing on long baas.

They finished by the time the day started to really heat up. The sheep had all been allowed to escape to the pecan grove. "That'll do, Wonder. That'll do," she said. The dog ran to a cutoff water barrel under an outside faucet, climbed in, and sat down for a soak. He rested his snout on the edge of the barrel and watched Salt and Wills.

Wills laughed and looked down at his jeans. "I might join him. This zinc sulfate?"

"Yeah." She nodded.

"Will the stain be permanent?"

"The stains will outlast the jeans. I'm sorry."

Sweat beads formed, ready to join and run down her chest. Through habit she had started to unbutton the work shirt she wore over an undershirt, but stopped when she looked up and realized Wills was staring at her with his mouth slightly open.

"The dog and I. I'm not used to company," she said, rebuttoning her shirt.

Wills didn't move or change expression.

"Wonder!" The dog jumped out of the barrel and ran to her, shaking water all the way. She squatted down beside him, realizing too late that Wonder's plastered wet fur outlined the fresh scars.

"What happened to him?" Wills asked, his voice heavy in a way she hadn't heard before.

She dropped her forehead to his back and took a deep breath. "Somebody broke in the house. He's territorial." She tried to smooth the wet fur.

Wills held out his hand, palm down, to Wonder's snout.

"Move slow. He's not much for petting."

They were both squatting down beside the dog. He tentatively sniffed the detective. The smell of sheep lanolin, wet dog, and summer dust floated around them. Wills moved the hand that he had held out to the dog and lifted a damp coil of Salt's hair. His fingers slightly touched the top of her ear. She quit breathing and looked down at her dog for safety.

"Don't make any sudden moves. He's wary."

"Salt," said Wills, just as Wonder sat back on his haunches and started a furious flea-scratching.

She laughed nervously, stood, and brushed her jeans. "He has about the same amount of social skills that I do."

Wills, still squatting in the dirt, let his head drop between his shoulders. He looked up at her.

"I didn't even make iced tea."

"Give me a hand up," he said, reaching out for her. "Do you have tea bags? Sugar?"

"Yes."

"I'll help."

"My only pitcher has tiger lilies in it."

"We'll switch them out." He took her by the elbow, easy, and walked with her to the house.

The sharp, clean smell of mint cut through the outside odors that hung on their clothes. They sat at the kitchen table. Mint leaves stuck to the inside of the cold tea glasses. The flowers were by the sink in a tall canning jar.

Wills looked good dirty. She liked the way he sat at her table, leaning forward, forearms spread. "Wills, ATF? Did the trace come back?"

"I didn't come out here today because I wanted to work on crimes." He pushed his chair back from the table, crossed one leg on top of the other, and pulled at the stains on his jeans.

She looked down at her hands. Even after all the sheep work two of her fingers were still yellow-stained from the lilies. "Flowers, pollen," she said.

"What?" Wills looked up at her.

She held out her hand to show him.

He smiled and took her hand. "We've both got something to remember the day." He pointed to his jeans and rubbed her fingers. "Salt, what about a report? Did you make a report? Does anyone know about your dog, about the break-in here?"

She shook her head. "You don't know how hard it's been for me to keep The Homes beat. In general, women have to work harder to earn a reputation for handling their beat. Some command staff still automatically want women cops riding desks and would jump at the chance to reassign me. I would resign rather than take an inside job."

He let her hand go and sighed. "There is a connection between Mitchell and Shannell."

"Shannell and the man I shot?" The morning light receded into hazy images of the city streets. "The guns?" She drew her hand back.

"Shannell was a straw purchaser. Mitchell was transporting guns back up north because, as you probably know, gun laws are tougher there and guns harder to come by, especially for convicted felons. Shannell had bought two of the guns found in his trunk. The rest had been bought or stolen by other people."

"She was a crack user and a prostitute. How could she buy guns?"

"She never had a felony conviction. She was perfect. Just under the radar for the background check."

"How many guns had she bought?"

"ATF found forty purchases she made over the past five years."

"Five years. So she couldn't buy many guns at one time. Whoever was pimping her probably had other straw purchasers buying for them. Could she have been holding the guns for pickup, storing them?" She thought about Shannell's red windows.

"What makes you think that?" Wills asked.

"Sister Connelly, you remember, lives across the street from Shannell's place, said that she saw a car with New York tags there."

"Some of the guns Shannell bought were recovered from crime scenes in New York. Mitchell had ties to a drug ring there that is believed to be distributing cocaine to points south, including our fair city."

"Do they know who the connection was or is here?" Salt asked.

"No, but whoever is receiving has to be handling weight."

"Then Man does know," she said, bracing herself, elbows on the table.

"You've been putting pressure on the Homes gang, haven't you?" Any trace of a smile was gone from Wills's eyes.

"Obviously not enough." She looked down at a chipped spot on the table.

"Who's got your back? Does Pepper know what you're doing? Does your sergeant?" His voice low and flat.

She stood and walked to the screen door, facing out.

Wills said, "Let me do my job, Salt. This is not the way I wanted this day to end."

She turned to him. "You're not gonna report what I told you about what happened to Wonder, and the break-in?"

"Would you let me come back if I did?"

She didn't answer, just looked out at the sheep.

He stood. "And if I don't let someone know, you will continue taking terrible risks. Salt, I'm the Homicide detective. This is my case." He stepped closer.

"How many open cases are you carrying?"

"I can make time for this case. But why do you care so much about this murder?" He reached his hand to the underside of her arm.

"She was the mother to a child I failed." She looked away, past Wills.

"We all fail children in places like The Homes," he answered. "Why this mother? Why this child?" He tilted his head, seeing her close.

"I don't understand exactly but when Mitchell's bullet scorched my head something broke loose. I didn't know he had ties to Shannell but somehow I'm not surprised." She looked over at the lilies in the canning jar beside the sink. The image of Shannell's kitchen flashed in her mind, an image of the girl, Lil D, and a green envelope. "I'm remembering things."

"It's my case. You don't have to put yourself at risk," Wills said.

"Shannell and her family have been special to me for a long time. About five years ago I got yet another domestic to Shannell's apartment—the usual—she'd cut Big D because he was ragging on her, probably about her crack use and whoring. They gave up their son, Lil D, years before, and then Shannell gave up her daughter and Big D got fed up. You know how it goes—just another Homes call, Big D bleeding, Shannell crying, face all smeary, I've already judged her because of giving up Lil D and on and on."

Wills shrugged his recognition of the scene and sentiment.

"So I trudge up those rickety stairs, five years on the job. That day Shannell, snot running down her nose, said, 'I couldn't take care no baby. I can't take care of my own self, much less no baby.' Something like that and then she said, 'I didn't think a baby would love me.'"

At the bottom of the steps, Wonder lay, head pointed at them, as if waiting for the next command.

Wills made a soft dog-calling sound.

"He still wants to work the sheep."

"Does he ever just want to play, have fun, be a dog?"

"Work is what he's wired for. It makes him feel good."

Wills put his hand to the screen door and opened it. "You won't back off, will you?"

Salt followed Wills to his truck. He opened the driver's door, then turned to her, his face different now, softer. She thought he might kiss her. She put her hand to her back pocket feeling for the hoof clippers, only to find that she'd left them beside the pen.

"Give me a chance," he said, and got in the truck. He turned on the ignition, set his hands on the wheel, and, keeping his eyes to the front, steered out of the drive to the road.

Salt watched the dust stir and blow into the fields. She weighed what Wills offered against what she needed, then inhaled to the hollow place that she was afraid of wanting him to fill.

24.

RED HIGH HEELS

The red high heels sat on the floor of Salt's closet like cardinals on a gray winter day. They were exotic-looking next to the dark navy uniform shirts and pants hanging above. Bright compared to the jeans and T-shirts folded on the shelves. Strange sitting there next to the work and sheep shoes. She stood admiring them, then thought of Wills taking his time on the tour of her house, wondered if he would have noticed them, smart detective that he was. He was on her mind a lot, and not just because of Shannell's murder. She liked Wills's steadiness.

She liked the company of men in general, partly a legacy of the companionship she'd had with her father. She'd had one or two close, intimate relationships: David, a college sweetheart, and a brief but intense one-year affair with a state cop. But she had felt something missing, or broken, likely having to do with her father's death. She understood enough to know that understanding wasn't the same as making things right.

This was the third night of the john detail. She laid out stockings, a garter belt, a pink short skirt, and a red knit off-the-shoulder top. Getting into the blouse and skirt, she began to anticipate the shoes. She'd manicured her rough work hands so they wouldn't snag the stockings while she slid them over each foot and leg, attaching them to the garters at mid-thigh. She picked up one of the shoes, the red leather soft, the spiked heel, four skinny inches. In some situations it might be a dangerous weapon. The insides of the shoes were lightly padded with soft leather the color of butter. She crossed one leg over the other, pointed her toes to glide her foot into the shoe, feeling the arch lift first her toes, then her foot as it narrowed to fit into the high heels. As she stood, the shoes moved her whole body to a different shape, her ass more pronounced, chest thrust forward, legs longer. She'd practiced and if her vision stayed clear during the eight-hour shift she hoped she could walk steady in the shoes, and not waffle or wobble. A small .38-caliber Airweight five-shot pistol tucked comfortably in her waistband was the only other accessory.

Salt had volunteered to do a week with Vice in order to look for Dirty Red, who had disappeared after their first conversation. Working the whore detail also gave her access to information she couldn't get in uniform.

Whores and police decoys aspired to a look that advertised body parts, not women, a look that appealed to fetishists and johns seeking a particular sexual act. So she had gone shopping for a cheap pair of shoes, something Shannell or Dirty Red might wear. She had been headed for a discount store when a mall window, displaying the extraordinarily expensive red heels, caught her eye. She stopped, then immediately wanted those shoes, somehow reasoning that it would help her feel less like a trickster if she wore shoes that even she couldn't afford. Trying them on confirmed her desire, standing up to watch her body change in the store mirror, a body she would be literally selling for the job.

She'd been loaned to the Detail before, when they needed fresh meat for the johns. She knew what was required to keep them interested and not suspicious, not letting the johns get too close until the takedown, small bits of free conversation.

"You dating?"

"Sure, what you want?" A light smile. Get him to name the act, no entrapment.

"What do you do?"

"What you need?" Another smile.

"Not regular sex. Can I pee (shit, watch, get you to beat me with this, suck, around the world, butt fuck)?"

"Sure, I can do what you need." Still smiling.

"How much?"

"What's it worth to you?" A little sex in her voice, get him to name the price, as the law required.

"One hundred (fifty, twenty-five, ten, five, food stamps, a shared crack pipe)."

Why did she let herself be seduced by the expensive high heels? All she had to do was step out into the street and she could become one of the women on the Avenue, unevenly lit neon signs reflecting off her skin, tinny music ringing in her ears. Even her perfume would turn and smell more like asphalt than lavender. Already she could taste the grit blown from the passing cars.

A platinum wig added protection against being recognized and covered her itchy scar. Behind an abandoned skating rink on the Avenue she got out of an unmarked that she'd gotten from the Vice Unit's motor pool. She tucked the shoulder-length hair behind her ears as she went up to the converted bus that served as a mobile office for the PD details, and was now parked at the command post location. There were other policewomen in whore clothes milling around the dark area behind the crumbling building. Even if she hadn't known the other women cops, it wasn't hard to tell them from the real street whores. The cops had better teeth. For several of the women it was their first time posing as prostitutes, and the rookies were laughing and admiring each other's ingenuity at finding the right wig or in daring to wear the shortest skirt or tightest pants. Salt smiled, waved, spoke to her colleagues, and acknowledged the requisite off-color admiration from the male plainclothes. They were bringing in the first of the real hookers, busted so they could be replaced on the street by cops. The in-custody whores looked like wilted flowers, faded a long time ago.

Salt moved her toes in the red shoes, watching for a minute, then decided and walked over to the lieutenant in charge. "LT, how long before you put us out? Love your hat."

He was a skinny, hyper guy wearing a baseball hat, which he habitually touched, the hat embroidered with the word *John*. "We got a late start so I think you have about an hour to kill before we're ready," he answered, moving the cap to the back of his head.

"Then I think I'm gonna go get something to eat." Salt's ankle turned and she stumbled.

"Hey, don't get hurt in those great shoes," he said. "You don't want to ruin your red slippers, Dorothy."

She gave an ironic salute and went to the car.

So in the hour before the reverse-Cinderella time she headed back to her beat, back to The Homes and to Marcy Street in the unmarked car.

. . .

Parked, ignition off, she looked in the car mirror to check her wig but couldn't see, so she switched on the overhead light. A fractured image met her eyes and for a moment it felt like someone else was in the car with her. She shook her head, careful not to dislodge the wig, switched off the light, and got out at Sister Connelly's.

Looking down at her shoes like a penitent, synthetic hair hanging around the sides of her face, she stood at the door and knocked. Sister opened the door wearing half-glasses and carrying an open Bible, its black-grained leather cover soft and pliable. She closed it using one thumb to hold her place and narrowed her eyes over the glasses. "You got the wrong house."

"Sister Connelly, it's Sarah, Officer Salt."

The old woman took her glasses off and looked at Salt hard. "My Lord, I thought for a second you were a street girl. I couldn't see your face clear."

"Can I come in?"

Sister moved back from the door but only slightly.

"Why you wearin' that whore getup?"

"I'm working Vice, undercover."

"You had me convinced." Sister closed the door behind Salt. "That where they send you when you don't do your job?"

"What job?"

"The other."

"What other?"

"You didn't arrest anybody for killin' Shannell."

They were still standing close in the small entranceway. A tobacco-and-coconut odor was coming off Sister, still taller than Salt in heels.

"Homicide detectives are the ones responsible for solving murders. I'm still assigned to my beat but I'm on loan, on special assignment for a week." She had to tilt her head to make eye contact in the close quarters of the hall.

"'Special assignment.' Yeah, it look special."

"I wanted to ask you a few more things about Shannell."

"What more?"

"Like who was around her place when she died?"

Sister led her into the dimly lit living room, to where they'd sat the last visit. She sat down in the same chair across from the sofa where Salt now took her same seat, careful of the short skirt. Again, the only illumination in the room came from the lamp beside Sister. Salt sat in the shadows.

"I save on the electric," Sister said. She let the Bible fall open on her knees. A small bunch of dried flowers dropped from the pages to the braided rug. Salt came off the sofa and knelt to pick them up.

Sister also bent to retrieve the flowers. Their eyes were inches apart. Salt looked down, picked up the blooms, and, still kneeling, turned the little flattened bouquet over in her hand. They weren't wisteria like the scattered petals on Shannell's floor or tiger lilies like Wills had given her. They were rose blossoms, tiny, faded, dried, and fragile.

"Are these from your garden?" she asked. Something was knocking around in her peripheral consciousness. The flowers were pinched together by a faded pink ribbon.

"Of course."

Salt handed them back, looking up into Sister's face again while struggling to get back onto her feet in the spiked heels and trying to keep her dignity in the short skirt. Slipping back onto the shadowed divan, she asked, "Sister, did Shannell come get flowers before Mother's Day?"

Sister looked up at the ceiling. "When you my age, Sarah, things tend to run together." She shifted her gaze past Salt to the window behind the sofa. After a minute she looked down, put her hand on the Bible, and said with flat firmness, "No, I'm sure she didn't."

"Could she have cut your wisteria without you knowing?"

"No. Even if I didn't see her. I know my garden. Nothing changes that I don't notice. I've put in every plant. Every day I weed what doesn't belong. I know every leaf, bloom, bug, and bird. I see the beginnings and endings, the causes of wilting and growing."

Salt sat in the dark, struggling to grab at fragments, trying to pull them together. "Mother's Day," she said to herself, then pressed her hand against the wig and wished she hadn't. The touch made the itching worse.

"What did you say?" Sister asked.

"Oh." She pressed the wig to her head. "My head itches where I got shot." Her eyes wandered around the room and settled on a wall clock that was wrong, both its hands up, stopped on twelve. She didn't have on her watch. Whores didn't wear watches.

"How long has it been?"

"What been?"

"Since you were shot?"

"I was shot in April. The man I shot had guns in his car. He was transporting, he'd picked them up from somewhere around here."

Sister's eyelids slowly closed, like someone who either does or doesn't want to see a memory.

"Sister?"

The old woman took a long breath, opened her eyes, and touched the little flower spray.

Salt glanced again at the clock, which was right twice a day. She felt like she was also stuck and only right occasionally. "I've gotta go, Sister. Thank you for the help." She was anxious now to get to the car clock.

"How did I help?"

"I don't have it all," Salt told her. "I just have pieces."

"You talkin' 'bout flowers has to do with what got her killed? You got pieces, huh?"

"Every once in a while you and I are speaking the same language."

"But you not sure?"

Salt got to the door, turned, and asked, "You said that Mrs. Mc-Cloud is your cousin? Please just answer me straight."

"Sometimes a crooked path leads you to where you need to go. She is. But we don't talk. Though I can't help but see her around."

"Crooked?" Salt, frustrated with the itching, pushed at the wig. "Is she good to Mary?"

"Mary is looked after better than most."

"I saw that, but is she good to her?"

"I think she uses the Bible *against* Mary, not *for* her. But she don't know but a narrow way."

"Sister Connelly." Now she was getting impatient. "I feel like I'm in Sunday school again, in the back row. I want to know if she is good to her."

"Truth is I don't see much of that woman. Frances is her given name. She avoids me."

"Why is that?"

"We go different ways. She was too hard on Shannell. Now she's got Mary."

"Hard? How?"

"She put too much on Shannell too young, and she uses the Bible like a whip, like a curse."

Salt was at the door and looked out into the night. "I think so, too."

"She does what she thinks is right." Sister sighed. Then she pointed her finger. "You know what might be out on the street there." She slapped the Bible against her thigh.

"But it steals the child," Salt said, carefully placing her feet as she went wobbling slightly down the steps in her high heels.

"You don't seem like you walk too good in them shoes. They belong to you?"

"They're new, for the job. I wasn't meant to be a high-heel kind of girl."

"Watch your step then," Sister called.

Salt headed to the car, its clock, and an evening on the Avenue.

Back at the command post the last sweep of whores were being loaded into the paddy wagon. They were lined up at the rear doors, a slow procession, wrists bound behind them with plastic flex cuffs. "The brides of the Avenue," the crew called them. A wagonful.

Some of the girls recognized her in spite of the wig: "Salt." "Salt, can I talk to you?" "Salt, you know me." "Salt, help me out here. I can't go to jail." All asking for a break, a trade, for information.

"Sorry, ladies," Salt said to the group, "not unless you got something to tell me."

One of the women cops, dressed and ready to take it to the Avenue, handed each woman a copy of her jail ticket as, one by one, they stepped up into the wagon. Voices inside complained about being crowded, about body odors, the "poleese," and life in general.

"You look good, Salt." Glenda stood at the end of the line with young Peaches. They were wearing matching outfits, red wigs, neon-blue stretch dresses that barely covered anything, and black heels and stockings.

Salt walked over. "I'm sorry, Glenda."

"Oh, I know the deal, Salt. I'm gonna help Peaches here"—she held up Peaches's hand—"through the jail and court." The young girl had tear tracks in her heavy makeup.

"I see you found Dirty Red," said Glenda.

"I'm still looking for her."

"Why? She in the wagon." The interior of the van was dark. Streetlight bounced off bits of jewelry, and irritated voices, amplified by the metal sides, jangled from the paddy wagon.

"Let me see what I can do, Glenda. I owe you twice now." Breathless, she walked up to the cop handing out the tickets. "Hey, Stacie. Have you got one, last name Stone?"

"I'll look." She sifted through the tickets. "Yep, here it is."

"I need to get her out. I need to talk to her."

Stacie handed over the green copy of Red's arrest ticket.

Salt looked in the wagon but didn't see her. Then in the corner one very thin body was squeezed between two other women, her head turned to the wagon wall.

"Red," Salt called.

Red turned, eyes wide, to see if Salt really meant her.

"Red, come on out."

"Come on, bitch." Another girl elbowed Red. "Get out so we can get going."

Red stood, bent at the waist, stumbling to the door of the wagon. She had on a long black wig that was tangled and had barrettes scattered in it for no apparent purpose.

As Red stepped out, Salt took a step back, caught her heel on a broken spot in the asphalt, and fell sideways, breaking her fall with the palm of her hand. Someone inside the wagon sneezed or laughed. "Shut up," said another voice.

"Shit," Salt muttered, pushing herself up. Her palm was abraded and little bits of dirt, glass, and asphalt were stuck in the scrapes.

"You not too good in them shoes," Red said, her rictus grin disappearing and reappearing.

"I'm not a professional." She picked a sliver of glass out of the pad of one finger. "Damn."

Red stood there with her hands cuffed, nose running, her body edgy and shaking. Salt could have passed her fifty times on the street and wouldn't have recognized her. The black wig nearly covered her face and it was like all Red's limbs had come out of joint and were just hanging by soft tissue. "Salt, you can see, can you please get them to let me slide on this bust? I can't do ten days. I'm hurtin' already. I stayed off the street as long as I could. I was too scared to work. But Big couldn't keep supportin' me forever. Help me."

"This bust is somebody else's case. I have to have a reason to let you go on a summons." Salt played it hard, way harder than she felt. She tried to brush some of the dirt from her palm.

Red stepped forward, like she would touch Salt if her hands weren't cuffed behind her back. "I know things, Salt."

"You know I don't need just 'things,' Red."

Red walked farther away from the wagon. Salt followed at her back.

"Okay, I know about Shannell."

Salt just barely heard her say it. She halted Red by grabbing the flex cuffs. "What about Shannell?"

"I know about what Stone had her up to."

The light around Red's wig went all fuzzy, the barrettes moving like moths in her hair. Salt started to raise her dirty hand to clear her eyes. Red seemed to recede, moving away without using her feet. "You didn't tell me anything before, when I came to see you at Big's." Salt's voice came out louder than she intended, like talking from a tunnel.

"I was scared. I been workin' for Stone. You gonna get them to cut me loose?"

Salt's feet felt mushy on the pavement. She shook her head. "If you give me good reason and you're gonna have to make a written statement."

"Oh, no. That would make me dead. I thought you were gonna look out for me. You gonna leave me to get shot. I won't testify."

"There's a good chance you wouldn't have to testify. If the feds can build a strong enough case, they wouldn't need you. But I'm not gonna lie to you and tell you absolutely you won't have to get on the stand." It sounded like she was trying to convince them both.

"Stone will kill me."

"I can't get you out of this bust if I don't have something written."

Even blurry, Salt could see that Red was in severe withdrawal, grinding her teeth on every word. She felt for Red, felt bad for using her pain.

Red bent over from the waist. "Oh, God help me, I'll write it."

Salt reached for the pen she normally kept in her uniform shirt pocket; forgetting her costume, her hand patted the red knit top.

"Hold on. Let me get the arresting guy and get a statement form. Which detective busted you?"

"That motherfucker," she said, pointing at Gregory, one of the regular Vice guys.

Salt passed Red to Stacie. "Can you hold on to her for a minute?" She went over to Gregory who was writing out more arrest tickets on the hood of a car. "Red give you any trouble, Greg?"

"Red, last name Stone? Naw," he said. "She's a pro. How you doin' Salt? I haven't seen you in forever."

"I know. First the shooting and I've been busy with the beat."

"How's your head?"

"About healed," she said, instantly feeling the headache spike. "Listen, would you be willing to cut Red loose on a summons? She's giving me good info."

"Since it's you asking, I can go with letting her appear on her own. You get her ticket, you change it."

"Thanks, Greg. I'll owe you one, maybe two. You got a pen I can borrow? I already got the ticket from Stacie."

"A freebie." He handed her a pen from his pocket.

"Did you get Glenda and the young one, too?"

"Nope. Those were Scrapler's arrests. You know you can have Red as far as I'm concerned but the LT will stop that if it's called to his attention by you trying to get three whores off. You're bleeding, Salt, your wrist."

Salt looked down and saw that a trickle of blood had begun down her wrist from her palm. "Damn, it's these shoes. I tripped on the pavement."

"I've got some hand wash in my gear bag."

"It's just a scrape. Thanks, Greg."

"Yeah, but out here you never can tell. Some of these girls carry some bad infections."

"Really, I'm fine," she said.

Glenda and Peaches were the last on the wagon so they sat across from each other at the doors. They had been last on and so would be first off at the jail. Glenda nodded to Salt just before the driver closed the doors.

Salt went back to Red, who was for the moment absorbed by the ends of her wig hair.

"Who's got the flex cutters?" Red, knowing the routine, asked as soon as Salt got back to her. "I can't think with my hands behind me."

One of the men brought over snippers and cut the cuffs.

"I have your ticket," Salt said, leading Red to a car trunk, careful now of the puckered and split parking lot pavement. Red checked over her shoulder, rubbed her wet nose, shook her head like a dog, and took the pen and blue form Salt offered.

"From the street nobody can see you."

Red bent over and tried to arrange her body to write. She swung her butt from side to side as she leaned on the car trunk, her shoulders twitching as she pressed the pen to the form. Her body was in constant motion, joints bent in unexpected directions, head rolling as she wrote. After torturous minutes, lips pulled into a hard grimace, she finished, stuck the pen in her mouth, jutted her hip till it looked like it hurt, and handed the blue statement to Salt.

The handwriting was childlike, printed with capitals in wrong places, misspellings and no punctuation, but it read like sacred text to Salt. Her heart rate revved with each word.

Me and cHanel bot guNs For stone
Four she di CHanel keeP the Guns at her aptment
Stone an som grill them
We can by guns cus we don got no Felnee rocod
At the gun places
Stone give us 2 rocks and 25 dolars for 1 gun each

After reading the statement Salt felt as jangly as Red looked but managed to write a series of questions and got Red to put an answer under each of the questions.

Q: How many times did you buy guns?
A: I don no. For 2 years, bout 10 times.
Q: What about Shannell? Do you know how many times
   she bought?
A: Mayb the same.
Q: Do you know anybody else that bought guns for
   Stone?
A: Thass not my bidnes. I don wan too no.
Q: What happened to the guns Shannell and you were
   buying?
A: Thass not my bidnes too.
Q: Was there anybody else in with Stone on the gun buying?
A: Les I no the bater I am.
Q: Is there anything else you can tell me about Stone
   buying and selling guns?
A: No.

Salt felt she had as much information as Red could give. She asked her to sign the statement. At first Red started to write, *dirt re—*

"Red, I need you to sign your real name."

She looked puzzled for a moment and then wrote, *Rose Lady Stone*, taking her time with loopy cursive on the signature line. She leaned back for a few seconds, looking at her name before handing the paper back.

Salt looked at Red's signature. "Your name is pretty."

"I didn't hardly remember it." Her voice was soft. "I like the 'Rose Lady' part better than 'Dirty Red' but I don't like folks to remember that my last name is same as Stone. I don't like that he's my blood brother." Then her twitches started. "Now can I go?"

Salt stepped close enough to touch Red, whose body held the street funk odor of the Avenue. Red handed her the pen.

Salt shook her head. "You keep it. Practice writing your real name."

Red's elbows came up, she clicked the pen, rotated her hips, clicked her heels together, clicked the pen again, turned, and started her stroll back to the Avenue.

Red's feet hadn't hit the sidewalk when Salt had Wills on the phone. "Hi, it's Salt."

"I know."

"I found Red. She wrote and signed a statement about Shannell. Get this, buying guns."

"Where are you?"

"Detail."

"Detail?"

"Vice—whores and johns."

"Amazing."

"She's a prostitute."

"I meant you on the Avenue. Damn. I'll call you back. Oh, and Salt. How are you?"

"I found Red."

Wills and the agent were waiting for her in a back booth of the Roadhouse. Over diners' voices and the sounds of dishes clacking, Jerry Lee Lewis screamed "Great Balls of Fire," spiking shards of light into her vision. Salt held her hand up, shielding her eyes against the bright lights of the faux 1950s-style decor: chrome, neon, Wurlitzer jukebox swirling colors off the mirrors. Prisms surrounded the tables and booths in her path.

Wills stood when he saw her. The blending images that at times obscured her sight and skewed her judgment were getting harder to ignore. Wills looked like he was too far away to be in the room. It seemed a long walk to where he was, especially in the trick shoes. Theater patrons, having after-show suppers, seemed to slowly turn, watching her walk. She hadn't taken time to change from the work wig or prostitute clothes. She touched her chest, where the statement was folded beneath her concealed badge. The hostess followed closely as she made her way to the booth.

Wills turned his head, scanning the room, watching the citizens and their attention to her progress toward him. *Shannell, shiny and skinny. Red, naked and hurting.* All she had to do was keep putting one red shoe in front of the other, each step closer to an arrest warrant.

"I almost didn't recognize you," Wills said.

The guy with Wills stayed seated, staring at her shoes and short skirt.

The hostess said, "Miss, are you—?"

"This is the man I'm looking for," said Salt.

"Sir, do you know this woman?"

"I'm not sure," joked Wills, smiling, winking at her.

She felt huge, standing there shifting from one hurting foot to the other, aware of the stares from the tables nearby.

"Yes, I know her, Miss. It's okay." Wills laughed and slid over to make room in the booth for Salt. They had the backseat so they could face the door. Wills must have won the cop version of musical chairs. Until she tucked her legs under the table the man across the booth kept his eyes on her shoes.

The smell of the Avenue clinging to her clothes, she tried to stay close to the edge of the booth seat, as far from Wills as possible. But Wills was his usual relaxed self. Everything always seemed easy for him.

He turned to her. "Go on, show her your badge so you'll get the discount."

"I can't," Salt said.

"Don't tell me you've worked a detail without a badge."

"It's pinned inside my shirt." She'd been flipping her low-neck blouse, the material now stretched and misshapen, down all night, displaying the badge to surprised perps.

The hostess said, "Well, if I don't see a badge I can't give you the discount," and turned and walked away.

"It's okay," Salt said to the woman's back. "I'm not that hungry." Her stomach growled.

"Agent Jim Thomas, ATF, meet Officer Sarah Alt, aka Salt, and tonight," Wills said, "obviously aka Hot Body." He gave her a comedic leer.

She reached across the table and shook Thomas's hand, remembering too late her sticky palm, still raw and seeping slightly. He drew back his hand quicker than she winced.

"I fell. And this—this getup was for a john detail tonight."

"You must have been very successful," said Thomas, brushing his hands and lowering them under the table.

Wills tapped the back of Salt's bad hand with a finger, then lightly turned it over, putting an ice cube in a napkin and closing her fist around it.

She crossed her legs, one foot outside the booth. Her feet were cramped from walking in the red shoes all night and she was trying to relax the muscles by arching them up and down. Thomas's eyes moved to her shoes again. "Great shoes," he said.

The waitress brought beers for Wills and Thomas. "Are you ready to order?"

She wanted a beer but there was already too much that was fuzzy, her eyes, her head. She asked for a root beer instead. Thomas and Wills ordered steaks. Salt asked for the catch of the day.

After the waitress left Wills said, "Salt is here with information, like I told you."

"I was just getting ready to leave the office, working on a big case, when my bud here called. He bribed me with a steak and a beer." Thomas reared back and adjusted his belt. He glanced from the red heels to a man and woman at a table nearby. The woman was watching the man watching Salt as she pulled Red's statement from her blouse, the blue paper curved and moist from prolonged exposure to her cleavage. "One of the other whores wrote this out for me tonight."

"Interesting filing system," Thomas said.

She unfolded the paper. "Have you heard of James and John

Simmons? They're called Man-Man and Johnny C. They run the dope gang in The Homes."

Wills reached for the statement and while smoothing the folds started to read.

"Yeah. We know about them. We suspect they have ties to gun dealers up north but so far we haven't been able to pin anything concrete on them," Thomas said.

"Read this." She tapped the form in Wills's hand.

Thomas took it between his thumb and index finger and started reading. "What? What is this word?" He squinted at the blue paper.

Salt leaned over the table to look at what word he was struggling with. She pointed to *bot*. "That's 'bought.'" Then pointing to *chanel*, she translated: "'Shannell.' She was murdered in May. That's . . ." Salt took the statement back. "I'll read it for you," and she began translating, first in Red's words then in cop-speak, pressing her finger under the hair cap, giving in to an itch near the front of the wig. She felt like bringing up a foot, like Wonder, and using the red heel to rake her head. "She and Shannell bought guns, twenty-five dollars and two hits of crack for each gun. Before Shannell was killed she kept the guns at her apartment and Stone and others 'grilled'—that is, drilled—them. I'm sure she means that they filed off the serial numbers." Salt finished, then looked at Thomas and then at Wills, waiting.

"How reliable is this Red?" asked Thomas. "This is only evidence against Stone, not Man or Johnny C." The agent leaned back, dismissively looking down, adjusting his belt again.

Salt touched Red's signature. Under the restaurant's bright lights Red's statement looked less credible, second-grade spelling, her large childish letters filling the form, leaving no margins.

The waitress brought their orders. Salt pushed her flounder to the side and leaned across the table toward Thomas. "She's telling the truth. It was hard for her to write this."

"Her reliability has to be established. Has she given you information in the past that proved true? You know how this works. I can't get a warrant on her word alone." Thomas shook out his napkin, picked up the knife and fork, and cut into his steak.

"But what about the information? Does it fit with what you already know about Man and Johnny?" Wills asked.

"Yeah, it makes sense. Your hookers, Red and Shannell?"

Salt nodded.

"They're straw purchasers," Thomas continued, covering his fries with ketchup. "They go to different pawnshops, gun shows, and stores, and buy guns, a couple at a time and with enough time between buys to not draw attention." He was gesturing with his fork. A drop of grease fell on the blue form.

Salt picked up Red's statement. "I'm familiar with some aspects of illegal gun transactions." She pushed the wig back slightly, to cool the tip of the scar on her forehead.

"They'd obviously be buying for someone else who sells the guns to a dealer, usually in the Northern states where gun laws are tighter, or they trade them for quantities of drugs." Thomas continued chewing and moving the food around on his plate.

"Mitchell, the guy you shot on the expressway, was a lowlife. He never bought guns himself because of his felony record, but he was a known mule. We traced the guns in his car to straw purchasers in a number of Southern states, including the ones bought by Shannell. But that doesn't tie her with Man or Stone."

Salt looked down at the shaky words on the blue form, thinking what Red had given up to write them. The grease stain was spreading.

Wills sipped his beer, his food untouched. "Do you know who his contacts were here?" he asked Thomas. "You're not eating." He pointed with his beer glass at Salt's plate.

"But what about the connection with Mitchell? Why isn't that enough to establish Red?" She focused on the agent, trying to will away what she knew was coming.

"We're not sure, but we think he'd been hooked up with Man-Man by some cocaine heavy in New York," Thomas answered Wills.

She sat back in her chair, silent.

Wills poked at his food. "What is the connection between the guns and Shannell McCloud's murder? It doesn't give me motive."

Salt held Red's statement in her raw hand.

"It doesn't do us any good unless we can establish Red's reliability." Thomas tossed a half-eaten fry onto his plate.

She realized that she'd known all along it would come to this but said anyway, "I told her she wouldn't have to do anything more, that this would be enough." She leaned toward Thomas. The table wobbled, causing the knife to slip off his plate, clattering on the Formica.

"You're not officially on this case. But if you want me to get this done you have to give me Red," Thomas said flatly.

"Why can't we just ride in and arrest the bad guys? This job has no happy endings, all our hats are black. There's always a sacrificial lamb," said Salt, looking down at her hand.

Thomas pointed his fork at her face. "You choose."

She thought about Shannell, about Red's real name, about Lil D, about the boards on the door to Shannell's, and remembered her dream about building with rough boards. Wills was staring straight ahead, his eyes not on Thomas or Salt, as if he were listening but not wanting to hear her decision. She dropped both her good hand and bad hand to her lap and said, "I'll bring Red to you."

25.

WILLS BRINGS DINNER

Salt woke up early, already damp and sweaty from the summer heat and troubled by a dream of a forest of dangerous flowers, spiky and poisonous, hanging, both huge and tiny, growing from the woven flowers on the rug in the upstairs bedroom. Some of the flowers resembled the crushed and scattered blooms in Shannell's crummy apartment. Another, a rose that sprang from Red's hair. Lil D stuck his neck out and his birthmark morphed into weeping thistle. Other dream flowers, tiger lilies like the ones Wills had brought, in time-lapse photography, wilted and faded. Anxiety and an odor greeted her as she woke. The smell of rot that had been faint a few days ago was now stomach-churning and intense enough for her to follow it to the living room, her bare feet leaving moist prints on the hardwood floor. Already hot daylight filled the air. The canning jar that held the bouquet sat in a stream of light, their stems mushy, leaves yellowed, curled petals littering the table. Most of the water in the jar had evaporated, leaving a chalky residue on the glass.

She picked up the jar and the odor of spoilage intensified. Breathing high and shallow, she brought the jar through the kitchen and out the back door. Near the sheep pen she pitched the whole thing, canning jar and flowers, to the top of a chicken-wire-encircled compost heap. An uncomfortable vision flashed of the seeds producing a profusion of volunteer flowers, a terrible bouquet, from the fertile pile.

By evening the painted table was set on the screened back porch. The ceiling fan kept the breeze flirting with the edges of a worn, freshly laundered tablecloth, embroidered with tiny faded-to-pink poinsettias. This time Salt had prepared, had tried. Wonder escorted Wills to the door, yelping with excitement. She let him knock on the porch door before she came out, wearing her best jeans, saved for special occasions because they were at the fragile stage, soft, right before the tears at the knees begin, a shade of blue just off white.

After Agent Thomas left them at the Roadhouse, Wills had stood with her at her car. "Can I come to your house Monday night?"

Before she could think about it she'd said, "Yes," then amended with, "but I can't cook. Remember?"

He'd smiled and kidded, "Oh, I'm sure you cook, maybe not with pots and pans." He lifted his eyebrows, Groucho-like.

When she had turned to put her key in the car door, he put his hand on her arm. "Here, let me do that," he said, taking the keys, unlocking and opening the door for her. She was surprised that she felt such pleasure from his chivalry.

"If you can chop up lettuce, I can grill. I think I saw a barrel grill in your yard. Right?"

And so that was the deal, easy for Wills, easy Wills.

At the door now he looked up from a CD clasped in both of his large hands. "Ray Charles and Betty Carter," he said with a wink and handed it to her. "I'll get the kebab." He left her looking at the recording while Wonder escorted him back to his truck. The cover showed Ray Charles on one side, wearing his dark glasses, hands lifted over a double keyboard, and Betty Carter on the other side, hands open, held waist high, a slender dress strap slipping off her shoulder.

She was still looking at the recording when he returned, carrying a rectangular foil-covered pan. She held the door for him. He said, "Betty and Ray, duets."

"Tofu kebabs—I don't think you found that recipe in the 'Homicide Detective's Guide to Grilling.'" She pointed her spoon at Wills.

He laughed. "No but you might be surprised at how many Homicide guys are vegetarian, or at least don't eat red meat."

They were still sitting at the table, finishing peaches and ice cream that she'd served in two mismatched bowls. Outside the lit porch, evening had glided to night. Betty Carter's voice carried from the living room: *"This evening has been . . . So very nice."*

"You know, you'd make a great detective. You've had me talking all evening about myself, my cooking, my dogs." Wills put his spoon in his bowl, pushed back from the table, silent, waiting for her response.

Salt pulled her index fingers across the underside of each eye, looked out to lights that could only be fireflies but that seemed now doubled up, blurry. After a silence she said, "I don't want to deceive you, Wills."

"Who are you protecting, Salt? You or me?"

"It's easier for me to talk about work. I wasn't going to, didn't want to bring Shannell into this, didn't want to confuse this—things." She quickly corrected herself.

"I don't want to talk about the job tonight. But when you talk about work you tell me more about yourself than maybe you realize."

"What do you mean?"

Wills reached into his back pocket and pulled out his worn leather badge holder. "You do have the right to remain silent." He smiled, opening the leather and showing the gold shield. "Inferences and deductions, tools of the detective. What you told me about Lil D. Not that many uniforms are as involved, know their beats as well as you do."

"I thought we weren't going to talk about work." Salt reached for Wills's badge.

"I'm not, I'm talking about you. You could trade on your looks, brains, anything. But you mark yourself with the streets. You risk the hurt to get close to someone like Lil D."

Her chest began to feel tight, like there wasn't room for her heart, which began to race. She tried to shrug her shoulders but they felt stiff. "It's how I work. How I am."

"That's what I'm saying, Salt."

"Look at this house, how I live." She stood up and went to the sink, looking out. "It's a legacy."

Wills stood and came to her at the window. "Let's walk." He took her hand and led the way out and down toward the pecan trees. The evening air felt like it was waiting for rain, thunder, lightning, hail, something to break the muggy heat. Even this far out in the country the city lights sometimes dimmed whatever stars might show through the shifting clouds. She felt like she needed to find her legs and catch some air. She began to walk around the trunk of the big oak, glancing to the dark upstairs windows of the house.

"You're just scared." Wills sat down on the bottom of the steps with Wonder hiding beneath him.

"That's nuts. I'm not scared in the street but in my own backyard." She swept her arm toward him, the house, and the orchard.

"It's what's in our backyards that scares us all."

She squatted and began to pull at blades of grass. Almost whispering, she said, "I think my heart or my head is cracked. That something is broken."

"I prefer cracked hearts and heads. Look, I'm not trying to fix you. I know special when I see it."

He stood up, walked over, and reached out his hand to pull her up. Then he let her hands go and touched the center of his chest. "With the things I've seen, my life, I have a heart that looks like a mosaic, all in pieces, held together with a little bit of hope." He worked his mouth into a smile.

Salt's hand moved to the hollow between her breasts and with a soft fist she pressed and a sound escaped, like a single tiny sob.

Wills gently pulled her against him. "Let's go in the house," he said quietly next to her ear. "You can open every door and closet and tell me about you. Then on some other day I'll lead you through the back door of my heart and show you the pieces."

Salt walked with him to the porch and paused, noticing that some of the porch floorboards had weakened and felt soft and springy, fragile under her feet. Before they reached the kitchen door she turned and said, "My name is Sarah Diana. I was named for both of my grandmothers. Well, for one of my grandmothers and for my other grandmother's breasts." Grinning slightly, she looked at him.

"With a beginning like that, Sarah Diana, the rest of the story can't be all bad."

Betty and Ray were ending, harmonizing: *"Baby it's cold outside."*

The porch light attracted moths. Wonder, following Salt and Wills, jumped and skidded, snapping at the ones that flew too low.

26.

ROADBLOCK

Salt, Pepper, Sarge, Blessing, Big Fuzzy, and the rookie were holding a roadblock at the bottom of the hill on Meldon Avenue at its intersection with Middleton Street. Vehicle traffic in The Homes was always light, not many of the residents owned cars. And people who knew anything about the area avoided driving through if there was another route. Most of the rest of the city wanted to forget The Homes existed. Where they were set up, cars cresting the hill from both directions couldn't see the police barricade until they were too close to avoid the waiting officers. It was that time in the evening when the sun is close to setting, sending the last light in bright vertical lines. This area of The Homes was called "The Shadows," a valley between two hills, its lowest elevation. Not only could drivers not see the cops and their cars until they were already headed toward the stop, but the cops' sight lines were also limited. They couldn't see what was coming until the cars were almost there. Here the evening shadows fell first. They could even claim headlight violations before the rest of The Homes, and the rest of the city, darkened.

Usually they made the best of roadblocks, turned them into a kind of goof. Command had ever-changing goals and strategies regarding where and how many would be conducted. This week it was one per shift, rotating through the beats. Even though it strained manpower, they were mandatory details. "May I see your license and proof of insurance," over and over. "Aw, Officer, I was just going to the store." "This is not my car." "These are not my pants." "I don't know whose shit it is." "May I see your license and proof of insurance." "My date of birth is wrong on that." "Some dude gave me this car, man." Like they'd never stopped people who were wanted, driving without a license, in possession of a stolen car, transporting narcotics, denied ownership of clothing wherein contraband was found. "These are not my pants."

"Sarge," the rookie called. "Guy here says the pants he's wearing aren't his." He held up a crack cookie in a clear sandwich bag.

"Ask him whose pants they are."

The handcuffed driver, without a license, shook his head. "Man, them's some dude's stayin' in the house."

Sarge walked over, playing the game. "Dude have a name?" His tone of voice implied cynicism tinged with happiness.

They riffed on the perps and on each other. Good riffs were valuable street coinage and could somewhat make up for a day of lost autonomy. They complained whenever forced to do anything structured, roadblocks being no exception. Making theater paid them off.

As usual, Fuzzy and Blessing were crackin' on Sarge. "You so old you knew Jesus as a corporal."

"He pees rust."

"And farts dust."

"Sarge, I think your name was mentioned in the Bible."

Finally Sarge tried to catch up. "You're both so stupid you'd fail your blood tests."

"That's lame."

"Yeah, he's so lame . . ." They carried on.

Salt would have felt safe but with the tricks her eyes were playing she worried she might somehow give herself away, that one of them would notice something was off with her.

Nearby, a group of little girls watched the cops between turns at jump rope singing to the beat.

> *"Sticks and stones can break my bones.*
> *But words can never hurt me."*

A scrawny tan dog ran up and began barking at the jumpers. A huge flock of birds in the two big oaks and one failing poplar erupted with a cacophony of squawks and screeches. Somebody in an apartment close by dialed up the volume on a static-riddled radio and Salt's vision responded, turning tricky and causing her to squeeze her eyes shut, then open them to see the jump rope blurring in double Dutch. The rope was fraying in the middle where it repeatedly hit the ground, and where a shadow image of the girl jumping appeared, a ghost girl, half a second shy of the real one.

Stone materialized from between two buildings. He walked by the hard-packed dirt yard, where the girls stopped their game till he'd passed by, headed toward Sam's, his eyes on the officers until he topped the hill and disappeared.

They'd been at it for about half an hour when the last of the orange sunset sprang off the chrome of a metallic-blue car, its engine revving, coming over the hill from the direction of Sam's. As they all turned toward the noise, the car's tires skidded and squealed on the asphalt. Gray smoke plumed from the burned rubber as the front of the car went right and the rear went left. It came to a stop sideways in the road, a football field away. The car jerked back a few feet. Stopped. Jumped forward. Stopped again and went silent. Pepper and Blessing started for their cars. They were halfway there when the car began to drift toward the roadblock slowly, motor off as it reached the bottom and the waiting cops. Even in the late light the birthmark stood out. Lil D was the driver behind a dead engine.

Stone was sitting high in the passenger seat. He turned away from Lil D and toward the cops outside his window as the sedan rolled to a silent stop, the flicker of a tightly held grin on his face.

Pepper walked up to Lil D, whose arms were stretched rigid, grasping the steering wheel. They all knew the car, knew it would likely have no insurance since it never had, and knew Lil D's license was likely still suspended.

"Aw, come on, Lil D," Pepper said. "Give me a break. Please. Your mama just died. Please don't tell me this car is dirty. Man, I do not want to take you to jail." Pepper was cuffing him as Salt walked over. "Let me talk to him," she said. Blessing and Fuzzy got Stone out and cuffed him.

They started the search of Lil D and the car. Lil D kept watch over his shoulder, toward the car, as Salt led him away to where the girls were jumping.

"They'll find it under the driver's seat, won't they?" said Salt. A quiet question to Lil D, not really asking, knowing.

"Nothin' to find," he said. His voice was low and tight.

The girls let the rope go slack in the dust. She turned toward them. "You know that guy over there?" The girls' mouths were shut. "The other guy that was in the car." Salt looked to the oldest child, maybe about eight years old.

She dragged the rope between her hands. "That Stone," she said. The girls were looking away from Lil D with his hands in cuffs behind his back.

"Did you see Stone earlier?" Salt asked them again.

"Why you axin' that? You saw him yourself, right when you and them other poleeses started stoppin' cars," said another girl.

Lil D sucked in his cheeks, his eyes going hard. Pepper was pulling a bag from under the driver's seat. "Whoa." He held it up for the rest of the cops to see.

Stone was standing next to the car, cuffed, facing Salt and Lil D. Salt softly asked Lil D. "Why would he set you up?"

There was no answer from D.

"You gonna take this hit for him?" she asked.

The muscles in his face hardened as he clenched his fists and strained at the handcuffs. He clamped his lips harder and didn't say a word. She waited, holding his arm tight, then, determined, she led him back toward the others, where Stone was now leaning casually against the car, one foot propped on the front tire.

So Stone would know, she asked Lil D again, "Tell us who put the dope in the car."

Stone gave Lil D a giddy, curious look, childlike. He grinned and jittered in place. Then he winked a watch-me wink, turned to her, and barked, "Rarff."

For a split second Salt was blinded by a wash of red. She was in his face, could see his jaw muscle jutting. "You saw this roadblock. You knew we were here, so you had Lil D drive. You had the crack.

You set him up. You walked by just a half hour ago." He turned his head, bunched his lips together twice, and barked again.

Sarge and the others stopped whatever they were doing and were watching her closer than they were watching their arrestees. They had never seen her provoke anyone and had no idea what the barks meant to her.

"Tell him, Lil D. Tell Pepper where the dope came from." She spoke to Lil D while still chest to chest with Stone.

"Salt. I need you to sign the ticket," Pepper said, trying to distract her.

"I'm not signing it." She was still in Stone's face.

"Salt," Pepper repeated, walking up to her with Lil D's ticket to jail. She glanced at the ticket book he was holding out to her and took a step back from Stone, her awareness of his rotten breath sudden.

Pepper faked a chuckle. "Big Fuzzy can sign it. He needs the case anyway. He's always short on felonies." Again trying to get back to their previous lightness, crackin' on the big cop.

It was too late. The last of the sun hit the corner of her eye. She looked over at Lil D. The sunset had washed over his skin and lightened his eyes, making him look more like his mother than ever.

"Give me the ticket. My name will be the only one on it though. I'll testify." She took the ticket and signed her name on the bottom line. Sarge and the rest, uncomfortable, looked anywhere but at her. Even Pepper just looked at his hand, still outstretched to give her the ticket she had snatched and signed.

She turned to Stone. "Your day will come, Curtis." She hit hard on the *Curt*. "The car goes to impound. You can walk." She grabbed his arm, spinning him, slamming him against the car. The key felt slippery as she searched for the tiny handcuff lock. Stone, free of the restraints, turned slowly and started up the hill toward the dope corner, barking and howling as he went.

Pepper lifted his radio mic. "Dispatch, start the wagon to this location."

In the background the little girls started their jumping again.

"One for the money.
Two for the show.
Three to make ready.
And four to go."

27.

THE THIN BLUE LINE
AND THE CHAPLAIN

The air conditioner in the precinct was stuck on too cold. An icy breeze blasted from a vent below the bulletin board. Salt rubbed her arms, warming them.

Sarge was saying, "The blue line will be very thin tonight, people."

They were standing roll call and there were only five officers for the early call. There would be even fewer for the late group. The beginning and end of each shift were staggered by thirty minutes so that cars would still be available and on the street during shift change.

Pepper was on Salt's left. Flower, Big Fuzzy, and Blessing were on her right. Sarge called them to attention and then walked down the line for inspection. "Goddamn but you motherfuckers look like total bums," he grumbled while he walked behind them. They all knew he wouldn't write them up. This afternoon Flower had on the same uniform pants that he had worn the night before, with the same muddy knees. Blessing's dark navy blue shirt was faded to the point that it no longer matched his navy pants. Big Fuzzy had on a winter shirt with the sleeves pushed up. Nobody's uniform allotment stretched far enough to replace pants torn in chases, shirts ripped in fights, or shoes scuffed and scarred by kicking in doors and scraped in street fighting.

He tapped her back, as he did each of the others', making sure each was wearing the vest, his tap like a good luck gesture.

The flyers, signs of desperation, held to the corkboard by pushpins, flapped in the cold blowing from the AC. One new flyer stood out: INFORMATION WANTED ON THE MURDER OF SHANNELL MCCLOUD.

Sarge gave them their assignments. "Salt, you'll be covering your regular and 305's beat. Pepper, you've got 307 and 303. We have no backup cars so hump it, folks, but watch out for each other. Fall out."

They broke rank and started out for the cars in line, handed over from the previous shift. Salt stopped at the board to look at Shannell's photo, probably the most recent, a blurry shot of her holding a beer can.

Big Fuzzy came up from behind and grabbed Salt. In one last moment of revelry, he slung her up in his arms and carried her across the precinct threshold.

"I've caught me a fair maiden, I think, but I better check."

"Fuzzy, put me down or I'll stick my scepter up your ass."

They were all laughing: the not-so-diminutive Salt being swept up by the blond giant, leaving the precinct like kids, tussling, play fighting, Fuzz dropping her. Outside the precinct door Salt trying out new swears on Fuzz—Blue Goon, Sumo Ass—noticed the chaplain sitting on the ground beside the lined-up cruisers. He was sifting through a stack of brochures, some of which had begun blowing across the grass and under the patrol cars. He tried to rock his rotund body to a standing position, grabbing for the glossy tracts. One, with the words *Post-Traumatic Stress* in large red letters, blew against Salt's boot.

The chaplain, gathering some of his papers and dropping others, said, "I came to ride part of the shift with you." He nodded at her.

That sent the guys, in exaggerated hurrying, off to their assigned cars, leaving Salt with the chaplain following her to her car. The ever-cynical cops didn't trust that his main allegiance was to God.

Salt began to check the cruiser for new damage from the previous shifts. As she lifted the bottom of the backseat, a favorite place for perps on their way to jail to ditch contraband, the chaplain told her, "Due to budget cuts, chaplains do the follow-ups now. Protocol requires that contact must be made within six weeks after a traumatic incident involving officers. It's been four months and you missed two appointments with the chaplaincy unit. I have to have documented follow-ups or the chief chaplain gets on our case." She remembered balling up two pink message slips.

The chaplain was wearing a suit coat, a clerical collar, and a vest, of the non-bulletproof variety. He carefully put one of the brochures inside the car on the dashboard and the rest he stuck inside his vest.

"Those won't save you if the bullets are flying," Salt said.

"I'm already saved." He patted the center of his chest over his heart.

"Yeah, but tonight, out here"—she looked toward the fading day—"you might have to be saved again, just a little, not the big salvation, I know, Chaplain. That's your department. But I feel responsible for you."

He looked at her like he wanted to say something but didn't. After an awkward minute she continued. "So you're going to counsel me while we ride my beat and answer calls?"

He pulled another sheet of paper from the pocket inside his jacket. "I have to be able to say I've observed you. I need to check off these questions and then after we're finished you can drop me back here at the precinct."

"Kinda like making a regular seventeen," she joked, referring to the standard crime report form.

"Oh, no. I'm also going to give you some advice," said the chaplain sincerely, opening the passenger door of the patrol car.

"When was the last time you worked the street?"

"Well, it's been five years, or maybe more, but I haven't lost touch."

"Where's your weapon?"

He blanched, then patted his pants pockets just in case he had remembered to carry his gun.

"I'll try to keep us out of trouble," said Salt, pulling away from the precinct.

As they drove the few miles to her beat, the chaplain smoothed the questionnaire on his knee and began to make check marks on the form.

"Officer Salt . . . that's not your real name. It's here on the follow-up form, Sarah Diana Alt." He was using his knee as a writing surface.

"3306," radio called.

"3306," she responded into the mic.

"3306, respond to a woman in labor at 1441 Jonesboro Road."

"3306 copies, 1441 Jonesboro."

"Your date of birth?" he asked, making another mark on the debriefing form.

"June 10th. We've gotta go deliver a baby, Chaplain."

"Couple of months ago, your birthday."

"Yeah."

"How did you celebrate?"

"Is that question on the form?"

"No, but I'd like to know."

"Let's just stick to required information, okay?"

They pulled up to a small tattered house with broken toys scattered around a bare-dirt yard bordered by a tiny fringe of grass. Two little girls in shorts but no shirts sat on concrete steps at the front door, centered on the middle of the house. Salt got out and started toward the entrance, then realized that the chaplain wasn't getting out. She walked back and stood beside the passenger window. He was staring at the form. He rolled the window down. As the glass descended, a woman's scream came from inside the house: "Jesus!"

"You coming in?" she asked.

Without looking up he said, "I faint if I see blood. Communion wine is as close as I come."

One of the little girls came running up and pulled at Salt's forearm. "You go help my mommy." She gave off a sharp tangy odor of urine and sour milk.

Salt leaned down. "The ambulance is on the way, sweetie, and I'm going in to help her right now."

The chaplain opened the car door. "You and your sister can stay outside with me."

The little girl backed away a little.

"Bears are in the trunk." Salt handed him the keys.

Inside the house, which was hotter than outside, a young woman wearing a loose green skirt sat on a soiled couch in the living room. Her legs were spread and her belly under an oversized T-shirt was huge. She was groaning. "Where's the ambulance?" she cried.

An even younger woman, hardly out of her teens, came from another room carrying a cloth dripping with water and began washing the pregnant woman's face. "You gone be all right, Shuffie." Close body smells hung in the air of the small room.

"How far apart are the pains?"

"Not no time," answered the younger woman.

"Oh, sweet Jesus," moaned Shuffie, rolling to her side. Salt watched as amniotic fluid soaked her skirt. The odors intensified.

Salt tugged at her shoulder mic and pressed the button to transmit. "3306 to radio. Can you give me an ETA on the ambulance?"

"Stand by, 3306."

"Easy for you to say," Salt mumbled without keying her mic.

The woman scooted down to the floor with her back resting against the ratty sofa. She rolled her head from side to side and then there was a sudden sharp tangy smell.

"The baby, the baby," she cried and slid farther to the floor, raising her knees and spreading her legs.

"Radio, advise on the ambulance," Salt demanded from dispatch while she knelt beside the groaning mother.

"ETA ten minutes," answered radio.

The younger woman had backed away to the wall of the room

and was chewing on the cloth she had been using to wash Shuffie's face. Salt turned to her. "Go get clean towels, clean clothes, anything clean. Now." She moved around to a position at Shuffie's feet. She'd delivered five babies during her time in The Homes. It seemed like not only did children have to grow up fast here but also they were often born too fast. The mother-to-be yelled, crunched her head to her chest, and pulled her skirt above her thighs. The top of the baby's head, slick with fluids and shiny black hair, was emerging.

Salt spread the fingers of her right hand. "I'm going to help your baby." She cupped her hands under the baby's head. The woman gave another cry and Salt was holding all but the feet of a squiggling baby girl. Salt's eyes stretched wide; shaking her head to keep sweat from running and making her blink, she whispered, "Wow," and touched the new skin of the baby's cheek. The tiny girl gobbled her first breath.

Just as the baby coughed and came completely clear of her mother, the door opened and the paramedics rushed in carrying their bags. They began unloading their med gear and snapping on gloves.

"Looks like a girl," one of the medics announced, tearing into a sterile blanket.

Salt looked up with the baby in her bare hands. "Accurate diagnosis," she said, feeling smiley. Her fingers formed a careful cradle around the newborn.

"A girl?" groaned Shuffie.

"A girl," Salt said with a second short prayer that this mother wouldn't go missing, go to jail, or die. A prayer that this mother might protect this child.

. . .

Salt had washed off with bottled antiseptic from the trunk. The baby was healthy and the whole distaff family had trundled off in the ambulance. First thing when she sat back in the car the chaplain shuffled his papers and without looking up said, "I should have at least baptized the baby." He lifted his head and watched the disappearing ambulance.

Back in service with the chaplain still trying to check off his questions, she drove the beat, her hands still tingly.

"Nightmares?" he read from the sheet.

"Nope."

"Flashbacks?"

"Only to my childhood," she tried to joke.

"What about your childhood?" He thought she was being serious. "And why do you mind if I asked about your birthday celebration? Did you get drunk?"

"I was joking." She turned the car down a narrow alley where abandoned stolen cars were often discovered.

"Officer Alt, can we stop here for a minute?"

"Sure." She put the car in park but left the motor running. The cruiser's headlights illuminated what appeared to be a new SUV about a block down the alley. The vehicle was jacked up, wheels missing.

"You have a job to do. So do I." He tapped the forms to align them.

She pointed down the alley at the SUV.

"I know it's a stolen car. Can't you just leave it for a minute?" he asked.

"Maybe it was used in a murder or robbery and maybe there's evidence in it that will solve a crime."

"Or maybe you don't want to be talking to me about your shooting." He made another check on the form.

The hair along her new scar felt like straw. Salt resisted the urge to rub her scalp. "There's nothing to talk about. He shot me. I shot and killed him." She reached for a paper towel in the side door compartment and began wiping the window in front of her, worried she had said the wrong thing.

"You're cleaning a clean window," he said, giving her a glance.

She stuffed the towel back in the door. "Your follow-up could get me transferred. Someone will look at that form you're filling out and make a judgment about my fitness for duty."

"That's not what this is about. Look, I might not be or ever have been a great cop but I know one when I see one. You're the real thing. I'm embarrassed that you delivered that baby with me outside."

"Chaplain."

"No, let me continue. I'm not even a good chaplain. I follow departmental procedures but they don't seem to be of help to wounded and troubled cops. So let me just say that the best I can do is to tell you that I hope you're not having any problems because of getting shot, or anything else." He folded the check-off sheet, put it in his pocket, faced forward, and swallowed hard. After a second or two she put the car in drive and pulled up to process the abandoned auto.

They hadn't said anything more on the way back to the precinct. In the parking lot Salt asked, "Which is your car?"

"Green minivan." He pointed to a battered older-model van.

A rear bumper sticker proclaimed JEWS FOR JESUS and featured a cross superimposed over a Star of David.

"Got a couple of major religions covered there." She tried for a lighter note, pointing to the sticker.

Still quiet, he answered, "I guess."

"Okay, Chaplain, you earn your stars today." Salt paused and drew a long breath. "I don't celebrate my birthday at all. Birthdays were hard for my father. I do have flashbacks about him. Maybe you heard talk. He was with the department. He committed suicide on my tenth birthday." She shrugged. "Really, the only birthdays I feel like celebrating are like—like the one today. I'll lift a glass of wine tonight to Shuffie's new baby. Do I fail the follow-up?"

They were both blue-and-white reflections on the windshield.

"No, you don't fail."

"Thank God." Salt let out a long noisy breath.

"That's my line." He laughed, a strange braying behind his hand. His odd laugh shocked her to laughter.

"You want to come to my office, drop by anytime." He got out of the car, stuck his head back in. "Anytime, anytime."

Salt put the car in drive and waved at him, without looking back, now recalling her dream of chairs, a more recent version of the dream—words appearing as a colliding vision on the boards, appearing on the rough boards for building the chairs in which she now longed to rest. The unknown person still walked forward from the misty dream woods, carrying a sign that she couldn't read.

28.

COURT, LIL D, SHELL CASINGS, AND MARY MARIE

"All rise," the bailiff called as the judge entered the dais at the front of the courtroom. Salt stood, along with citizens, cops, and lawyers, cops behind the lawyers in the never-turn-your-back-to-them tradition.

She wasn't exactly surprised when Stone entered the courtroom, loping without grace, his shoulders folded inward. When he saw her across the room he stopped, turned, and just stood, no expression, flipping his cap between his hands. Court didn't allow hats. Stone's hat hair was mushroom shaped.

A cop behind her tapped her on the shoulder. "What's that asshole's problem?" He thumbed in Stone's direction.

"He's having a bad hair day."

Her colleague laughed and relaxed, telling her a bit of the latest gossip around his precinct, until the bailiff called the first case.

Waiting to be called for Lil D's first appearance on the "Posses-sion with Intent to Distribute" charge, Salt felt nervous for the first time since her rookie courtroom days. The headaches were becom-ing more intrusive. Her vision was increasingly populated by phan-tom lights and floaters.

As they sat, the court continued to fill with families of suspects, victims, and victims' families. There was rarely a difference between the accused and the accusers. Very young women with babies on their hips and grandmothers with babies on their hips were in abun-dance. Shannell's generation was missing but the courtroom was packed.

Too much of the culture of The Homes was being shaped by Budweiser commercials, the celebrity of the moment, what they were driving and wearing. Bling over substance. Modesty had gone the way of mules. Quite a few of the women and girls who came to court were sent out by the judges for improper attire while others barely made the cutoff.

Case after case, young men, slouching in defiance, were led from holding cells. When Lil D's name was called he was led out blinking, looking thinner and hungrier than ever. Stone stood up and went to lean against a wall in Lil D's sight line. He covered his mouth with his cap. His face muscles moved like he was talking behind it though he made no sound. Lil D looked at Stone, then turned back to stare at the floor.

The judge recited, rather than asked Lil D, the questions regard-ing his ability to afford a lawyer. Asked if he had held a job in the past six months, Lil D was barely audible when he answered, "No." His voice sounded weak and unused when he answered, "Yes," to needing a public defender.

The judge postponed the hearing for another week. Before the bailiff corrected him Lil D tried to turn so that the stain on his neck was away from the courtroom audience.

Out in the parking lot, as Salt opened her car door, Stone popped up between cars and strutted toward her. There were too many cops leaving court for him to cause her any real trouble. He strolled by inches away, his bony shoulders moving back and forth, like a large bird of prey, dancing.

By the time she told radio she was back from court, the late afternoon bloodbath in The Homes had begun without her. Domestic quarrels were the theme for the night. On Thirkeld a woman held her jaw as she related between sobs her story of abuse, her baby's daddy having fled before Salt arrived. She took the report while a tall thin man watched, leaning on the corner of the building. It was not Stone. On Shaw, Salt arrived as the paramedics were holding a pressure bandage on a young teenage boy's face. The boy had gotten between his mother's knife and an uncle. Salt arrested the mother. As she was sitting behind the wheel working on the report and waiting for the wagon with the caged mother in the back, she flinched when someone slapped the patrol car, her puff of relief audible as an old man stumbled by and she saw it wasn't Stone.

By nine the assaults had turned deadly and Salt was stringing yellow tape to preserve, protect, and defend another dead body. The crowd chorus again complaining about the slow ambulance arrival time and "Poleese don't care 'bout nothin'," the crowd working into a frenzy, potential witnesses scattering.

Around ten the "shots fired" calls weren't even being dispatched, but the sounds of gunfire ricocheted throughout The Homes. Salt sat under a streetlight finishing paperwork, documenting the facts, leaving out details like the color of blood under halogen lights. She kept glancing in the car's mirrors and out the windows, but her night vision couldn't adjust from the reports. Fully automatic gunfire erupted from behind the closest building. It was too much and too close for her to ignore.

"Radio, hold me out on shots fired at 1412 Middleton Street."

"Radio copies. Can any unit start for her location?" The familiar dispatcher knew Salt wouldn't have bothered to call it in if there hadn't been some significance to the gunfire.

"3307," Pepper responded. "I'll hold my paperwork. Show me en route."

Instead of getting out on foot, Salt put the Crown Vic in low gear and punched over the curb. The patrol car's undercarriage scraped the ditch as she rounded the corner of the building. Her headlights dipped as the car wheels bumped in ruts and over a drainage pipe. A sports field down the hill was wide, spread out, the center of The Homes. Just outside the illumination of the patrol car's lights, dark figures darted in and out below the direct beams, scattering from the center of the ball field. The car door made for good cover as Salt opened it, the beams of her flashlight adding more specific light to the scene. Her boots skidded on shell casings, the ground littered with shiny brass.

What little ambient light there was reflected off Pepper's silver buttons as he walked around the corner of the building. "Smart girl. It's too late to be chasing gunmen on foot," he said, noting the position of her car. He added his light to the glitter on the ground. "Goddamn war zone here," he said, bending down to pick up one of the brass casings. He examined the casing, rolling it between his thumb and finger.

"We've gotta collect all of them."

"Why? We never collect casings on just 'shots fired.'"

"We do these, Salt. They're armor-piercing. Remember the flyer the Gun Unit passed out at roll call last week? These have the markings, same as the ones in the flyer." He stood next to her, his flashlight shining on the brass in his palm.

Salt's stomach turned over. Stone didn't need words. From an open apartment window the theme song from a popular police drama started up. Dropping shell casings in an evidence bag on the downbeat, she and Pepper kept time to the music.

The rest of the week continued with the usual hard and sad life in The Homes. Stone was conspicuous by his absence.

Her nightmares got so that she'd wake up and find Wonder staring. She trembled in her bed, in her house, where she now felt more on edge than in The Homes.

Another summer downburst was flooding the streets just as the bus lumbered to a stop. Salt watched from under the tattered awning of a nearby pawnshop. STEREO EQUIPMENT, JEWELRY, GUNS, AND MORE! advertised fading painted block letters on the concrete wall at her back.

The school bus delivered Mary at 4:22 almost every day and it was all Salt could do to get out of roll call, load her gear, and get to somewhere near the bus stop so she could watch the girl, always the last one off the bus and never with another child. Today was the same.

Mary never seemed to see her. Salt didn't hide but did take

pains to always park away from the stop, in different places, and walk to some vantage point.

On the opposite side of the bus from Salt's view, the children clamored out and dashed down the sidewalks. The bus pulled away, splashing water from the gutter. Mary stood alone, rain sloshing her up and down, running from her braids. A crack of lightning threw the scene into a negative. Mary didn't startle or even move.

Salt looked down at her own feet. Bits of wet weeds clung to her black boots, but she could feel the wet socks in Mary's shoes, the ribbing printing itself on her ankles. Memories of her own childhood washed over Salt as she stood watching Mary get soaked. She put herself back against the warm storefront wall as Mary took the first of her plodding steps toward the house where Shannell had once been a child.

Mary didn't flinch at the second blast of lightning, either. She stood still, rain streaming down her cheeks, and lifted her face as another strike flickered close. The girl seemed more reluctant to go home than to stay in striking distance.

29.

TESTIFYING

The city had lit its courtrooms like live theater. Recessed lighting was dim in the audience and bright up front. The judge's dais was large and raised above a waist-high wooden island on either side of which the prosecution and defense held forth and negotiated.

Salt sat three rows back in the far-right section. The thunk of leather-covered metal against the wood benches sounded as other cops arrived. Her gear belt with cuff cases and baton holder at her back filled the normal curve of the bench so that she had to find purchase with her boots to keep from slouching, to be able to see above the front rows of lawyers. She scuffed the floor, letting off nervous energy.

In the other two sections of the dim area, a flux of family members, of both the victims and the accused, and a few witnesses, moved either to the front as their cases were coming up or to the back and out once a disposition was rendered. These were preliminary-hearing courts. No trials. No Bibles were sworn over. No gavel was struck. Impatient cops waited their turns. Mothers tried to quiet crying babies and restless children.

"Officer Alt," called the solicitor, her cue to go forward and play her part, testifying against Darrell Rafael Mobley. She had practiced her lines often enough in similar cases, knew the rules of search and seizure. She stood and walked toward the front of the room.

Lil D was led, shuffling, into the courtroom, leg restraints inhibiting the exaggerated side-to-side tough walk. He was wearing the orange jail jumpsuit, pant legs too long and bunching at his ankles. The bailiff positioned him opposite Salt, across the island. The brighter light revealed lint in his hair, which unaccountably provoked Salt's fury. She dug her fingernails into her palms in frustration that there had never seemed to be a way out for Lil D. Lil D, head bent, squinting and looking from the corners of his eyes, upper lip raised like he smelled something bad, looked like she felt.

The solicitor and Salt stood on one side of the polished wood peninsula. Lil D and his court-appointed lawyer stood on the other side. When she turned her head toward Lil D she involuntarily blinked from the glare.

Above them all sat the judge, a bored, cynical veteran of the city courts. The back of a laptop computer was visible on the judge's desk to his right. His hand moved quickly over the track pad, the light from the screen playing across his face, rapidly changing from green to blue. "Next case," he called, his eyes not leaving the computer. Salt thought he was playing a video game.

The solicitor, who knew Salt well, didn't bother to ask about the arrest. He assumed that this case would be like others she brought to court, it would be solid. His words ran together. "Your Honor, Darrell R. Mobley is charged with 'Possession with Intent to Distribute.'"

The judge, a blue glow on his chin, frowned at his computer, then plopped back in his high-backed chair, waving his hand for the solicitor to begin.

"Officer Alt, tell us about how you came in contact with the defendant on August 28th of this year."

Salt looked at Lil D. He'd tried to hide his birthmark by turning up the collar of the prison suit.

"Officer Alt," the solicitor prompted, shuffling through the stack of charges on the shelf beside him without looking at her.

"Myself and four other officers were manning a roadblock at Meldon Avenue and Middleton Street when the defendant, driving a 1974 Oldsmobile, came through the location." Salt felt something caught in her throat. She covered her cough with a fist and continued. "There was a passenger, Curtis Stone, with the defendant."

The solicitor, who'd been at ease because of their familiarity, now cut his eyes. *Stone?* he mouthed silently at her. They both knew it was the job of the defense attorney to bring out the fact that Stone had been in the car, suggesting his relevancy. She was volunteering information unnecessarily. The defense attorney didn't miss "Stone" either. A public defender, he also knew Salt from previous cases. He cocked his head to look at her, now also more attentive to the case.

"And Officer Alt"—the solicitor's voice had tightened ever so slightly—"did you have reason to arrest the defendant?"

Salt looked again at Lil D, who didn't know the script, was unaware of the misplaced lines. Like a lamb to slaughter, he stood there testifying without saying a word.

Salt missed several more beats. "Officer Alt?" the solicitor prompted her again. He'd now put down the other paperwork and was looking at her with the same cocked head as the defense attorney.

"Yes, yes," Salt answered. The solicitor moved toward her, making eye contact. "On what grounds did you arrest the defendant?" His words were clipped, precise, and impatient.

"He didn't have a driver's license or proof of insurance," she answered. The words sounded tired, even to her.

The solicitor's mouth had fallen open. He turned to the judge. "Your Honor, if I may take a minute to confer with my witness?"

The judge snapped forward in his chair. "This is a preliminary hearing. You should have talked with Officer Alt before she began her testimony. Proceed." He leaned forward toward the computer, his whole face now a light shade of blue. He smiled at the screen.

"Thank you, Your Honor," the solicitor replied automatically, thanking him for nothing. He knew his lines.

"Officer Alt, in the process of arresting the defendant did you witness the recovery of any contraband from the defendant's vehicle?"

"It wasn't his vehicle," she answered.

The solicitor's lips stayed parted over his very white teeth, speechless. She was choosing another way of looking at things, the way it should go, giving Lil D's attorney a gift, the facts for a defense for Lil D. She wasn't lying. She was telling the truth. But it was out of order, not according to the script, and definitely not for the state.

Beyond the lights of the front of the courtroom, the odd congregation, which included her fellow cops, had grown unusually quiet. Even the uninitiated sensed the cops' attention to her testimony. Salt felt the grains of her reputation shifting.

The leg irons around his ankles clinked on the hardwood floor as Lil D shifted his feet. He looked frail under the courtroom lighting. She rubbed her hand across her eyes. It was as though every move she or Lil D made was spotlighted.

"Officer Alt, please answer the question." Now the solicitor sounded mystified, annoyed, both. "Were drugs recovered from the vehicle the defendant was driving?" His mouth stayed open again, staring at her over the top of his glasses.

"Yes," Salt answered without elaboration, which sent the solicitor into a quick spin on his heels. Turning to the judge, he recited, "Your Honor, I have the results of the crime lab analysis. The analysis found that the drugs recovered from the car the defendant was driving were positive for crack cocaine." He waved the report at his side.

The chains on Lil D's ankles clattered.

"Duly noted for the record. Continue with your case, Mr. Solicitor," urged the judge.

The solicitor turned, stared straight back at Salt to get the answer that was required. "Were the drugs in the possession of the defendant?"

Salt's next line was supposed to be *Yes, they were found under his seat, within his wingspan.* She drew a large breath and exhaled. "No."

Lil D lifted his head.

"Officer Alt"—the solicitor flapped his arms twice against his suit—"what was your probable cause to charge the defendant with possession?"

"They were found—they were found within his wingspan." Her voice was limp, without conviction.

"No further questions, Your Honor," said the solicitor. Then he whispered to Salt, "I'm unhappy," although they all knew probable cause was established, enough to bind Lil D over for trial.

Except now the public defender, who usually wore an air of resignation, walked upstage and in a loud voice asked, "Officer Alt, were the drugs found within the wingspan of Curtis Stone also?"

"Yes, they were." Blowing her lines, she answered, not bothering to disguise the satisfaction she felt in telling the whole truth, nothing but.

The solicitor had turned his back to her, looking out at the audience, playing to the cops. Lil D's eyes were squinched like he was trying to see something he didn't understand. For a brief second he raised his head and looked around wide-eyed with what might pass for hope on his face.

The public defender, quite aware now of Salt's cooperation, quickly asked, "Was there any indication that Curtis Stone might have been in possession of the drugs?"

He had gotten the question just right.

"Yes, I don't think Lil, Mr. Mobley, would have come toward the roadblock if he knew the drugs were under his seat," Salt answered.

The defense attorney did not ask what she had seen to lead her to say yes. He had the good sense to quit right then. "Move to dismiss, Your Honor."

The solicitor threw up his hands while still looking at the other cops. "No objection, Your Honor," he said with disgust. And in a bit of melodrama he let the charge ticket for Lil D fall to the floor.

"Charges dismissed. Next case," said the judge, monotone, pushing up the sleeve to his robe and leaning closer to the light from his computer.

Lil D turned to scan the courtroom, the first time during the hearing that he showed an emotion, his eyes wide, white around the edges. Salt followed his glance, ignoring all that he ignored, focusing on what was his focus, watching until he was led out of the courtroom, to the back door and freedom.

The city attorney turned to Salt and watched her walk past through the swinging gate that led from the front of the courtroom to the aisle. She could still feel him watching as she walked past her fellow cops, who, for now, were silent and also watching her. She stared straight ahead, eyes on the red exit sign above the courtroom door.

All through the shift, the calls, she thought about the restraints being removed from Lil D, his release, and wondered if she had given him a dangerous chance.

30.

ANSWERING TO PEPPER

From a clothes-tearing skirmish between a teenager and her mother to a box-cutter duel, two fender benders, backing up Blessing on a chase involving an eighteen-wheeler, a break-in at a cathole shanty, and a community meeting at the church, the rest of Salt's Friday was, well, Friday. The air murky with heat and humidity, she could smell herself, the funk that steamed between the Kevlar vest and her damp undershirt, .38 rusting under her left arm.

Back now at the empty church, she slid her spotlight over the old stones of the building. The African Methodist Episcopal congregation kept the door a freshly painted shiny fire-engine red. At night the door took on a darker, blood-red hue. Turning the spotlight handle, Salt illuminated the stained-glass windows, each of which depicted one of Jesus's disciples: Judas leading lambs to slaughter, Peter's window shattered by bullet holes, his fishing boat patched with cardboard. Navigating the driveway that circled the church, steering with one hand, she swung the spot up and down, side to side with her other hand.

This was Sister Connelly's church, where the funeral for Q-Ball had been held, where the funerals for other drug boys were held. Salt had been to many community meetings in the sanctuary and felt more at home here in some ways than in the rural church she had attended growing up. The choir here was better, more enthusiastic, louder, and with stirring rhythms. When the calls allowed, on some Wednesday nights she parked to hear them practice, just outside the window of John, the beloved disciple, shown with his hands over his heart.

Gardenias that grew beside the stone façade were dropping the last cream-to-brown petals, the intensity of their scent not too far off the too-sweet odor of decomposing flesh. Other than echoing gunshots, the Homes' equivalent of wolves howling, the church grounds were silent. Radio wasn't reporting the shots fired. Nobody bothered calling them in.

The only lights around the church were two dim streetlights, too high up on their poles, and the portable electric sign at the drive entrance. It announced next Sunday's sermon: "Feed My Sheep." Except for the white noise of the expressway in the distance, there were no sounds at all after the distant gunfire ceased.

She swept the side of the church before checking around the corner and back wall under the window of Simon the Zealot speaking to a crowd. The church groundskeeper's name was also Simon. He worked on Saturdays keeping the outside of the church pristine. There wasn't a scrap of trash anywhere except under the window of Matthew the Tax Collector, bronze now from the flash of her light, where the back basement stairs were littered with crack bags and used condoms from Saturday night. She checked the stairs.

The third window on the back belonged to James the Martyr, his head falling under a sword. With the engine idling, small night noises emerged, tree frogs, crickets, and the odd night bird calling in the dark.

"3307, radio, raise 3306." Pepper's voice over the mic was empty of its usual smile.

"3306." She sounded formal even to herself.

"3307, name a location."

Salt hesitated, knowing he'd heard about court today; the tone in his voice confirmed it.

"3307 to 3306, location?" he demanded again.

"3306, Meldon and Lansing," she said into the shoulder mic.

"Meldon and Lansing," he replied.

The window disciples were silent dim shadows, set back into the stone walls, and of no help as she tried to find the words to make sense of this for Pepper. *We meet to talk about what just happened, what we did or didn't do and why. We try to make sense of the sorriness, the hilarity, the stuff we witness, by telling stories, trying to find some moral or meaning, something that will save us next time.*

A dim glow from one streetlight fell at an angle, illuminating the passenger side of her cruiser. Her uniform hat sat on top of her gear bag. She picked it up and turned it over. Their hats had plastic liners in the center of which was a clear pocket intended for a name card. Most of the cops kept photos there of their mates and children. Salt had a close-up of Wonder smiling, his small, strong front teeth in a bit of an overbite. She pulled out the picture of her dog. Behind it was another photo, a girl, herself as a ten-year-old, the focus a little blurry, the camera too close, her skinny legs stiff and straight, locked in an awkward pose, red shorts stretched in the legs, making her look even thinner. But it was the eyes that hijacked the photo. Some quirk of light had given her blue eyes an odd cast, like a version of red-eye, only whitish. She looked like a haunting child, glowy-eyed, like she had some superpower or X-ray vision. Salt felt an unreasonable affection for the photo, remembering her father aiming, clicking three times, to be sure one would be good.

Pepper's headlights caught her off guard. She hadn't thought he'd be so close by. As he pulled into the lot she put the photos in her left shirt pocket. He stopped driver to driver beside her and pushed the gear arm to park. Then he just sat there staring straight ahead, not looking at her. Then finally: "What are you doing?" He turned, his dark face shiny with sweat from the hot busy night.

"Nothing," she said, lowering her hand from the itchy scar. Insects flew furiously in the widening beams from the cars' headlights. She blinked and the lot came alive with jumping and flickering cicadas and moths.

"What was that about in court today with Lil D?"

She cut the engine and pushed the light knob to off. "What did you hear, Pepper? I just told the truth and the case was dismissed."

"I heard you threw the case." His voice came out too loud.

"You know Stone set Lil D up." Her voice right on top of his.

"What I know is Lil D sells dope in Man's gang. Whether Stone had his hands on that dope first is irrelevant. Lil D sells it."

"It's not irrelevant to me."

"You've let this get personal. Stone, Man, Lil D. They've gotten to you. Who are you trying to save?" A cloud passed over the moon, further dusting the church and saints with darkness. "Stone set Lil

D up. Lil D knows it. Now Lil D is out. How do you think that's going to play in the street? So if it's Lil D you wanted to save, he's directly in the vulture's sight now. You're not thinking clear."

"I'll go to Man." She snuck a rub at her scalp, her fingers finding the ribbon of bunched skin.

"Stop it, Salt," he barked, and banged on the steering wheel. "Goddamnit and quit clawing at your head. You're going to rub it raw. Stay out of the gang's business, let Homicide work Shannell's murder."

"But they don't know The Homes like I do." Her scalp was now furious with itching but she kept her hand down.

"Nobody knows The Homes like you do. Nobody should. You're too close. We're supposed to have each other's back. You are my friend, my partner, but you've been keeping things to yourself."

She could still feel the touch of Pepper's fingers parting her hair along the bloody wound. "I've been given this beat, this . . . assignment." She'd wanted to call it her "mission." She turned on the ignition, felt the gears. At first Pepper didn't move, just sat there watching her. Slowly she began to back the car with her head out the window, trying to readjust her vision. The light from the pole did a double halo and she was distracted just for the second it took to drive her cruiser an inch too close to his car. The side-view mirrors on both cars cracked.

"Damn," she said, backing up and pulling up again. A sliver of pain, like a tiny glass shard, pinched in her head. "How many years of bad luck have I brought us?"

Pepper's mirror fell and hung by the wires. "How many years have you been in The Homes?" He reached for the dangling mirror and tried to pull it free of the wires. He finally just let it hang and drove on out of the lot.

Salt pulled past the funnel of light from the pole and glanced in the cracked side-view mirror. There were three crack lines in the glass and she couldn't recognize anything reflected there. She touched her pocket with her right hand but thought of Lil D's face right before he left the courtroom.

31.

ESTABLISHING DIRTY RED

oddamn, I hate this," Salt announced again to Thomas. ATF had called someone in the department to get her a temporary assignment to Wills's guy, Agent Thomas, so they could find Red.

"Come on. You know the rules. Information from an unreliable source cannot be used as probable cause for a search warrant," Thomas argued.

"I know. I do know. But Red has to live here after you're gone."

"What do you care? She's a crackhead whore."

They were sitting in his Taurus, the federal car, all shiny, without a speck of dust. A cloying air freshener polluting the new-car smell, making her nauseated. Unlike her patrol car, there were no bullet holes, no lingering body odors.

"Nice car," she said flatly. "Couldn't you get it washed though?" She ran a finger over the spotless dash.

The light changed and Thomas, at her direction, turned off Lakewood onto Jonesboro.

Thomas was wearing a white knit shirt and tan khakis, like he had just come from the golf course. His scalp was pink under a buzz cut. She was wearing her best jeans but her herding boots were mucky from the night before.

They passed the drunks at the liquor store, the dope holes, the whores, and just folks trying to get by. Agent Thomas looked out at the people on the street and the crumbling architecture, cut his eyes, and gave his mouth a twist, a sneer that looked practiced rather than earned. Salt liked the idea of Red as an informant less and less.

The bleak eyes of the people shifted as the Taurus drove by.

"Turn right at the next street," she instructed.

On Red's sister's narrow avenue an older-model Buick slowly passed them, farting exhaust over the clean Taurus that screamed, *Cops.*

Big Red was in the yard cooking something on a homemade ten-gallon drum grill.

"Stop here."

Big looked down through a cloud of smoke coming off the grill.

Thomas sensed Salt's hesitation. "What?" he asked.

"Just so we're clear, neither of us is fooling anybody around here," she said, then opened the door. He got out and followed her up the steps to the yard.

"Hi, Big," she said, lifting her hand and walking over to the grill. "This is Officer Thomas."

"Agent Thomas," he corrected.

"Agent," said Big. "What you an agent of? Double O? I know you ain't no secret agent." Big was wearing the same shapeless dress she had had on when Salt was there before, and she was sweating rivers down her chest and arms.

Thomas looked around at the yard like a tourist from another planet.

"What he doin' with you and why you comin' back to my house in that car?"

"Sorry, Big. I'm looking for Red again."

"You gone get that girl killed coming here in that car with Mr. Double O."

"Uh, ma'am—" started Thomas.

Big snapped, "Don't you talk to me while I'm cooking." She pointed a long grilling fork at Thomas, who took a step back, his elbow against the butt of his gun. But Big had turned back to the grill and started stabbing at some chicken wings. About two dozen wings were beginning to brown.

Salt stepped closer to the grill and Big Red. "We don't want to mess up your dinner. Man, that smells good." She leaned over, inhaling deeply.

Big Red busied herself swabbing sauce and turning wings.

"I need Red's help," Salt told her. "I need her help quick. It's already dangerous for her."

"You gonna help her?"

"I'm not promising anything."

"I know you ain't."

"If I can just get her quick and get her out."

Big bent over the grill. "So it's like a race. You quick enough you win. But what do Red win? And what if she lose? Do you lose, too?"

Salt couldn't tell if her eyesight was acting up again or if it was just the increasing smoke from the grill making her eyes water. She

looked through the hazy smoke over at Thomas, who had turned
away and was standing there with his back to them, watching the
Taurus.

Big was furiously flipping wings.

"I'm not going to lie to you. I might be putting your sister between a rock and a hard place, but she might be able to help us
catch a killer."

"What if the killer catch her?" Big stabbed harder at the wings.
Grease sizzled and popped on the coals.

"Can I have one of those wings?" Salt pointed at the grill. "This
is what heaven must smell like."

Big speared and lifted a black-and-brown crispy wing off the
grill. "Careful, it's hot."

Salt took the end of the wing between her thumb and finger,
holding as little of the hot chicken between her nails as she could,
blowing on the steamy skin, inhaling its smoky tang. Her teeth
were already touching the meat when Big stopped moving the
wings and said, "She in the house."

The skin of the chicken was crisp, the meat juicy and full of
smoky flavor. She took her time stripping the meat and then started
chewing on the end knuckle. She bit down hard to the marrow, her
teeth crunching the bone. Thomas just kept staring at the Taurus,
as if it might leave without him.

Big pointed her grilling fork at Thomas. "I ain't givin' him one
of my wings."

"Where are your manners?" Salt said, grinning at Big.

Still sucking on the bone, she walked over to Thomas. "I'm
going in the house while you chat with Big. She wants you to come
over and have a wing."

"I'm not going near that woman, much less eating something she cooked."

"Suit yourself, then. Watch the car. I'll be inside."

She took her time walking toward the house, keeping watch for movement around the outside and behind the curtains. Up on the porch, she reached for the doorknob but found the knob and the lock were gone. Now there was just a round hole in addition to the busted lower part. She pushed the door open.

Dirty Red was sitting on the sofa in the living room waiting, this time wearing clothes, a loose pair of men's plaid shorts and a pink T-shirt with the sleeves ripped off.

"You said I wouldn't have to do any more." Red tried to stand, already trying to talk her way out of something.

"Red, I—" Salt started.

"Who that man out there drooling over Big's wings? You bring a date?"

"Agent Thomas from ATF."

"What he got to do with anything?"

"The statement you gave me was good, but to use it we have to get you to wear a wire, to get Stone on a recording."

"No way." Red flopped back on the worn sofa. "No, no, no." She slumped and swung her head.

Salt took a breath then turned her back on Red. "There's money," she said, and waited, watching the smoke from the grill blowing in the hot evening air.

Red coughed twice, then sniffed.

"I'm sorry." Salt turned to face her.

Red wiped her nose on her hand. "How much money?" she asked.

"Paid informants for the feds can earn a lot, for as long as they can provide information." The muscles in her face felt like rope and her eyes stung.

Red stood on her wobbly legs. "What I got to do?"

"Wear a wire and deliver guns to Stone. And get him to talk about you buying the guns for him." The grease from Big's wing had turned to a bad coating in Salt's mouth.

Red looked over at the window. The smoke rose into the leaves high above the house. Salt had to lean down at the window to follow the plumes that drifted in the oak that must have been growing since before the Civil War. One limb of the tree had broken off, rotted, and was caught in lower branches. The next storm would bring it crashing down.

Red sighed. "When?"

"Now." Salt turned from the view outside. She could make this work. "We've already got the guns and the wire ready. Do you know where to find Stone tonight?"

"Probably, but I ain't leavin' here with you and that agent. Stone likely already knows you been here, with that car out front."

"Just walk up to the corner in two hours and we'll have an agent posing as a john pick you up in a white van. He'll have the wire and the guns. Where do you put them for Stone to pick up?"

"We use that old run-down yellow house at Thirkeld and Meldon. There's some boards loose in the closet wall. I put them there. He goes and gets them when I tell him."

"Do you owe him guns now?"

"Yeah, he give me a hundred dollars two weeks ago to buy two guns and I smoked it."

"He gonna hurt you?"

Red shrugged. "He hurt me sooner or later anyway. Maybe not too bad if I have guns for him to pick up."

"'Not too bad.' Shit," Salt mumbled.

"What's wrong with you? You ain't got to do it," Red said.

"I'll be listening on the wire, like I'm there with you."

"Yeah, you'll be listening but when you gonna open the door and come in?"

"I won't say 'trust me.' You know the deal. I've put you exactly where I didn't want you to be." She walked quickly to the door, as she talked, afraid that if she were there any longer she'd spoil the agreement, untie the knot. "Two hours, at eleven, on Jonesboro."

Red followed to the hall then had to lean against the doorsill to the living room. Salt put her hand out for the knob of the front door, having forgotten it was missing. She turned back to Red and tried to think of something more to say.

Red said, "Push."

Salt pushed the flimsy door and walked out.

"What's that noise?" Thomas asked.

"Whee." There it was again, a breathy injured-bird sound coming from the monitor. "Whee."

Salt, Thomas, and the tech agent, Marandoza, were in a mud-spattered van marked ABC PEST CONTROL with a logo of a large insect with Plexiglas eyes. The van rolled slowly through the dark, narrow streets along the back side of The Homes. Marandoza had Red on the speaker so they could hear as she met up with Stone and hopefully got in and out without harm to herself, as well as getting Stone to incriminate himself and establishing her legal reliability.

"It's her, Red. Sounds like she's trying to whistle," said Marandoza.

Dirty Red was struggling with each note, flat then sharp. The rustling coming over the speaker reflected her disjointed walking, walking and whistling. She kept repeating wrong notes: "Whee," times eight.

"She's not very good at it," said Thomas. "She sucks." He laughed. "Get it? She sucks. She's a whore. She sucks."

The vehicle was soundproof. Their voices couldn't be heard from outside. Salt and Thomas sat across from each other on metal built-in benches, where they jostled and slipped as the van made turns and pumped over potholes. Bending over made the five-shot .38 stuck in the waist of her jeans bite at her skin. The bubble windows, the bug's blind eyes on the outside of the van, limited her view; the streams of moonlight were distorted, as if viewed through water, or tears. She strained to focus on the usual streets and buildings of The Homes. Things looked even worse through the bug's eyes. Broken toys looked spit onto the littered yards. Sad cars, jacked on concrete blocks, sat in uneven suspension, hopeless. Nothing could be seen that might recommend a life here. She sat back, closed her eyes, and tried to imagine what Red looked like whistling.

"Whee."

"She's trying to comfort herself," Salt said.

Red was wearing, in addition to the wire, a homing device that allowed the agents in the pest control van to follow at a distance. Salt didn't know when she'd see Red again since she'd be leaving the surveillance devices with her big sister and didn't want to be put at risk by having any further contact with any of them. Red had walked off down Meldon, having told them that she would meet Stone in an apartment on Shaw Street and that he often took her to other apartments nearby after the initial meeting place.

Thomas said they'd play hell trying to pinpoint the exact apartment.

Salt leaned her head back against the soundproofing wall blanket. She had an image of Red, naked, like she'd been at her sister's, wearing the red heels Salt had bought for the john detail. "How many apartments can you narrow it down to?" she asked, not for the first time, hoping the answer would change somehow.

"We can follow her to the building. That's all," Marandoza said. "You can probably figure which unit after that. You know who lives in most of the apartments. You also recognize the gang members."

So it might all come down to her. Again. And she was stuck in the van. She slid down the bench to be nearer the rear door.

"We're not going to have to go in the apartment anyway. We just need her to get him on tape about the guns." Thomas stood up bent at the waist. "What's the worst he'll do? Slap her around some?"

"I'm not listening to him slap her around," Salt said. Now Thomas seemed to have more experience than she'd given him credit for. Even though the van was air-conditioned, her face felt like it was near a fire. Her palms began to sweat and she wiped them on her jeans, over and over until her hands stung.

Red stopped whistling.

Thomas looked over at Marandoza.

Then Red started again.

The agents alternately watched the speaker and Salt as they followed Red on a parallel street. In the midnight hour, along the way, they'd passed a few lone stragglers and an unfamiliar beater, bass booming from its trunk. Nothing or no one that seemed likely to report suspicions to the gang or Stone.

Eight notes, over and over, until finally Salt didn't know if she was beginning to recognize the tune or if she was creating the notes of an old hymn. She'd almost get the words to come but then Red would hit a flat note. Then another note would go wrong when she ran out of breath. Her world narrowed to what she could hear from the speaker. She closed her eyes and kept them closed in order to concentrate but the edge of the hard bench in the van began to reach her bones.

Six notes. Silence. Three knocks.

"Don't slow down. Keep moving," Thomas said to Marandoza. Red was one block away on Shaw, behind two rows of Homes buildings, according to the homing device.

Locks clicked. The sound of a door separating from the sill.

They heard something thud. Salt tensed, ready to stand. A whoosh like a silent cough sounded through the speaker. Salt inhaled sharply but the van ceiling was low, and her lungs couldn't fully expand with her head bent.

"Bitch." Stone's voice a between-the-teeth hiss.

Salt reached for the handle of the van. Thomas threw one leg out to block her before she got to the latch. She reached around him but couldn't see to grab it.

"I got two," Red said, sounding out of breath.

Salt spread her legs for balance and stood facing the back door, head tilted to listen to the speaker.

"You owed me a gun two weeks ago." Salt could almost see Stone's mouth as he spoke, lips tight over his gritted teeth.

Another sound, like material ripping.

"Where's the mic on her?" Salt asked, looking at both Thomas and Marandoza. She put her hand to her waist, to the small pistol.

"He won't find it," Marandoza said, eyeing her hand and glancing at Thomas.

"Where is it?" she repeated.

"You ugly bitch." Stone's voice sounded farther away from Red and the device.

The sound jumped. "I got you two this time."

Stone's voice again. "Turn around."

"Where's the bug?" Salt reached for the latch. Thomas moved his whole body, which put Salt's hand at his waist. His previously crisp shirt was limp. Her fingertips hit hard muscle.

"I need money or hit me up with a rock, Stone," Red pleaded. "Why you got to see me naked? Why you got to put you hands all over me? You my half-brother," Red cried with almost a glimmer of dignity.

"The tracer and bug are in her hair," Marandoza said. "They're tiny. He wouldn't know what they were even if he saw them."

"We got what we need," Thomas said. "She established herself when he said she owed him the guns."

A cartoon melody sounded from the speaker. Salt sat up rigid. The same melody again.

"Oh, God, no," Salt whispered.

At once the agents looked at the speaker. "Ring tone." Marandoza nodded.

"God, get her out of there," Salt said. She slumped to the bench. She'd underestimated Thomas's willingness to sacrifice Red. "He didn't move her because he has a lookout." She looked directly at him, yet was blaming herself for having missed something.

The ring of the phone was cut. Stone's one syllable, "Yo."

Now even Thomas and Marandoza froze. "We didn't see any-one following us. You didn't see any lookout," said Marandoza. But he was whispering also, as if the speaker could hear, or as if whispering could protect Red.

Stone's voice, "What you mean?"

Salt began to pant in anticipation.

"Shit, man." Stone's voice roared into the van.

This time she didn't try to go around Thomas, she moved toward him, use of force, street, one hand moving while she stretched out a sheep boot. The agent driving downshifted, grinding a gear. In the same second Thomas was out of her way.

"Wait, I think I heard the call-end tone. Wait," said Marandoza.

Salt already had the door open, the van still in motion, when she heard Stone. "You late again, bitch, I'll kill you skinny-ho ass."

"Nobody saw us. The call wasn't about us." Marandoza spoke to equipment.

She looked back at the monitor, trying to pull confirmation from the air.

Stone again, closer to the bug. "Those guns where they supposed to be?"

The agent driving stepped on the brake. Salt used the braking momentum to swing the door shut.

Sounds of movement over the speaker. "They at the yellow house, like always." More rustling.

Thomas looked at Marandoza, rolled his eyes. "You city police got to hold on. Have a little faith." He reached out, took Salt's fore-arm between his thumb and fingers, and gave it a friendly waggle.

She jerked away and slumped to the bench.

"Pick it up, ho"—Stone's voice—"and get the fuck outta my sight."

Salt exhaled, then gagged. Stone was letting Red go. More movement and the sound of the door slamming, then one note of a choked whistle came over the speaker. Red was out, walking again. Three notes. Silence, then five notes, then all eight, over and over until finally she hit the note she had been flattening. Salt sat upright. She remembered the words, from a Sunday school hymn: "I Come to the Garden Alone." Red hit all the notes right.

32.

HARD TIMES

The odor of metal lockers always reminded her of high school, as did the clacking of the doors catching, slamming open, then shut. Salt leaned her weight on her left hand, head bowed. Pepper brushed by and it took her a few seconds to realize he'd said something. "... more than you think ..."

Asshole, Pepper mouthed at Big Fuzzy across the precinct workroom.

Sarge was signing and compiling paperwork at the long writing table. "Get those reports over here before I retire. I wanna go home tonight, too."

Metal ticket book holders clattered on the table. Half-written reports littered the floor. Adding to the locker room odor was something that smelled like a wet cigar. The shift dumped, then stumbled over each other's gear bags. They left boot prints on the fallen reports and tickets.

"Who you callin' 'asshole,' asshole?"

Their karma was fucked tonight, as sometimes happened; they were getting on each other's nerves. Not shy about letting emotion show. One emotion—anger—was the acceptable one.

"Goddamn, she's PMS-ing and I swear you all go on the rag." Sarge jerked reports and tickets from Pepper and Big Fuzzy.

"Nice, Sarge," Salt said to her open locker.

"Rough around here tonight." Salt turned to find Wills standing behind her in the locker aisle. "I thought we might console each other."

She slammed the locker door. "Yeah, well, it's a lot rougher out there every night for Red." She picked up her bag. Wills's tie was loosened and there were perspiration marks on the sides of his white shirt.

"I came to tell you that we got the warrants for Stone."

"Fuck the warrants. It's not worth the risk of getting Red killed." Blessing walked by, cutting his eyes at them. The others lingered, scowling and growling at one another and at Sarge across the room.

Wills glanced toward the uniforms. "I did—we did what you wanted."

"What I wanted. You did what your ATF buddy wanted."

"Come on, Salt." He reached out to help her with her gear bag. "We just have to find Stone."

"Before he finds Red?" She swung the bag from his reach.

"Who are you angry at?" he asked as she walked past him.

The shift stood staring as he followed her through the precinct door. "If you had done your job in the first place, Red wouldn't have had to go through what she did. You don't care about her or Shannell." She left him on the precinct landing while she continued toward her car.

She had her bag stowed in the trunk and was unlocking the driver's door when he confronted her, pounding his fist on the fender. "I'm just a man, not a superhero like you. I've got ten homicides I'm working. And I actually try to have a life other than this job."

"And I don't have a life. Well, you're right, Wills. I go home to my dog every night. I'm sure you've got women stacked up waiting, like your unsolved homicides."

"I don't deserve this crazy bullshit."

"Crazy?" she repeated, then turned her back on him, got into her car, and slammed the door. Wills receded in the rearview mirror, watching as she tore out of the precinct drive.

Salt twisted her neck, turning to face the living room and checking for Wonder on the floor beside her. The green sofa cover was bunched under her thighs. She groaned thinking about the harsh words between her and Wills last night.

Wonder stirred, stretching in his sleep. She had a hunger pang and an ache from her full bladder.

Her fist was balled tight under her tank T-shirt, between her sweat-sticky breasts. She scanned the entrance to the room from the shadowed hall. The sun through the curtains threw lace patterns on the dark green hooked rug and its warmth amplified the odors of her own night sweat and Wonder's fur, sweet, like drying silage.

The ticking of the mantel clock echoed off the beveled mirror behind it. Wonder moaned at some menace from his dream.

Her fingers found the flat bone of her sternum and pressed to slow the drumming from her heart. She curled her short nails into damp skin between her breasts. Feeling the bone, she remembered how, after her father died, she had wished for colds, so her mother would rub her chest with mentholated ointment and cover it with a cloth warmed by the bulb of the bedside table lamp. She'd lied, faking colds, to get her busy, nervous mother near her. She'd felt guilty wanting her mother's attention when her mother had her hands full cooking, washing, taking care of her baby brother, and reading the Bible. Wrong to lie about having a cold just to steal her mother's touch. Her mother's hands had grown nervous and too busy to soothe, pat, or give caresses. It had become clear to Salt that she was on her own.

Salt dropped her hand to the dog's smooth head. He lifted his snout, pushing his cold nose to her hot palm, his dreams forgotten. The thumping in her chest began to subside as she synced her breath with Wonder's waking breath. He didn't worry about intruders, and only reacted when need be.

Salt's hunger motivated her empathy for the dog and so, untangling from the afghan, she shifted her feet to the floor.

33.

CONFRONTATION

In other regions of the country the hot weather would be over. But in Atlanta, summer was dragging her dry skirts into late September. The green leaves had turned brittle and brown at the edges, covered in red dust. In The Homes, parched grasses strained to hold ground; what little survived was beaten down and trampled by the feet of residents who longed to be outside, out of close apartments, away from potential confrontations that often boiled over in the heat. The hot wind blew Styrofoam food containers, lottery tickets, eviction notices, and cheap advertisements through the rutted streets.

Based on the information obtained from Dirty Red's wire, the feds had secured the warrant for Stone, who hadn't been seen for weeks. Salt hadn't even felt him lurking. She watched for Red during her shifts, and hoped that Red would survive both Stone and the crack that the ATF money could buy.

Her Thursday shift was over and exhaustion soaked her to the bone, looking for Red, looking for Stone, watching the gang, Lil D, her eyes straining more and more to see clearly.

The sheep were fed and in the paddock. Wonder followed and watched as Salt shed her jeans and boots, turned out all the lights, then padded to the kitchen in T-shirt over panties for the nightly glass of wine. The wide plank floor of the hall felt cool on her feet as she walked back to the living room. Wind from a yet distant storm whipped the branches of the big tree beside the house, their shadows flailed on the blue gray of the front room wall.

A door slammed somewhere on the unused second floor. Salt set the glass of wine on the lowest step and faced the upstairs. Her mother had closed the house up and moved with her new husband and Salt's brother to North Carolina before Salt had left for college. Salt's mom and her brother had never come back, never, even for a visit. The ghosts that haunted these rooms belonged to Salt alone. The full-moon light coming through the windows ebbed and flowed as clouds rushed in front of the storm. Even in total darkness her feet could find the familiar worn places in the wooden steps. She started up without realizing she was lifting her feet. The wine on an empty stomach was in her bloodstream so quickly. Wonder followed, watching her step by step. At the top, the hallway stretched out just as long as it had seemed when she was small, the carpet runner woven in green and lavender wisteria vines. The hall walls were lined with old portrait photographs, some turn of the century, her father's people. A faint odor of wilted flowers still tinged the mustiness of the hall, bereft of furniture. None of the benches and tables had been left.

The doors to all rooms were closed, four bedrooms, two on each side and, at the very end of the hall, the sleeping porch. She felt unarmed. The moonlight shining in the downstairs windows didn't reach the upstairs hall. Trying to see in the dark, her vision began to blur from the edges to the center, the bedroom doors seemed to shift closer, then farther away. Wonder kept stepping in front of her feet, herding her in no particular direction. She tripped or stepped on his paws whichever way she turned. Thunder rolled. The dog made a new sound, like a whine. "It's okay. It's far away," she told him. As she reached to smooth his back to calm him, his static-infused fur rose to her palm.

Her brother's bedroom was first on the right. When she pushed the door open, although the moon was on the other side of the house, the room was filled by ambient light from the windows. She passed through the bathroom that adjoined their bedrooms.

"Baa. Bleat. Baa, baa." The sheep in the paddock below this side of the house were getting worked up, cueing one another. Wonder's ears twitched, almost vibrating.

The carpet on the floor of her old room was faded and there were permanent indentations where her chest of drawers and bed had been. The old rug had once been sky blue with all kinds of birds winging their way across the floor. Now in the dark, the bright night outside lit up a window-shaped portion of the floor and the two birds in the shadow frame seemed to float on night air.

She left her room by the hall door. Directly across was the guest room, which in her memory had never been used. The hinge whined as the door swung inward. This room was the only one that didn't have a rug. The shades were pulled but the moonlight snuck around the edges, like it itched to get in. She shut the door and turned to go back toward the stairs, walking quickly past her parents' bedroom door. At the head of the stairs she stopped. Determined, she turned back and pushed open the door to the big bedroom. Moonlight filled the room, filled every corner, while the wind tossed shadows high on the walls. The roses on the rug were in full bloom, as bright in the night as they had been on the day her father shot himself.

Salt shut the door on the moonlit room and stood there, mixing up memories, thinking of dead Shannell on the other side of the door, her hair tangled in a garland of briar roses and dangling wisteria. Wonder gave a short woof and skittered to the stairs. His nails clicked on the downstairs hall floor. When she turned to go down, the door frame of her parents' room shifted and framed the hallway. Her eyes were at it again, merging images, mixing present with the past. She steadied herself on the banister going down.

Wonder was at the back door, still giving the short woof sound that meant he didn't have anything to growl at but was saying *What? What is it?* In the distance, heat lightning sprang up from and down to the ground. A low rumble sounded from the direction of the city.

She put her hand on the dog's head. "It's still a ways away." A little strange: he'd never been troubled by storms before. Was she spooking him? The sheep increased their bleats, every one of them, each familiar by their individual shout and tone. They were pushing against the paddock boards and clanking their hooves on the metal gate. Wonder went into a full growl.

The first volley tore across the entire back of the house. Salt fell, grabbing for Wonder's collar and rolling them both back toward the kitchen. The refrigerator's skin had holes, not dents. Pepper's words registered in an instant: *armor-piercing.* There would be no cover. The shooter didn't have to aim or even be a good shot—the weapon was fully automatic.

The second volley was lower and ripped through the back porch and kitchen. Toaster, canisters, and the empty blue jar that had held Wills's orange flowers exploded on the counter. Wonder pulled at his collar to get to the screaming, terrified bleating sheep, their hooves frantic against the fence.

She had to move, but standing up to run for her gun hanging on the closet door in the bedroom would make her an easy target. She calculated the seconds it would take to go the twelve yards.

There was another fully automatic blast but this time not at the house. The silent seconds afterward were broken by the sound of only one sheep, bitter but precious information. The gunman was, in those moments, pointing away from the house, killing the sheep. She grabbed the dog and sprinted for the bedroom, just as the next spray ripped through the walls.

She scrambled through the hallway, her hand on Wonder's collar, dragging him along as he was working against her, trying to get out to the sheep, whose cries were fewer and fewer. "That will do," she commanded him while throwing both herself and the dog into the bedroom.

The gunman, still outside, was closing in. Glass shattered in the hallway, the family photos. Salt snatched the gun from her belt on the door hook and shoved the dog inside the closet. "That'll do," she repeated, latching the closet door.

The back screen door slammed. Without looking she came out shooting toward the kitchen with one hand while tearing from the bedroom to the living room.

Another spray of bullets followed her. Then there was silence, except for the sound of a gun clip dropping, the click of another magazine shoved into a weapon and the bleating of one sheep, the smallest dam.

Then Stone's voice. "Here, doggy, doggy," high with false sweetness.

Salt threw her arm around the stairwell wall, fired into the hall, and ran for the second floor. Rounds raced her, tearing through the upstairs floor behind her.

She reached the double doors of the sleeping porch, looked back down the hallway of broken glass, splintered wood, her bloody footprints, and the top of Stone's head appearing from the stairwell. Aiming, forcing herself to breathe and bring into focus both front and back sights, she fired just as the sights doubled in her dominant eye. The upstairs hall shattered as she leaped over the rail of the second-floor porch onto the slanting roof.

Faintly the wail of a siren entered her consciousness before she began rolling, weapon flying, nails grabbing for purchase, hearing that one bleating dam calling from the paddock.

There were puddles under her arms, rain pelting her face. The heat had been washed by the storm and she was cold. A voice drawled, "She's ah-openin' her eyes." Somebody call Central Casting. That was the voice of a Southern sheriff if ever there was one. Then a matching voice in the rich black range: "Tha am-bu-lance Eee Tee A, one away."

Salt squinted from a flashlight's glare but could see very clearly the fine white wires that joined together in the bulb of the light.

34.

MEDICINAL PURPOSES

The rolling bed of the CAT scan machine delivered Salt out of its tomb and into the bright examining room. Pepper, sitting in a plastic chair against a near wall, leaned forward. Wonder, wearing a Red Cross rescue saddle, was on the floor beside him, the whites of his eyes showing, watching the technician.

"Good boy," she said. Wonder trotted over and licked her lowered hand. "Thank Mr. Gooden for bringing him," she said to Pepper.

"You can do that yourself. He's in the waiting room." Pepper's smile, as always, warmed the room. "The dog's good medicine; he just needed a cover story."

"Hey guys, just because we got him the disguise doesn't mean he can take over," grumbled the burly nurse, helping Salt off the machine and onto another exam table. Her muscles were beginning to stiffen. Bloody abrasions down her right arm and leg stung when she moved. The hospital gown didn't do much in the way of concealing the scrapes and scratches. Her mother's huge hydrangea bush had apparently broken her fall, as well as hidden her from Stone, before he fled the sirens. She was scratched and bruised and there was what the doctors called "suspicious tissue" in the area of the old head injury.

"The doc will be with you in a few," the nurse said, hitting the automatic door panel and leaving the room.

Blue paper hospital slippers covered the cuts on her feet. Salt pointed them toward Pepper. "Self-inflicted. I ran through the broken glass of family photos."

His expression didn't change, his eyes studying her, his mouth set. "Something's catching up to you. Does it have to do with family? You ready to tell me what?"

The automatic door sounded and a young guy with an energetic walk almost jogged into the room. "I'm Doctor Quake. Don't say it. You're Officer Alt. How's your eyesight?"

Salt blinked, squeezed her eyes shut, then opened them. No fuzziness on the periphery, no ghosts floating in the light. "I think it's actually better."

"How long since you've been having problems with your vision?" The doctor seemed very young to be a specialist. He had blond hair, blond eyelashes, his blue eyes clear and sharp.

Pepper was looking at her with his head slightly cocked and his eyebrows raised. He was not smiling and his scar moved up and down as he clenched his jaw.

"Honestly, I've kept thinking it would clear up. Since I was shot in April, Doc," she answered, still looking at Pepper.

"Salt," Pepper said. He and Wonder both lowered their heads. "Do you know how this makes me feel?"

"I know, I know, I should have said something."

The doctor stepped to the side. "Guys, I'm gonna go check on another patient. I'll be back shortly." He backed out of the room with a small smile and a wave.

"Pepper." She rolled her head toward the closing door.

"It makes me feel like you don't trust me."

She sat up, holding the open-backed gown to her chest. Her legs dangled. She felt very like a child, throat muscles tightening. "It was just," she croaked, "my father."

"What about your father?" Pepper sat up straight. She noticed that he was wearing jeans but instead of a shirt he had on a pajama top covered in little white clouds on a sky-blue background. He must have dressed in a hurry.

"He— You mean you hadn't heard about him?"

"All these years, girl, I've left it to you to talk about him. Figured you would talk about him when you could."

"I needed him. I needed to keep him close."

Pepper came over and put his hand on her head. Then she cried. The clouds on Pepper's shirt held the rain and she started to laugh.

Salt didn't have to be admitted but the doctor insisted she return for further tests regarding her head injury. The clarity of vision that she had recovered in the previous night's encounter remained. By ten a.m. Pepper had her and Wonder in his minivan headed for last night's scene of destruction. When they came within sight of the long drive to the old white house, Wonder stood up on the backseat and began that short woof again, the woof that had been the warning before Stone's assault.

There were cars and trucks, a lot of trucks, parked along her drive, Blessing's Dodge beater, Fuzz's red truck, Sarge's new SUV. Almost every guy from her shift.

Pepper looked at her when she turned to ask. He said, "The other zones are covering our calls tonight. Command approved it."

"What?" she asked.

"This was never your problem alone." As he pulled beside the house, Blessing, Big Fuzzy, Sarge, and all the rest, wearing dirty jeans and filthy shirts, stood at attention in front of a truck that blocked her view of the sheep paddock.

Ten cops spent ten hours fixing most of what Stone had spent ten minutes destroying. They hauled furniture, splintered and torn beyond repair. They swept glass, sanded holes in wood and plaster, removed rugs laced with shrapnel, replaced panes of glass. They also dug a grave and buried four sheep.

Ten cops plus one Homicide detective. Wills stayed after the last of her thin blue line had left.

Boots off and sitting in the old metal glider in the backyard, he moved over and handed her a glass of whiskey when she and Wonder walked in from the paddock. Wonder was at a loss. "It's hard to herd one sheep," Salt said.

Although she had been ordered to stay out of the way, her friends had consulted her on every item from the house that had to be trashed. She felt bone tired but the adrenaline still lingered from the night before. Also, she hadn't been able to bathe since before Stone's attack.

"Bet I smell worse than a sheep," Wills said, echoing her thoughts while pulling at his shirt.

She sat down beside him and took a sip. Wonder stood directly in front of them, staring.

"What's he waiting for?" Wills asked.

"We have a routine every night and he's confused."

Wills took a sip of his drink. "Are you?"

"Just a little lost."

Wills took her drink from her hand and put his on the ground. He dipped his index finger into the whiskey and leaned his tired face close to hers. He traced her lower lip with his finger, wet with the whiskey, and when she closed her eyes instead of smelling blood, sheep, dogs, and a hard time, she was reminded of murky green ponds, cool nights, and wood smoke.

Moving closer, he said quietly, "My granddaddy used to say the bourbon he drank was for medicinal purposes."

"I think I'm on the mend," she responded, her voice like a long-overdue sigh.

The only sheep to survive gave out a lonely call, then another, and another, until Wonder gave a commanding woof in the direction of the paddock. The dog stood and stuck his snout between her and Wills. Salt looked down at the dog and said, "Go to place, Wonder." The dog looked up at her to see if she meant it. "Go to place," she said gently. He trotted off to the back steps and lay down.

35.

TAKING LIL D TO BIG D

They were glowing, jerseys shiny under the streetlights. Orange, green, blue, red, all with white numbers: 37, 28, 54. New dealers, new gang members. Man had recruited quickly. They sparked like aberrant fires in a dead forest and junkies flitted around them, drab moths to deadly flames, hoping to catch some artificial light. Steamy heat snakes squirmed up off the pavement.

Salt was back again, watching the action on the corner, seeing clear-eyed. She lowered the binoculars, pushed back from a squat, and rested her butt on a cinder block in the smelly hidey-hole apartment. A light gold bruise the shape of a shrunken Texas was fading on the underside of her forearm, reminding her of the patches of new paint on the walls at home, places where the guys hadn't quite blended the new with the old.

"Damn, this place stinks," Blessing called from the outside doorway.

The new members were center stage. Little kids with big eyes and round open mouths tugged their mothers' arms as they walked past in obvious fascination for the colorful allure of the gang. Sneakers so white they seemed to float over the asphalt. No color in The Homes was so brilliant as those jerseys. No energy existed in The Homes to match theirs. This gang, these brothers that brought color, like nothing on TV.

She watched as Pepper rolled through the lot. Like air let out of birthday party balloons, the crowd shrank away. Stone, Lil D, and Man were nowhere around.

"Okay, I'm done here," she announced to Blessing, but when she turned he was right behind her. "Damn, you scared me. I thought you were still waiting outside."

"You a lot of trouble."

The shift wouldn't let her alone, not until Stone was caught. Calls backed up, paperwork turned in late. They raised her on the radio. "3320 raise 3306." "3303 raise 3306." It was all night. It was comic, annoying, and welcome.

The doctor had cleared her fit for duty after a week at home. If command had plans to transfer her, they'd not made it known; punishing a cop who'd been assaulted would be an affront to every cop in the department. Instead of seeing ghosts she'd spent time appreciating the repairs the shift had done, each patched place reminding her of their care.

As she and Blessing climbed the hill back toward their cars, she was conscious of stretching out the last of the soreness from the fall. "You're off duty now." She gave Blessing a friendly pat.

"Trouble," he mumbled with exaggeration, shaking and hanging his head.

.   .   .

In the patrol car going down Shaw Street, the wide alley rarely used except by the few residents with functional cars, she found Man walking alone. When she was close he stopped, gave a sharp exhale, and tossed a cigarette to the gutter. There was an odor of something burning in the air, something layering over the smoke from his cigarette. His white T-shirt was wet around the neck. A drop of sweat hung on his left earlobe just below a simple diamond stud earring.

She pulled alongside of him. "Where's your ride?"

He stopped and closed his eyes in exasperation, as if he could blink and she'd be gone.

"I'm still here. Where are your boys?"

People on the stoops stayed on the stoop. They watched Man, some lifting a hand in tentative greeting, but when he didn't acknowledge any of them, they leaned back into the shadows of the overhangs. The sounds of TVs turned to warring stations added to the pollution of the burned smell in the air. He turned and faced her through the window of the patrol car. Salt had her nine in her lap, hand on the butt of the gun. "I didn't know you smoked."

"You got your gun ready to shoot me."

"I don't want anyone killed," she said.

"Well, looks like we agree on somethin'," Man said. He held his arms from his body and pointed to a pocket in his jeans. "I'm reaching for my phone." He punched at the phone and put it away.

In the yards tired children fought and called each other names. "Fat Nose." "Flap Mouth." "Ugly Ass." "No, you ugly."

"Smells like somebody burned dinner," she said.

Man sniffed. "I don't smell it. Somebody always burnin' something."

He turned and started walking again. Salt put the cruiser in gear and rolled along beside him. Old cars, beaters, lined the narrow street on both sides, narrowing the gap between the cruiser and Man.

"You missed your place," Salt said as they passed by Man's girlfriend's apartment.

"You don't know my place."

"You and I, Man, are both part of The Homes. Actually all of this is our place."

"You just work here. Just like me. It's business." He stopped and patted the pocket with the phone.

Salt braked to a stop and put the car in park. "It's not just business for me. I want to know who killed Shannell and I won't let it go. That's why your new recruits won't last. I'll bring heat on them, like Bootie, your brother, and all the rest. Your new boys will be out of work, too. Pretty soon either your business will go to Englewood or somebody will move in on your corner." Her words spit themselves out. Being careful wasn't keeping her safe anyway.

"Why you got to keep at this? Don't you have something better to do? Don't you have a place?" he sneered. "Don't you have a life, a man?"

Salt felt a buzzing pressure behind her eyes and started to come out of the car, then realized she was still holding the gun and that her grip had tightened reflexively. "You send someone else after me and every cop—city, state, and federal—will be in your business."

"Send someone after you? You crazy. I'm not stupid. I'm not risking business to get a cop killed." He stopped still in the road but continued to face forward, not looking at her.

"Well, maybe Stone is trying to take over. Somebody sent Q-Ball after me. Q was too stupid to think of something like that himself. Did Stone brag about hurting my dog and shooting up my house, killing my sheep?"

Man still wasn't facing her. She holstered and snapped in her nine. "So which is it, Man? Did you send Stone and Q? Or are you losing control of your boys?"

As she got out of the car she felt the molecules move around her, heard the springs of the car seat uncoil, smelled the engine oil, noticed the slip of sweat on Man's cheek, felt a tightening of stomach muscle under her gun belt.

Man hadn't moved. She stepped around directly in front of him and watched his face until he focused his eyes on hers.

"Stone not gonna do nothin' I don't tell him," he said, sweat and a flush along the light beige of his neck betraying his discomfort.

"I think you don't realize how terrible Stone is. He's a problem, a curse. He sees you stressed because I'm pushing, and he pulls, whether you want him to or not. I don't think you've ever really had control of him. This is also my place, Man, here, here in The Homes. Give me who killed Shannell. Tell me where I can find Lil D or Stone."

"You want Lil D. I don't care. He at Latonya's." He plucked at the wet neck of his shirt.

"Lil D, Stone, Bootie, Q. They're all just business for you. Right, Man? You just turn them loose and then don't care if you lose them."

"Business," he said, turned, and walked away from her, his expensive work boots crunching pebbles on the asphalt. She got in her car, put it in gear, and watched Man recede in the rearview mirror. A tiny reflection of streetlight, either off the diamond in his ear or off another drop of sweat, sparkled, ready to fall. She headed for Latonya's.

Latonya was a beautiful seventeen-year-old Salt had known since she was a little jump-roping champ. Her skin was as light as fresh dinner rolls and her hair a cinnamon swirl. But there was no other word that described her better than skinny. She was at least five feet nine and couldn't weigh more than a hundred and twenty pounds. Her baby, however, was fat, a coffee-and-cream color with only thin fuzz for hair, and enormous eyes. Latonya now had her own apartment in The Homes, right next to her mother's on Thirkeld. Lil D was sitting on the small six-inch-high concrete stoop. The door was open to the apartment behind him. He watched, squinting in the darkening evening, as Salt got out of the patrol car. The towel he used to cover his birthmark was limp and damp. Salt tried not to hope for too much but tried to still hope. Just as she got to within speaking range of him Latonya came out of the apartment with the baby.

"What's wrong, D? You goin' to jail?" She didn't sound like a girl or a champ anymore.

Salt told her, "I'm not here to take him to jail."

The baby started to cry. "Give him to me," Lil D said, and reached out for the baby.

"I need some Pampers," Latonya said.

"I just gave you money." Lil D sounded annoyed, old, and he seemed thinner every time Salt saw him.

"I had to use that money for his milk," Latonya said.

Lil D turned to Salt. "Just 'cause you after Stone don't mean you can just come here expecting anything from me." He didn't mention his—her—day in court and neither did she. Lil D tried bouncing the baby, who was watching his father's face. As Lil D became more agitated, so did the baby. His mother went inside, slamming the door behind her. The baby opened his mouth to cry again.

"What's his name?" she asked Lil D as she walked closer. The baby, maybe a year old, turned with fat tears on his cheeks and stopped crying. His eyes focused on her shiny badge. Before Lil D could stop him, the baby leaned out and latched on to the shield with one tight little fist. Lil D was holding him with one arm and Salt reached out as he leaned toward her. She and Lil D each had an arm under the baby.

"Dantavious," said Lil D. "He bad." But Lil D was smiling as he said it, trying to gently pry his son's fingers from Salt's silver badge without touching her.

"No," Salt said. "He's perfect. He's perfect." She let go of the baby.

Lil D ran his right pointer finger gently along the baby's creamy neck and put his lips to Dantavious's fingers.

"I've been looking for you, D."

"Why? I ain't done nothin'." His face began tightening again and Dantavious started looking back and forth between her badge and Lil D's face.

"I want you to talk to Big D."

"Now he ain't around to talk to, is he? Nobody seen Big D since he kill."

"He didn't kill her."

Dantavious started to reach again and Lil D jerked him back. This time the tears dropped out of the baby's eyes and he began a serious cry. Latonya came out of the door and snatched the baby from Lil D, who didn't seem to have any fight left.

He sat down on the stoop. "Why you callin' me 'D'? And how you know he didn't kill her?" He pulled the towel from his neck and twisted it.

"I'm callin' you 'D' because you got your own Lil D now. Remember when Shannell stabbed Big D that night I found him bleeding and you came up with the knife?"

"Yeah. What that got to do with anything. They fightin' all the time. Just more proof he killed her."

"No, remember what she said to me that night?"

"You took her to jail over that bullshit." He spat out the last word, blaming her all over again.

Salt had to get at it quickly. "She said Big D loved her cooda potpie."

"That's just the way she talk." He lowered his head and turned it to one side.

"I know, I know. What she was saying was that Big D loved her, period. And you and I both know that if ever he was going to kill her it would have been that night. But he walked away, almost dying. And she risked jail to get me to find him so he wouldn't bleed to death."

Lil D wouldn't or couldn't lift his face. She waited. He swallowed hard several times. Finally she said quietly, "Do this with me for Shannell, for your mama. I know where Big D is. Come with me."

Lil D swallowed hard again and when he answered he sounded like he was fourteen again and his voice changing. "Where he at?"

"He took himself away from The Homes so neither of you would hurt each other. Just like he took himself away from Shannell that night."

"So how I'm gonna talk to him if he ain't around?"

"I'll take you to him."

"I ain't getting in no cop car. I been tricked like that before."

They both heard Dantavious's sudden cry from inside the apartment and just as suddenly he stopped.

"D, you've heard a lot of things about me since I've been in The Homes but you've never heard anyone say I've ever lied to anyone."

He looked straight at her before he said, "No, they all say you tell the truth but one time you lied to me."

"So you remember?" She didn't turn away or feel worse.

"Yeah, you said you'd get me out."

"Yes, I did. But I didn't lie. I just couldn't do it. I couldn't do it alone and I couldn't find anyone to help."

Lil D clicked his mouth with disgust and hung his head. Salt noticed a pulsing vein beneath the wine mark. He looked back up as if he was ready for whatever was next, his face as suddenly changed as Dantavious's.

"Front seat." Salt opened the front passenger-side door and moved her gear to the back. He got in, sweating, smelling of baby pee, the white towel pulled close around his neck.

"This stupid," he said.

"3306 raise 3396. Permission to make a courtesy run to the Haven House shelter."

"Af-firm," Sarge growled.

Thank God, she thought, for once they weren't slammed on calls or Sarge would never have given permission to leave the zone.

A light mist began just as they pulled away from Latonya's. Lil

D's eyes took in the console that spit radio jargon, the switch box for the emergency lights and siren. He found the AM/FM radio and tuned it to a gospel station.

They passed the Moury Street alley where scores of athletic shoes swung from telephone and power lines. A slanted pickup, loaded with scrap metal, was parked on the corner.

Lil D's fingers tapped his knees on the two and four beats.

"You go to church?" Salt asked.

The dirty laundromat on the corner spilled foamy water into the street.

"Naw, Latonya take Dantavious sometime."

"But you like gospel music?" She nodded at the console.

"My mom had it on all the time 'cause she still believe in Jesus."

A whiff of fried fish made its way into the car from the Muslim take-out. "You hungry?" She glanced at Lil D and turned on the wipers to the slowest speed. Gray rain trickled down the sides of the front windshield.

"I cooked some spaghetti just before you came."

"You cook?"

Lil D patted his stomach. "Been cooking since I was little. I sometimes make up recipes."

"Will the circle be unbroken." The song ended as the cruiser bounced over the tracks at the three-way crossing. Warehouses of corrugated metal stood empty and rusting along the weed-hidden rails.

Near the sports stadium, closer to downtown, fans ran for their cars in the light rain.

When they got to the shelter Reverend Black was in the same spot out front, banging away on his Bible. Rain soaked the shoulders of his suit coat. He didn't seem interested in saving the occupants of the cop car and hardly looked their way.

Lil D stared out at the soaked street preacher, the dingy men hovering under the shallow overhang, and the broken grocery carts. "I used to think Jesus would save me." His chest and shoulders rose. He drew the towel from his neck, folded it, and laid it on the floor by his feet. As they crossed the street Lil D lifted his chin like he was trying to keep his head above water.

Reverend Gray was at his post in the entryway, smoking and checking the ledger book. He looked up as they approached. "I've seen you before," he said, tapping his temple.

"I was here some months ago. I helped you with a blond guy in DTs?"

"Oh, yeah. You were looking for somebody. Yeah, the man in the back. Have you brought me a new resident?" He nodded at Lil D.

"I ain't no bum to stay in no dump like this," Lil D snapped.

Pressure flared behind Salt's eyes. "They're not bums. This is where men on crack end up before they die. This is where sick men come who have no family left. The bums are the ones selling the crack."

Lil D turned. "You cops nuts." He started to go back out.

"Wait." She followed him and reached out to grab his arm but circled in front of him instead.

"This shit depressin', man." He clicked his mouth, grimaced, and shot quick glances at the shabby men slumped along the hallway floor.

"You're right."

Just then there was a sudden downburst of rain. Lil D turned back. "Okay, just get it over with, Miss Poleese."

The Reverend looked up at her, one eyebrow lifted and one eye squinting from his cigarette smoke. "You here for visiting hours, Officer? What's this about?"

"This is the son of the man I came to see last time."

Reverend Gray reached his hand across the desk. "His father. Okay."

At first Lil D didn't seem to know about men shaking hands but then he reached out and took the Reverend's hand.

Reverend Gray stood. "I'll take you."

"Is he in the same place? I remember the way."

"Yeah, we moved a cot back there for him. He's not in good shape. I have his real name written in one of these books but everyone here calls him 'Father' and some of the Catholics even try to get him to hear their confessions. 'Course they're crazy, too." He dusted ashes off his belly. "My house is your house."

They started toward the sleeping area, with Lil D following her, glancing around and checking behind them.

Salt said, "Keep up. I know the way back."

The cavernous room was the same as it was before, except that the light was different. Instead of the early morning sun coming in the huge windows, rain-diffused streetlight shone from above. Most of the tin funnel lights hanging from the metal rafters were turned off. Only a few lights along the brick walls had been left on; they helped staff avoid trampling on the worn men on the mats. Lil D stepped carefully, following Salt's footsteps to where Big D had sat before in his metal chair, looking out at the city.

The cot grew visible but looked unoccupied. Closer she could see that Big D had become so impossibly thin that he barely made an outline under the blanket. As they approached he said without opening his eyes, "May the Lord bless you and keep you. May the Lord make his face to shine upon you and give you peace now and forever. Amen."

Lil D looked at Salt, then toward the way back out.

"Big D," she called softly.

He opened his eyes and saw his son. "You," he said. Lil D took a step forward, stopped, and waited. Big D pushed to raise himself up on his elbows but one arm slipped on the thin edge of the cot. Lil D went down on one knee to catch his father's fall.

Salt stepped back.

It had begun a hard rain while Salt sat in the patrol car waiting for Lil D. Gutters rushed trash, dirt, and heavier debris toward sewer grates. The streetlights in front of the shelter were reflected in raindrops falling into black street water, creating tiny craters that sank dark, then lifted with glimmering edges.

Lil D appeared in the entrance and pulled his ball cap low on his forehead. He dashed across the street, dropped himself into the passenger seat, and slammed the door shut. He faced straight, staring out at the rain. "Don't say nothin'." His face had been kept dry by the cap but his jersey was spotted with wet splotches.

Salt drove slowly back toward The Homes, She stopped at every yellow light. Lil D took off the cap and kept staring straight ahead, and clenching his jaw muscles. City lights shone through the windshield onto his face. His skin glowed with light streaming rain. His birthmark appeared as a continent cut by a river.

When they were getting close to The Homes, Lil D dug a fist into the seat. "Ain't you gonna say nothin'?"

"Big D can't help dying." Her voice held an even tone that she didn't feel. They were silent, stopped at a light. "Where do you want me to let you out?"

"I wanna go to Latonya's."

"You're not worried about being seen?"

"Just take me back. Latonya be tired now, she need a break. Dantavious need his daddy."

He looked out as they passed Sam's, the laundromat, and the alley hanging with shoes, until they got to Latonya's apartment. When Salt stopped the car Lil D sat there.

"Do you still believe he killed your mother?"

"He told me. No, he didn't." He brought his arms up to the dash and locked them stiff. In silhouette, his eyelashes were back-lit, clinging together, damp.

The radio on Salt's shoulder began the traffic that always accompanied the rain. "3307, 3309, 3310 respond to accidents at . . . respond to an accident with injuries . . ."

"I've got to go," Salt said quietly. The calls couldn't wait. "He told you what?" she asked, trying to keep her voice solid. "Did he know who might have?"

Lil D grabbed the car door handle and leaped out. He didn't go to Latonya's door but ran up along the building, then broke toward the empty field in back and disappeared into a sheet of black-and-white rain.

36.

STONE MAN

The early October days held hints of cool and the shift went to long sleeves, rolled up in the afternoon and down when the sun ducked behind the city. Salt sniffed the breeze as she and Pepper stood outside their patrol cars at Big Red's. Sometimes she thought she was so close to Stone she could smell him.

Pepper was saying, "Every cop in the metro area has heard about what happened at your house. His mug shot is all over the place."

Big wasn't outside. The grill was closed. There was an old wooden Adirondack chair turned over on its side. The late-day sun was warm. A slight wind ruffled the orange leaves that still clung to the branches of the tree above the blue tarp on Big's house.

"He's here, in The Homes." She tilted her head upward toward the tree.

"Yeah, but gone to ground." Pepper's eyes followed an old bow-legged woman walking by with a toddler's gait.

"Guys like Stone have never been anyplace, wouldn't know how to buy a bus ticket, much less a plane ticket."

An old man pushing a baby stroller followed behind the bow-legged woman. The stroller was full of cans to be sold to the recyclers.

"Stone's probably never even been to the north side of the city, much less to some other city."

Easy-to-steal American sedans were parked facing the wrong way on the narrow one-way street.

"Even if he had money. And you know nobody's gonna front him. Man's not exactly a charitable guy."

"He's here all right, and you'll probably be the one to find him. But you won't be alone. Not this time." Pepper tapped her forehead right where the scar tipped out of her hairline. She couldn't breathe into her radio these days without backup appearing. Pepper was trailing her on every call.

"I wish I could find Red. I'm worried about her. She's just disappeared."

"The shift has her photo, too. Share the load, girl." Pepper waggled her shoulder.

Salt tugged at her vest and pulled her shirt collar to let some of the breeze under the uniform while her eyes wandered to Big Red's curtain-covered windows. On the days that Red's sister had been in the yard she'd just shaken her large head and they had rolled on past. If they knocked on the door she would come to the front window and shake her head in the same giving-up way. It had been weeks since Salt acquired her Pepper trail, two weeks checking every day at Big Red's.

They were about to leave when Big Red came out into the yard. She was wearing a tool belt, overalls with nothing underneath so that the sides of her breasts swung loose beneath the front bib, and a rope around her waist. She walked over to the chair without acknowledging them and began pounding one of the backboards with a hammer. The sounds of the day, car engines running, the click of the air-conditioning, Pepper's voice, traffic on the adjacent streets, all became muffled. Salt heard the hammer strikes as if in a tunnel, the echoes, the sound of the hard steel on old wood. The cool, edgy October air, a woman in overalls, nailing boards on a chair. Salt stood entranced, then looked off to the near north. The swinging boards of a broken door. Her blood rushed, adrenaline finding receptacles ready for the run.

She turned to Pepper. "I know where he is."

Pepper reached for his radio mic. "I'm calling SWAT."

"Hold on."

"Don't start. You're not doing this by yourself."

"No, it's not that I don't want help. I think he has Red and I want to try to get her away. SWAT, really anybody, won't care who's in there with Stone."

"What place?"

"I should have known. They're at Shannell's."

They didn't have to wait long for the night. Even with the last of the autumn sun there would have been plenty of cover for Salt to make her way unseen from the street that paralleled Marcy. She took the back way on foot to Sister Connelly's, weaving between trees, vines, and kudzu, her boots catching on low, dark vegetation, dodging tree limbs. The fighting voices of drunks on the corner came from several streets over, nothing out of the ordinary.

A quarter-man moon had risen, glowing large with spiked tips, shining on the trail that addicts had worn, a cut-through to Marcy Street. Salt stepped into the familiar path, the flashlight on her hip banging gently against her leg as she made her way in the moonlight. Sister Connelly's house was dark, backlit by the waxing moon. Closer to the house, a small soft glow from inside was barely visible. She tapped softly on the panes of the old woman's back door, then, not hearing any movement, put her face to the glass, trying to peer past the dark kitchen to the yellow light coming down the hall. A figure appeared with an odd silhouette, its arm too long. The door suddenly swooped inward.

"Good thing I don't shoot first and kill you later." Sister Connelly pulled the cord for the overhead light. The shotgun, pointing directly at Salt's belly, gleamed in the glare of the bare bulb. Salt stepped quickly into the kitchen and pulled the cord back to off. She felt Sister Connelly lower the gun.

"Ask questions," corrected Salt, saving her breath.

"You here to ask questions?"

"No, I meant that the saying is 'Shoot first and ask questions later.'"

"Now you ain't here creeping up in the dark to correct my speech." Sister Connelly had her hair unbraided, flowing over her shoulders and down her back, and was wearing a nightgown that left her chest, shimmering with scars, exposed.

Salt tapped her own protected chest, then touched the scar at her hairline and, trying not to look at Sister's old crisscrossings, said, "I just need to use your house for a few minutes. I need to watch what's going on at Shannell's."

"Ain't nothin' goin' on there 'cept that Red whore using it to flop in."

Salt started moving down the hall toward the small parlor,

feeling the rush intensify, and was relieved to see the shades over the windows pulled.

Sister followed her with the shotgun by her side, pointed toward the floor. "Now I don't think I invited you into my living room," she complained, dignified, indignant.

"I know," Salt said, turning out the one lamp by the reading chair, "but I don't have a lot of time to use manners. So please, ma'am, may I use your house for a few minutes? Just for a few minutes. I need cover." She carefully pulled back the shades, trying to find the window that gave the better view.

Sister Connelly was behind her. "I heard what Stone did to you. It's a wonder you weren't killed."

A streetlight on a pole near the end of the building illuminated a cone of night. Shannell's apartment door was now missing the plywood cover. The broken screen, hanging by the one hinge, swung in the fall wind, a sharp scratching sound. No lights were visible in the ruined apartment. The light over the door had never worked. A slight movement, the dark door gained a darker, wider trim. Someone was coming out.

"3306 to 3307, stand by," she radioed Pepper, two streets away.

"How is it you weren't killed?" Sister Connelly continued at her back.

"Stone's a bad marksman at distances," Salt responded, distracted, trying not to blink her eyes for fear of missing any crucial movement across the street. A dark shape stepped from the apartment door, followed by another. Man, followed by Lil D.

"3306 to 3307, there's movement. Hold." To herself she whispered, "Lil D," aware that her breath was taken by a sudden, sad hollow in her chest.

"I told you 'bout seeing too much evil. Those who see turn to a pillar of salt."

"Or stone," Salt said as she watched the third man, with wing-shaped shoulders, descend the stairs. She heard the ignition. Lil D was in the driver's seat again.

"3306 to 3307. Move. Three to the car." Unholstering her weapon in the two strides it took to get to Sister Connelly's front door, she grabbed for the knob.

"I'll be watching," Sister Connelly said as Salt went out, down the steps, into the street, taking cover on the side of the building while Stone slipped into the back of Man's car.

Pepper's engine sounded like warm thunder, his headlights lighting up the street, tires throwing dirt, spinning and fishtailing toward the gang, driving straight for the front of their car. Lil D in the driver's seat, Man the front passenger. Salt ran, bent at the waist, toward the metallic-blue sedan.

The alley lights of Pepper's patrol car snapped on. He trained his searchlight straight at the car. White light washed them. Lil D and Man threw their arms and hands up to shield their eyes. The car interior filled with arms bent and heads turning from the glare. Pepper's cruiser jerked to a stop five feet from the front grille of the beater. He bolted out and took position at the passenger side, opposite Salt on the driver's-side rear. All the car windows were down. Some part of Salt's brain registered the interior smell of the car, fast food grease, and sweat.

Pepper ordered, "Reach for the ceiling and keep your hands up," his pointed gun reinforcing the command.

Salt used the flashlight in her left hand to illuminate the backseat. The trickle of adrenaline became a river roaring in her ears.

Stone was facedown, stretched across the floorboard with his arms beneath him.

"I'm watching every twitch you make, Stone. Don't make a wrong one. I want to see your right hand first. Do not move anything but your right hand. Do it." Her voice loud, like she had to be heard over the rushing of her blood.

Stone's right shoulder folded out slowly, upper arm, elbow, then he showed his right hand, thin bony fingers spread wide.

"Now the left," she told him, her voice steady in the current.

The seat constricted his left shoulder but he showed his left hand by crawling it up the back of the front seat, one finger, two, then five fingers moving upward. She sensed him tense, not thinking about life or death but judging her and the weapon in her hand. She focused her muscles, her mind refused any distraction.

Stone continued to unfold, still lying on the floor of the car with his right arm spread. Pepper had his gun drawn, trying to cover Lil D and Man in the front seat, his attention torn from them to Salt and Stone. The car was still running. From a hole in the muffler, heavy gray exhaust swirled around the car and came close to choking her.

The headlights of the two cars beamed against each other, smashing light rather than making it clear. In her side sight there was a slight movement of Lil D's head, turning toward Man or maybe Stone, who at that moment began to use his left arm as leverage, rolling to his side as he reached his left hand toward the floor beneath him and a flash in the shape of a gun. She began the trigger squeeze, felt the first of the metal coil yield and then the sound of an old clock tick as the car lurched forward and the metal window-frame shoved her gun arm up with a blast. Space entered where none had been and Stone disappeared from view. Her flashlight rolled onto the pavement. The car rammed into Pepper's parked vehicle. Lil D and Man jerked forward. Stone began rising. The car seemed in slow motion as it recoiled from the collision. She was back up at the rear door in one stride, her eyes even with Stone's, his hands not yet visible. She raised her weapon level with his face. Stone turned his head, screeched at Lil D, "Motherfucker, give it up," and lunged for the gun that was now in Lil D's right hand. Stone's wide shoulders blocked the space between the back and front seats. Salt snatched at the driver's door, Pepper opened the door next to Man. In one sure movement Salt caught Lil D's arm, scooped his thin elbow with her left arm, like a mother removing a child in the street from the path of an oncoming car. The gun dropped in the gutter. Stone grabbed on air.

She shoved at the backs of Lil D's legs to force him to the sidewalk. Her gun still trained on the inside of the car, she stepped over Lil D and picked up the gun from the street.

Man threw his hands up as if surrendering the game, as if distancing himself from what he ultimately had set in motion. Pepper had a cuff around one of his wrists and Man was offering him the other.

Inside the car Stone raged in a frenzy of slapping, banging, and flapping, his whole body beating itself against the insides of the car, his furor so intense that Salt half-expected feathers to fly. Stone bloodied his face against the windshield, the skin of his leg cut in contortions with the steering wheel, his fingers tearing at the car ceiling. But worse than his acts of fury were the sounds he made, like a scream mixed with the whimper of a child when its pain is immediate and pure. Ordering him out of the car would have been futile. In his rage he was beyond comprehension.

Then it stopped. The moment seemed to hang. Salt and Pepper moved only when Stone lay with his arms and shoulders up and draped over the backseat, and his only movement the rise and fall of his ribs. Salt blinked away tears, moved forward, holstering her gun, tucking the other gun in her waistband and drawing her second handcuffs from the case on her belt. Pepper covered.

Stone's panting slowed. He barely flinched, lifting only one finger as Salt clamped the metal cuff over one wrist slick with blood. She crawled into the car to reach for his other wrist. Her body, heavy with gear, pressed against him, securing him in the close confines of the car's front compartment. He'd tried to kill her, he'd killed her sheep, hurt her dog, and stolen her peace. She collapsed against him, the lingering echoes of his rage ringing in her ears. She glanced out at Lil D's face, his eyes wide, his mouth tight with incomprehension.

The headlights and alley lights of beat cars lit up the street. Most of the shift seemed to be arriving on Marcy just to see Stone in handcuffs. No citizens had ventured out to witness an arrest of one of the gang. Lil D and Man were leaning against Man's car. Stone was sitting on the curb, cuffed behind his back, his feet in the gutter. Flanked by Blessing, Sarge, and Fuzz, Salt lifted Stone, like deadweight, by his elbow. She stood him on his feet for the walk to the wagon. He kept his glare on Lil D, who said to Man, clearly so that Stone could hear, "My foot slipped." He turned to Stone and grinned.

Trying to break away from her, Stone lurched at Lil D. "You whole family fucked. Ask that prissy sister of yours what she doing at yo mama's the day before—before she claim to found her." Lil D and Man kept their practiced masks of nothingness. She jerked Stone toward the wagon, pushed him in, and closed the inner doors. Through the grate she asked, "You wanna make a statement to me about what you just said to Lil D? Or you just blowing smoke?" She was beginning to feel the ebb of energy, to notice how the street dirt was sticking to the dried sweat on her skin and she thought she could detect the clinging odor of something decomposing.

"Since it seem to matter to you, Mrs. Poleese, I ain't got shit to say." He spit on the cage door.

"You haven't read him his rights." Sister Connelly stood on the sidewalk beside the wagon. A thin, loosely buttoned housecoat covered her nightgown and those old scars. She had left the shotgun in her house and was now armed with a Bible.

Salt slammed the outer paddy wagon door, then turned toward Sister. The wagon took off for the downtown jail. "Sword of the Lord," Sister said, and raised the Bible.

"Did you hear what Stone said to Lil D?" Salt asked.

Sister looked past Salt. "My hearin' not what it used to be."

"He said Mary was at Shannell's the day before Mother's Day." Salt moved closer and tried to make eye contact. But Sister Connelly kept searching the darkness, her eyes squinting, swiveling her neck.

"Well, if she was here he must have been here to have seen her," Sister said.

"What did you see? What do you know? Don't you want justice for Shannell?"

"Ain't no justice for Shannell." She turned.

"What about for Mary?" Salt asked.

Sister walked away, up her steps, and, without looking back, closed the door behind her.

Salt glanced across the street and there was Dirty Red, looking like a ghost of herself, sitting on the top step of the stairs to Shannell's. Salt started toward her.

She passed Lil D and Man, who were standing in the light of the single street pole like they were stranded on their own street. "D—" she began.

"Can I go now?" He cut her off.

She wanted to ask him if his foot did slip, wanted to ask why he had grabbed the gun. He pulled the towel from around his neck and walked away.

"Man." She nodded to the gang leader, and turned to the stairs. In those few seconds Dirty Red had disappeared again.

Salt, Pepper, and two other officers searched the area for Red. At Shannell's they lifted every loose board and checked behind every cabinet and door. They canvassed the neighborhood and searched the wooded areas around Marcy Street. Red stayed missing.

37.

SUNDAY MORNING

The sky above the AME church was bright blue and cloudless. The voices of the choir and congregation, accompanied by a fuzzy, too-loud organ, carried on the slight breeze through the windows, open to the cool fall day. Salt leaned against her car in the parking lot and lifted her face to the sun. The shining rays warmed her cheeks, her hair, the scar. A soloist began.

> *"Blessed assurance, Jesus is mine.*
> *Oh what a foretaste of glory divine.*
> *Heir of salvation, purchase of God,*
> *Born of his spirit, washed in his blood . . ."*

Then the preacher's voice rose, reassuring the flock that they were in Jesus's hands and that they would be led to the Promised

Land. The congregation prayed in unison: "Thy rod and thy staff, they comfort me."

The people began filing out of the church. A large percent of the congregants were older women dressed in all white with elaborate hats, some with feathers and sequins. One woman had an artificial dove perched atop her wide-brimmed crown.

Sister Connelly stopped to shake the preacher's extended hand. Her dress was bright white, as if it had been bleached by the sun. She was wearing a matching hat with a simple veil covering the top part of her face. No one would ever mistake her for anyone else, her dark skin, her height, a shadow surrounded by a cloud. She didn't say anything to the minister, just changed the Bible she was carrying to her left hand and shook his hand while she looked out at the parking lot. She made her way through the churchgoers, who nodded as she passed, acknowledging her, showing respect to a woman who knew and kept their history.

Sister stopped a foot or so farther than conversational distance. "Why didn't you go to church today, Officer Salt?"

"I came here for help." Salt straightened off the car. She was wearing jeans and a T-shirt, had left her gun in the athletic bag on the passenger seat.

"The Lord helps those who help themselves." Sister lifted her already dignified carriage. "You got your man. That Stone never stood a chance," she said, shaking her head. The hat and veil, tied and pinned, stayed firmly in place.

"He was charged with assault and violation of gun laws."

"I thought you arrested him for killing Shannell." The old woman's eyes were hidden by the now slightly shaking veil. Her lips folded inward, holding back.

Salt reached out her right hand without touching Sister. "Sister Connelly, you remember that you told me Shannell picked flowers from your yard to give to Mary when she would visit?" she spoke to Sister's lips beneath the veil.

"Did I tell you that? Well, it's true then." Sister crossed her arms, holding her pocketbook and Bible in front of her waist.

"I went back and looked at the crime scene photos. There were wilted wisteria blooms scattered on the floor. I remembered the smell. Did you see her pick the flowers? Did she say Mary was coming that day?"

Sister Connelly's hand with the Bible rose and she pressed it close to her chest. "Ain't you seen enough evil? Why you got to go lookin' for more? I'm truly tired of it. You'd think God would come on and send us the Savior."

"Did God send a savior for Shannell? Was there a chance for her and she just didn't take it? I'm just trying to do my job. Did you see Mary at Shannell's the day before, like Stone said?"

"You think Mary might have seen who killed her mother? Then why wouldn't she tell it?" The old woman dropped her arms to her sides. All kinds of little dried flowers fell from the Bible. Sister snapped it shut. "Just leave 'em." Sister turned and took a few heavy steps back toward the church, not toward her house down the street.

"I don't know the answers," said Salt. Sister's back was to her. "Maybe she was afraid. Did Shannell say Mary was coming? Did you see Mary that day?"

The old woman, armed with the Bible and scars, turned and took one step back. "Why I got to be the one to bear witness? What do you want?"

"I want it to stop. I'm going to talk to Mary again and I need more than Stone's say-so that she was there the day her mother was killed. I need to be sure. She's a child who may have witnessed her mother's murder. I have to be sure. I can't take a chance that I'd hurt her more than she's already been hurt."

Some church members turned toward them with brows wrinkled and narrowed eyes. Some knew Salt. "Sister, I swore an oath when I took this job. Old-fashioned as it might sound, I feel a sacredness about it, like I've been given a trust, a legacy, you might say. Mary isn't just a piece of a problem to me. I swore to protect and defend her, you, Lil D, even Man and Stone." She paused, pressed her palm to the scar in her hair. "But I can't do it alone."

"Can I be of assistance, Sister?" The minister close at hand now. "Officer Salt?"

Sister Connelly turned her veiled head, looking at the other members of the congregation. She looked past them and the minister to the stone church and the window of James the Martyr. "No," she answered him, then turned to face Salt. "There's no problem. This police officer has the answers. She just doesn't know which ones." She lifted the veil. The dark, dark skin of her face reflected the sun and the years. The deep paths under her eyes were running like old creeks. She wiped a finger under each eye. Her chest rose and fell. "Salt," she said, "the truth may set us free but it also binds us. I've tangled with truth before." She patted her chest where the white dress covered her. "You have to be mighty careful how you unravel a mystery. You go pulling one thing and we all feel a tug. We're all bound together.

"Do you want me to tell you the answer you already know? I did see Shannell the day before she was found, on the top stairs to her place, where that screen door hangs. And her daughter had wisteria in her arms."

38.

ANOTHER VICTIM

The children tumbled out of the school bus doors into the sunlight, stumbling into one another, doubling up in the doors, jumping and tripping over themselves in their excitement to be free. Salt watched from the porch of the McCloud house. Mary Marie was again the last off the bus. Mary eyed a group of girls stopped on the sidewalk in front of her, slapping their look-alike sneakers on the pavement, trying to make squeaking noises. She stayed back, didn't pass, but reached down to pull up white ankle socks that had been eaten by her brown loafers.

At her vigil on the porch, Salt's legs gave way and she sat down with a thud. Mary was so marked. She took a deep breath and entertained a brief fantasy of having Wonder herd all the children to include the girl.

The sidewalk girls giggled and cast coy eyes outside their circle to see if anyone worth noticing was noticing them. They covered their mouths and elbowed one another, laughing at laughing. Mary hunched her shoulders to get past, on the edge of the sidewalk. They didn't seem to notice the black sheep, like Salt—a child who was kept separate—like The Homes, cut apart from the city. As Mary passed, another girl with long coltish legs in a short pleated skirt parted from the group and started down the sidewalk almost beside Mary.

"What you know anyway?" the girl, grinning, called back to the others.

Following behind, Mary matched her step for step, her socks slipping down again. Her focus was so intent on the girl that she almost passed by her own house but pulled up when she noticed the police car. She glanced in the car, then looked up on her porch and saw Salt. She canted her head then watched as the receding girl turned the corner, out of sight.

Images of Wonder watching the new lambs, holding them gently with only his eyes, came to Salt again. He was tender while they were learning their legs. It didn't take much to make them skittish, to send them into an uncertain run, dangerously bolting. Salt wished she had a way for Mary to learn what to hurry toward and when to stay back.

"My grandmother told you not to come here again," Mary said, her face flat, her eyes hooded. She came up the steps. Her braided hair looked painfully tight, her clothes too clean for a twelve-year-old who had just come home from being at school all day. The slipping socks were the only things out of place.

"Should we wait for her?"

Mary swung the backpack from her shoulders and sat it down. "Know what?" She unzipped it and took out a large black three-ring binder. "I keep all my tests from the beginning of school till the end." She balanced the open notebook in her left hand while flipping the dividers with her right. "We worked on fractions today in Math. I got all ten problems right the first time. I always make one hundreds on my tests. I show my notebook to my grandmother every school day. You see? I make As in English, Social Studies, and History." She looked up from the notebook, looked down once more at her schoolwork, and closed the binder.

Salt stood beside her, her boots heavy on the wood planks. Mary handed Salt the notebook and left her pack where she'd dropped it. "It doesn't matter, does it," she said as she unlocked the front door. The cheap socks were halfway gone into her shoes. Salt picked up the pack, tucked the binder under her arm, and went in behind Mary.

Inside the door the girl slipped off her shoes, straightened her socks, and watched Salt put the backpack and notebook down beside her loafers.

"You did it wrong. That doesn't go there. You better not knock my shoes against the wall." She turned down the hall. "Are your shoes off?" Mary said over her shoulder.

"Not this time," Salt said, mostly to herself. "I can't."

The girl turned into a room to the left. The house was close and airlessly warm. When Salt came to the doorway she found Mary standing in front of a dresser mirror, holding her arms wrapped around herself, shivering. The room was all white: walls, bedspread, throw rugs, and a picture of a white Jesus hanging above the bed. Salt unloaded the books. As she placed the books on a white desk, Mary came over, patting them as you would a dog, and began to arrange them, weighing each book in her hands, then stacking them according to size. "What you know anyway?" Her voice sounded high up in her throat, a parody of the girls she'd left at the bus stop. With Salt following, she marched out down the hall and into the sterile kitchen that was filled with so much light it was hard to see through.

"I know you were there that day, Mary. The flowers. I know your mother gave you the flowers like she always did."

The girl went to the kitchen sink and grabbed the rim hard with both hands, holding on, the shivers turning into a tremble.

"The wisteria was on the floor." Salt pushed on, matching Mary's stiffening muscles with her own body loosening to the point that she felt her bones disappearing.

Mary bent over the sink and began to heave. But it was words she brought up. "I asked her, it was Mother's Day, the next day." She turned and there was a strand of spittle coming from one corner of her mouth. "I asked her to let me come live with her, to be my mother." She wiped her hand across her mouth and started to choke. Then her eyes widened suddenly and focused past Salt's shoulder.

Salt turned.

Mrs. McCloud was in the doorway. "I told you. Go past my door; you're not to be in my house." She headed straight toward Mary. "What you tellin' this cop?" Her voice echoed. "What have you been telling?"

The light from the window was brilliant, hitting the floor in a wavy shimmer. Mrs. McCloud came through the light at Salt, who put a hand up, against the grandmother's chest, to hold her back. In the halt, her fingers struck and hit something hard beneath the old woman's dress, an old-fashioned corset. Mrs. McCloud startled at Salt's hand, drawing quick breaths into her hard chest. No one spoke. Her chest heaved against Salt's palm. Slapping at Salt's arm: "Get out," she said.

Salt didn't move, the feel of the old woman's corset still impressed on her fingertips. The house was very quiet. Salt still stood between the old woman and the girl. She directed her words to both, but facing Mrs. McCloud she said, "Tell me the rest, Mary. You tried the first time I was here."

Mary's words floated up. "She'd picked those ugly purple flowers." The afternoon sun struck through the kitchen windows, yellow bars pinning the three of them in place. Mary turned toward the window with her back to them. "Wisteria's not real flowers, they're vines. They fall apart before I even get home. She give them to me because she don't even know what are real flowers. I feel ashamed of her and mad at me 'cause I was ashamed. I'm mad at me and her." Mary sounded like a little girl. "Her hair was all sticking up. I could see her head in places where she didn't have hair."

The grandmother pounded her fist against her hard chest. "Don't she have the right to remain silent?"

Salt, fingers shaking, fumbled the Miranda card out of her pocket and recited mostly from memory, her voice like it belonged to someone else, "You have the right . . ." When she asked, "Do you wish to speak to me at this time?" the final question on the back of the card, Mary turned and looked straight at her grandmother, standing her distance, her voice loud, so distinct, like someone in the last seconds of a spelling bee, and said, "I will for me and my mother."

"She wasn't no mother, she was a whore," Mrs. McCloud growled.

"Mrs. McCloud, you have the right to remain silent."

Mary turned to the sink and lifted her head to the window above it. "That's why she wouldn't let me come live with her. You made her believe what you said, that she was no good. She believed you, Nana. Why she said no. She said, 'You know your nana says this is no place for a child to be.' Her arms were all snappy and she was knocking things over, trying to find a jar for the flowers. All her head bopping, I wanted her to be still, to quit banging around." Mary put her right hand over her eyes, blocking her view.

"I won't hear this," Mrs. McCloud said behind gritted teeth.

"I can't be nobody's child ever," said Mary.

"You don't know nothin'." Mrs. McCloud pointed a crooked finger at Salt, ignoring Mary Marie. "You ain't had to raise up your own self while taking care of everything and everybody else. I didn't have no mother." The old woman took a step and planted herself firmly. "Shannell wasn't fit. And now Mary. And I just got myself. I wash my hands. Ain't no good in nothing. The sin just keeps passing on."

The radio crackled on Salt's shoulder, a unit was being dispatched on some children found home alone. She shifted under the weight of her gun belt and vest. It seemed that her armor had never weighed so much. Salt pressed on, "What happened?"

Mary tucked her right hand under her arm and looked harder out the window. "I just left her. I left her." She pushed away from the window, her voice broke apart; crying, she sank to the floor beside the sink. She put her hands over her face, muffling her words. "I had to go back on Mother's Day. The next day."

The grandmother stood rigid. Salt knelt next to the girl, flashlight banging against nightstick, keys clanking against handcuffs, radio transmitting, stiff in the bullet-resistant vest. "I'm sorry, Mary, but I need you to tell me how your mother was shot."

"'Stop it,' I told her." Mary jerked her hand from her face and again coiled the fingers of her right hand. "'Stop it.' Then she dropped the glass with those stupid flowers and slipped on spilled water. Couldn't be still long enough for me to see her eyes." Mary looked up from her squat on the floor. "There was a gun and beside it on the counter was a bunch of rolled-up baby diapers. I wondered was there a baby there, was she keeping a baby and not me? She screamed crazy when I grabbed a diaper. A gun fell out. I pulled at all the diapers. They all had guns in them. Why guns? My mother so scared of guns she always go after Big D with knives. I picked up one of the guns. She yelled, 'You gone kill me. You gone kill me.' And she ran like she was scared—of me! I went after her to tell her it was just the drugs making her think I would hurt her. But really I did want to scare her. To make her stop. Scare her like she scared Big D with knives. I yelled, 'Where's the baby?'"

With a moan the old woman dropped to one of the kitchen chairs.

Salt, cross-legged on the floor, reached out to uncurl Mary's hidden fingers.

"She was yelling, bumping into the wall. I found her in the closet, hiding. I felt sick and ashamed. She looked silly, pitiful. She couldn't do anything right. She was never going to be quiet and still and be my mother. She would always run away from me. I lifted the gun like a finger. It did make her be still. She was quiet. I could make her see me. 'I found you, Mama.' Then her eyes came wide open on mine and there wasn't any of my mama there, just something that took my mama. My finger pulled twice."

Salt was as still as Lot's wife until the girl put her hands on the floor to stand. They stood together. The grandmother kept her head turned away. Salt placed two fingers on the underside of Mary's wrist, as if taking her pulse, then keyed the radio mic, "Radio, hold me out en route to Homicide." And to Mary, "You can come with me."

"My mama wasn't there."

Salt walked out with her arm around Mary Marie.

Salt stood by Mary in every step of the process. She held her hand while the girl made a transcribed statement to Wills at Homicide. She rode with her in the back of the unmarked car while Wills drove to juvenile detention. And she stayed with her until she was taken to her cell. She'd probably never see the girl again. Department policy dictated law enforcement separation from arrestees prior to their trials. Salt and Wills did have friends at the district attorney's office who they'd call on to ask that Mary not be tried as an adult. But it would be years before Mary would be out of some kind of institution.

Her last view of the girl was the back of her loosening braid.

"Hey, Homicide detective." Wills was gently shaking her awake. They were in his unmarked, in the parking lot of the precinct.

"You snore." He laughed.

"I was dreaming," she said, her words heavy from sleep. She sat up. "I fell asleep."

"I know. Happens to me all the time when I've been involved in a case and I finally get the bad guy. They say you can always tell the guilty perps 'cause they're the ones who fall asleep in the interview room. The hunter and the hunted, exhausted after the chase." He turned toward her, propped his arm on the steering wheel. "I know you're tired, but give me the short version. What led you to Mary, to think she might have killed her mother?"

"Flowers." She inhaled, pushing up from her knees. "But I kept hoping she'd only witnessed Shannell's death."

"Flowers?"

"The wisteria in the photos, the fragrance beneath the stench of the apartment. Sister Connelly across the street said Shannell would pick flowers to give Mary. And then when we arrested Stone he taunted Lil D by saying Mary had been at her mother's the day she was murdered."

"Which meant Stone had been there, seen Mary, and that probably he'd gone in after Mary and gotten the guns."

Salt lowered her face to her hands.

"Sarah." Wills's hand was on her shoulder. "We'll do the best we can for Mary, whatever help, therapy, treatment the state can provide."

Salt covered his hand with hers.

Wills gently pushed her upright. "She would have had a hard row to hoe no matter. I think she stands a chance now."

Salt tried to stretch out her legs, her mouth sticky. "I am really tired. I must look like hell."

"You solved my homicide. I wouldn't care if you looked like Gardner. I'd still want to kiss you." He turned toward her.

"Oh, no." She put up her hand, covering her mouth. "First, if you're into kissing Gardner for solving your homicides I'm not sure we're on the same page."

He laughed. "I kiss Gardner all the time. He doesn't take it personal."

"You're ruining the image of homicide detectives." Now she did grin. "But second, my mouth feels like I've been licking sheep."

"Well, that lets you off the hook," Wills said, moving as close to his door as he could, laughing. "But not for long. It's high time for you and Wonder to meet Pansy and Violet."

She faced him. Over his shoulder she could see the shift pulling in for the night, the line of cars forming for the next shift. "When?" she asked Wills.

"When?" he repeated. "I'm making sure I heard you."

"When? You've made your case. I watched the way you tried to soften everything for Mary."

"Saturday," he said, then leaned over and kissed her woolly mouth anyway.

39.

HOMECOMING

Salt watched from the front window as Wills's shiny truck, pulling a tail of red dust, turned off the highway into the drive. She looked around the living room at the sparse furniture. Plenty of breathing room. Wonder would have felt crowded otherwise; fewer tables and chairs for him to skid into. She'd felt guilty that she'd enjoyed the absence of her mother and brother after they'd left. She'd come home from college, torn the boards off the windows and doors, moved back in, and put in her application at the PD. Like Mary Marie, she'd slipped and slid down the hall in her sock feet. She let the curtain fall, took a breath, walked to the back of the house and out to greet Wills.

As she came out Wills was parking under the great oak. The late afternoon sun was shining and there was a definite hint of winter in the air. The windows of the truck were rolled up; Wills's voice was muted as he sang along with the radio and gathered bags from the seat. Salt stood at the driver's door, waiting with Wonder at her side. When Wills turned, window still up, his mouth opened in an O of exclamation. Recovering, he opened the door. "Startled me."

"Maybe I ought to call you by something other than your last name, Wills." Salt reached in to help with a thermal bag.

"How 'bout 'Handsome.'" He shifted the bags. "Hello, dog." Wonder came nudging and nuzzling his way under Wills's out-stretched hand. He ruffled the dog's ears, sunshine warmth still on the dog's fur from a nap in the sun.

"I hear lambs." He turned toward the paddock and orchard. "How are the new sheep?"

"Why don't you come on in? Something smells good." She lifted one of the bags to her nose. Wonder followed, yelping and snap-ping, herding them on their way toward the back porch.

A chill wind picked up and blew some of the bright yellow leaves from the pecan trees. Wonder stepped carefully beside them as they walked, keeping them together.

"I still smell new paint." He put his things on the kitchen table.

She pulled the food from the bags. "Cold ham, potato salad, cucumber. Where did you get these late tomatoes?" She laid the dishes on the counter and began taking the covers off.

The screen door rattled. The setting sun sent rays straight up off the horizon so Mr. Gooden stood there in an orange aura. "Hello, hello," he called.

"Why, Mr. Gooden."

"I don't want to intrude but I saw the truck pull in. I thought you could use some flowers. He handed Salt a bouquet of lavender chrysanthemums and went over to shake hands with Wills. "Don't get up. I'm Wayne Gooden, from next door."

"Bernard Wills. People just call me Wills." The two men shook hands.

"I'm proud of this girl." Mr. Gooden reached his arm around Salt's shoulders. He was as tall as her father.

"They're beautiful, thank you." She held the blooms close.

"We're all proud of her," Wills said. "But she keeps us on our toes."

"I'm sure she tries not to worry you." Mr. Gooden was headed for the door, smiling, winking at Salt, like they shared a private joke. "Good to meet you, now. Have a good visit." He was out the door, long legs halfway across the yard.

The table was covered with half-empty plates and serving bowls.

"Bernard?" She grinned.

"Why did you move back here? Yes, I'm changing the subject. I'd never live it down if I was known as Bernard."

"It's home."

They were silent for a few minutes. The dog looked up. It was time and time was passing.

"I heard your dad was a good cop until he got sick."

She took a bite of Wills's cold ham. Her teeth sank in. The mustard in the potato salad was strong and good.

"Are you sure your head's all right?"

Salt swallowed and took a breath. "I'm too nervous not to get this right out. Let me give you the tour."

Wills held his hands out, palms up, ready.

"I need to tell you about my dad, so it won't be something hanging, some big secret or taboo thing. Come on. Upstairs." She took his hand and led him down the hall.

Twice a year she gathered all the necessary cleaning supplies. She would carry a boom box to the far end of the upstairs hall. The music was always the same, always gospel, the Blind Boys of Alabama, the Staple Singers, blues gospel that transported her to the baptizing banks of a river. While she cleaned and washed the walls and floors of the scene of her nightmares she sang along with the voices of sanctification and salvation.

They stopped at the top of the stairs. "The rooms are mostly bare. My mother took a lot of the furniture with her." Crystals from the small chandelier overhead cast tiny darts of yellow, pink, and green light along the walls and patched boards of the repaired floor. "You all did good work." She opened each of the doors on the right. "My old room." They peeked in from the doorway, then on to the sunporch: "My escape hatch," and on to the guest room. And then to the closed door of her parents' bedroom. She put her hand on the brass knob, tarnished to black. When she was ten years old it had been level with her chest. She heard the familiar click as she turned the knob to the left.

Wills covered her hand with his own and opened the door for her.

The old flowered rug was the only thing left in the room. When Salt was Sarah and five years old she had misheard *Red rover, red rover* as *Red roses, red roses.*

> *Red roses, red roses*
> *Let flowers grow over.*

She'd sing while she walked a secret path in the floral pattern on the rug, pretend it was an enchanted garden where her father was the king, and the language he spoke a magical one.

Salt walked part of the secret path from the door of the room. "I used to sit on the bed while he took off his uniform. He'd tell me funny stories about things that happened on the job." Standing at the windows on the other side of the room from the door, she turned to the closet. "He kept his uniform cap and his gun on the top shelf.

"I think I tried to stay close to him with the job, like it was just me and him, our mission. More recently"—she looked out to the orchard—"I've come to realize that it's not the job. I have memories."

Salt dreamed that she left her mother in the house and that she and her father walked arm in arm from the back porch, Wonder at their side. The sheep acknowledged their coming with baas or bleats, rustled a little, then settled back against one another in the paddock. The rising moon, a smooth yellow scimitar, was large against the trees, a nursery rhyme moon. A cow sat with her legs crossed over the crescent.

They walked through the orchard, the first leaves off the trees crackling, oval nuts rolling under their feet. The branches and dry grasses gave up the sharp peppery odor of sticky green pecan shells and sweet sheep dung.

"Smells different when the moon is out," her father said.

"You've got a fine nose there, Pop."

"I've learned to appreciate what I've got left."

She drew apart from him, turned to face him, to find out what he meant. She could see nothing but two moons reflecting out of his blue, blind eyes. Salt turned away and looked off past the end of the tree line. Wonder had run ahead to the edge of the field and was sitting, nose pointed up, silhouetted by moonlight. "I wish you could see him out there. He looks like the classic canine, wolf dog." She swallowed hard.

"It's almost enough to hear you describe him."

"Wonder's a great dog. I'm so sorry, Pop." She was trying very hard not to cry.

"Sorry? Sarah, my head was cleared when I shot out the demons. I may be blind but the clouds were blown away that day. Should have shot myself sooner." He smiled into the night.

She tried to swallow, shivered, then took her father's arm again, this time leaning a little bit on him. He felt warm. She rubbed her cheek on his flannel shirt and somewhere in her chest there was a small release. They walked on a little longer in the crisp night with the moonlit dog keeping them company.

Wonder, curled in a ball at the foot of her bed, moved his quivering ears back and forth. His eyes were open but he, like she, stayed curled up. Since they were almost always past midnight going to bed, the sunrise felt a little early. They heard kitchen noises.

Salt called the dog to her pillow. She thought he pretended to like his head on a pillow the way he saw hers. She opened one of his ears and whispered, "Heeeee's uuuuup."

The dog waved his ears, stood up on the bed, and shook out the night fur. Salt pulled on her jeans under her nightshirt and padded, barefoot, into the kitchen, letting the dog out the back door.

Wills was standing at the sink, staring out the window. He had thrown an old quilt over his bare shoulders.

"Mornin'."

He opened his arms as she came to him. She tucked her head to his chest and breathed in his scent as he wrapped the quilt over her shoulders. She turned her back to him and he encircled her in his arms and put his hands in her jeans pockets, pulling her close. "Know what you get when you work your fingers to the bone?"

"What?" she said, knowing the answer to the old joke.

"Bony fingers."

She tugged at the quilt and went over to the glass-front cabinet to get a cup. The day was already bright, trees in the orchard giving off their crisp fragrance, the leaf dust peppering the air. A jay screeched and on the highway an eighteen-wheeler changed gears. The muscles of her legs began to tense and she wiped her hands on her jeans.

The tick, tick of canine nails sounded at the porch door. Wills let Wonder into the kitchen, the dog making his sound like a low train whistle, "Woo, woo," a signal for someone to do something for him. He slid his head into Salt's lap. The grace of his simple affection made Salt's chest hurt. Blinking her eyes she looked up to see the trim on the kitchen door, patched by her friends. She smelled Wills's ham on the counter, on a grass-green platter. She heard a solo baa from her surviving sheep, then a chorus of bleats from the four new members of the flock. The clouds outside reminded her of Pepper's pajamas. Little salvations, like the air around love. She drew in a long breath of it and put her hand on a frayed flowered square of the quilt Wills was wearing, her mother's quilt. "Let me show you the new lambs." Salt took Wills by the hand and pulled him up, the quilt sliding off his thick shoulders.

"Come on," she repeated, feeling as eager as a kid.

Wonder followed and when he saw they were headed for the sheep, he ran past to the pen, eager to work, his snout inches from the ground, eyes unblinking, focused, his shoulders and head lowered.

Salt led Wills to a section of the fence that was catching the first few rays of sun. The sheep protested Wonder's intensity and bunched into a corner of the paddock. She hated to disappoint the dog but led him back to the porch anyway. He dropped to the floor when she closed the screen door.

When she entered the pen the sheep gathered around her. Even the new ones had become accustomed to her as their shepherd. She put her hands in the dirty white wool of the little dam that had survived Stone's slaughter and led her out to Wills.

He reached out to the sheep. Salt reminded him, "All sheep stink."

He bent down and moved his hands over the dam's knotty head. The normally placid little sheep stomped her hoof, let out a quick belch, then bent down to nibble at some weeds.

"I've named her Red." Salt thought of her last glimpse of the lost woman, her thick hair the same color as red clay. "'Cause this sheep, she's usually covered with dust," she explained, vigorously patting the woolly flanks, sending up a halo of dust and the memory of a whistling whore.

Wills touched the knobby head between the horn remnants. "Her head's like a rock, a hard head." He spread his fingers into Red's woolly neck. Red lifted her nose, sniffing. "Hello, Red." The sheep moved close to sample one of his shoelaces. "She does stink," agreed Wills, wrinkling his nose and pulling his foot from the sheep, but smiling and continuing to circle the sheep's head with his hands.

Together they fed and watered Red and the lambs. While they were spreading the grain and filling the water trough, the sun, full and bright, came 'round the house and covered them with something like warmth.

40.

TURNING THE CORNER

Salt and Pepper had been able to finish a complete thirty-minute meal from clear broth to fortune cookies that neither had unwrapped. They talked about the new sheep, about Ann and the boys and how they were doing in school. For once radio had not interrupted to order them to calls.

"You gonna take the detective exam?" Pepper got down to it.

"Wills says he'll pull for me to get to Homicide and he thinks because of the Shannell solve that I'll be a shoo-in. You?"

He smiled, looking down. "Yeah, it's time for both of us to do something career-wise. I'll probably get sent to Narcotics if I make the cut. You know all us black guys get sent to drugs." He shrugged, still smiling.

"Pep, it'll be the first time in more than ten years we won't be working together. It's kinda like we've been a couple and now we won't be."

He stretched against the back of the booth, arms wide, and looked out at the room. "Let's cross that bridge when it crumbles. It's not like we won't be spending time together, at least off duty. Although I see, happily I might add, that Wills is taking up some of your time."

She openly grinned back at him. "Don't forget that I'm gutting half the upstairs at home for the dojo. You promised to bring the boys over and we'll all work out together. They can hang with Wonder and the sheep, pick pecans, whatever. Ann says you can, so that seals it." She motioned for him to wipe a crumb from his chin.

He took a swipe with his napkin then, reaching out his hand to her, said, "Deal." But instead of doing the buddy handshake he covered their clasped hands with his left hand. "You've got to promise though that you'll always remember who's got your back."

"You do, Hot Pepper. You do."

Embarrassed, they untangled their hands. "Check," they simultaneously called to Mai.

Standing in the parking lot at their cars, she brought up what she hadn't at the table. She wanted it said when Pepper didn't have time to argue. "Help me watch out for Lil D," she said.

He shook his head with frustration.

"Nothing big, Pep. Just if you see a chance. He needs to get his GED. Talk to him about a real job, something he'd want to do."

"I guess I know where you're off to. I don't know why you're so determined on that kid. Just seems you set yourself up for disappointment. But we're in this together. You know all the guys will help somehow." He gave a little salute, touching his fingers to her forehead instead of his own, and went back to his beat.

As usual Salt had the windows down, riding up the perimeter of her beat on Pryor. An almost cold wind worked with the last of the warm afternoon sun to keep her comfortable. She rode past Sam's, where the corner crowd was gathering. A couple of bright cars with oversized wheels were tuned to the same rap station and blasted in stereo across the parking lot. The girls had traded their summer shorts and skirts for tight pants and jackets, unzipped to reveal firm cleavage. They snapped colorful fingers to the beats coming from the broadcasting cars. The out-on-bail gang members, plus some young new recruits, were working the deals, rolling up to the cars, palming hits to the walk-ups, pausing only briefly as Salt slowly drove by, hand raised in an unreturned wave to the crew. She made a right, then right again to get to her usual place where she could keep watch for him. She concealed the car two parallel alleys over, thumbed the car door locks, and began on the downward path toward the abandoned building.

"You got company." Man fell in beside her, a big smile on his handsome face. He pointed to himself, smile widening.

"You gonna try to hold my hand?" She laughed. "Dispatch, hold me out on a suspicious person." She gave radio her location and Man's name and description. Her eyes all the while were steady on his face.

"You don't trust me." Man gave her a mock frown.

"Yes, I do. I trust you to be you." She put two fingers over her left shirt pocket and the phone there.

"I didn't put that scar on your head. That was a white man shot you." Children's voices came from somewhere close by, screeching, yelling, and laughing.

"He bought the gun from your boys."

They got to the abandoned apartments where she generally kept watch on the gang. She turned instead and led Man toward the hill overlooking the corner. As they rounded the building a gang of seven or eight grubby little boys scurried like feral cats from the broken windows and missing-plyboard door of the building. One of the littlest caught his palm on a jagged piece of glass. She went over to help the kid but all the boys, including him, dashed to a nearby scrubby magnolia tree, shoving each other to be the first up.

"You checking on my boys across the street or you meeting somebody here?" Man said cheerfully.

"Meeting you," she said.

He stood a bit away, watching his drug corner. She touched the phone again. The little boys in the tree settled on a limb, swinging sneakered feet.

"There's always the possibility that Stone could turn." She faced him straight on.

"He won't. Ever. He'd die of natural causes. I ain't been charged. There ain't no proof. Anyway, you say the man who shot you was buyin' guns from me. Even if that's true, you know he was buying for some other white man, your side I mean." He bent down, picked up a rock, squatted, and threw it down the cracked, dry red clay hill. They both watched it kick up loose pebbles and dirt.

"I'm not going to argue blame. There's enough of that for every-body." The boys in the tree hung close enough to be able to hear. She sensed that she and Man had their attention.

"So what's changed, Officer Salt?" He turned his head and smiled at her. "I'm doing my job, Lil D and the boys still doing theirs, and you, you just passing through."

"We're all passing through, Man."

"Yeah? So what's different?"

"Some of us are changed."

335

"Who else?" Man stood up and dusted off his brand-new baggy jeans. "Like I told you before, don't nobody give a shit about this place. This city, people, don't care 'bout no Homes." He left her, walking off down the hill. "You ain't even made no dent of a difference in this place," he said, not looking back, even to wave goodbye.

She hummed a few notes of a gospel tune and turned her attention to the boys in the magnolia and hummed a little louder, loud enough so the tree boys looked down, put their hands over uncertain grins, poking at one another for what to think about a cop standing on a rutty hill in the projects humming a church song. The children dropped to the ground like ripe fruit. Laughing, they ran up the hill in the opposite direction from the corner below. She hummed the chorus again.

The phone buzzed in her shirt pocket. Man was walking toward his gang. She pressed the phone close to her ear.

"That Merrill guy that you lookin' for on that robbery?"

"Yeah," she answered, recognizing the reliable informant.

"He on Thirkeld across from Sam's right now. He scrapped," he said, alerting her in the vernacular that Merrill was armed.

"D—" was all she got out before the connection was gone. Salt closed the phone. "Be careful," she prayed for them both.

ACKNOWLEDGMENTS

I have tremendous gratitude for my agent, Nat Sobel, who has believed in Salt from the beginning. Thank you, thank you, Sara Minnich Blackburn, my editor; Katie McKee, my publicist; and the entire team at G. P. Putnam's Sons. As always, I'm thankful for the support of my family—Noah, Viki, Gabriel, and Sadira. I am so fortunate to have my husband, Rick Saylor, along on this journey.

31901061127439